JUSTIFIABLE

New York Times
Bestselling Authors
WES
SARGINSON
AND
DIANNA LOVE

DEDICATION

We'd like to dedicate this book to the
Philadelphia Police Department

ACKNOWLEDGMENTS

We'd like to thank Philadelphia homicide detectives Timothy Bass and Stephen Buckley for answering our many questions. Thanks also for the tour of the Philadelphia police firing range and other locations that might otherwise have been off limits. We also appreciate the time and patience of longtime Philadelphia accountant Nelson Mishkin and his wife Barbara for giving us insight on the city's many characters, one-of-a-kind dining establishments and its neighborhoods that are a unique blend of cultures and personalities not often seen. We'd like to thank Dr. William F. Gayton, the clinical psychologist who answered questions and shared insights on the mind of our villain. Sometimes details have to be altered for fiction so any mistakes are our own. And a special thanks to Hal Lichtenwald for the clever nickname Tusk.

Much appreciation to Mary Buckham, whose very early read and brainstorm suggestions spurred the idea of a significant secondary character. Dianna works on no story without the sharp eyes of her amazing assistant, Cassondra Murray, whose feedback is always spot on. Thanks also go to early readers whose feedback made a tremendous difference in this book – Steve Doyle (thanks for the weapon notes), Danny Agan (thanks for the detailed feedback from a former homicide detective), Manuella Robinson, Joyce Ann McLaughlin and Michael McLaughlin. Kudos to Kim Killion for a great cover, to Jennifer Jakes for formatting and Judy Carney for copy editing.

Last, and most important, thank you to Karl Snell and Ann Sarginson for putting up with two crazy writers who love them dearly.

Thank you to all the readers who have emailed asking about this book. We appreciate your support. If you'd like a free Keeper Kase™ Cover card (glossy card with this cover image and signed by Wes and Dianna on the back), go to www.KeeperKase.com for details.

We love to hear from readers –

Snail mail either Wes or Dianna at 1029 N. Peachtree Pkwy, Suite 335, Peachtree City, GA 30269
Email Wes – Wessarginson@gmail.com
Email Dianna – dianna@authordiannalove.com

Chapter 1

"Didn't mean it. Didn't mean it. Didn't mean to hurt my baby – "

"Sally." Frigid air badgered his skin and snatched frosted breaths from his lips. The gas camping lantern beamed a pocket of light into the night. Everything else was swallowed by darkness.

"Sorry, sorry, sorry – "

Not sorry enough, Sally...but you will be. "I understand, and we'll pray your son recovers quickly." He offered her what she needed – a smile meant to reassure.

The hefty thirty-two-year-old mother cowered at his feet, sobbing, eyes downcast and searching, as though the concrete foundation would open up and save her. Tree shadows waved across her hunched form wrapped in a dirt-brown coat. Renegade snowflakes sprinkled around them, whispering optimism for Philadelphia and a new year just twenty-five hours old.

Sally had not started hers off well, but he'd give her a chance to prove she could do better. One chance for redemption.

He shifted his numb feet on the frozen slab where a house had once stood years ago. Charred remains surrounded him, a testament to living too far out in the woods for a fire truck to reach. Too remote for rescue teams to save anyone.

The perfect location for an honest confession.

Sally Stanton babbled the same watery apology in a woebegotten voice. "I didn't. I didn't . . ."

More lies, like so many fabrications whispered in a

confessional booth. He'd persevere against evil for the sake of the weak, even for pathetic lying women. He crooned to her in a soothing baritone. "It's all right, my child, God understands your failures. He sees how difficult life is for you and your son. I'm here to ease your pain."

Her red-rimmed, button eyes glowed with a spark of hope, like stirred embers. Words sputtered from her lips in a choked gurgle. She wiped her runny nose with the back of her pale hand spotted with freckles.

The vacuous mask of another sinner who lacked remorse.

"It's important for you to be truly repentant to receive absolution, Sally." His jaw muscles ached from holding back what he really wanted to say.

"I sorry...sorry, sorry – "

"Enough!" The constant lying bruised his ears.

"Please, *sir*." Greedy desperation crawled into her voice.

"*Sir*? You dare to call me sir?" Wind gusted violently. His black cassock billowed. The linen robe snapped as if issuing a reminder of how to properly address the right hand of God.

Even this dim-witted ox should be able to get it right.

"I m-mean father." She clutched her throat with pudgy fingers the size of Goliath's. Filthy, broken fingernails.

Standing upwind spared him her usual noxious odor. He could overlook a lack of hygiene, but not her sin.

A child had been harmed, a penance due.

As God said, woe to the man who harms a single hair on the head of one of these little ones.

She coughed and peered up cautiously. Brittle wind lashed her limp hair that wrapped around her head, swatting her face.

Sally deserved so much more than a slap on the cheek for not taking care around a child she could crush. Her skinny five-year-old boy had gone to the hospital with cracked ribs.

"Father?" Sally whimpered, wild eyes staring past him, confused. Her chest lifted and fell with one shaking breath after another. "I-I'm sorry I hurt Enrique when I fell on him. He should'na made me run after him. He was crying...lost my job today...not my fault...I need money."

Another ridiculous confession. *"Cease!"*

This woman would sin again and again and...patience, he had to be patient. First they repent then they pay penance.

Still kneeling, she posed in meek supplication. Her soggy voice dribbled out a pitiful whisper. "Don't let police take me. Please. We got no family. Enrique needs me."

Blessed are the meek, for they will inherit the earth.

But St. Catherine's Outreach Center would never survive and thrive unless the sinners atoned for their actions.

Sally quivered, an earthquake in a coat.

He had a responsibility to everyone – God, the community, even this woman and certainly her child. She needed help, relief from lugging her cross.

Come to me, all who are burdened, and I will give you rest.

She'd broken a commandment. Thou shalt protect the children. Not one of the original ten, but one he was sure God demanded every adult obey.

"You gonna talk to police, fix this?" she begged.

"Yes, my child. I shall fix this, but you must repent and pay penance." He had to go through all the steps, assure the sinner was given every chance to prove true remorse.

"Accident, just an accident...love my Enrique." Her voice jumped a pitch higher, hysterical. "Not my fault. Not my fault." Sally's hiccupped sobs rocked her body. The keening noise squeezed from her lungs might be another "sorry."

He tried to see her as one of God's creatures instead of maternal vermin that bred like rats then killed their young when food became too scarce. He lifted his hand palm out to quiet her, but fury clenching his muscles whipped along his arm.

His fingers curled into a tight fist.

Her eyes caught the movement. Her gaze slashed upward to meet his then her face flared with surprise, fear, panic. She dropped down on all four limbs and scrambled backwards on her knees, moving quickly for a big woman on rough concrete. Her doughy palms dragged across rusted nails sticking up through the foundation. She cried out, scooted faster, leaving a bloody streak. "Love my baby, love Enrique

_ "

Even an animal knows its baby is fragile and needs to be sheltered from harm. He stepped toward her. "Calm down, Sally. I understand and so does God. I'm going to help you."

Ignorant relief etched deep vertical lines between her eyebrows. "Now? You help me now?"

"Yes, now." He reached through a slit in the side of his robe to feel cold wood and metal. Withdrawing his hand, he raised the .38 Smith and Wesson, pointing the barrel at the center of her forehead.

Sally's mouth fell open. Six rotten teeth chattered soundlessly behind her quivering lips.

He gently squeezed the trigger. Just like practice. The explosion rocked across the empty foundation and echoed against the trees.

She crumpled into a brown heap. Garbage.

He took a moment as she drew her last breath then shoved the weapon through the opening in his robe and inside the waistband at the back of his pants. From a hip pocket, he fished out the vial of oil and poured a drop on his latex-gloved finger.

First, he drew a cross of oil on her forehead then a second cross in oil on the inside of her open wrist. He offered a prayer for her soul.

Sally lay still as dead wood, eyes stuck wide open, pleading for mercy. Now, she could ask God for mercy in person.

Time to return to St. Catherine's Church.

So little time.

So many deserving sinners.

Chapter 2

Does pulling off the perfect murder count if the victim is a welfare mother?

Riley Walker stared out the foggy passenger window of the news van where early morning traffic slugged toward downtown Philadelphia with all the enthusiasm of a funeral march.

What if I'm right about the killer? What if...

The hell with that. What-ifs came with a high price tag.

Don't dwell on the past.

He focused on the cars caked in winter grime, the low-hanging clouds and water streaks fingering the dirty glass inches from his nose...anything to block the gruesome images that barged into his mind at any reminder of one hideous day he'd never live down.

What he wouldn't give to be just another working stiff with a normal life, like the ones jockeying for position along Martin Luther King Drive today. To have spent yesterday recovering from a New Year's Eve celebration, piled around a television watching football games with friends.

To turn back time and feel human again.

This time last year, he'd had plenty of reasons to celebrate as the number one anchor of the top television station in Detroit.

That life was gone. Taken by a killer's bullet.

And my stupid drive to do what I believed was right when everyone else just went for a story.

That was yesterday's news for everyone in the world except one family – *and me* – who would never forget.

Dwelling on that wouldn't help Riley get through today or save this bottom-of-the-barrel job.

He needed to break a major story. Now.

And damn if the news fairy hadn't dropped a big fat juicy one in his lap just after midnight.

Dumb luck and opportune timing was more like it. All he had to do was get to the freakin' press conference in time to question the DA and force her hand the minute she tried to dismiss the Sally Stanton killing as domestic violence.

No other reporter knew what he had on this story and Riley would use that leverage to turn this into a blockbuster.

And because Sally Stanton deserves a voice. Deserves justice.

He closed his eyes to silence a conscience he hadn't yet forgiven for getting him involved the last time. He needed to just get the damn story. Nothing else.

What about Sally? You just going to let this go once you get your story? Let the DA bury the investigation?

A conscience with a motor mouth. Damn it. *Shut. Up.*

If he hadn't gone into the WNUZ archives last night to dig around in the news files for something he could turn into a story with teeth, he wouldn't have this problem.

But working beat sleeping, where nightmares waited to ambush him.

Riley stifled a yawn, but he was ready for the press conference, and DA Van Gogh. She'd try to bury this killing as another unfortunate death. But she'd have a tough time brushing off why the body had been left on the front lawn of a prominent judge's home.

Sally Stanton's death had to premeditated. Not a domestic violence incident. Riley had more information than the other newsies, something exclusive that would throw a kink into the DA's domestic violence angle, too.

All he had to do was toss out a few suspicions at the press conference to make it tough for her office to back off this case.

That wouldn't happen if the traffic didn't start moving. Even the clock had it in for him these days.

A low curse seared the quiet. Riley glanced at his driver.

Cameraman Ron "Biddy" Bidowski maneuvered their news van from lane to lane, jockeying for any forward position. Buzz-cut black hair and six-foot-one, Biddy carried his two hundred and twenty pounds in all muscle and attitude.

Scowling at snarled traffic, he was in no better mood than Riley after getting called to cover the early-morning homicide tip. Except Biddy blamed Riley for dragging his ass out of bed to film a crime scene in the bitter cold.

Frigid air wailed through the cab from the driver's side. Biddy had rolled down his window, proving ice water ran through his veins.

Riley hunched his shoulders. "Dammit, Biddy, shut that pneumonia hole. You trying to freeze my ass?"

"Nope. Trying to clear the windshield and not ram the picture of that grinning jackass." Biddy nodded forward as if Riley hadn't noticed the image advertising the anchor of WNUZ's fiercest competition in the city. "When you getting *your* picture on the back of every bus in Philly?"

Riley ignored how the question had come out thick with sarcasm. "One more ratings point and four more share points should loosen Lehman's choke hold on the advertising budget. Then the only place you'll see his – " he lifted his chin toward the bus poster " – ugly mug will be on garbage trucks."

"So you say."

"Don't think I can do it?"

Biddy's chest moved with a heavy sigh. "Shit, I'm banking on you doing it. Literally."

That made two of them and Riley's time was running out. He had to jack WNUZ's ratings *before* next week when his contract came up for renewal. He needed to keep this deal so he could stay near his foster father, Jasper Owens, who was going blind – the main reason Riley had accepted this job.

That and this being the only station to offer him an anchor position three months ago after his career crashed in Detroit.

Not like he was trained to do anything else.

No regrets. He'd have dug ditches to be here for Jasper, the one person he'd never be able to repay, but digging ditches wouldn't cover home care costs.

Biddy muttered a pungent curse under his breath when someone cut him off. "You really think this Stanton death's a story?"

I know it is. "Got a feeling about this killing."

The nod Biddy gave him said he'd heard Riley but was reserving judgment. Biddy had busted his tail for the past three months to boost ratings, too. Had more than earned the pay hike that would filter down to the team responsible for a jump in the station's revenues.

And Riley would make sure Biddy got his due, no matter what.

The cameraman had some kind of money problems he kept to himself, which suited Riley. He'd made the mistake of becoming friends with coworkers in the past.

That had blown up in his face.

But lumping Biddy in with that spineless bunch in Detroit would be wrong. He was one of the only people at WNUZ, or in Philly for that matter, who didn't treat Riley like he butchered kittens for a pastime.

The only person who didn't give Riley a daily jaded look to remind him that Detroit had destroyed his career and shredded his sanity.

No, the blame fell to me, not Detroit. A bad decision for the right reason didn't change the outcome.

One that had broken a family's heart and left him hollowed out. He might have a chance to rebuild his reputation some day, but he'd never outrun the nightmares because...nothing would bring back a dead child.

He rubbed his temple where an ache had set up camp.

Wondering about that little boy they'd never found kept Riley awake at night.

Always the boy.

Amazing how one decision could go so hideously wrong.

Can't go back and change the past when it's written in blood. Just get through another day. Right now he had thirteen minutes to make downtown and drop an oh-shit bomb on the DA. Get the story. Let others worry about justice.

Nobody else cares about a dead welfare mother. Why should I?

Because he still felt an ember of passion for helping the victims of crimes. But for the first time in his life, getting involved scared the hell out of him. Someone else would have to champion the pitiful woman found dead in a ragged brown coat.

He would not survive another Detroit.

Biddy wheeled off the interstate and zigzagged along surface streets.

Riley let go of his mental wandering to grab the passenger door handle and brace himself. "Can we make the press conference on time *and* in one piece?"

Biddy ignored the jab, maneuvering the van's steering like a NASCAR driver on holiday. "How come that new DA bitch calls a news conference at nine anyhow? She knows we all covered the killing last night and halfway into breakfast. What's the damn rush?"

"What? You think she cares if you get another hour to snuggle your wife?"

"Sore topic," Biddy grumbled. "One more weekend working and I'll be snuggling a six pack on the couch."

Riley had no advice to offer. He didn't have baggage. Not after divorcing a woman who had thought her wedding vows were optional. Add that to becoming a social pariah three months back, and demand on his personal time had fallen off significantly.

His new motto had been an old saying years ago – a rolling stone gathers no moss. Damned lonesome existence, but one where he wouldn't get his balls nailed to the wall by a divorce attorney's Mont Blanc pen.

Biddy slid around the last corner, catching the curb with his rear tires and jarring Riley's teeth. He slammed their "Nuz You Can Uze" van into the press parking lot at the courthouse with ninety seconds to spare.

There wasn't a parking space to be had.

Undeterred, Biddy jumped the curb and parked on the sidewalk. He slapped his NEWS CREW AT WORK sign on the dashboard and piled out of the van.

The rear doors squealed open and slammed shut as Riley reached the back bumper.

Biddy chortled. "Hope they take the two grand out of Lehman's yearly bonus."

"Two grand?"

"Annual parking fines." Biddy stumbled and almost dropped the camera and a bundle of equipment he juggled.

Riley grabbed the tripod.

Biddy's lurid curses should have melted the snow banked around the sidewalk. "All this just to hear the DA's latest dribble about Philly's tourism image." He turned a hard glance loaded with challenge at Riley, impatience loaded with a hair trigger holding it back. "You got a plan?"

Not one that would make Biddy happy. "I'm giving Van Gogh one chance to tell me why that body was placed on the judge's front lawn. I'm betting she'll blow us off. That's all I need to break the story I have in mind."

Had the murder been a message for the judge?

Or someone else?

Hell, he had a slew of questions *everyone* should be asking. Such as why the killer had placed the body with hands crossed as though posed for the morgue.

And why the killer had called Riley instead of the police.

Chapter 3

Riley set an urgent pace down the sidewalk to City Hall's front door, careful not to lose his footing on the icy surface. If he did take a header, chances were Biddy would pause first to inspect the tripod he carried for damage *then* check Riley for a broken bone.

Covering several quick steps, he reached the door first and waited for Biddy to knock the snow off his boots.

His cameraman belonged to NABET and Riley was a member of AFTRA and both were broadcasting unions. No anchor had to carry equipment for his photographer, but Riley showed any camera staff the same consideration by helping with equipment regardless of his position. Biddy wasn't social to begin with, but in a show of mutual respect he'd told Riley early on, "If you ever get turned in for union violations, you can bet your ass it wasn't me who dropped a dime on you."

Riley's kind of guy, especially Biddy's "get the job done and screw the rules" mantra. Cutting edge news reporting meant scars on occasion. Just part of the job if a person did it right. You had to put it all on the line to get to the facts.

At least, that's what Riley had believed until...

Shit. *Focus on today. The next five minutes. Now.*

Biddy passed through the open doorway and headed for the elevator. He mumbled in a tired voice, "Another suck assignment."

"Trust me. This beats the hell out of missing child assignments." Riley snapped his jaws shut. *Breathe.* He shook his head to clear his mind and stop the backward fall into a black mental hole. *Get your shit together.*

If he wanted to prove everyone wrong who had declared his career over, he had to stick to reporting news...*and* keep a lid on his temper.

Three major network affiliates in ten years.

His foster dad had called him passionate.

Others called him a hot head.

Riley called it cutting through the crap to find the real story. Especially with murders.

The chatter in his brain gave way when a cacophony of voices reached him. Press conference. Briefing room up ahead.

Got it.

Riley walked forward, eyes level. He banged Biddy's tripod on the door jam outside the press briefing room where the commotion picked up volume. Slowing, he pulled up short at the entrance.

Newsies already packed the pressroom. All four of the camera slots positioned at the front of the room were taken.

Three slots had cameras set up to roll.

That fat slob and newspaper muckraker, Henry the Whore, occupied the fourth position.

Henry weighed about three hundred pounds, smelled like last week's ashtray, and loved to piss off TV people. He'd probably been sitting there, holding court until the press conference and disappointed he hadn't had a chance to screw with someone.

Henry had splashed a damning print article the first week Riley took the anchor desk for WNUZ, alluding to the dangers of allowing *some* in the media to go unchecked.

And here the newspaper pig sat in the spot reserved for Riley and Biddy, making it clear whose chain Henry wanted to jerk. Biddy might be a surly partner, but he was loyal to people who helped him. When someone at the station had shown Biddy the scathing article Henry had written, he'd looked as though his fist might go through a wall.

Same way Biddy looked right now.

Riley ground his jaw. He had to deal with the blowhard or face another slam in the rag Henry wrote for. Normally, he didn't care what the hack wrote, but with everything riding on renewing his contract with WNUZ in a week, Riley didn't have time for battling on multiple fronts.

Before he could decide what to say or do, a wink of bright color down the hallway snagged his attention.

The sexy investigator for the District Attorney's office, Kirsten Willingham Massey, stood in a doorway two offices away speaking to someone. And wearing another snug business suit. Today's outfit was a nice silk number in Corvette red. She hooked a lock of chin-length black hair behind one ear and tapped an unpolished fingernail against the doorframe.

Exotic and unapproachable. Riley had heard both terms used to describe her. He'd tried to interview her once, but she'd seen him coming. The look of disgust she'd given him right before she vanished into the closest office made it clear she wasn't a fan of the media.

Or maybe just of him.

As if she'd felt his eyes on her, Kirsten Massey turned her head slowly for a brief glance his way, paused, assessed, then dismissed him with a curt flick of her chin.

He looked down at himself. What? Where'd she come off dismissing him out of hand?

An "uh oh" sound whispered through the press conference room, yanking him back to the present problem. When Riley turned around, Biddy had already dropped his camera and lens bag, heading for the newspaper pig. Tossing the bag strap over his shoulder, Riley stepped forward and lifted the camera.

"You're in our spot, Henry." Biddy glared the rest of his thoughts, but to his credit he'd been semi-polite in spite of a short night's sleep.

Henry answered with a pissy shrug.

No survival instincts in that gene pool.

As a former Navy SEAL, Biddy wasn't boasting or joking when he said, "Move your fat ass or I'll move it for ya." He took another step toward Henry.

Biddy got the same shrug...no, it was worse.

Henry chuckled.

Big mistake. Riley took a step inside the room to diffuse the situation, but he didn't move fast enough. For all Biddy's bulky muscle, he moved with the lithe speed of a panther and cupped both hands under Henry's sweaty armpits. He hoisted the pig and walked him backwards like a rag doll with shuffling cartoon feet.

Then let go.

Henry stumbled. Momentum took over. When his feet lost traction, the only thing to slow his backwards velocity was a forty-plus-year-old window with a thick wood frame.

If his ass went through that window it'd make one hell of a splat on the sidewalk four floors below.

But even Henry's elephant butt couldn't break glass that thick. Right?

Henry's body slammed the window.

A loud crack rent the air.

DA Investigator Massey marched into the room with an arm full of files just as Henry's grimy nails started dicing window trim like a carrot through a Vegematic.

She took in the scene with a horrified gaze.

The room froze. Wood cracked and splintered.

Chapter 4

Shedding camera equipment, Riley dove toward Henry. The window cracked again and every newsman in the pressroom made the sound of sucking air and scrambled to help, but Riley and Biddy were closest.

Riley grabbed a handful of belly fat as the big man kept sliding out.

Dammit. He hooked his fingers through Henry's belt, planted his boots against the wall and stopped the fall. Barely. Biddy clutched a handful of loose skin that might be Henry's neck, which he used to help haul him back to safety.

Henry wheezed and coughed. His face glowed heart-attack red, wimpy hair scattered in all directions. Steam should be coming out of his ears to match the snarl he turned on Biddy and Riley. "I'll...see you bums...in court – "

Useless threat.

" – and tonight's paper."

Bigger threat.

Riley swung around, calculating damage control as Henry stomped out. That's when he noticed that every newsman in Philly – except him and Biddy – had the episode on tape.

Investigator Massey stood with one hand clutching file folders and the other fisted at her hip. The imperturbable calm she wore like a new accessory fractured with a hint of anger in her jade-green eyes.

Biddy's chest heaved twice more, an adrenalin rush clear in his sharp gaze, then his eyes quieted with realization of what had transpired. His shoulders drooped. He mumbled, "She's going to kill me."

Riley felt for the guy. Biddy wasn't talking about the hot DA Investigator standing with chilled silence between them and the door to the hallway. His cameraman would have to explain to his wife how he got canned with Christmas a too-recent memory and credit card debt eating up every free penny already. Trouble like this piled on marital problems and laid the groundwork for a nasty backlash.

But from the way Biddy talked about his wife, she at least cared for the cameraman and not just his paycheck.

She hadn't married with ulterior motives the way Riley's ex-wife had.

Biddy thumped Riley on the shoulder and cocked his head at the DA's stuffy male assistant who rushed into the room apologizing that DA Van Gogh had been called away. Oblivious to what had just transpired, he handed everyone a typed press release about the most-recent murder in Germantown.

"Don't that figure?" Biddy shook his head. "Freakin' DA don't even show after what we went through to get here."

Riley scanned the sheet. Sally Stanton, the thirty-two-year-old welfare mother of a five-year-old boy was found dead of a single gunshot wound to the forehead. An APB for the woman had been issued just hours after she delivered her child to the hospital then left before police could question her. Police believe the victim was killed in a different location, then moved to the upscale area just off Germantown Avenue. Police were interviewing neighbors from where Stanton lived in the Northern Liberties neighborhoods, searching for a possible boyfriend or family member connected to what appeared to be a domestic violence crime.

Not a word about the body being on the judge's lawn. Or any note of questioning the judge's connection to this death.

Or that Riley had been the one to inform the police of the body's location.

The omission about the phone call worked in Riley's favor. Did Van Gogh know *he'd* been the one to tip the police on the body? That should have been in the police report.

Didn't matter. He knew the score. DA Van Gogh hadn't

been called away at the last minute. She just wanted to get her name in the press without having to actually answer a question.

The mayor's narrow focus for the past year had been tourism for the city and schmoozing industry. He painted all the trashy-looking problems with a brush dipped in happy colors and stuffed the dirty laundry down the garbage chute rather than deal with it. Van Gogh needed the backing of Philadelphia's favored mayor for any hope of climbing the political stairway. She'd belt out any song that favored the mayor.

What about the DA Investigator? Would Massey bury her head in the political sandbox and play nice to keep her superiors happy?

The pressroom emptied on a trail of snickering and jokes.

Didn't it figure? With the press conference over, the Henry debacle had just become bigger news than the dead woman on a slab in the morgue.

Riley moved toward his cameraman, but Massey intercepted him with indictment riding her frown.

So she finally wanted to talk to him?

"You two might be up on charges by the time Henry gets to his office." Honey coated her steel voice, but what Riley heard beneath all of it was money and education. Her backbone straightened to the point someone could use it to iron a shirt.

"You *know* I kept Henry from crashing out the window." Riley crushed the worthless press document in his clenched fingers.

What the hell did he care what she thought?

What anyone thought?

"Might not sound that way on the news tonight." She arched one graceful black eyebrow that dared him to argue.

"I'm well aware of how something insignificant can get blown out of proportion in the media." Like turning today's event into an unprovoked altercation.

"Must have been something to it. Henry left before he got the press release."

"What press release?" Riley waved the crumpled paper in

one hand. "You calling *this* a press release? Van Gogh could have emailed it."

Embarrassment colored her cheeks for just a second. "Things come up that can't be avoided. Just the nature of the business." Massey shoved a lock of hair off her face in a feminine motion he'd find sexy as hell if not for the irritating holier-than-thou attitude clinging to her rigid control. "Isn't there enough violence to report without having to manufacture more? Trouble seems to follow you, Walker."

Riley's insides clenched at an obvious reference to his problematic history...and Detroit. So what if he had a rocky background? He never proclaimed himself a saint. Far from it.

And Detroit was none of her business.

He'd seen that closed expression too many times on others unwilling to hear the truth or taking his silence as an admission of guilt, like when he'd been threatened with jail time for defending himself as a teen. Jasper had stepped in and offered to take Riley into his home.

Riley had faced plenty of prejudiced you're-an-asshole looks over the years and answered every one with the patent stick-it-where-the-sun-don't-shine smile he broke out now.

"Thanks for the quote, Investigator Massey." He nodded at Biddy who sidled up to him with his camera running. "This will play far better than that dribble the DA had printed up."

"What quote?" Massey stilled. Her confident mask flickered with confusion.

"I couldn't agree more about the violence in the city," Riley continued. "If the mayor paid less attention to opinion polls and tourism, maybe Philly PD could get enough financial support to do something about nightly murders in low-income areas. Of course, that would involve showing a sliver of interest in what happens to women like Sally Stanton – "

"The Stanton case is being reviewed."

" – and not brushing off her death as domestic violence when she was killed in one place and her body moved to Judge Berringer's front yard. Want to comment on that?"

The investigator kept her chin tilted up and her voice neutral, acting unaffected by his assertion. "The details of this case are not open for discussion."

"Maybe this case *should* be open for discussion." Riley should be more worried about the story and finding out if this mess with Henry was going to affect his contract, but all he could see in his mind right now was Sally's dead eyes stuck wide open in terror. "Maybe the mayor should show as much interest in the crime rate as Philly's tourism."

Massey's fingers made indentions in the files she held. "The mayor *is* concerned about any loss of life, but he's also dealing with the highest unemployment rate in this city's history. Bringing jobs to Philadelphia is critical to those out of work. Just because *you* can pull a job out of your hat anytime you want – regardless of how you performed at your last position – doesn't mean the average citizen has that luxury."

Riley bit down on the retort he wanted to fling, determined to keep his temper locked tight until he got out of here. He tried to glare her into silence.

Didn't work.

She continued her canned statements in that same righteous tone. "As for the Stanton killing, we give every case equal treatment – "

That lit up his bullshit meter.

"Be serious." Riley shouldn't care, not about a woman he didn't know or a city he'd held no attachment to three months ago, but since returning he'd been amazed at how much the police accomplished with antiquated equipment and a dismal budget. "Sally Stanton was *murdered* and dumped on a judge's lawn." He shook the paper. "Not a word about investigating *that* in this joke you call a press release. What about Judge Berringer? What's his connection?"

She went perfectly still as though reacting in any way would be a tactical error. "We're looking into all aspects of this crime."

Riley leaned closer to speak softly and gave her an insincere smile. "In other words, you'll find some way to keep the heat off the judge and mark this off as another unfortunate death." He lifted Biddy's tripod. "Watch for the story at six."

Massey's eyebrow arched a tiny bit more. She smiled with supreme pleasure. "I'll be watching the other channels where *you* will be the lead story."

Biddy clicked off his camera and headed out, toting equipment bags. Riley held his don't-give-a-shit grin as he stepped away, turning his back to Massey. He brightened his smile as he passed a pair of young ladies, hiding his churning-gut reaction from curious onlookers until he exited the building.

In three steps, he lost his smile.

With the DA shuffling off the Stanton case as domestic violence, law enforcement wouldn't spend the additional hours investigating. The story would die along with Sally unless the police could be convinced her death could have been premeditated.

Based on his brief discussion with the killer, this didn't resonate as a crime of passion. It hadn't been much of a discussion this morning, now that he thought back on the call he'd received while in the archive room.

The male voice had been calm, flat and scary quiet.

Street noises playing in the background and the tinny sound of the connection had left Riley with the impression of a pay phone.

Those phones were rarer than finding an honest politician.

The caller had told Riley to film the body first and report the truth, *then* contact the police. The call hadn't lasted a full minute.

All the while, Riley had been seconds from shutting down completely, his heart thudding loud in his ears at the flashbacks ricocheting through his mind. Shock had swamped him at being contacted by another murdering bastard. He couldn't recall how long he'd sat there holding the phone until someone banged a door shut at the station, shaking him out of his stupor.

Riley had ignored the killer's demand that he head to the crime scene first. Screw that murdering asshole. He'd dialed

9-1-1 immediately then headed out the door, replaying the one-sided conversation in his mind, trying to recall the words.

The killer had muttered something about, "Her fault."

Fault for what? That calm and clinical male voice hadn't sounded like a distraught lover or an angry boyfriend.

Riley had shared everything he could remember about the call with J. T. Turner, the investigating Philly PD Detective he was getting to know after covering a steady run of murders for WNUZ. But little things buried in his subconscious kept creeping into his mind. Like the killer saying, "We have a job to do."

Had he meant only last night or something more? And what about the "we" reference? Did the killer have a partner?

The call had let loose a flood of anguish that clouded his mind the whole time, but Riley could swear he'd heard the word, "Soon."

A job to do *soon*?

Stepping outside into the brisk January morning, he sucked in cold air that burned his lungs. If this wasn't a DV, then finding this killer might stop another murder.

Get the story. Stay out of everyone else's business.

But the receptionist who'd put the call through last night had said the guy asked specifically for Riley. He had a feeling, a news hound's sixth sense, that told him he'd hear back from this guy. Not if he got canned. What if the guy called and Riley wasn't at the station?

A psychopath's ego made him dangerous and unpredictable. Riley knew that too well.

There wasn't a damn thing he could do about any of this unless he could convince WNUZ to spin the Henry incident at City Hall.

He paused, just remembering something crucial. The CEO of Henry's newspaper hated the CEO of Riley's network.

Damn. Some things might be beyond spinning.

Chapter 5

DA Investigator Kirsten Massey's teeth clicked when she snapped her gaping mouth closed.

The retreating profile of Riley-damn-Walker stood a head above most City Hall staffers, attorneys and uniformed police moving along the corridor outside the pressroom.

Too bad he had such a nice profile. What a waste for a man like that who oozed testosterone to end up in the news business, the one occupation she detested almost as much as she hated dealing with the new DA.

That was saying something.

Two women heading her way slowed as they passed Riley, who trailed several steps behind his cameraman. He flashed a my-place-or-yours smile at the pair without missing a step. Both women gave him a long, appraising once over, then faced back around. One fanned herself and smiled wickedly.

As the woman fanning herself passed Kirsten, she mused conspiratorially to her friend, "I bet he'd be fun – "

Kirsten flung a silent "get a life" eye roll at the females. If they looked beyond the broad shoulders and wavy black hair that curled carelessly around Walker's neck, they'd find the cold-blooded shark swimming inside that skin. Those women only saw deep blue eyes, not the calculating mind behind his laser gaze.

Kirsten had grown up around the media and knew exactly what that rascal smile hid. Riley was no different than every other newsman in search of the next big story that would push up ratings.

Like he really cared about Sally Stanton's death or Kirsten's caseload? He only jabbed at her to spin her off balance.

And she'd let him, blast it all.

"Massey."

At the sharp sound of her name, Kirsten turned to face her chew-on-my-ass boss. Her muscles constricted, preparing for another battle.

Now that the media had dissipated, DA Cecelia Van Gogh covered the stretch of hallway from her office to the pressroom on long legs beneath the skirt of her tailored navy blue suit. How she walked in that pair of ice pick stilettos all day was beyond Kirsten. She'd never be a slave to fashion over comfort. Before she could say a word, Cecelia started in on her.

"What have we got on the Germantown murder?"

"Not much more than we released to the media until I get the final report from Philly PD." Kirsten shifted the stack of documents in her arms. "I plan to speak with Sally Stanton's neighbors today."

"When am *I* getting the full report?"

Kirsten squelched the hit of irritation at Cecelia's I-want-it-ten-minutes-ago abrasive tone. "Soon as I can. Takes time to sift through all the information, but you know that."

"We're on a deadline here, Massey." Cecelia's lips rippled like a petulant librarian discussing an overdue book instead of a dead woman. "The Mayor wants these domestic killings out of the news before his address on the state of the city in six days."

Did the mayor really think this case would just fade away with the other urban killings because he had a speech to give? Or was this all Cecelia?

Kirsten stuck to the issue. "A deadline? To solve a murder? You've got to be kidding. What's this all about?"

"Do I look like I'm joking? We're on a deadline to get this out of the news." Cecelia paused for affect, head tilted to emphasize her point. She wore her honey-blond hair twisted in an attractive upsweep style intended to show off her chiseled beauty. "He's hosting an early reception for reps of several major corporations at the international business symposium next week. Two national brands are looking at Philly as a possible city for relocating their headquarters."

"That's all good news for Philly, but I don't see how that should affect the way our PD solves cases."

Cecelia tightened shoulders already soldier straight. "I do not want this Stanton case blown out of proportion in the media because the body was dropped at Berringer's house."

"I haven't even seen the police report – "

"My assistant got the bullet points by phone for the press release. Preliminary ME evaluation is the body had been killed somewhere else then dropped on Berringer's yard. Probably someone the judge had put away killed his girlfriend of the week then decided to dump her on Berringer's lawn to screw with the judge. Similar killings have happened before. Berringer's squeaky clean, one of the most respected judges in the country. He's the true victim in all this. The sooner you get humping and put *this* murder behind us the sooner he and his wife will get their life back."

Put the murder behind us? Kirsten managed not to snarl at the obvious meaning beneath Cecelia's words – deep six Sally Stanton's death as just another unavoidable mishap amongst Philly's less fortunate.

Not until Kirsten was convinced this was domestic violence.

Cecelia gave her a look that was the equivalent of snapping her fingers. "I gave you help by dealing with the press conference. Make this your priority and get it done."

"There are limitations to what I can do on this case to begin with."

"Then step outside those limitations if you need to. You have my authorization."

Great. That just meant Cecelia would have more reason to complain if she didn't get what she wanted. "That shouldn't be necessary, but I'll keep it in mind."

That must not have placated Cecelia who unloaded her impatience. "If you've got anything else on the Stanton case I want to hear it."

"This is the *second* killing of someone from Philomena

House in Northern Liberties." Unsolved killings rode Kirsten's conscious with a whip, lashing at her to find a way to stop the criminals. "These deaths *might* be connected."

Cecelia lifted a hand to silence Kirsten then looked around them. No one stood closer than twenty feet away, where two attorneys spoke quietly with an Assistant DA. When Cecelia's attention swerved back to Kirsten she kept her voice just as soft.

"Don't start making noises about connected killings. This Stanton was a welfare mother with an out-of-wedlock kid. Why do you think St. Catherine's put Philomena House in Northern Liberties?" Cecelia's unstable attention flitted past Kirsten then to the side as a group of men passed. "You so much as hint at a connection and Philly PD will be up to their armpits in people claiming other killings are connected. You want that for our PD? That area is full of drug addicts and urban outdoorsmen for crying out loud."

"They're *homeless*, Cecelia, not urban outdoorsmen." Kirsten despised the DA's flippant reference to Philly's less fortunate.

Cecelia waved her hand to dismiss the reprimand. "We closed the last homicide case from Philomena as drug related and Stanton's murder probably is, too, if it's not a DV."

Labeling Stanton's murder as either drug related or domestic violence based on her socio-economic level was morally wrong and negligent.

Plus, the prior related killing from Philomena House was *not* a closed file. Not yet.

"As I said, I haven't had a chance to even review this morning's police report," Kirsten countered. "I want to go through all the evidence *first*, consult with the investigating detective and find out if there are any other similarities – "

"What similarities?"

"Both had single shots to the forehead of similar caliber, both were Philomena residents and both bodies were moved after the vics were killed. Once I finish my investigation, I'll be ready to make a recommendation about how to move forward on this case. We have a responsibility to make sure there isn't a connection."

Condescension came in many forms with Cecelia, like the way she shook her head and paused an extra second. "You really want me to believe a welfare mother from an area known for B&Es and drug deals was popped by a serial killer? That's a stretch. Do you realize what raising that unrealistic possibility would do to the image of this city? That's sensationalizing a death."

Focusing on the city's image was the tourism bureau's job, not Kirsten's or the DA's.

And being ordered to hump harder than the sixteen-hour days Kirsten already put in just to help the mayor save face with corporate America had her grinding what enamel was left on her back teeth. This reminded her too much of the one directive above all others she'd grown up with – protect the family name at any cost. Image. Image. Image.

She'd left that life behind. She'd thought.

From her point of view, she had an uncomplicated job description – find the evidence necessary to convict criminals.

End of statement.

Kirsten met Cecelia's uncompromising stare with an equally determined one of her own. "I can appreciate the timeline you and the Mayor are facing for his speech, but I'm *not* going to perform a faulty investigation to hit a PR-inspired deadline."

"*Every* investigation for this office had better be top notch, but be careful what you discount." Cecelia drew her thick lashes together, cranking the threat in her glare to gladiator level. "There's nothing trivial about this deadline. Bringing tourism into Philadelphia shows industry this is a thriving city, a place people want to visit and a place their employees will like to live. The mayor can't get new industry to come in if people think this is a war zone."

"I'm more interested in making sure we have a safe city for our citizens to live in *now*."

Cecelia's animation quieted abruptly with a chilling change. "Don't ever make the mistake of insinuating that the safety of our citizens is not my first priority."

There was the face and voice of Cecelia's dangerous

political ambition. Kirsten was duly warned, but she wouldn't bow to pressure. "I didn't insinuate anything. *If* we're both after the same thing – protecting Philly's citizens – then I don't understand rushing due process."

The unflattering look Cecelia gave her questioned Kirsten's IQ before her gaze swept the hallway that grew more crowded with people. "Step into the pressroom."

Once Kirsten entered the room, Cecelia followed her and closed the door. She swung around and crossed her arms. "We aren't rushing due process, just being efficient. All of these businesses and people pay taxes that finance salaries, as in money for *your* position that will be the first cut when the coffers run dry. Solve this murder ASAP and put a lid on the media so we can focus on the higher-priority news of an expanding tourism program."

"Not until I get my questions answered," Kirsten persisted.

"Such as?"

"Why was the body of a destitute woman dropped on Judge Berringer's yard? We need to interview his neighbors – "

"No, no, no." Cecelia shook her head like a dog splaying water. "I told the judge we'd keep him and his wife out of the limelight. Reporters are camped out there as it is. Don't give the media anything."

"The media is already digging around. If we shove this under the rug they'll cry foul and how will *that* look in the news?" Kirsten understood both sides of the media, better than most in the DA's office.

"I'll worry about the press. You worry about closing this case, Massey. You've got to learn how things work around here. You've been here a year. That's long enough to have a clue on how we roll in Philly. They may do things differently in Chicago, but here we protect our innocent VIPs – and that includes judges – from being harassed by news vultures."

That was how Cecelia *rolled*, not the city.

Kirsten tapped a finger against the files she still carried. "If the Stanton murder fits a domestic violence profile, we'll limit city resources on investigating, but – "

"There is no *but*," Cecelia sliced in. "Judge Berringer has had no case involving Sally Stanton. I checked that out *myself* this morning. Stanton was probably just in the wrong place at the wrong time. Process the paperwork, declare it DV and move on."

"I'll file my report once I've finished – "

Cecelia released a hiss of frustration. "This wouldn't even make the news if not for being a slow news day. Don't be so anal."

Kirsten slapped her head. "Yeah, I'd hate to be that invested in finding a killer."

Cecelia gave her a don't-be-so-dramatic eye roll. "What about St. Catherine's? They're behind Philomena House. You want to stir up trouble for that little church after all the bishop has been through?"

She *would* poke at Kirsten's empathy for someone publicly humiliated, blast it. "No, of course not – "

"Then don't," Cecelia snapped. "Even the media has enough sense to leave them alone after victimizing St. Catherine's *twice* in the past year. The embezzlement case practically closed their doors. Why do you think they brought in the Enforcer?"

Who? "You talking about the new monsignor?"

"Yes. The city loves this guy. How many times do I have to remind you not to screw with good press? Seems like you'd know that with your family background."

Anything else Kirsten said at this point would not serve her purpose, but she wouldn't budge another inch on this investigation. Cecelia could shove her ridiculous opinion where her head was obviously planted.

Kirsten's cell phone rang, saving her from having to respond. She answered, "Massey."

"Detective Turner, Philly PD. I'm at the morgue. Coroner found something odd on that body from Germantown – "

She did not want to discuss this in front of Cecelia. "Excuse me, detective. Would you please hold on?" Kirsten cut him off and made a point of glancing at her watch. She had a morning full of interviews and meetings, but she wanted to find out what the detective knew about this case.

Talking in front of Cecelia would only cause more problems. She pulled the phone back to her ear. "I'm in a meeting right now. Can I meet you there at 11:00?"

"Meet? Here?"

"Yes, I'll meet you there." She wanted Cecelia to think the call was about asking for a meeting and she could get more done on this case outside the office.

"*Fine*."

She flinched at Turner's curt answer. Add him to the list of people she'd rubbed wrong today, but she'd smooth it over with Turner when she saw him.

"Something on the Germantown murder?" Hope for confirmation of a domestic killing curled in Cecelia's voice.

"Possibly. Catch you up when I get back from the morgue." Kirsten squashed the guilt fingering her neck over letting Cecelia think this would be positive news.

She'd done more than her share of stretching the truth since entering the investigative field, but she still felt the slap of a ruler on her hand from back in Catholic school.

If she were a good Catholic, she'd go to confession

No. If she were a good Catholic she'd have taken this position just to do the job and not for her own agenda – to find the truth behind a missing person.

Cecelia headed for the door. "Unless you receive indisputable evidence at the morgue that proves otherwise, this case is DV."

Kirsten considered using the stack of files getting bent in her grip to beat some sense into this woman. Refusing to allow Cecelia's threat to burn a hole in her control, Kirsten gave a noncommittal, "I understand."

Once Cecelia disappeared down the hall, Kirsten headed to where she'd left her purse and coat with the receptionist outside the conference room. She took a minute to hook up her cell phone Bluetooth receiver on her way out of the building. She considered swinging by her office in Three Penn Square to pick up her emails, but that would run her late with meeting the detective she was already inconveniencing. Besides, he could catch her up on the case in person.

Her cell phone beeped with a call coming through on her way to the elevator. When she hit the receive button on her ear piece, she heard, "Hello, Kirsten?"

How had *he* gotten her cell phone number when she'd just changed it? "Hello, Dad."

Chapter 6

Kirsten exited the elevator on the ground floor of City Hall, waiting to find out why her father was calling. What game would he play this time to get her to come home?

"I left messages for you." Her father said that in his lecture tone, the one he used on employees who revered Theodore Massey.

They didn't recognize it as the voice of a man who could be cold as the Grim Reaper when someone refused him.

Especially his daughter.

She hated how the Bluetooth earpiece made it feel like he was inside her head. Flexing her jaw to loosen her clenched teeth, she tried to sound civil to the man whose voice turned her stomach inside out. "No, your assistant left voice mails. None that stated what you specifically wanted."

"I want to know how you're doing."

Hadn't taken long for his first lie to surface.

"I'm fine. Anything else?" Kirsten clutched her trench coat close and wove her way around slower-moving pedestrians while brittle silence answered her. *Don't like it that you can't bully me?*

"Your mother would want us to be together, to support each other."

No, she wouldn't. Kirsten worked around the pain lodged in her throat. Her mother had rarely uttered her own opinion about anything when Kirsten lived at home, always parroting whatever her father said. The last time Kirsten had seen her mother at the family home in Chicago, her mother had cautioned her not to provoke her father.

Kirsten had replied sarcastically, "I'm twenty six. What's he going to do? Ground me?"

Her mother's voice had carried a chill of warning when she said, "You have no idea what your father is capable of."

Years of watching her petite mother live in the shadow of her father as nothing more than a doormat trophy wife had blown the lid off Kirsten's patience. She'd stopped packing her clothes that last day at home and said, "You're still very attractive. Divorce him and find someone who appreciates you. You deserve to be loved."

Hope had flared in her mother's eyes before she looked away. "I can't."

"Sure you can. I'm taking my bar exam in a week. I'll represent you myself and – "

"No."

"Why are you so afraid of him?" Kirsten had finally asked.

Her mother just shook her head. "I made my bed and can't walk away from it. Just don't cross him. He wants you here in Chicago and working with his company. Give him what he wants and you won't have any problems."

Kirsten had heard that all her life. *Do what your father asks. Mind your father. Your father is right.*

"I am *not* you, Mom. I will not live under his thumb like a helpless bug," Kirsten had said in a snarling tone she regretted two weeks later as she'd watched her mother's casket lowered into the ground.

Four days before the unexpected funeral, Kirsten had received a cryptic voice mail from her mother saying, "I'm sending a friend to you who needs help."

After two hours of trying to locate her mother by phone, Kirsten had finally dropped what she was doing and driven to Chicago. By the time she'd arrived, her mother was in the hospital in ICU after having suffered a major stroke from which she died six hours later.

The doctors had no idea what caused the seizure in a forty-eight-year-old woman who was an avid tennis player in optimum physical condition.

Kirsten wanted an autopsy.

Her father refused to have his wife's body desecrated, but he'd had no problem cremating her.

"Kirsten, I miss you," her father's voice said from the Bluetooth, yanking her back to the present. "Come home for a visit."

She inhaled a quick breath of icy air that froze her lungs. "I've got a heavy caseload and little time off."

"You don't take time off."

"What do want from me, Dad?"

"I feel like I've lost my whole family. I need to see you."

She struggled against all the things she wanted to scream at him. The audacity of his acting as though *he'd* lost a loved one. *She'd* lost her mother, *because* of him. "We never were a touchy-feely family. I do better working all the time. Like you."

He allowed the quiet to fill in for a few seconds, something he liked to do to put his opponents on edge. Didn't work on her. She waited him out until he finally spoke again.

"The new marker is finished. I thought it would be nice for us to be together the day they set it in place."

No, it would be nice to have her mother back. Kirsten couldn't care less about the elaborate statue he'd probably had carved in honor of his wife. She'd bet the media would be involved as well, but refusing him would only raise his suspicions. "When do they plan to set it?"

"Next Monday afternoon."

That only bought her a week. "I'll ask about getting off work." Kirsten moved on shaky legs toward the parking lot where she'd left her car. She squeezed the files when she wanted to have her hands around her father's neck. He'd guilted her into doing what *he* expected of her since childhood, to make her perform according to his vision of a Massey woman. Her rebellion had started before her teens, when she'd recognized her mother's meekness as fear.

But what she felt now went way beyond rebellion and she was no longer a child.

"I have a dinner party planned for this weekend. Why don't you come home and just stay over? Everyone misses you."

"I'll have to work this weekend just to get off Monday."

"That's ridiculous. There's more than one person who can do the busy work."

Busy work? She kicked a dirty snowball out of her way. "I'm not a flunky. My job entails more than pushing papers around."

"Why are you always so hostile, Kirsten?"

Oh, I don't know. Maybe it's because I'm pretty damned sure you killed my mother for something she knew. Kirsten forced herself to take a breath. Maintaining control of her emotions was paramount in dealing with her father, who would attack a weak prey. She pushed calm into her voice so she'd sound reasonable.

"I'm not being hostile. It's cold and I haven't had much rest. And discussing...Mom doesn't bring out the best in me."

"I understand, honey. I miss her, too." Her father allowed another one of those lapses in conversation to stretch for a bit. "Your mother would have been happier if you were here. Even if you didn't want a position at my company, you'd make a hell of a lot more money at a prestigious Chicago law firm."

"We've had this conversation one time too many already. You're not looking at this from my point of view."

"What I'm doing is protecting my family and my companies. It's embarrassing that my daughter wants to work for slave wages and do grunt work...especially in a city like Philadelphia."

Her father and Cecelia Van Gogh had the same skewed set of principles when it came to protecting an image.

Kirsten liked this city and believed in the work she did with law enforcement.

She'd go home on Monday and suffer standing next to him at her mother's grave while she bided her time in hope of gaining the one thing that would bring her father to his knees.

A murder conviction.

She had to suck it up and play nice for now to keep him from realizing the sole reason for her taking this job wasn't simply to thumb her nose at him. She needed this job in this city for any hope of finding out what had happened to the woman her mother had asked her to help.

Kirsten cleared her raw throat. "I'll get home for a visit as soon as I can." One lie to combat so many of his. Now to stay in character so he knew he was talking to his argumentative daughter when she really didn't care what he thought. "But I'm proud of what I do with the DA's office. I would think you'd see putting away criminals as being positive for the Massey image."

"You're *proud* of being nothing more than a gopher after graduating Magna Cum Laude from one of the top law schools in the country? Any law enforcement grunt with a law degree could do what you're doing. Massey women do *not* take pedestrian positions. You had an exceptional opportunity waiting for you here. Still do."

That had worked to shift his attention. He never missed the chance to point out that she had a position in the legal department of his international communications firm waiting for her. If she let him continue, next he'd remind her that he paid the Pennsylvania Law School on the other side of Schuylkill River a hefty amount for Kirsten's degree, which meant she owed him. After all, he'd threatened to cut off her financial aid when she told him she was moving to Philadelphia.

He'd thought since he controlled her trust fund and, thus, the checkbook, she'd come to her senses.

Big mistake.

"I've never been interested in corporate law," she said, digging for her keys when she reached the parking lot. And, more specifically, she was not interested in *his* corporate legal issues. She *hated* anything to do with the heartless media business where the end justified the means – to quote her father's philosophy – and wouldn't have taken a position with his company for any enticement.

Admittedly, she'd gotten her stubborn genetic coding from this very man.

"Kirsten – "

"I really have to go. I'm running late for a meeting. What time is the...event on Monday?"

Another long pause. "I've got a call holding. I'll let you

know as soon as I have the exact time."

The call ended, saving her from acting on the urge to shout, "Liar." He wouldn't have called if he didn't know the time of the new headstone placement down to the second. She could not give in to his badgering and guilt dumps. Not if her hunch was correct about her father's culpability in her mother's death.

Especially if she found the young woman Kirsten's mother had sent to her for help. Right before the funeral, Kirsten had received a call from a frightened woman who'd given her name as Jane Doe and sounded like she was in her late twenties. Jane said she'd only talk in person and only if Kirsten could help her deal with the FBI. That's when Kirsten knew in her heart that her mother hadn't died of natural causes.

Kirsten had told Jane to meet her at an apartment that belonged to Elicia Halladay, the first person Kirsten had made friends with in the town where she'd attended college.

Her first and only friend outside the Massey influence.

After the funeral, it had taken until the next day to get away from her father's house under the pretense that Kirsten needed time to mourn alone. When she'd arrived at Elicia's apartment it was empty and both women were gone.

Did she believe her father was capable of murder?

Yes.

And she'd make him pay for it.

Powerful men just fell that much harder when brought down by the law.

Finding Elicia was key to locating Jane Doe, if either one of them was still alive.

Kirsten spent some part of every day searching for her friend. Elicia trusted one person who lived here in Philly and, based on what Elicia had said, she'd never move away. Kirsten hadn't found that person yet, but she would.

Right now, her job was investigating Sally Stanton's murder and keeping the media – specifically Riley Walker – from interfering while she did. If Walker knew she was taking a closer look at the Stanton murder and agreed with him on several points, he'd dig harder than a dog after a juicy bone.

The minute he turned this case into anything news worthy, the mayor would come down on Cecelia who would make Kirsten's life hell. She could have her choice of jobs with her degree, but Philadelphia was the only place she could find out what happened to Elicia and, possibly, Jane Doe.

Being a DA Investigator gave her access to information and suspecting foul play in her mother's death gave her a legal reason to be searching for Elicia.

Kirsten wouldn't let anyone – especially an ambitious newsman – cost her this position. Nor would she allow Sally Stanton to receive anything less than her best effort in the meantime.

Walker was no slouch when it came to reporting. He had a dangerous background in the media that someone like her father would respect. Not her. With twenty-four hour security squatting outside Judge Berringer's residence, there was nothing Walker could get from digging around that location.

Walker had used his anchor position to film a special that helped Philly PD get some badly needed equipment, but Detective Turner wouldn't talk to the media about a case either.

That meant Riley Walker had no more information than the rest of the reporters who'd left with Cecelia's lame press release and he didn't give two hoots about a welfare mother's death. He'd only come to the press conference to harangue Cecelia about the mayor's economic and tourism programs.

Riley Walker should be out of her way for a little while with the assault charges the newspaper reporter was probably filing at this very minute. The idea lifted her spirits until she wondered again how her father had gotten her new, unlisted cell phone number.

She had only given it to a few people, all of whom were either in the DA office or law enforcement.

Not for the first time, Kirsten wondered just how far her father's powerful fingers could reach.

Chapter 7

Sunshine finally won the battle over fog, leaving the mid-morning skies bright blue beyond the windows of George Lehman's eighth floor office.

Riley sat with his arms crossed, waiting on WNUZ's general manager to finish his rant. *Yada, yada, yada...you're making my life difficult ... yada ... yada...*

Lehman walked to the window that looked out over the west side of downtown Philly where the traffic was probably mangled along Independence Boulevard. He raked his fingers through the few hairs left on his balding head. "I will not have this station in constant legal battles over bullshit."

Not much to say to that, but Lehman didn't want a reply.

Riley had a grudging respect for the general manager even if the man was as abrasive as sharkskin rubbed the wrong direction. Most of the staff and newsies hated the GM's micromanaging, but the station had shown significant improvement since this hardass had taken over operations.

People rarely liked the person who had to make the tough calls.

"I didn't agree with bringing you in, Walker."

"I know that. Think I've proved my value." Riley let that sink in. Lehman might not have agreed with WNUZ's board of directors' decision, but even he had to admit that Riley had increased revenues for the station.

But would it be enough to hold onto this job?

Lehman scratched the heavy jowl that belonged to a man who had enjoyed a daily quota of hard liquor for most of his sixty years. His beady eyes hadn't lost any fire. "This stunt at

City Hall could tank the ratings you gained."

"My special last week on child abuse didn't hurt us." Maybe Riley should keep his mouth closed, but he had to point out some silver in the cloud lining.

"That rating spike was Dr. Ziegler's. Not yours. Now with this City Hall incident . . . "

"*And* Dr. Ziegler is now our new expert on child abuse."

Lehman released a terse sigh. "Fine. You came up with the special, but any doctor on child abuse – "

"No. Ziegler's different and you know it," Riley argued. The woman had almost a sixth sense about knowing if a child had really been abused or not and how to get down to the truth.

"This isn't about her." Lehman's cold glare was low on patience. "This is about you not managing a volatile situation today."

Riley hadn't caused the problem, but Lehman had to give the board a scapegoat. Regardless of what happened, Riley wouldn't point a finger at Biddy.

Enough was enough. He asked, "What do you plan to do?"

Lehman paced back across the room and stopped at the side of his desk, tapping the files stacked on the surface with a long finger. "*No one* is worth putting this station in jeopardy. Your contract is clear as glass about confrontations."

Lehman was a bottom-line kind of guy who wielded his power over anyone who stumbled in his path, but Riley had *some* juice with the board of directors right now. This station hadn't seen a consistent ratings hike in the two years prior to his showing up.

He was also a bottom-line kind of guy.

"You firing me?" Riley asked calmly.

The GM straightened to his full height and whispered something vile under his breath. "You deserve it. Should have expected something like this out of you after that last fiasco."

Lehman's voice had trailed off but Riley caught the insinuation. He ignored the stab in his gut every time someone referred to Detroit as if he'd been going after ratings when he met with the Kindergarten Killer. He'd have gladly handed off the story to another station and lost his job without a peep if they'd saved Sammy Dell.

But Biddy's future was at stake here, too, so Riley kept his eye on the goal and countered the slight with facts. "I've given you solid reporting for three months."

Lehman held up his hands, palm out. "I actually argued against firing you."

Huh? "Why?"

"Because it sets a precedent for a news man to get canned over confrontations. I don't want anyone making my people in the field a target just to get them fired." He paused, facing Riley straight on. "I back all my people, but not if they're reckless."

That isn't what I'd call a vote of confidence, but it's better than I expected. "So the board agreed?"

"Not exactly. The board's giving you a week's suspension with no pay, but there's no leeway on the terms of your probationary contract."

"Fine." Riley could live with that. He still had a story to turn in that would only get stronger once he figured out the connection between the judge and Sally Stanton.

Lehman's faced twisted with puzzlement. "You're awfully confident for a guy one step away from getting canned."

Riley shrugged. "I'm meeting my contract commitment so far." All he needed was for the station's PR department to show some balls and for legal to negotiate a quick settlement with the newspaper. With that, Riley would be back in the anchor seat in a day, maybe two. This whole fiasco might play into his favor for gaining that last point.

In this biz, everything revolved around points and money.

If the Stanton murder turned into a real story, he'd ace that last point and more. That would give him the power to negotiate a *new* contract with some meat to it.

"I wouldn't be so sure about meeting your contract commitments." Lehman said in a voice that almost sounded genuinely concerned. "If you don't deliver three points in eight days you – "

"I know the contract terms," Riley cut in. He had his sights set way beyond the probationary 90-day contract finishing up next week. Why would Lehman think he wouldn't make that last point? "This thing with Henry at City Hall will kick up the last point, maybe more, *if* it's handled right."

Lehman lifted his eyebrows in a "not so fast, buddy" look. "The board wants today's incident downplayed so we don't lose advertisers, too. We spent the first two weeks you were here dealing with picketers. The specials you did on the police and that charity event finally shut them up, but we lost a major advertiser because they felt our station had turned into a media circus of its own."

The advertiser was right. You brought me in to perform like a carnival freak. He kept his thoughts to himself and let Lehman finish his discourse.

"To make that last point count, we have to also maintain our market share over the next eight days. And there'll be fallout no matter how we spin it. Don't think even Tom Brokaw could pull a ratings hike out of his ass in so little time."

"Don't underestimate Brokaw," Riley countered in a tone a hell of a lot calmer than he felt. "Or me."

"You don't understand. You're out on unpaid leave for *seven* days. Still think you're sitting pretty?"

What the hell? He thought he was only losing a week's pay. Riley kept his temper wrenched under control, but every instinct warned him the tables were rotating in a way he wasn't going to like. "You're locking me out of reporting for a *week* when you could use this to boost the station? Does the board realize what keeping me off the anchor desk means?"

"Let's get something straight. The board brought you in for a quick hit in ratings, nothing more. You've handed in some stories with meat and brought up our market share more than anyone expected, but the board's made up of financial gurus, not newsies. I convinced them to keep you, but until you do something that puts this station in the lead, you're just another anchor that can be replaced. Getting the station hit with an assault charge makes you very replaceable."

Riley hadn't caused this latest problem, but he refused to throw Biddy out as shark bait. "That's exaggerating what happened this morning."

"This isn't about just this morning. You're combative with everyone downtown from the DA to the mayor."

"WNUZ afraid to take a poke at City Hall?"

"There's poking then there's damaging," Lehman said. "Having a WNUZ anchor in conflict with the city and other media isn't going to play well with the viewers over a long period of time. People will get a thrill out of watching the Henry incident on the news tonight, but if this gains momentum it'll poison the station's presence in the community and the backlash could undermine everything we've managed to build."

Un-damned-believable. *Who'd I piss off in a past life to end up with this one?*

Lehman shoved his bottom lip up in a bulldog stubborn frown. "If we don't see another point this week we'll still hold our own, but if we _lose_ ground because the viewers think WNUZ is a bully in the media community I can assure you the board will not renew your contract for any length of time."

Riley had never bullied anyone in his life. This was just another example of the power of the media and how it could turn on anyone. "What if I bring you a story no one else in the city can touch?"

The interest that flared in Lehman's eyes died beneath some hidden thought while he debated for several breaths. "If you care about what happens to this station, you'll hand over any news opportunities to the rest of the staff while you're off the desk."

The unspoken implication was that if he didn't share information he was only bluffing about having a story and if he sat on something big he clearly had no investment in the station's future.

Nice move, Lehman. Riley had never let anyone see him sweat and wouldn't give the GM that satisfaction. When in a corner, bluff. "I have a source who won't speak to anyone else."

"If you can turn a big story *legitimately* then I'll be the first one to congratulate you, but if you pull some razzle-dazzle crap that puts this station in a jam I'll be the first one using a shovel to bury you."

Detroit was not razzle-dazzle, asshole.

Riley let it go. He had one more concern. If he was getting a week off without pay, Biddy might face two since he was the one who had gotten physical with Henry. "What about Biddy?"

"Bidowski? Can't be saved." Lehman's voice hummed with finality.

"*Firing* him?" Riley couldn't make that compute. Sure, Biddy shouldn't have let Henry bait him, but altercations happened in the news business all the time, especially to camera operators in volatile situations.

Legal had dealt with far worse and not lost a cameraman.

Lehman was crazy if he thought he could get away with giving Riley a deal and Biddy the axe.

Not going to happen.

"Biddy didn't shove the guy out the window. It was an accident."

"Don't you understand? The board isn't foolish enough to let you go, but they don't want picketers on every station this week. Someone's got to be responsible." Lehman sank into his leather chair and leaned back. "Don't make a stupid mistake. You're getting a break. Worry about your own neck and keep your opinions to yourself if you expect to have *any* chance at a contract in eight days."

Probably good advice, but Riley had never taken the easy way and didn't intend to start accepting career tips from George Lehman.

He had an idea for how to keep both his and Biddy's job, but like any gamble it could backfire. Riley still had Jasper to think about since he couldn't help the aging man if his next job was two thousand miles away in a town with a three-digit population.

Riley forced the tight muscles in his chest to relax so he could sound calm and sell this with confidence. "Biddy and I were together at City Hall this morning. You shell out two different penalties, won't go well with the unions. Raise a ruckus with them, and I doubt the board will like that either."

When that didn't generate a response, Riley clarified, "Biddy goes, I go."

Lehman studied him for several long seconds before he asked softly, "You trying to blackmail *me*, Walker?"

"Me?" Riley shook his head and allowed a smile to creep into his voice. "I'm helping you. If the unions get involved, the board will be looking for a scapegoat. Who do you think they'll toss under the bus then?"

Contempt seeped into the GM's watery eyes. Not a man to be bested by anyone. But Lehman knew the station's public relations department *could* spin this incident if their legal team made a cash settlement to quiet the newspaper blowhard.

On the other hand, if the unions teamed up against the station in a blue-collar city the board would need more than money to appease the viewers.

Lehman should be thanking him, because Riley's suggestion protected his job, too, and the bastard was still locking him out for the next seven days.

Standing up abruptly, Lehman shuffled to the window again as if some answer would fly by outside the glass.

Riley had one hope of saving his future while he was off the anchor desk – nailing a story that rocked. Something big would have to break on the Stanton murder this week to meet that requirement.

Riley liked a challenge but this was the end-all-be-all of challenges.

Three solid ratings points in eight days to save his job and Biddy's, too, since he wouldn't be far behind Riley getting tossed.

Could be a slamdunk.

Or a major shut out.

First, they had to have jobs to lose.

Chapter 8

Kirsten dodged patches of ice as she cut a heel-clicking path down the empty sidewalk toward Philadelphia's morgue, a nondescript two-story building on University Street with unloading docks on one side. She'd blown the last red light to reach the parking lot by eleven on the dot.

Finding the front door was a challenge for anyone walking erect. Since most visitors arrived laid out on a gurney that was weighed then wheeled into a giant refrigerated space, the complaint box didn't get much action. Once inside, Kirsten whipped past the examination rooms on her left where an ME snapped photos of a colorless victim sprawled along a stainless steel table.

Good thing she was on time since Detective J. T. Turner waited near the suite of autopsy rooms, one boot impatiently tapping. With skin the rich color of warm molasses, he stood in contrast to the reflected fluorescent light bouncing off shiny white walls and polished tile floors. Turner's slate gray suit showcased his beefed-up, six-foot body in a way that made her wonder when he found time for the gym with his schedule. He wore a fedora cocked with an air of confidence befitting the detective named as one of Philly's finest. The keen intelligence in his brownish-black eyes struck her as the most remarkable part of a face that was quietly attractive.

The closed door on his left did its best to shield odors of the examination room, but Kirsten knew from experience, the lingering smell of death couldn't be gotten out of clothes, hair or skin without a thorough washing.

She offered a conciliatory smile. "Thanks for meeting.

What have you got, Detective?"

"Might not be much, ma'am." Detective Turner was as nice a person as his clean cut looks promised, but his tone suggested he was not happy about a second trip to the morgue.

"I'll take *any* information on the Germantown case at the moment." Frustration slipped through her voice before she could stop it.

Turner's gaze snapped with annoyance. "I emailed you a copy of my report, *ma'am*."

Kirsten ran her fingers up to shove a lock of hair behind her ear and frowned at his reaction. Her fault. "Sorry. That came out wrong. I know how prompt you are in filing reports. I wasn't at my office when I spoke to you so I didn't get a chance to access my computer before I headed over here. I haven't read your report yet. Would you, please, give me the short version?"

The subtle lift and softening of his black eyebrows indicated he understood and allowed his anger to slide away. He lifted the notepad in his hand and flipped back a couple of pages then started reciting in a monotone.

"Vic is Sally Stanton, mother of one, a five year old boy. 9-1-1 was called at 12:52 am this morning with a report that a woman's body would be found in the Germantown area. Fully clothed corpse, no sexual abuse noted, single gunshot to the forehead. Lack of blood near body indicates victim was killed at a different location than where the body was discovered. Hole consistent with a .38 caliber bullet, which the ME dug out of her skull an hour ago. Location of body identified as the residence of Judge Earl Berringer."

"Did the judge find the body?"

"No, ma'am." Turner glanced up from his notes, those sharp eyes holding something back, but he continued before she could pinpoint what it might be. "Want to know what I called you about?" He indicated the examination room behind him with a tilt of his head.

"Sure."

"One of the ME interns found oil on Stanton's head."

"What kind of oil?"

Turner rolled one of those wide shoulders in a shrug. "Won't know until further testing is performed, but the tech said the clear appearance and viscosity is similar to cooking oil."

Kirsten turned that over in her mind. "Maybe Stanton was killed at home while cooking?"

"No idea. I have men searching Stanton's apartment at Philomena House and interviewing neighbors. No sign of blood or struggle reported from there so far. Be a while before we get the ME's final report."

Probably a long while with the ME's backlog of work.

"Any guess on when they'll have that report?" Of all people, she knew how strapped local law enforcement and everyone else involved in the investigation was for funds. Having worked part-time during college at a small police station to gain experience for being a DA Investigator, she had an appreciation for how much Philly PD accomplished with so little.

Turner drew a deep breath and expelled the lung full of air while he thought out loud. "Two, maybe three months. If interns weren't here right now and hungry for details after watching too many CSI shows we wouldn't have heard about the oil at all."

Without strong forensic, or any evidence to the contrary, this played into Cecelia Van Gogh's hands, blast it. The DA would leap on any chance of writing off Stanton's death as DV, which the case was starting to sound like.

Not that Kirsten wanted to turn Stanton's murder into anything it wasn't, but neither did she want City Hall forcing her to close the case prematurely.

"Is that all, *ma'am*?"

She really hated to be called ma'am in that tone when she was only twenty-seven. Turner couldn't be much older and probably considered his address professional, but every time Kirsten heard *ma'am* she got a vision of her mother in clothes by the same designers who outfitted Queen Elizabeth.

Kirsten didn't overdress. In fact, she wore clothes with a little attitude. Screw the Massey name and image.

But she needed to make allies in Philadelphia not enemies,

especially with the police department.

"Yes, that helps a lot, Detective Turner. Thank you for waiting. I know you're busy and appreciate your time." Kirsten had bent over backwards to show the local PD she was not Cecelia who thought playing hardass around law enforcement was part of her job description. The DA didn't seem to care that she rubbed people on the government's side of a case raw as lye soap. "I'll find out if we have any funds available to send this out to a private lab and cut that time."

"Good luck with that."

Kirsten had her doubts, too, about getting any help on this case in particular when the evidence was pointing toward a domestic crime. There was no strong tie between this and the drug-related killing of a young man from Philomena House ten days ago except the bullet hole in his forehead and bodies being moved, but something kept pecking at her conscience.

Coincidental or a connection?

Damn Cecelia and her get-this-behind-us attitude.

Kirsten had a duty to all citizens, no matter where they fell on the socio-economic totem pole. "I won't know about funds until I ask."

"Fat chance of getting an extra nickel for lab work." Turner's wry smile turned the sarcasm into a friendly taunt. He tapped his closed notebook against the palm of his hand in a silent rhythm.

She didn't blame him. "I know you and your men do miracles with a shoestring budget. I'm not making promises, but I'll do what I can." She'd have to go through Cecelia, but anything was possible. Was this the time to pick a battle? "I'd like your honest opinion on something."

"Okay."

"I'm more than willing to go to bat for the money, but I don't want to do it unless you agree that we should investigate further on this case."

He didn't answer at first, allowing his gaze to travel past her shoulder before it returned to her. "What's *your* honest opinion?"

Her answer could be the difference between gaining his respect or being dismissed as clueless, but she would only give him the truth. "First of all, I think everyone deserves our best on solving a crime, but I know there are so many you have to prioritize. Second, I can see how a welfare mother's death wouldn't rank high on most people's lists."

He stopped tapping his notebook, but didn't comment.

"To be perfectly honest with you, Detective, I don't think Sally Stanton was a victim of domestic violence though I don't have anything solid to offer as evidence. And I can't in good conscience let this get brushed off as DV when it feels like more."

Turner studied her a minute. His tough shell cracked a bit when his mouth softened further. "To tell you the truth, I have the same feeling. Moving the body to another location doesn't fit with DV."

She enjoyed a charge of encouragement. "I'm glad to hear that. Okay, I'll get moving to see if we can pull some funds and please let me know if you hear about anything else."

"Will do." He slipped his notebook inside his coat. "By the way, nothing's turned up yet on that hooker with the chewed up ear."

"Hooker? Oh, right, Lucy. Thanks for keeping her in mind." Kirsten suffered a moment of guilt over having told Turner a friend of hers was searching for a woman called Lucy whose right ear had been bitten half off by some man. The dangers of being a prostitute. That's how Elicia and Lucy had met eight years ago, before Kirsten and Elicia became friends. Kirsten first met the brassy Elicia in the police headquarters near college where Kirsten had been working part-time to gain law enforcement experience while finishing her degree.

Elicia later told her they *both* had degrees, but Elicia's was from the school of hard knocks.

There couldn't have been two more unlikely women to become friends than Elicia and Kirsten, but Elicia never met a stranger. She had more backbone and grit than any woman Kirsten had met before, and none of the advantages of the women Kirsten had grown up around. Elicia soon became a fount of information on how to spot illegal activities *and* how to cook great spaghetti sauce.

Elicia's friend Lucy said she'd always stay near her baby girl who lived with relatives in Philadelphia.

All Kirsten had to go on to find Lucy was a chewed-off ear.

Turner tipped his head in goodbye. "Got to run."

"Of course. Thanks again for meeting me."   Kirsten remembered one more question about the dead welfare mother as Turner sauntered off two steps. "Do we know who called in the 9-1-1 on Stanton?"

When he turned around, she could swear he sighed from the lift of his shoulders. "Yes. A television station received an anonymous call just after midnight with the body location and instructions to contact the authorities. It's all in my report, Ms. Massey."

"What television station? Who took that call?"

"WNUZ." He hesitated. "Riley Walker took the call."

For the love of...

Walker hadn't said a word to her at the press conference. Kirsten ran back over their brief conversation in her mind. Not a word. That sorry scumbag had hidden this detail and toyed with her the whole time. But wasn't that the way her father's reporters were trained?

Give up nothing. Use any means to get the story.

The world of media revolved around who won the race for the story or came up with an exclusive. Her father had once joked, "I'm thinking about offering a new Mercedes to any reporter who gets a killing on film."

Wouldn't dear old Dad have loved someone like Walker in his stable? A reporter who could sleep at night after that live interview with the Kindergarten Killer? She shuddered at the sick memory. Her heart ached for the family.

Riley Walker was about to find out she had no sense of humor when it came to a dead welfare mother.

Turner's phone chimed while he waited in solemn silence. He answered it, nodded a couple of times, then his mouth flattened into a grim line. He hung up and lifted eyes that had lost all warmth. "That was about Sally's little boy. He's missing."

The fist gripping Kirsten's heart squeezed. "I thought he

was admitted to the hospital last night."

"No. My report stated that Sally took her son to the hospital then left with him before the police had a chance to question her."

Kirsten wanted to strangle Cecelia. The press release had neglected to mention *that* detail. Or that someone had called the tip in to Walker. If Kirsten had read the police report this morning she'd have known that Walker had taken the call. Had he shared everything?

Would a reporter *ever* share everything willingly?

Based on what Kirsten's assistant had said when she called on Kirsten's drive here, Walker's station intended to suspend him, pending investigation of that little debacle at City Hall. If he did end up suspended, he'd have plenty of time to come in and review the phone call he took one more time.

And if anything happened to that little boy because Walker withheld information about the phone call to get a jump on a story, she'd bounce his balls back to Detroit.

Chapter 9

Within minutes of leaving Lehman's office, Riley found Biddy leaning against the wall in an alcove near the break area of the executive level of WNUZ. Biddy held a cup of coffee that had to be gourmet up here in "carpet land" as the reporters called it. The eighth floor of the Liberty Building was a world apart from where the newsies hung out three floors down.

Quieter than the news pit on the fifth floor where police monitors chattering in the background made shouting a necessity.

The only yelling on the eighth floor came from George Lehman. But even he was quiet now.

Riley strode forward, grinding mentally on a way to turn this fiasco around.

His cameraman stood alone, his casual dress and dangerous stance out of place among fragile pieces of glass art and a wall with a smattering of Emmy statues.

Biddy lifted his head when Riley reached him. The look of despair hovering in his eyes punched Riley in the solar plexus. He wouldn't expect a former SEAL to fear much in life, but Biddy was clearly worried about losing his job.

Lehman wanted to dump the blame on Biddy for the Henry incident at City Hall, but to be honest the cameraman hadn't done anything Riley wouldn't have done himself at one time.

And wanted to do badly this morning.

And Biddy wouldn't be in near as bad a jam if not for being caught in the crosshairs of Lehman's attitude against

Riley.

"They getting rid of me?" Biddy stood away from the wall, thick forearms crossed, ready to accept the decision.

"Not yet."

"Yet? What does that mean?"

"He wanted to dish out separate penalties until I reminded him our unions would kick a fuss." Riley watched as understanding settled in Biddy's face that Lehman *had* wanted to fire him. "We're both suspended for a week."

"Guess it's not as bad as it could be. Still got health insurance."

Riley studied him for a minute, but didn't push for details. Since Biddy had grumbled once that he didn't like his wife working so hard, Riley assumed she had insurance, too.

Biddy's gruff exterior folded briefly under the weight of his gloom. "The wife's had a couple problems already, needs to stay off her feet. We've maxed out our credit cards." He shook his head. "She quit work as a temp and is doing what she can by computer from home, but even *with* insurance it's already going to be tight to have the baby we're expecting."

Riley nodded. He doubted he could say anything that would lighten Biddy's load.

"We can make a week on money we got stashed, but it's a high-risk pregnancy. If I lose this job, insurance won't cover a lot of extras she needs and Lehman's gonna hold my insurance hostage during a suspension. We lost two babies already. I'm more concerned the stress will cause her to miscarry."

Well, damn. No wonder things were tense at home for Biddy.

Biddy stared off for a minute. "It was a helluva lot easier facing down terrorists than dealing with assholes and corporate bullshit."

More bad shit would twist the knife in his gut right now, but a man like Biddy would want to know exactly what he faced.

"That was the good news." Riley considered how much to share about the terms of his 90-day contract for a nanosecond. The terms didn't matter. If he failed to pull a story out of his bag of tricks he and Biddy would both be gone.

"What's the bad news?" Biddy scratched his chin, eyeing Riley closely.

"I've got eight days to hand the board a third ratings point jump. If not, they'll have the ammunition to get rid of me...and you."

Two suits strolled past the alcove, chatting, just as Biddy released a lethal curse.

The men went dead silent and turned stern faces to the cameraman who glared them into submission. When they continued on, Riley cocked his head toward the elevators. "Let's get out of here."

Biddy followed him, neither one speaking until they reached the bottom level where the elevator doors opened to the parking deck. A wicked breeze howled around the concrete pillars and slammed Riley in the chest with every step to where he'd parked his Tundra pickup truck. No one hung around long with temperatures in the low thirties.

He hated this weather. "God, feel that wind. One thing I hadn't missed about Philly."

"Cold as a witch's tit in a brass bra face down in the snow." Biddy didn't so much as rub his arms in spite of wearing no jacket.

"Wish I could convince Jasper to move somewhere warm like Florida." But Jasper wouldn't leave Philly, which weighed heavily in WNUZ's favor when the station made Riley what amounted to a pity offer. Jasper needed Riley's help whether he'd admit it or not.

"Philly has personality." Biddy stopped next to the Tundra and turned on Riley. "What're you not telling me about this deal?"

Riley would have been surprised if Biddy had let it go with a superficial explanation. "Lehman will do damage control, but the board is running scared about the advertisers. I think he doubts the board will renew my contract, but if I can land a big story this week the station *will* pick up that third ratings point. All the board cares about is what translates into profit. No advertiser will walk away from that."

Biddy hooked his thumbs in the front pockets of his jeans. "You did a favor for me with Lehman and the board so I'm in this with you. We need a hot story. How do we get it?"

Riley hadn't expected the "we," but wouldn't turn down help from a guy with Biddy's military intelligence skills who had grown up in Philly. "The only thing I have right now is the Stanton murder, but I think it was premeditated."

"I don't see somebody killing out of rage and taking the time to move the body, but what else have you got?"

"The caller said something about 'her fault' at one point, which makes me wonder what Sally did. When I asked the caller who he was and how he was involved, the guy said 'I'm cleaning up.' He was calm and sounded like he was just taking care of business. None of that fits the MO for a domestic killing. I'm going to find out what I can about Sally and her son, and anyone connected to them."

"I see your point." Biddy scrunched his mouth to one side, pondering on something. "I know this ain't your favorite topic, but what about a piece on Sally's kid?"

"No." Riley answered so fast and hard he expected Biddy to snap right back at him. "I'm not doing anything with any kids. Ever."

I thought after you did that special on the child abuse doctor you might – "

"No kids."

"Okay, your deal." Biddy raised his hands in a just-trying-to-help motion. "If this don't work out, I might have a lead on another story."

That surprised Riley. "Like what?"

"Pope's visit to Jersey in a couple weeks."

"Old news and we need something in Philly."

"There's some behind-the-scenes scuttle going on."

He wanted Biddy thinking much bigger. "I haven't heard anything significant about the Catholic Church recently and pedophilia is yesterday's story – "

Biddy shook his head. "Not that. Let me check out what I got and I'll get back to you."

Screw it. If the Stanton murder fell through, Riley needed

something so he wasn't about to discourage Biddy. His cell phone played the default jingle, meaning caller unknown. He pulled the phone out of his coat pocket. "Walker."

"This is DA Investigator Massey."

Riley lifted his eyebrows in surprise. "What can I do for you Investigator?"

"Be in my office in an hour."

"Why?"

"To answer questions on the Stanton case."

Riley checked his watch. A little before noon. "Why don't you meet me for lunch?"

The hesitation should have warned him, but the control behind her smooth voice didn't waver. "This is not a social call, Walker. Be in my office at one o'clock or I'll send an officer to give you a ride. Got it?"

"Consider it a date." The phone line died.

Riley killed the call on his end. What had happened in the last couple of hours for Massey to want to talk? "That was Investigator Massey. Wants me in her office at one. That might produce some answers."

Biddy gave a little shake of his head. "Better be careful with her. She ain't been here long, but longer than you have and she's tough as nails. Not a good one to jerk around. Doubt even your slick routine will charm her."

Riley grinned. "Ye of little faith."

"Telling ya, she ain't got a soft corner on her."

"The bigger the challenge, the sweeter the prize."

Biddy scowled and walked away. Not that Riley expected Biddy to turn into a happy guy any more than he expected Kirsten Massey to give up one of her secrets without a fight.

Or did she have word of Henry's newspaper legal eagles filing an assault charge?

His cell phone rang. Another unknown caller.

He keyed the button to talk and smiled when he asked her, "Change your mind about lunch?"

"Careful who you talk to. You're being followed." The line died.

Riley pulled the phone away slowly and stared at it. He raised his eyes and took in the parking deck, but no one loitered.

He'd heard that voice before. Just after midnight this morning. The killer had his cell phone number.

Chapter 10

"Bless me father, for I have sinned. It's been two weeks since my last confession. I...I had impure thoughts about the teenage boy who shovels my driveway." Crying and sniffles, then Mrs. Feldman cleared her throat.

Here it comes again. Same thing I heard two weeks ago.

"I know it's wrong, but my husband travels all the time with his job."

Can't criticize him for that, besides getting away probably keeps him sane around you. Change of place, change of perspective.

"He doesn't appreciate me, father. I'm stuck home raising three kids and doing their homework at night, plus dealing with anything that needs to be fixed around the house or the car while he takes people to dinner."

Get a life. Or better yet, get a job during the day while the kids are in school. He waited through the pause as she made squirming noises.

"I tried to talk to him about it, but he just ignores me, or if we argue he tells me to find something to do during the day."

See?

"I know it's wrong to think about a seventeen-year-old boy, especially being a married woman, but Cody makes me feel special."

Not special, young. You want to relive your youth.

"He makes me happy, but not like we've done anything, just that he brightens my day. When I'm happy, I don't hit the dog or my kids."

You hit the kids?

"My husband doesn't understand how tiring it is to raise three children alone. I'm exhausted all the time and stressed out. I deserve some peace and rest, too."

Yes, you do deserve rest. Eternal rest.

Chapter 11

If I died right now I could ask God why humans hurt one another.

Margo Cortese considered praying for a swift death before her brain exploded from an excruciating headache. She could suffer the pain in her head better than that in her heart.

Poor Sally. And what about Enrique? Where could the wee one be?

Swallowing the lump in her throat, Margo licked her dry lips and kept trudging down the street toward St. Catherine's. Thankfully, temperatures were still in the mid-thirties at lunchtime, warm by Philly standards in January. Her black dress pants, raspberry cotton turtleneck and sturdy canvas jacket were ideal in this cool breeze, but she could do without the endless blue sky and bright sunshine she'd send a prayer of thanks for on any *other* day.

How about a few clouds, huh? *Just until my head stops feelin' like a swollen melon about to split.*

Sunglasses spared her the worst of the glare blazing off the snow, but the bright light still aggravated her pounding head as she picked her way along the narrow strip of half-shoveled walkway running from Second Street to St. Catherine's stone-and-mortar chapel.

Had to remind Valdez to clear a wider path for church and outreach center visitors. This would be a treacherous walk for the elderly, who seemed to make up most of St. C's parishioners. Not that St. C's was much different from any other inner-city parish, but after only seven months here, Margo was still adjusting to feelin' so young in comparison.

At her last parish in a suburb of San Francisco, she'd been considered middle-aged at twenty-nine years.

She was *not* middle-aged.

Just as Monsignor often said, "Change of place, change of perspective."

When she reached the steps to the chapel, Margo made a right turn, taking the walkway that led to the entrance of the three-story, brick addition attached to St. C's by an enclosed breezeway.

Her head throbbed, but her heart hurt more.

If vengeance belonged to the Lord, she wanted to ride shotgun for him.

Tomorrow. When she felt better. Hopefully.

Extreme stress triggered really nasty head-bangers that forced her to spend some nights slumped over a toilet. Hearin' about Sally Stanton and wee Enrique qualified as extreme. Margo swallowed the misery climbing her throat over the news she had to be givin' Monsignor soon.

And over havin' to explain her delay in returning from lunch. Opening the weathered pinewood front door to the administrative offices and outreach center, she kept her dark shades on when she entered. No one should have to face all that yellow paint in the foyer without eye protection.

Couldn't Baylor have chosen a different color than sunshine? But Baylor was so indispensable to St. C's running, not to mention the restoration work goin' on, he could have painted the whole interior Pepto Bismol pink and Monsignor would have only nodded and been happy.

A glare flashed off the newly stained hardwood floors.

Did *everything* have to reflect the sun?

Just kill her now.

Her queasy stomach balked at the smell of fresh paint. More of Baylor's doin'.

Maybe she should be passin' out a memo – Margo Cortese, not the mornin' person. The school clock on the wall corrected her. Okay, not a just-past-noon person either.

She snatched off her glasses when she reached the quieter central hallway that fed to all the offices. The hall ended in front of the door to the kitchen and had an exit door on the left for the parking lot in the rear...that Valdez was slipping out of at the present moment.

Wasn't he supposed to be upstairs tidyin' up the construction area? The smattering of freckles across his nose and cheeks, partnered with carrot-red hair, didn't look like the mug shot of a young man convicted of burglary and assault. She couldn't reconcile the name Valdez with all that red hair either.

But then she was Irish as the day was long and didn't have the first freckle – and hair more auburn than red.

Valdez was Father Ickerson's problem, not hers. She hadn't figured out Valdez yet and was willin' to give anyone the benefit of the doubt, but she knew lazy and sneaky when she saw it. Father Ickerson, on the other hand, had high expectations for his protégé.

She would leave it to the good Father to deal with his underling. Dismissin' Valdez, she headed to her office that smelled of history like the rest of the original building. Of being inhabited by many others long before her time, quite a contrast to all the remodeling happening on the second floor.

The remodeling was going slowly, but construction workers were donating their time and skills, plastering and painting the new outreach center up there. All under Baylor's watchful eye for detail work and his love for St. C's.

Not that she didn't appreciate his skill and sincerity, but...did he have to be so talented?

Monsignor loved art and admired the man's ability to shape things with his hands.

The only thing she could do with her hands was type.

Jealousy is not attractive. Especially when the old guy just wanted to do a great job. And he was far more spry and pleasant than some people, like Icky.

Just thinking about the cantankerous Father Ickerson sharpened her headache.

Rolling her shoulders, she worked on mind control, fighting the potential migraine that had become an unpleasant companion since her first menstrual cycle. Almost as unpleasant as when she reached the third doorway on her right to find Father Angus Ickerson inside her office with his back toward her.

Icky stood too close to Monsignor's door on the far side, his head cocked at a snooping angle, hands squeezed together behind his back. No doubt trying to look more clerical and less like an accountant with a perpetually pinched expression.

What was Icky doing in here? Waiting to see Monsignor? Wasn't Icky supposed to be listening to noon confessions? St. C's always had a few on Tuesdays.

She stepped inside.

Icky swung around, startled, then lifted those chicken lips into a tight little grin. What had him all in a tizzy?

"Can I help you, Father?" She paused several feet from him, shrugging out of the faded red canvas jacket that had been a decade old when her brother passed it down to her. She tossed the coat over file folders blanketing the top of her desk.

Father Ickerson, who boasted of havin' studied in Madrid and Rome before comin' here, smelled like garlic or curry most of the time, the reason the kids nicknamed him Icky.

She had other reasons.

"Big news about the Pope," he tittered, hands now squeezed together just beneath his weak chin. Wavy brown hair, wide-set small brown eyes and a mass of freckles. If not for the pale skin as a backdrop he'd look like a tree trunk. A tree trunk listenin' in on phone calls happening in the next room now that she heard Monsignor Jack Dornan's voice.

That sneakin' stinkpot Ickerson. She ground her teeth. She should have been here sooner. Monsignor expected her to watch his back and protect his privacy. To be the layer between him and everyone else when necessary.

"How would you be learnin' this big news about the Pope?" Margo asked, crossing her arms. "And what news might that be?"

A loud thump, thump, thump on the ceiling pounded as though God drove nails the size of railroad spikes into steel beams. Plaster chips trickled down over her jacket and desk. Her ten-foot high ceiling had yet to be covered with the new hanging tile system, but that was a low priority with so much more goin' on.

Right now, though, construction workers remodeling the second floor were turnin' her office into a torture chamber.

Father Icky, obviously not sufferin' from a killer headache, angled his chin as if a peasant had dared to question him. Just into his thirties, he acted his shoe size most days.

She might not be a deacon or priest, but she *was* chief of staff and deserved his respect as such.

Before Margo could press Icky, Mr. Baylor came in whistling. She recognized the melody as *The Eucharist* and turned slowly, her only speed until her stomach stopped threatening to play volcano. Just another side effect of her ambitious headache.

Baylor's bushy silver mustache hovered over a jutting bottom lip and rigid jaw. St. C's quiet, but oh-so-competent handyman, maintenance man, do-whatever-man wore faded coveralls. He raised intelligent eyes to her that had seen close to six decades of livin' and were still bright with life. St. C's would fall apart without Baylor, even if he sometimes demanded as much of Monsignor's attention as Icky wanted. Men could be just as difficult as unruly boys. He placed a stack of mail on the only open corner of her desk.

"Thank you." Margo smiled at the old guy who never complained. He didn't smile much, but he always did his work and the kids liked him. Much better than they liked Icky.

But then, few people liked Icky.

Guess she'd have to confess that uncharitable thought.

"Want me to clean up in here this week?" Baylor asked. "I could do the Monsignor's office, too."

"No thank you, Mr. Baylor." She answered nicely, the same way she did every time he asked to clean her and the Monsignor's offices. She didn't like people touching her things and never minded maintainin' her own space. And Jack Dornan? He was a stickler for his private sanctum.

Before Margo could resume questioning Icky about what he was doing here and why, the Monsignor's gray-green door opened with a squeak of admonishment that made her jump. She gritted her teeth at the sharp noise.

The Monsignor's slightest move exuded power and careful decision. His casual greeting commanded attention. At six feet, three inches tall, with shoulders so wide his crisp black clergy shirt and Roman collar had to be custom made, he didn't look his fifty-six years. Nodding first at Icky, Monsignor said, "Father," then he turned to Baylor with a smile. "Always a pleasure to see you, Mr. Baylor. How's the scroll work coming in the chapel?"

Baylor scratched his beard and said, "Quite fine, Father, but I'd like your opinion on a section when you have a moment."

Margo squelched the urge to roll her eyes, which would have drawn Monsignor's attention, and in the wrong way. The Monsignor did not have time to inspect every little –

Monsignor nodded. "Be happy to take a look this afternoon." Then his gaze slid to Margo. "Didn't hear you come in from lunch, Margo."

Might that be because I slithered in, silent as a mouse with stolen cheese?

"Good afternoon, Monsignor." Margo didn't let her pain or frustration show. She admired this man above all men but the Pope. "Your door was closed when I arrived. I'd have called to let you know I'd be a few minutes tardy, but there's a problem with my home phone." She told the truth. Wouldn't lie to him any more than she would to God.

But the truth took a crooked turn when she omitted the part about forgettin' to pay her phone bill at her cottage down the street, thus the dead line this morning.

"You're fine." His voice held no rebuff, which it rarely did for others, though he allowed himself no room for error. "The schedule is still casual here until the construction is finished, which should be soon."

Monsignor's blue eyes were so clear she could practically see through them. Shiny gold hair fell in gentle layers, just long enough to suit all the members in the parish from young to old. The few lines at the corners of his eyes had formed from years of quick smiles and narrowed concentration.

Just one of many expressions Margo had witnessed in the past eight years.

"I'm here." Deacon Grizzle entered softly for a six-foot-five man who towered over her five-ten and Icky's six feet. Baylor sort of disappeared in the midst of these giant men. A quiet mid-sixty year old, Grizzle wore his standard khaki pants, beige cable-knit sweater and button down shirt, pale yellow today.

What was it with this place and yellow?

"Here for what?" Margo muttered, glancing past Grizzle as Baylor turned and left. She hated how the man moved around skittish as poor relations at a feast. She knew how that felt, but appreciated his respecting parish business by leavin'.

Icky, on the other hand, had no compunction about enterin' private conversations.

"I have news that must stay between the four of us since it isn't confirmed yet," Monsignor answered.

Icky vibrated with excitement.

Overhead, pounding started up like a competition between two hammers, out of sync.

Most women wanted cosmetic surgery. Right now Margo would take a lobotomy for relief from her head and Icky.

"Everyone step into my office." Monsignor led the way then closed the door once they were all inside. The finished ceiling filled with insulation dulled the noise some.

Monsignor's familiar scent reminded her of early autumn and citrus. Some smells would always instill a basic animal reaction. His conjured up a sense of peace and comfort for her in the worst of times.

Dark-stained panels covered his walls, not yellow.

A man with a man's taste. He propped a hip on his cherry wood desk that held one tidy stack of folders, a reading lamp and writing accessories. How did he accomplish so much without ever looking disorganized or rushed?

Margo straightened her desk each night, but she'd never been accused of bein' OCD.

Margo, Icky and Grizzle spread around the Monsignor's desk, waiting for what he had to say. His smile started from deep in the heart and broadened. "I just got off the phone with Bishop Gautier who told me the pope may stop *here* during his visit to America."

"Sweet Mother of Mary." Icky bounced on the balls of his feet as if he'd been told he would become the next pope.

Grizzle ran a hand through his salt-and-pepper gray hair, his voice in hushed awe. "A dream come true."

"'Tis an amazing honor for St. C's," Margo said. A tremor of excitement raced along her spine. The pope. Here. The Monsignor must have had a hand in this, but he'd never say. For a man whose reputation knew no boundaries, a man who inspired awe in everyone around him, he wanted only what was best for his flock.

In the eight years she'd known Monsignor, he'd been the only one to inspire her to become more than a clichéd result of a dark past. He'd spearheaded changes in the church many never believed possible, all with the blessin' of those above him. Some said the Cardinal, and even the pope himself, supported Monsignor's pushing the boundaries.

Monsignor switched gears just that fast and moved to the next phase of this meeting without missing a breath. "Exciting, but it also means we have a lot of work to do. We've got to get this parish cleaned up, push the work upstairs to have it completed on time and show the pope how St. Catherine's is the flagship program for more inner city outreach centers across the U.S."

Margo soaked up his enthusiasm, ready to tackle anything he wanted.

"The young man I brought in to mentor, Valdez Gibson, has been asking for more responsibility," Icky announced. "I can have Valdez spend time upstairs overseeing the men since he used to work in construction."

Before he was paroled, Margo added silently. Icky loved to be in charge of something or someone at all times.

"We want to include everyone in this endeavor, but we will be under a microscope when this visit becomes public knowledge and can't have a misstep." Monsignor had directed his words at Icky whose smile lost spark.

"Valdez is dependable and honest," Icky argued. "He deserves a chance to prove himself."

"I won't deny him that opportunity," Monsignor assured Icky. "But we also have Mr. Baylor to consider. He's doing a fine job and it would be uncharitable to demean him by favoring someone else with less experience."

"But Baylor is so...so – "

Getting on your nerves, Margo wanted to finish for him. Icky had a competitive streak a mile wide, especially when it came to Monsignor's attention.

"Father Ickerson," Monsignor soothed. "There will be opportunity and responsibilities for all when the right time comes. Perhaps you could speak to Mr. Baylor about sharing some of his workload with young Valdez. Keeping in mind you're responsible for Mr. Valdez and anything he does."

Icky nodded, mollified.

Monsignor continued. "We also have to be exceptionally careful with the media, especially after the embezzlement incident. I came here to rebuild St. Catherine's reputation and to do that we must avoid bad press."

Margo knew better than anyone in this room just how capable Monsignor was, how many times he'd been the catalyst for unbelievable changes. Like in San Francisco, where he'd spent most of the past year before coming here.

"I want Margo to field media requests and contacts, to create press releases as necessary and to report everyone's progress to me."

Press releases were among her least favorite job duties, but if that's where she could help most, that's where she would.

Icky did protest this time. "I'm senior here beneath you."

Monsignor could have just said his decisions were final, but he turned on his charm and showed why he'd become a respected leader by smoothing the friction. "So noted, Father Ickerson, which is exactly why I would never impose on your time to do busy work our chief of staff can handle. You're needed in a higher capacity."

Bullseye. That appeased Icky.

Grizzle coughed, a raw sound as though his lungs were ripping apart.

Monsignor paused. "Deacon Grizzle?"

"You should be seein' a doctor, Deacon." Margo considered patting his back, but that required touching.

When Grizzle caught his breath, he said, "Yeah." Cough. "Think I got bronchitis again."

Monsignor's brow creased with concern. "Better stop by the health clinic and see to that before you get worse."

Grizzle nodded though he rarely took time off and didn't seem eager to do so now either.

Moving ahead, the Monsignor addressed Grizzle again. "If you feel up to it, I'd like you to start interviewing teachers for our preschool program. We only need a couple for now, but I'd like to show the Bishop and the pope that we'll be ready soon to take in children."

Grizzle quieted, uncovered his mouth and took a shallow breath. "If that's all, I'll get to work."

"We're through here." Monsignor's gaze slid to Icky who would remain planted in this office for as long as allowed.

"I'm very busy, too." In a show of importance, Icky hustled out with Grizzle right behind, hacking again.

Margo figured Monsignor had more to say and she had news to share with him. "Much as it pains me, I need to tell you about Sally Stanton."

Monsignor was already picking up a thick file. "Who?"

"The mentally-challenged woman with a little boy named Enrique? They were here last week. You took her confession."

"Oh, yes. A Philomena House resident." Monsignor frowned. "What about her?"

"She was killed last night."

He paused, no doubt as stunned as she was. "That's tragic." His voice was calm, but sounded like he paid only half attention to her words. "How, where?"

"Gunshot wound and her body was left – "

He shook his head, a growl of frustration escaping. "We have to do something about Philomena House. Ickerson isn't doing a solid job of vetting people for that place or here. We can't have people getting shot every other week." A deep frown marred his face before he glanced back at her. "The pope will think we're running a crack house instead of a halfway house for the indigent. His visit is going to affect all of us, you in particular."

"Me?"

"Yes, I've informed Bishop Gautier I'm giving you more authority. You've gained tremendous experience from all the different projects we've tackled. I've been laying the groundwork for you to become the director over a program and I think this outreach center is the perfect place for you to show what you're capable of doing. I'd envisioned your position eventually expanding into a regional one, as we open more centers."

Not a position that would normally go to a woman.

"Thank you, Monsignor." She couldn't swallow. The director. That meant...

"The job comes with a load of responsibility, as does anything worth having. You asked me for a platform, the opportunity to prove yourself. That's one reason I accepted this appointment at St. Catherine's, *along with* paying back the support I've received from Bishop Gautier."

"I'm beholden to you for all you've done for me."

He waved off her adoration. "You've earned everything you've received, but you need to know this new position and the pope's visit are both golden opportunities you may not see again. You can't fail."

"I won't." Not when she had a chance to take on more responsibility. She was already in what was considered one of the highest positions for a woman in the Catholic Church. Only a fool would squander this chance. "I just need to know what's expected of me."

"The bishop will be watching how you handle the pope's visit and how well St. Catherine's is progressing. This pope can understand Bishop Gautier's vision, but he will only support that vision if he is shown a successful operation that makes a difference in this community."

Translation: This pope would take a risk on a female director.

He was the same pope who titled Monsignor and thought outside the box in so many ways. Her skin tingled with anticipation...and her headache tiptoed back a few steps.

"Stay on task and protect my back. Remember, your star rises with mine. This is your proving ground."

She wanted to salute, or do a happy dance. She'd worked so hard for the last eight years and now she had a chance to prove she was capable of more.   A chance to serve a community and help others the way Monsignor had helped her in her darkest hour. A place to belong.

St. Catherine's would shine when the pope arrived.

Chapter 12

Where was Miss Be-Here-On-Time-Or-Else?

Riley sat in a semi-uncomfortable office chair facing Kirsten Massey's desk at a minute past one, according to his banged-up Rolex. He knew a power play when he saw one. Kirsten Massey might be soft and sexy on the outside, but he'd watched her in action in the courtroom several times.

Tough, but fair.

And she had to know more about this case than the DA had shared in this morning's press release.

"Hello, Mr. Walker." Investigator Massey swept into her office, still wearing that smoking red Jones of New York suit and a downplayed perfume, something original yet subtle. Nice.

Not that he was noticing.

"Investigator." Riley had met her type plenty of times, a woman bent on holding the reins of this meeting.

She moved to place the files on her credenza and his gaze latched onto the way her black hair shimmered in the light shafting through the narrow window on her left.

Interesting woman. Rigid and feminine, just like her office decorated with slick black frames around paper touting her education, right alongside original watercolor paintings of outdoor settings and some intricate animal sculptures by an artist Riley couldn't remember. Her preferences ran to horses and large cats like mountain lions and cougars.

"Let's talk about your conversation with the killer." She spun around with a legal pad in hand and settled in her office chair so fast it was as if she'd been planted there the whole time.

He'd expected that little detail to be in the police report, which she must not have read before she'd seen him in the press conference earlier. As long as the other newsies didn't know about his speaking to the killer, Riley still had a lead over the other stations.

A small lead but he wasn't going to be picky at this point.

"I'm not sure who I talked to," he hedged, wondering if she'd been trying to trick him since they had no proof it was the killer.

"Fine. The anonymous call you received about Sally Stanton's body just after midnight."

"Gave the details to Detective Turner at the scene. Should be in his report."

She smiled, but not the kind meant to encourage a man, if he correctly read the irritation forming in the slant of eyes almost hidden by thick lashes. "I'm giving you a chance to repeat what you heard here instead of in an interrogation room. Your choice."

Since she put it that way. "When I answered the phone, the guy said, 'Send someone to pick up a body a block off Germantown Road on Berringer's front lawn.' I asked who had died. He didn't answer so I asked why this person was dead. He said, 'Her fault.'"

"Whose fault?"

"I can only assume the caller was talking about Sally."

"Go on."

"I asked who he was or what his connection was to the woman. He said, 'I'm cleaning up.' I tried to ask another question, but he hung up." Should he tell her he *thought* the guy had said, "we have a job to do" and something that ended with "soon"? Or keep that to himself since he might have imagined the words in his zoned-out state this morning? In her shoes, he'd think that line was something added to sensationalize the story. The next thing she'd think was that he was holding back information.

Besides, telling her he had a case of night sweats and disorientation when he'd realized he was talking to a killer again would sound like he was fishing for sympathy.

Not even.

Riley sat forward as Kirsten made notes. She was left-handed.

He kept his hands relaxed and non-threatening, cooperating like a good ass-kisser. "I don't think the caller sounded like a distraught boyfriend or someone who killed out of passion."

"And you would know this how?" She stopped writing, laid the legal pad on the smooth dark wood surface of her desk and placed a hand on each side of the pad. Her thumb never moved, but the other four fingers on her right hand tapped one, two, three, four, over and over slowly.

"Just speaking from experience." And not second guessing himself for the first time in months.

"Or are you trying to turn this into a news-worthy story?"

"It's already a news-worthy story. The question is why the DA's office wants to downplay this and keep it out of the media."

"Our job has nothing to do with the media, Mr. Walker. We're only interested in putting criminals behind bars. We can accomplish that much more easily without the media's interference."

"Hey, all I did was accept a phone call. You *charging* me with interfering?" He gave the words levity, but she didn't smile.

"I don't find death humorous." She spoke in a soft voice filled with compassion and held his gaze in a locked-eye-version of chicken.

She would lose.

The seconds ticked until her gaze dropped to her notes.

Never challenge a man who had fed himself on scraps from a restaurant Dumpster at fifteen. He drew in a deep breath and exhaled, refusing to be pushed or rushed, but determined to keep his temper in check. "You wanted me here for questions. I'm here. What's your next one?"

She added an extra thump with her thumb between the finger taps that kept time to some unknown beat. "What else happened last night?"

"Nothing."

"Tell me more about the call." She held the pen in her left hand, waiting.

"Like what?"

Kirsten glanced down at her notes and spoke to him without lifting her head. "Background noises, his voice, a cough, anything."

Riley thought for a moment. "When I thought back on it later, it seemed like he was trying to mask his real voice to sound average. Noise around him made me think he stood outdoors. Reminded me of how payphone calls used to sound so I'm guessing he might have been calling from one."

She scratched out more notes, eyes still down. "Odd when burner cell phones are so easy to get. What else did you hear?"

This was a pain-in-the-ass waste of time. He'd given J. T. everything he could think of this morning. Kirsten Massey just wanted to posture, play who-wielded-the-bigger-axe by making him go through this again. Would she believe him if Riley told her he thought the killer had just called again on his cell phone this time or accuse him of trying to create a story?

Either way, he had to go through this hoop once more. "The guy called right after midnight. No cars driving by, no one really talking. No sirens. Just light ambient background sounds." Something clicked in his mind. "Might have been near a neighborhood. I think I heard a kid whining nearby like maybe walking past, but that could still be anywhere."

Kirsten stopped tapping. "A kid? After midnight on a quiet street in the dead of winter?" She raised eyes that held no tolerance. "You heard a *kid* and are just *now* informing us?"

"Hey, I'm sorry. I didn't remember until *now*," he snapped, but his gut told him something was important about that kid's voice.

"Sorry? That's your best answer? Sounds like selective memory to me, Walker. Something that runs rampant in the media industry."

"Now, wait a minute."

She didn't so much as take a breath. "Isn't that how the

media works, doling out information in sound bites? Doing whatever it takes to get the story regardless of who pays the price of their ambition, right? Even a child."

He'd never hold back a sliver of information that could help someone, especially a child.

Did everyone think he'd forgotten Detroit? That it was just another story? That he hadn't paid for that mistake every waking minute of every day and would for the rest of his life?

The frustration he'd choked down for months threatened to explode. *Not now.* He needed to get out of here and think. He clenched the arms of his chair, taking in shallow breaths drawn through locked jaws.

Kirsten's breathing wasn't much calmer, but she had no idea how close she was to seeing true fury.

He spoke past the tight muscles in his constricted throat. "Let's get something clear between us. Detroit's in my past and has nothing to do with this case. So what does a kid's cry have to do with anything?"

She leaned forward, that spooky control in place like an invisible tether of propriety holding her back from making the mistake of an emotional reaction. "Sally Stanton left the hospital with her five-year-old child last night and was never seen again until her body turned up this morning. We have confirmation her son is missing. He was probably alive when you received that phone call. If we'd known about the child's voice in the background we would have put out an APB on a man with a small child immediately. Might have gotten a jump on this case."

Ah, shit.

She stood then, bending down and forward, hands flattened on the desktop. "*If* the police had done that, they'd have realized they had an APB on a woman that fit Sally's description and put it together sooner, and started a search for that child."

A missing child. Riley lost his anger with his next labored breath. Had the killer taken the little boy?

What had he done with the child?

Bile rushed up Riley's throat so fast he thought his head

would burst from the pressure.

Detroit hovered at the edge of his sanity, ready to blast into his world with the slightest invitation. Riley saw it all again so clearly, sitting in the woods with a man who had kidnapped three children.

Two dead and one small boy buried alive, waiting to be rescued.

Dots swam in Riley's vision.

Going there stretched his frayed control. *Push back, run, dive away from those images*. He couldn't let the nightmare get a claw hold. Not now.

"Mr. Walker?" Kirsten's voice faltered. For the first time since entering she didn't sound combative, but concerned.

He didn't want her concern. Didn't deserve anyone's.

With iron control that had gotten him to this point, he dropped a blank mask in place and regrouped mentally. "Had no idea. If that child's voice had registered when I spoke to J. T. this morning I'd have told him immediately." He cleared his throat and met Kirsten's unyielding gaze. She'd confirmed one thing a moment ago. She didn't dislike just him. She despised the media. "You made your point. I'm a trained observer. I should've caught that. What else do you want?"

"I want this child back *alive*. If you truly mean to help this investigation, no games and no grandstanding with live interviews."

Damn, he didn't think she had any more daggers to throw, but that one nailed him in the center of his chest. Only a fool would rush in waving a red flag in front of her now. Riley had been called a lot of things, but fool wasn't one of them. He changed his mind on telling her he thought the killer had his cell phone number since he didn't even know if that had been the guy for sure. Could have been a crank call. Hostile as Kirsten was right now, she'd probably confiscate his phone.

Then where would Sally's kid be if the guy called and a stranger answered? The killer would know immediately that the police had Riley's phone.

Dammit, though, he'd missed that child whining in the

background of this morning's call. He wouldn't make another mistake like that. Or let this kid down.

Riley smothered his sick disappointment under a hard layer of professionalism, determined to get the information he'd come for. "I'm concerned about this missing child, too, but I think there's more to this killing than domestic violence."

Kirsten sat down, elbows on her desk, hands clasped. "Of course you do. Otherwise, how could you make this into a major story for your station."

Getting damned tired of that tune. Sure, he needed a story, but that wasn't the only spur driving him as of right now. "If you figure out who killed Sally you might find the kid. Isn't that worth looking harder at this case? Philly PD is stuck trying to find yet another killer on no budget. This is where the media *could* help."

"Help? Like you helped in Detroit?"

Fuck. This. He had sources she didn't and wouldn't use if she did.

Without another word, he stood up and walked out.

Chapter 13

Lucinda Myers parked her silver 560 SL Mercedes in the circular driveway between perfectly trimmed hedges dusted with snow. A charming neighborhood, but then most of the custom-built houses in neighborhoods on the northwest side of Philadelphia were pleasant and attractive. Zip codes with a mix of new and old money where social standing ruled.

But the address had nothing to do with why Lucinda lived here. She'd fallen in love with Stan, a man who worked hard for every penny he earned as a television executive and strived to give his family – her and Kelsey – the best.

Providing a home in a safe neighborhood meant more to Stan than social standing.

Unfortunately, all the money in the world wouldn't fix her little girl's problems.

Clouds gathered densely overhead. Lucinda hoped the impending snow would entice a six-year-old into leaving the house to make snow angels or build a snowman.

Kelsey loved the snow, or had until recently.

Lucinda climbed out of the car and prayed she'd found a way to pull her child out of her depressed state. Everything in the tall shopping bags piled along the back seat was for Kelsey. Lucinda enjoyed perusing malls about as much as she'd like to give birth standing up.

But she and Stan desperately searched for anything that would turn Kelsey into the bright and cheerful child she'd once been. She loved Stan even more for trying everything the school counselor advised that might help Kelsey.

They were running out of options and had considered therapy, but that suggestion had scared Kelsey so badly she'd hidden from them for a whole day until they'd relented. That had caused Stan to be even more frustrated, but he refused to make Kelsey go to the therapist. Said he feared she would lapse into a deeper depression if they pushed her.

Lucinda gathered up the bags. Maybe the dresses and games she'd found would at least put a smile on her daughter's face.

For a child who had always been outgoing, Kelsey became more withdrawn each day. Lucinda would not stop until she figured out what to do. She'd poured her heart out to the priest where they worshipped at the Cathedral of Saints Peter and Paul, who suggested spending more time with her. But she and Stan already included their daughter in everything they did.

In fact, Stan doted on Kelsey. He'd treated her as if she were his own flesh and blood from the moment their relationship turned serious and he'd asked Lucinda to marry him.

Stan had gotten more involved with the church in the last few months. He volunteered on the weekends that Kelsey attended programs there. Lucinda couldn't want for a better father for her child. A guardian angel had sent her a man who'd fallen in love with her *and* Kelsey.

But Kelsey had stopped going near the computer, the one special thing she and Stan had shared.

Lucinda juggled the bags and headed for the front door and climbed the steps. The Colonial style, two-story brick house was ten times the size of the one-bedroom apartment she and Kelsey had called home when Kelsey's father had died. Opening the front door, she stepped inside and deposited the bags on the marble floor of the entry.

She started to call out for Kelsey to come down when a high-pitched wail echoed from above.

Every mother knew her child's cry. Lucinda rushed up the steps. *"Kelsey!"*

"No, Daddy, stop it!" screeched from way down the hall.

Lucinda reached the upper floor and raced toward the

sobs.

"Don't! Daddy stop!"

A chilling fear gripped Lucinda's heart at the shrill cries of her child. When she burst into her daughter's bedroom, Kelsey jerked away from her father and ran to hide in the space between her canopied princess bed and the wall.

"What's wrong?" Lucinda wanted to run to Kelsey, but stopped when she took in Stan's tense eyes. He stood between her and Kelsey.

Surprise deepened the worry lines in his face.

His gray eyes had never looked that kind of frustrated before, but this was his first time at being a father and frustration came with parenting. He'd never had a flash temper, but something clearly bothered him now. She could see anger in the way his jaw muscles tightened.

The dark storm permeating his gaze didn't give her the feeling of just a bad day at the office.

He swiped his hand over his face. "Nothing's wrong. Kelsey tripped walking with that blanket she drags around. I tried to check to see if she had hurt herself and she freaked out." He turned his face to where their daughter hid. "Are you okay, Kelsey?"

Muffled sobs answered him.

He covered his eyes with the palm of his hand, muttering something through his clenched jaw.

Lucinda blurted out, "What are you doing home now? Where's Janeen?" She struggled to pull the scene together in her mind and come up with anything besides the first explanation for her child's terror. As a single mom, her biggest fear had been dealing with so many babysitters and caregivers who might hurt her child. But she'd stopped worrying about that since marrying Stan.

She'd been paranoid for so long. Had she gotten too comfortable and let her guard down too soon? If so, that would mean...Stan had...

Not Stan. He wouldn't hurt her child. She was embarrassed at the direction her mind had gone. She lived in a constant state of anxiety with Kelsey, but even accidentally thinking that way about Stan was wrong.

Lucinda trusted Stan with her life.

With her daughter's life.

Her question finally sank in because Stan was frowning at her now, looking at her like she had three heads.

"This is my home, Lucinda. It's where I come to decompress...or try to. Thought you'd be glad I came by early." That last part had come out gritty and irritated.

She rephrased her question. "What I mean is that you have so much work to do I'm surprised...to see you this early." She clamped her mouth shut to keep from rambling like an idiot. Stan had said many times about employees that he couldn't tolerate idiots.

He dropped his hand from his eyes, stretching his fingers from where they'd fisted. "Why should we pay a babysitter to stay with Kelsey once I get home?"

Lucinda had no answer to that, but Stan had been the one to suggest a regular babysitter when she'd first married him so that they'd have a person Kelsey was comfortable with when they needed a night out. Now that she thought about it, he'd been popping in more often recently. Kelsey's sniffling broke Lucinda's heart and scared her.

"Why are you so angry, Stan?" she said with as calm a voice as she could muster. His face was actually red, and his hands had curled into fists again.

Stan took two steps toward her and Lucinda backed up a step then stopped.

She'd fought to keep her and Kelsey fed and clothed on her own before marrying him. Fighters didn't back down.

But what was she fighting him about? The babysitter?

Stan's voice went dead flat. "So now *you're* afraid of me?"

The sadness in his voice broke her heart.

"No, honey, of course not." More than anything, Lucinda wanted to get to her child and comfort her. Arguing with Stan in front of Kelsey wasn't helping her daughter.

Kelsey hid in the smallest places if she got upset. Lucinda had thought she'd lose her mind the last time she'd spent half a day hunting for her child. She'd almost called the police before she'd found Kelsey inside a pantry cabinet.

Nobody in the media wanted that kind of attention, especially Stan, so she'd kept a closer eye on Kelsey since then. He didn't need anything else to add to his stress and frustration right now.

Lucinda didn't care if the babysitter went home early. This whole moment was spiraling out of control and it was her job to calm everyone down so she could get Kelsey in her arms and assure her baby that everything would be okay. Just as Lucinda had so many nights when she'd had no one else to turn to as a young widow. "I'm worried about both of you. I was just rattled hearing her cry out. I didn't mean to annoy you further."

Stan let out a heavy breath, looked away then back at her with guilt-filled eyes. He raked a hand through his thick golden hair and kept his voice low. "Ah, hell. Look, I'm sorry, too. I'm not angry with you or Kelsey. I just wanted to hug her and she backed away."

Her heart tripped at the pain in his voice and she wanted to hear what else he had to say, but first she had to see about Kelsey. "Can you give me a minute to check on her?"

When he just nodded glumly, she stepped around the bed to her daughter. "Come here, sweetheart."

"Go away." The tears poured down her baby's face.

Lucinda took a step forward.

"*Go! Away!*" Kelsey rolled into a ball.

"Okay, it's fine. You can stay there." Lucinda lifted her hands in surrender and backed up then she motioned for Stan to step out into the hallway. She had to bite the inside of her cheek to keep from crying herself. Stan didn't need a weepy woman on top of this at the moment.

He started in the minute they were clear of the bedroom. "I really am sorry. Just try to understand. It's been a long week at work. The damn ratings are yo-yoing, we just lost one of our best salespeople to a competitor, and the anchor's demanding too much money to re-up his contract. We may lose him."

When he paused, she kept silent, not sure what to say after witnessing his unusual outburst of anger.

Shaking his head at some inner thought, he said,

"Anyhow, I only came home to pick up some papers. After Father John said to spend more time with Kelsey I figured I could stay here until you got home from shopping and let the sitter go early. When I went into Kelsey's room and tried to hug her, she backed up dragging that damn blanket and fell over the tail of it. So I picked her up by her arms. She started yelling at me and crying. I hate to see her afraid. I hate to hear her cry and that...on top of everything that happened today, I just lost it."

She'd watched Stan handle the pressure from work over the three years she'd been married to him, but the past four months had been really rough due to the hammered economy.

Added to that was Kelsey's problems that had started twelve weeks ago.

If she looked at it from his side, the man wasn't getting any break at work *or* home.

Stan's hand moved from his hair to his neck. "I told you about that lunatic woman I married the first time."

"Only that you were married for like seven months and didn't know she was on medication when you met her." She hoped he wasn't comparing *her* to the crazy woman he'd been wedded to almost ten years ago. "What's she got to do with this? Us?"

He kept his voice low. "There was a lot more to it than I've ever shared. I'd come home back then and say one wrong word that would send her into hysterics. She'd cry and scream for days. It was awful. I didn't know what to do for her."

Just like he didn't know what to do with a child who had developed emotional problems overnight.

As if hearing her thoughts, he added, "I don't want to make a mistake with Kelsey and miss something that would help. She started crying today and I guess I just snapped. I shouldn't have tried to deal with her like this after the day from hell."

Now Lucinda felt like an inconsiderate wife for jumping to unkind conclusions. What was wrong with her? She'd have to confess to Father John that she'd taken such a wrong mental leap about her own husband. Lifting her hand to his cheek, she kissed him on the lips.

"I understand, sweetheart." She matched his soft tone. "I'm sorry I yelled, too."

He cupped her hand to his lips and kissed her fingers then met her gaze with pain-filled eyes. "I kept trying to convince myself I could find a way to fix the problem with my first marriage. But she was psychotic and drove the car through the front wall of the house. Almost killed her and would have killed me and a neighbor's child if I hadn't just stepped outside a minute before to talk to him about mowing the yard."

Lucinda was speechless. She had no idea why Stan would ever have married again. "I'm so sorry you went through that."

"I just wished I had signed the papers to admit her to a mental health facility. Everyone tried to get me to do it. But, I couldn't even bring myself to talk to our priest about it back then. I regret the one time I was indecisive."

He'd told her his first wife had died when her car ran off the road into a deep lake during bad weather. But Lucinda now realized Stan thought the woman had probably committed suicide.

She didn't know what to say that wouldn't cause him more pain so she hugged him. Stan was a private man. His relationship with God might not be as open-door as hers, so he had nobody to talk to.

Lucinda told Father John everything that worried her. But now that she thought about it, could she really confess how quickly she'd jumped to an unfair assumption about her husband today? Especially to a priest she had to face outside the confessional booth?

When she pulled back, she gave Stan a little smile. "I'm fine. Go ahead and do whatever you have to do at work. I brought Kelsey some clothes to try on and some games I'm going to play with her. Give me a call if you think you'll be late and I'll hold dinner for you."

He put his hand up against her cheek. "Don't hold dinner for me, babe. We're ordering sandwiches for the team. We need to kick up the ratings. WNUZ is becoming a real pain in my side. Go on to bed when you're ready and I'll slip in once I get home." He gave her a peck on her forehead and the Stan Myers she knew was back. With a glance into Kelsey's bedroom, he shook his head then strode down the stairs.

She gave it a minute, listening for him to leave. When the front door opened and closed, all the tension went out of her shoulders. When Stan came home tonight she'd be waiting for him with a bottle of wine and late night snack. All would be back to normal.

Lucinda tiptoed back into the bedroom and around the end of her daughter's bed.

The look of betrayal on Kelsey's face when she lifted her head ripped Lucinda's heart apart. What was going on with her baby? "Kelsey, honey, want to see what I brought you?"

"No."

"Did you hurt yourself?"

"No."

"Want to play a new computer game with me?"

"No."

Lucinda wished for the days when she had to hound her daughter to get off the computer and go outside for fresh air. Kelsey wouldn't even go near the computer now, which was another disappointment for Stan. He and Kelsey had first bonded over a mutual love of computer games while Lucinda preferred reading a book. That had been his and Kelsey's special time together. "I got you some new clothes and – "

"No." Her daughter's pretty blue eyes were swollen from crying and her strawberry blond hair fell in limp strands around her shoulders.

Lucinda moved forward slowly. Kelsey had curled into almost a fetal position. Her lacy dress crumpled where she'd caught the skirt between her legs.

"Sure you didn't hurt yourself?" Lucinda asked. "Want to show me?"

Kelsey shook her head, wrapped her arms around herself and started sobbing again.

Heartbroken, Lucinda reached down. "Come here, baby." She started to hook her hands under Kelsey's arms to lift her when her daughter screamed, *"Don't touch me!"*

Chapter 14

Based on the vehicles crammed into the visitor parking lot in the spaces cleared of snow, it looked like a fire sale on meds at St. Joseph's hospital. Riley parked his truck and started the quarter-mile walk to the emergency entrance.

A hike might take the edge off.

The hell with Kirsten and her damned high-horse attitude. Did she think she had the corner on right and wrong, just because she worked for the DA's office?

She thought she knew what happened in Detroit? Only what she heard on sound bites sprayed across the country from every major station. She might have read the police report, but even that wouldn't tell the story.

If she'd ever gone through what he'd been through she'd realize that. He paused his mental ranting. Had Kirsten been involved in a lost child case before, or lost a sibling? He hadn't considered that. Dammit all. Maybe he was the one with the hair trigger today. Walking out of Kirsten's office hadn't helped anyone.

He sure as hell hadn't charmed her as he'd boasted to Biddy.

Flashing red lights cut across his vision. A load of pain squealed up to the hospital in an ambulance. Medical personnel scurried.

He slowed, hesitating. Maybe he should let this go, leave the investigation to others. To do so would be admitting Kirsten had rattled him. Had him questioning himself, his actions.

Like everyone else, she couldn't see past Riley's news

credentials. Yes, he needed a major story now, but he wanted Sally's kid found more. If it came down to missing the story or endangering a child, there would be no story.

But people like Kirsten convicted him of having no conscience without seeing all the evidence.

They had no idea just how brutal his conscience could be. He saw that interview over and over again. Night had cloaked the two of them, alone in the woods, camera on a tripod, silently transmitting the live scene. Riley pointed a microphone toward the Kindergarten Killer who pointed a .357 Magnum at Riley in return.

He could still smell the crisp outdoors, the gunpowder and blood.

Everything moved in agonizingly slow motion at the point the Kindergarten Killer swung the gun up under his own chin and pulled the trigger. The explosion from the killer's suicidal shot slammed against Riley, the trees, the ground, in deafening finality. Blowback of brain matter scattered in red droplets.

Then the silence. The empty, frozen silence.

And the sick realization that the chance of finding a kidnapped child had just died with the only person who knew the child's hidden location.

The police found a note on the Kindergarten Killer that said the little boy had been buried in a four-by-six wooden box with only seven hours of air left.

Cold chills danced over Riley's skin. He lifted shaking fingers to drag through his hair.

The Detroit television station had gotten what they wanted after all – ratings through the roof – but the story of the year had cost a mother her baby and Riley his sanity.

Standing outside St. Joseph's hospital, he swallowed the sour taste of regret and pressed his mind back on task. Search for information that could help the police find Enrique Stanton first. Worry about the story next.

Stay out of the way of law enforcement no matter what.

Riley might not have been in Philly long but he'd built up a network of contacts, people who might know other people. The network wasn't broad or deep, but he had a place to start digging for answers of what had happened to Sally Stanton the night she disappeared and was killed.

Unearthing information on Sally would put the police one step closer to finding her son.

When Riley reached the emergency room entrance, glass doors slid away to each side. Air bulging with antiseptic anxiety slapped him in the face.

Some people associated a hospital with the joy of a new birth or saving a loved one. The too-clean smell and hushed sounds would always remind Riley of human suffering.

Like now. He'd heard a couple of his sources were here, one of them injured. Riley had just given a name to the admission clerk when he heard a low shout of "Hot shot!" from his left.

Only five people called Riley that and all five knew each other. He'd found his source.

He swung a wry smile at Romeo, the street name for one of the tight-knit group of teenagers ranging in age from fourteen to sixteen that Riley played basketball with at least once a week in Northern Liberties. Romeo had on the same black, gold, blue and red Philadelphia 76ers sweatshirt Riley saw him in most of the time. Romeo and his team lived, breathed and dreamed basketball.

He asked Romeo, "Why's Baby G getting patched up?"

With skin the color of cappuccino, almond-shaped eyes and tight black curls covering his head, Romeo ignored Riley's question and swaggered forward. He came by the grunge look naturally, the legs of his oversized jeans dragging the ground. His thick-lashed gaze strayed to something more important than Riley – the ample backside of a tall African-American woman leaned against the wall talking to another female.

"Hello, you hot mama," Romeo purred.

The twenty-something woman, who stood close to six feet in her four-inch heels, cut a you-can't-be-serious glare over her shoulder down at Romeo's cocky grin. Full dismissal.

Oblivious to anything else, Romeo smiled as though she'd blown him a sexy kiss.

Riley sighed at the five-foot-eight teen whose mix of

African-American and Mexican parents had rewarded him with an exotic face that fed Romeo's oversized ego.

The kid's no-limit confidence had sucked Riley in the first time they'd met. Riley had been on his way to visit the local Boy's Club, like he did in every city, when he saw Romeo and his "team" playing on an improvised basketball court where weeds grew at will and a rusted wire hoop served for a basket. The five boys bounced a ball that should have stopped holding air a million dribbles ago.

Riley had left and returned an hour later in a ratty T-shirt, faded shorts and nasty sneakers for a pick up game. He got a resounding "no," the same answer he'd received on his next six attempts.

Each time he'd hang around and watch them play.

When Romeo's curiosity finally got the better of him, he gave Riley a chance to match up against "his team," which Riley knew meant an opportunity to be knocked over, stepped on, elbowed and run into the ground.

He hadn't been disappointed.

That had been four months ago. Now they gave him hell if he only showed once a week. Weather was no deterrent to them or an acceptable excuse for missing a game.

Romeo sidled up to him, every muscle in his body bragging he had something to offer any woman. "She'll find me later."

Riley lifted an eyebrow at him. "That might not be good news if she busts your chops with a sexual harassment suit."

"*That* don't happen to me." Romeo broke out the smile that had probably saved him more times than his quick wit.

Romeo would continue in this same vein for as long as he had an audience so Riley changed the topic to what brought him here. He'd swung by the pseudo-basketball court and the other three on Romeo's team would only tell him that Baby G had gone to the hospital.

"What happened to Baby G?" Riley asked again. He'd only recently found out that G stood for Ginormous. Any other kid his size would take up football instead of basketball.

"Cut himself playin'."

Riley might be tempted to accept that if not for how Romeo's eyes shifted away when he lied.

"Show me." Riley waited for Romeo to make up his mind first, then followed the boy to where a nurse pointed out a curtained-off area. Baby G – a five-foot-eleven, two-hundred and ninety pound, Asian kid who reminded Riley of a Sumo warrior with bad acne – lay on his back with his shirt off. One side of his enormous gut had a bandage the size of Riley's hand just above the elastic on his baggy green warm up pants.

"What's up, Hot Shot?" Baby G's sixteen-year-old voice had changed already to a deep radio announcer's baritone.

"Hanging out. What happened to you?"

Romeo and Baby G exchanged a guarded look before Baby G answered. "Got cut screwin' around."

A knife fight. Riley had a scar riding his shoulder from "screwin' around" on the streets as a teen, which meant just trying to survive. He crossed his arms and asked in a tone of camaraderie, "What was being discussed during this screwin' around?"

"Told you he'd figure it out," Romeo whispered under his breath to Baby G.

"Usual bullshit." Baby G lifted his hand to his face and tapped a cheek with his thumb, a motion that meant he was thinking.

Riley let him think. These kids were used to being interrogated by everyone from parents to teachers. He let them talk to him in their own time.

There was no better resource for anything that went down in Northern Liberties. To get a lead on the missing Enrique Stanton, he'd wait as long as it took.

Baby G stopped thumping his cheek, angular eyes slanting at Riley. "Blades showed up at our court when they heard Romeo was forming a regulation team. Their leader *suggested* we were wasting our time." In complete conflict with his generally unkempt appearance, Baby G surprised everyone who didn't know him when he opened his mouth and spoke with such precision.

A regulation team? Ah, hell. Riley had planted the idea in

Romeo's head to consider building a full team to compete in a city league...at some point. He figured if you gave kids a goal they spent less time hunting ways to get into trouble.

At least that's what Jasper had believed when he'd found Riley and brought a wild fifteen-year-old foster child into his home.

But Riley had thought Romeo wouldn't act on it for a while yet, not until they actually *attended* a city game. He'd been thinking about taking them to some games later this year.

But Baby G wouldn't be talking about this if the "team" hadn't made a decision. No one acted solo in this bunch.

All five of the boys had potential to do better in school, and a couple of them showed exceptional athletic ability, but any decision was made as a unit. No one in their group would consider moving ahead and leaving the other four behind.

If they organized a league team, they had a chance to expand their world beyond a scrappy parking lot. Find out how to battle in a healthy way, how to interact with other males without using fists. Or knives.

Another lesson Riley had learned from Jasper.

But didn't it just figure some rival gang would throw a kink into a simple plan to get these boys invested in something productive?

"What'd you tell the Blades?" Riley asked. Baby G's smile formed slowly, climbing his face to pinch his eyes. "I mentioned their flawed ancestry and suggested to their leader he should attempt sexual penetration upon himself."

"He didn't like that shit one bit," Romeo interjected, shaking his head.

"So he stabbed you." Riley wanted clarification. "Did you call the cops?" That earned him a round of snorts.

Romeo waved his hands back and forth like he washed a window. "No. That fool was all jacked up yellin' shit. When he flipped out his blade, Baby G didn't see it under his gu – " Romeo paused, catching himself. "Chest. Baby G moved in on the fool to shut him up. That's when he got cut. But not bad."

"I'll be able to play this week." Baby G made that

announcement then met Riley's gaze and added, "But we need to acquire a sponsor in order to submit our team for the league."

"How about your brother-in-law, G?" Riley hadn't met any family, but he knew Baby G lived with his sister and her husband.

"He detests sports. The man's an anomaly of nature." Baby G lifted his shoulder as in "go figure."

Romeo shook his head. "We don't want some suck bag draggin' us around like a ball and chain."

Riley needed to shift this conversation. He couldn't get busy with being a sponsor for this bunch, but that was the direction of Baby G's subtle pitch. Riley had bigger problems and might not even have a job in a week. "Let's kick around some ideas next time we meet at the court."

Romeo and Baby G exchanged one of those silent message looks again, but didn't press the subject. These kids weren't used to asking for anything or expecting to get something for nothing.

Once he knew where he stood with WNUZ, Riley would come up with a way for them to be sponsored so that it didn't sound like charity.

Baby G lifted his chin at Riley. "Why are you here?"

"Looking for information on someone from Northern Liberties." Riley didn't say a word about being on suspension since they hadn't heard about it yet or he'd be getting an earful.

What kind of role model ended up losing his job over an altercation?

"Who you lookin' for?" Romeo's eyebrows lifted with interest. He liked to be the one in the know on everything.

"Either of you know Sally Stanton or her little boy Enrique? Five years old. Lives around here."

"Why?" Romeo again, always cautious.

"Sally was killed last night and Enrique is missing."

Romeo shrugged and Baby G's guarded face didn't change.

Not that Riley expected any type of reaction from them. "So you haven't heard a word about Sally's death?"

"Didn't say that." Romeo studied his fingernails as if he sported a manicure instead of skinned up fingers and dirt under his cuticles.

"What can you tell me?"

Romeo cut his eyes at Baby G who moved his head in some nod of okay then they both looked at Riley when Romeo answered, "Depends on what you've got to trade."

Riley dug in his pockets, not at all surprised to pay for information. "I've got cash."

Romeo cocked his head. "Uh, uh. Not good enough."

Riley squinted in thought. "What do you want?"

Baby G smiled. "You sponsor our team. We share information."

The little hoodlums were blackmailing him. This was what Riley got for running a couple of pick-up games with these renegades. His temper built, a slow boil, percolating up his neck. If he let them get away with this, no telling what they'd do next time. He flexed a jaw muscle, considering.

Romeo and Baby G didn't say a word. Didn't have to. They'd set their price and wouldn't budge. Right now, Romeo's team wasn't just Riley's best hope at getting anything useful on Sally's murder and Enrique. It was all he had.

And to be really honest? In a twisted way, he admired their underhanded ingenuity.

"Okay, I'll sponsor the team." Going to be hell to do that if he lost his job and had to leave town to get another one, but he'd worry about that later. "What do you know about Sally and Enrique?"

Romeo puffed up, the man of the hour. "They live in that Philomena House over on 3rd Street. Sally didn't come with a full tool kit." He spun his index finger next to his head.

"She's mentally challenged," Baby G corrected.

Romeo frowned at his teammate.

"What do you know about Philomena House?" So far, Riley hadn't heard anything worth getting stuck with footing a sponsorship. "Is it a crack house or what?"

Romeo took over again. "Nuh-uh. Church runs it. St. Catherine's."

"Have any idea why someone would want to murder Sally?"

Baby G moved his shoulders in what could be called a shrug.

Romeo quieted, his eyes turning thoughtful, old for his years. "Why you care about some Northern Liberties brat?"

"He's a little boy who's lost his mother and could be in danger. I figure anything that helps the police find Sally's killer will help them find Enrique." Close enough to the truth without opening a wound that would never heal. Riley had found the killer once and still lost the child.

Medical staff scurried around on the other side of the curtain. Someone moaned, followed by words of comfort.

"But why do *you* care," Baby G pressed.

Riley always kept it straight with these boys since they could smell bullshit a mile away, but he didn't have an answer for that question. Not one he wanted to explore and dissect right now. That didn't stop the weight of their stares from crowding him into a corner.

"The DA's office is burying Sally's case as domestic violence, which means hunting for her son will fall so deep into the cracks he'll never be found. The police don't have the money or the men to hunt for Enrique. They need all the help they can get. I'm not going to ask you to talk to the police, ever. If you'll help me, that's enough."

Romeo exchanged a glance with Baby G then nodded. "Sally didn't have jack but that scrawny kid. Saint C's took her off the street, put her in Philomena and kept her fed. She didn't have *no* money, nothing worth stealin', didn't hurt nobody. She wasn't dangerous, just – " He looked at Baby G then continued, "Mentally challenged," saying the words as if they barely fit inside his mouth. "Don't know why anybody'd kill her. Just damn meanness."

That helped, and it didn't. Riley scratched his head and took a step to the side, thinking. The police should have questioned everyone at Philomena by now. "Who knew Sally besides her neighbors?"

"Folks at Saint C's."

Riley lowered his hand to hook a thumb in his pocket. "St.

Catherine's?" He got another yes nod. "Who runs that place, and don't tell me God. I need a name, someone I can talk to."

"Top dude's name is Monsignor, but he may not be there now."

"Why not?"

"He's a Philly PD chaplain." Romeo said the words like a curse. He glanced at Baby G then back at Riley. "We watch the cops shoot. Seen that Monsignor there on Tuesday afternoons a few times around two, three o'clock."

Riley checked his watch. Closing in on two-thirty. He'd made inroads with the police and had been invited to shoot at their range a few times. Not much of a lead, but somewhere to start. And he'd rather ask questions away from the church if he had a choice. But before he left, Riley wanted to make sure these two shysters got home. "Who's coming to get you?"

"My sister," Baby G told him. "She'll be here soon."

Riley pinned both of them with a no-nonsense stare. "I want more information than this if I'm going to sponsor the whole team."

Romeo crossed his arms and gave a grudging, "Okay."

That one word stood as a signed contract with these boys who lived by their word.

"See you later." Riley started to leave until Baby G said, "One more thing."

"What?"

"Be careful." Baby G slipped easily from his perfect diction to the street kid he was underneath it all when he said, "Word in Northern Liberties is, Monsignor's called the Enforcer on the street. They say he's one scary mother fucker."

Chapter 15

Why do you care?

Baby G's question still haunted Riley twenty minutes later as he drove mindlessly through the Rhawnhurst section of Philly. He passed one plain gray government building after another. Overcast skies washed in the same dull gray as the buildings swallowed the sun. The bloated clouds crowded together, reminding him the weather forecast had been for sleet. He doubted a chaplain would hang around outdoors long if that happened.

Unless the priest fit Baby G's colorful description.

Knowing Baby G's sense of humor, he'd been jerking Riley's chain about the chaplain being scary.

The area turned more grim by the minute the closer Riley came to the jail and shooting range. Fifteen-foot, chain-link fence with curled concertina wire piled on top would razor the skin of any detainee foolish enough to climb over.

Unlike most of the city's police training and administrative facilities, the jail was a fairly modern building. Nice break for street vermin from terrorizing the citizens. Everyone from burglars and rapists to drug dealers, murderers and mobsters, all awaited trial or court appearances in these buildings.

The criminals had it better than the crime fighters.

Riley had a story to whip into shape and needed facts for that, but first he planned to do what he could to tip the scales of justice in Detective J. T. Turner's direction. To do that, he needed background information on anyone connected with Sally Stanton.

A block before he reached the shooting range, Riley called Biddy on his cell phone.

"Nothing to tell you yet," Biddy answered in his usual don't-waste-my-time voice.

"What do you know about a monsignor at St. Catherine's Church in Northern Liberties?"

"Nothing. Not my area, but I got a buddy who drinks over at Race Street Café. I'll find out." And Biddy was gone just that quick.

Riley turned into the paved lot for the police shooting range, the western-most structure on Rhawnhurst and furthest from the Delaware River. He parked his truck, turned off the engine and opened his door.

Gunshots interspersed with gaps of silence pelted his ears. He'd climbed out wearing his worn leather flight jacket that covered a shoulder holster. Unclipping a panel on the driver's door, Riley fished out a black plastic case with his favorite firearm, a Smith and Wesson .41 Magnum. Once he'd holstered the weapon, he shoved extra ammo into his jacket pockets and reached for a pair of protective earphones and a set of shooting glasses in the back seat before locking up.

Riley strolled through a sea of vehicles, visually searching the range. No chaplain in sight, just a training session going on.

"Not going postal on us are you, Riley?" Sergeant Flynn chuckled from the other side of the chain-link enclosure, reaching for the gate latch.

Riley gave him an indulgent half smile and stopped just inside at an unloading table. He dumped the shells out of his .41. No one walked to a shooting position with a loaded weapon. The officer on duty assured that didn't happen, which was why Flynn counted each round, including the ones Riley pulled out of his pocket.

"Guess you heard about Henry's elephant ballet act at City Hall." Riley joked to keep from giving the story any weight.

"Oh, yeah. Saw the news at lunch. Henry didn't waste no time getting a shot in at you and Bidowski. Called you a TV prima donna and Bidowski an out-of-control thug."

Riley shouldn't be surprised. He knew the way some in

his business twisted the facts. Didn't stop him from curling his fingers into a fist that felt deprived with nothing to slam.

Flynn locked the gate behind him. Riley surveyed the landscape, looking for a white priest collar. Nada.

Instead of clay backstops, high banks of ground-up tires flanked the range. The waste material absorbed lead and suppressed ricochets from cops getting their annual qualifying rounds in. The rubber was toxic as hell, but the city didn't have the funds to replace it.

None of the experienced officers shot here during rookie training for fear of being wounded. Dense banks could protect only so much. A stray bullet fired by a rookie was more likely to drill a hole into his own boot than to hit the target.

"What about the Stanton murder in Germantown?" Riley asked Flynn. "Anything on that on TV?"

"Didn't catch nothing on it."

The Stanton murder gets buried and a rumble in the courthouse leads the news. Riley shook his head.

"Sounded like talk radio's playing fair and square with you, though," Flynn added while he logged in Riley's name on the books with a stubby pencil. He finished, closed the log and said, "Shoot, they're makin' you the hero and downplaying Biddy roughing up Henry. One radio jock said Henry stumbled and cracked a glass window, called it an accident. Your station's saying the incident is under investigation. First reports have you saving Henry's life and some saying it was more of a misunderstanding than an altercation."

Good to know some newsies called it straight.

Riley made a mental note for later to touch base with Lilly, the one person at the station who would give him the skinny on viewer reaction.

A fresh round of gunshots ripped the air like an attack. Sulfur odor stung Riley's nostrils, a familiar and welcoming smell.

"Didn't realize you were training today." Riley sized up the range where uniformed officers worked through a fast-paced sequence of skill. Everyone started at nine feet from the target then moved back together in one long progression to fifteen feet away then twenty-one feet, finishing with their last shots at seventy-five feet away. The targets on posts were perpendicular to the field of officers, and flipped to face the shooters in two-second intervals.

"Yeah, be a while before we start the next group." Flynn turned his round body to the left. "Go down to the long range on the far side."

Riley hadn't specifically come to shoot, but he needed information without raising anyone's curiosity. "Heard your chaplain comes by on Tuesdays. He here?"

"Yeah, he's here but doubt he has time to hear all *your* sins." Flynn chuckled.

Riley smiled at the dig. "Just want to ask him about Philomena House." As safe a reason as he could give without sharing his real purpose.

"He's always looking for donations. Go on down to the long range. He's there."

Riley rotated his gaze, focusing way past the line of officers training nearby to the area for fixed shooting that the Secret Service used when the president was in town.

One person stood at a firing position.

"That's a priest shooting targets?" Riley couldn't hide his surprise.

Flynn shrugged. "Likes to shoot and keeps to himself unless you talk to him. 'Course he might have time to hear a confession if you're feeling bad about Henry."

Riley frowned. "I don't think so. In fact, you got a target with Henry's fat head?"

"'Fraid not." Flynn chuckled.

A priest who liked to shoot, huh? This should be good.

Riley clipped on his ear protection and ambled along the training range, then past the dirt and recycled-tire embankment that separated the training range from the long range. Each inhale of sulfur residue and the rubber refuse reminded him of every officer's determination to keep Philly safe.

When Riley reached the shooting stations, a big man wearing a black down jacket and black pants occupied the center one.

Not Riley's stereotypical image of a priest.

He chose a spot on the right side of this guy – the monsignor – who either couldn't see Riley with his body turned to shoot right handed, or didn't want to acknowledge his arrival. Accustomed to no loading tables after a couple of trips here to shoot, Riley reached in his pocket, grabbed six shells, and loaded.

The popping sound of the priest pumping six rounds from a .38 into the head of a silhouette seventy-five feet away came through Riley's headphones.

Whoa. Hell of a shot for a priest.

The priest stood in police profile, both hands on his weapon and feet shoulder width apart. The guy had to go an easy six-feet-two, maybe three, with a wide build.

Riley loaded and emptied a round into his own target.

A steady pop, pop, pop from the .38 and thunderous kaboom, kaboom, kaboom from Riley's .41 Magnum ensued.

He noted the tight pattern of holes when he stopped shooting.

Pushing the release on the cylinder of his weapon, Riley glanced over to the padre who also reloaded. Sandy-blonde hair styled short, angular cheek and strong jaw line would easily be taken for a powerful CEO or groomed sports jock announcer. The monsignor moved with confidence that circled arrogance.

Even if curiosity hadn't been part of Riley's DNA from his first breath he'd still have to know more about this guy.

"Nice shooting, Padre." Riley lowered his weapon hand until the barrel pointed at the ground.

"Thank you." The priest's voice came across educated and assured. He methodically reloaded his weapon, closed the chamber, nodded at Riley still without eye contact then resumed his shooting position.

Guess Flynn wasn't kidding when he said this guy didn't talk.

Riley smiled. He was so accustomed to people *wanting* to gab to a newsman, he found being ignored somewhat amusing.

Leave it to a priest to humble him.

Riley eyed the priest's target. The center of where the head *should* be was shredded. Who would have thought a man of the cloth could shoot the pit out of an olive?

Not to be outdone, Riley proceeded to demolish the center of his paper target's head. When he stopped, the only shooting he heard came from the training range. Riley cut his eyes sideways and caught the priest checking out *his* target.

The monsignor's eyebrows lifted in surprise. A smile of respect creased his lips. His gaze drifted further right until he realized Riley was watching him as well. The smile vanished with the priest's attention. He ejected his spent casings.

"Where'd you learn to shoot like that?" Riley asked.

"My father."

"Was he a cop?"

The priest paused, resignation heavy in the lack of motion. He raised sharp blue eyes that took Riley's measure, processing his evaluation in one glance. Fast and decisive as a predatory bird deciding to attack or pass on a prey that could inflict damage. "Yes. He was a cop in another city." An unreadable thought flickered across the priest's face before he slowly nodded as if he'd decided there was no way around it. "I'm Monsignor Jack Dornan."

"Riley Walker." He nodded, moving into the I'm-just-curious route of questioning as if he didn't know anything about Dornan. "You at St. Mary's or St. Joseph's?"

Monsignor thought for a moment before answering. "No, in Northern Liberties. St. Catherine's. We serve a more modest crowd. I'm here to develop an outreach program."

Philly's middle-to-upper class attended mass at St. Mary's or St. Joseph's Catholic Churches. The money exchanged in some areas of the north side like Northern Liberties, Eastwick, Kingsessing and Mantau had to be washed at night to disinfect it.

"St. Catherine's?" Riley added just enough inflection to sound sincere then shifted gears. "And St. Catherine's is behind Philomena House, right?"

"God is behind Philomena House, but we do aid the residents."

Riley noted the noncommittal sidestep. "Know anything about one of your parishioners who lived at Philomena who was killed last night?"

The monsignor's nostrils flared. The scent of media must have reached him. "May I ask why you want to know?"

A civilized version of who-the-fuck-are-you?

Riley let a smile spread and extended his hand. "WNUZ anchor." He kept his hand out, dared the priest to ignore it.

No alpha backed down from a simple challenge.

Monsignor clasped hands in a firm grip that tightened like hardened steel, giving no leeway for Riley to misjudge him as an easy target. "Tragedy strikes all families at some point. St. Catherine's is there for every member of our parish in time of need. Nice meeting you."

Riley had been rejected by the best, including his family. The rebuff affected him less than a drop of water on a hot skillet.

Monsignor turned away to load, his hands flexing with each deliberate movement. Impressive show of being unbothered by the reference to the killing.

"I was on site this morning when they found the body. Since you didn't ask who had died, I guess you wouldn't know about Sally Stanton."

Monsignor turned his head, his jaw muscles so tight his smile looked squeezed into a small jar. "Yes, we know about Sally."

Riley took the opening. "Gunshot wound to the head..." Just for the hell of it, and because he enjoyed pushing buttons on a man who clearly knew his way around media, Riley dropped his gaze to the .38 in Monsignor's hand. "Small caliber bullet."

"If you're looking for a story on Sally Stanton, Mr. Walker, I have no comment. Talk to the police."

"What about her missing child? Care to comment on that?"

Confusion broke through Monsignor's steady gaze before the window into his thoughts slammed shut. It took a vicious level of control to regroup on the spot, ready for another strike.

Riley had seen professional politicians pull off that reaction under fire in front of cameras. He recognized a kindred spirit in the business of power, a player who knew his pitch point – a front man who wouldn't panic. All qualities of a Teflon leader. Not because others protected him, but because this man would know how to protect himself.

If not for having a trained eye from covering big dog politicians, Riley might not have known he'd made a clean hit. Good to know he still had the touch to upset a power player's game.

Small joy in a day lacking any.

Monsignor broke the silent standoff. "I realize you have a job to do, but I ask that you avoid putting further hardship on the family."

"How can helping to find Enrique Stanton put hardship on the family? The police are working double time to find this child and the killer. I'm sure they could use your help. Any comment on that?"

Monsignor showed his experience by not rushing to answer any question, taking a couple of seconds to sort through his answer. "Of course, we'll assist the police in any way possible. I'll have my assistant prepare a statement for the press."

"When?"

"We'll have something ready within an hour."

Riley did his own assessing. Smooth answer, nothing-to-hide attitude, even a press release. All very well articulated and a great maneuver...if not for the way Monsignor's eyes had averted past Riley's shoulder when he spoke.

A sure sign this man was hiding something. Interesting.

"I'll get in touch. Have a nice day, Padre." Riley stowed his weapon and walked away, but as he reached the barricade between the ranges, he took a quick look back.

The monsignor stood with his shooting arm at his side, weapon pointed at the ground, his eyes staring down. Not thoughtful so much as determined.

Powerful. Capable. Revered.

Had Baby G nailed it?

Was Monsignor someone to fear?

Chapter 16

"Monsignor's looking for you."

Margo turned to answer Baylor after signing the receipt for a lumber delivery that had just been unloaded in the back lot of St. Catherine's. "Thank you."

He waited, reminding her of messengers from back during the dark ages when they were expected to return with a reply. Thinning salt-and-pepper hair fell to one side above his oval shaped head.

"Would you be wantin' anything more, Mr. Baylor?"

"Think he wants you right now." No smile, not a joker that Baylor.

"Is there an emergency?" She had no idea what would cause Baylor to spend so much time speaking with her when the height of their conversation most days was limited to "hello."

"Don't know, but he's not happy 'bout something." Baylor shuffled a couple of steps then looked at her again. "If it was me, I'd be double-timing it."

But Margo wasn't Baylor and did not need to kiss up as Baylor sometimes did.

"Excuse me then." Margo refused to rush down the hall like some kid in trouble headed for the principal's office, but that's exactly the way she felt right now. Her stomach squeezed with a moment of concern. What had she forgotten or messed up? When she reached her office, she squared her shoulders and crossed the room to Monsignor's open door.

He sat at the same polished-wood desk built in the 1920's that he'd had for the past eight years she'd known him. Had the antique possession shipped everywhere he went. He held a pen in his hand and stared at the blank legal pad in front of him as if waiting for inspiration.

"Looking for me?" she asked and started to chide him for having writer's block on some speech when he lifted his head, his blue eyes stern and uncompromising.

Baylor was right. Monsignor did not look happy.

"You're supposed to make sure I stay informed on everything." He lowered the pen to his desktop and stood.

What the devil? "I do keep you informed. I – "

" – didn't tell me about Sally's son missing."

She'd planned to finish discussing Sally and Enrique along with a few other things as soon as Monsignor returned from his appointments. He'd dashed off a list of preparations for the pope's visit for her and the other staff to get hopping on, then took a phone call as he left the office.

Would have been a bit hard to interrupt him when he was on a roll, but telling him that right now would sound whiny.

She hated whiny and so did he.

"I'm sorry I let other issues sidetrack me." She wanted to ask why he was upset, but pointing out that something or someone had rankled his normally imperturbable calm would not improve his mood. "Has something come up?"

"I got blindsided by a reporter at the gun range about Sally – which I thought I had under control – but he asked about her missing son. Why didn't I know about that?"

That's right. Today was Tuesday, the day each week he stopped at the police range where the officers were more prone to share their troubles with him in the less formal setting. She'd suggest that Monsignor pass off the duty of being the PD chaplain to Icky if Icky wasn't so abrasive. That and the fact Monsignor wanted to make inroads into all levels of Philly government.

Margo ignored the bite in his voice and moved forward to initiate damage control. "What did this reporter want?"

"What they all want. A story. He gave me the 'I'm concerned about this missing child' bit, but that's nothing more than an opening to sensationalize Sally's death." Monsignor lifted his hands, palms together and touched his fingers to his lips in thought. "We're going to have heavy media focus on St. Catherine's and Philomena House the minute news of the pope's visit goes public. The last thing I want is this guy turning an unfortunate death and a missing child into an abuse story."

"Some people judge the mentally challenged with an unkind eye." Margo couldn't abide an unfair accounting of anyone's life. The first time she'd met Sally she made sure Monsignor took the woman's confession so that Sally received advice wrapped with compassion.

He raised a piercing gaze to Margo. "The media is capable of much more than being unkind. Do we know for sure Enrique is missing? What details are circulating about the disappearance?"

She brushed off the feeling of once again being back in school where she'd handled pop quizzes with as much calm as a live hand grenade. Expecting to have her world blown to bits if she gave the wrong answer and failed the test.

Silly reaction. Monsignor always wanted as much information as possible when dealing with a potential problem.

Lifting her hand, she counted off things she knew on each finger. "Miss Betty took Sally and Enrique to the hospital last night after Sally fell on Enrique. Sally was supposed to call Miss Betty to pick them up after the doctor saw Enrique, but Sally never called. When Miss Betty heard the news about Sally this morning she called the hospital. They said Enrique's rib was either bruised badly or cracked, but he was released to Sally with pain medication. They don't know where she and Enrique went after that."

"Poor child and Sally." Monsignor massaged his forehead with two long fingers. "Sally had her problems."

"Sally didn't abuse her son, but the hospital visit and Enrique's injury has been foremost in the news reports." Margo shook her head to herself. "Of course, WNUZ trotted out their new expert on child abuse."

"Dr. Ziegler." Monsignor nodded. "That's actually a good thing. She's one of the best, who can identify whether a child is suffering from abuse or some other emotional issue.

I've referred families to her since I arrived in Philadelphia."

That Monsignor referred troubled souls to Dr. Ziegler said a lot about the doctor in Margo's opinion. Monsignor was a savvy judge of people.

Monsignor stared out his window and murmured, "Even when abuse happens we must remember to hate the sin and love the sinner."

Margo longed to have his capacity for love and compassion, the reason he hadn't chewed her out over getting caught unprepared by the media. "What can I do to help with the media?"

"I need some uninterrupted time. I've got to write a press release right now."

"I thought you wanted me doing press releases."

"This one's too important."

That stung, but Margo had told him a long time ago to always give her the truth. She couldn't fault him if he failed to sugar coat his words to spare her ego. He considered her on the same side of the line as him when it came to taking a stand, that she'd take her licks and not complain.

"Don't let me walk out of here uninformed again, Margo."

The good thing about an honest relationship was, she didn't pull punches either. "Fine. You want to be kept informed? Sally is dead, Enrique is missing and Bruno beat his wife into submission again. Lisa's in the hospital and Bruno is here for his usual confession." *Usual* because Bruno was about as redeemable as a hyena.

Monsignor's frown pulsed with impatience. "Bruno normally sees Father Ickerson."

"Ickerson isn't here." Her tone said truth-can-be-a-bitch.

"Bruno will have to wait until I get this press release written. I told the reporter we'd have one ready and I expect him to call soon."

Margo wouldn't admit it out loud, but she enjoyed a certain relief at not dealing with writing that release. Not that she couldn't write one, but her expertise fell more along the lines of presenting program issues for community awareness and positive publicity releases. Death was personal to every family, something she'd never consider writing about publicly.

Wasn't it just like some heartless reporter to use another person's misery for a stupid news story? Those people should get a life.

"You're needed in the chapel, Father."

Margo spun around at Baylor's deep voice. How long had he been standing there? His feet were planted in the hallway to the side of her office door that was a straight shot to Monsignor's office.

She answered for Monsignor. "Please tell Bruno that Father Ickerson isn't back yet."

"I told him." Baylor didn't come in or leave, just kept eyeing the interior of Margo's office as though he would see something new after working on buildings like this one since Noah got into the boat business. They were fortunate he'd been around this old structure prior to its being turned into St. Catherine's. Baylor seemed to be the only one who could coax the heat to work or keep water flowing through pipes that should have been replaced years ago.

He had hands capable of doing a simple repair, or restoring the fine detail in the architectural carvings scattered throughout the church.

Baylor's gaze swept back to her. "Bruno ain't acting patient."

"I'll only be a few minutes." Monsignor sighed and sat down, lifting his pen to write.

"Bruno's getting agitated. He kicked the confession booth wall when I told him Father Ickerson wasn't here. Valdez was in the chapel and got onto Bruno about how he should act right inside a church. They're...having words."

Monsignor rose to his feet. "I will *not* have fighting on these premises." His words were low, rather than loud, a sure sign of his agitation.

Baylor lifted his shoulders and looked away as if giving words to his thoughts might get him in trouble.

"Fine." Monsignor ran his fingers across his hair, ruffling the neat layers. "Tell Bruno I'm coming."

Baylor nodded and left.

Monsignor turned to Margo. "Write the press release."

What?

He continued, "Keep it brief. Make sure to express our concern for Sally and Enrique. Ask for everyone to participate in a prayer vigil for finding Enrique."

Shoot. So much for dodging the sensitive press release. Now it was back in her lap and she had no idea where to start. But if she backed away from this, Monsignor might start looking at her differently for shirking a simple task.

One that a director should be capable of and he believed she was. She'd write the press release and make it the best he'd ever seen, even if it took the rest of the day.

He crossed the room to where his stole, the white scarf priests wore, sat folded on a wrought iron and marble side table. With the stole looped across his shoulders, he walked toward the door, slowing long enough to tell her quietly, "Be very careful. I've heard about this guy before. Riley Walker is a barracuda. Do *not* give him anything he can sink his teeth into. Shut this guy down."

She felt her future slipping into quicksand. "Maybe we could – "

Monsignor released a stream of air so tense it sounded like a pressure cooker ready to blow. "The last thing I need is the police called in to break up a fight in the chapel. I told Walker we'd have a statement by 4:00 PM. Get it done and get rid of him. I trust you to do this."

Monsignor strode away like a general heading into battle.

Consulting her watch, Margo felt the first shiver of a panic attack. She didn't have a prayer of pulling this off in twelve minutes.

Chapter 17

"Bless me, father, for I have sinned. It's been three weeks since my last confession," Bruno said without sincerity.

That would be three weeks since your wife got out of the hospital the last time, you son of Satan's whore. His heart raced, pumping angry blood through his body. The air he breathed reeked of all the souls that had passed through St. Catherine's begging for forgiveness, spewing lies upon lies until the very wood stank with the deceptive words.

The dull thrum of hammers working on the outreach center reached even here, where all should be peaceful, contemplative. The way a holy place was meant to be.

Clean, well ordered, an oasis in a world gone mad.

"I didn't mean to hurt her, Father," Bruno continued in his slow, plodding way. He'd drag on, complaining until he broke down in tears, then calm down and go back to life as usual for a bully. "I didn't. But she kept pushing at me, and pushing. I get off the job site after a long, hard day. All I want is a cold beer. Want to sit down. Not that much to ask. But what does she do? She's yammering at me about the plumbing and the kids and her stupid sister."

What's a good penance for a man who uses his fists on the person he's vowed, before God, to honor and protect?

Bruno Parrick was a thirty-one-year-old ironworker built like a bull who could probably lift a bus and throw it. Lisa needed a protector. Talking to Bruno was a waste of oxygen.

Maybe punish his hands? Make it hard to slam Lisa across a room.

Or Bruno's mouth...to stop the spew of lies and self-pity.

"I just want some peace and quiet, Father. I'm a good father. A good provider." Bruno's whine deepened. "I come to church every week. All I want is what's coming to me. Is that too much to ask?"

No, my son, it's not.

Chapter 18

Why would a monsignor be in a place like this?

Two blocks north of Race Street and the Ben Franklin Bridge overpass, Riley pulled to the curb in front of a Catholic church, once ornate and crafted with loving hands, now dowdy and faded. This was a far cry from the type of place a bishop of the monsignor's caliber normally hung out.

Jack Dornan's name surfaced in the news, often connected to Philly's prominent citizens.

A monsignor was the most exalted of priests, Dornan rumored to be among the top of even *that* heap based on what Riley had learned in the past hour.

Why wasn't Dornan in a power location like New York or even in the Cathedral of Saints Peter and Paul, the most distinguished parish in Philly's Catholic Archdiocese?

Why here?

The three-story brick structure to the right of the chapel looked like it might have once been a school. Riley had never followed any religion, but even he knew a lot of inner city schools had closed down when families fled to suburbia. But this building appeared to be undergoing a transformation if the action behind the upstairs windows was a clue.

Riley gave his truck engine a little gas and turned onto the narrow drive that ran alongside the church. When the potholed thoroughfare funneled him into a parking lot, he spied a restored Mercedes sedan, the full-size one like they made in the 90s. Same one he'd seen at the shooting range. The sedan and four unremarkable vehicles sat in the paved lot. Two late-model white pickup trucks, a rusted-out green beater step-side Chevy, and on an adjacent weed-covered lot, a utility trailer carrying a load of 2 x 4's covered with a blue tarp.

Someone in coveralls, with the hood of his coat shielding his head and face, walked out of the back door of the church and over to the truck. He lifted something small like a cell phone from the cab then hurried back to the church.

Riley circled the vehicles and stopped when his cell phone rang. He kept the truck idling for warmth, noting the time at almost four. Temperatures were dropping with the light sleet falling. No point in sitting in the cold while he talked.

He got "Walker" out of his mouth and Biddy started in.

"Got something for ya on Monsignor Jack Dornan."

"I met the guy. A slick number."

"He's a badass."

Riley sat back and scratched his chin. "I keep hearing that. He's a priest." *Who shoots like a pro.* "Where'd he get that reputation?"

"Here's what I heard. The bishop over St. Catherine's brought Dornan in from San Francisco to clean up after the embezzlement mess in Philly and to spearhead their outreach program."

"What mess?"

"That's right. Happened before you got here. St. Catherine's had a deacon handling the books and incoming donations. The city partnered with the bishop to set up Philomena House. Everything was moving along fine until the bottom fell out of the stock market."

"Were city funds tied to the market?" Riley asked.

"Nah. The deacon was tradin' stocks on the side, playing the market big time when it crashed. He got in serious money trouble and cooked up a scam with a bunch of guys he found to bid on the remodeling materials for Philomena. The president of a supply company that got knocked out of the bids heard from the contractors doing the remodeling that supplies were substandard and coming in missing materials. That ran up a red flag. By the time the bishop heard from a city councilman about the rumors and investigated it, word had already spread that the church was running a scam."

"So this St. Catherine's bunch is suspect to begin with." Riley watched the landscape blur under a layer of sleet on his windshield. "There might be more of a story here than I first thought."

"Oh, hell, no."

"What? Why not?"

"The media hosed the church, slamming them for bleeding the city and Philly's citizens for funds and donations on the heels of the recent national economic fallout. Henry-the-Whore smeared the church in the paper, called for audits of money donated. TV stations ran nasty sound bites. Got really bad."

"No surprise there. Anything's game in this business." For some, but Riley had a personal code he lived by that didn't include harming the innocent. There were plenty of stories about the corrupt and dangerous without hurting someone unnecessarily. "Was the church guilty?"

"No. In the end, the bishop did bring in auditors who cleared the church of any mishandling of funds. Basically, the only one guilty was the deacon, who went to jail. The bishop suffered a heart attack. The mayor said the media owed the bishop and St. Catherine's an apology and said the city was behind Philomena House. It finally died out just about when you showed up."

That had to be why Riley hadn't heard anything about it. "Did Lehman issue any apologies?"

"That's the funny part. WNUZ was the only station that didn't sling shit at St. Catherine's because one of the board members had gone to church and school there as a kid. He made it clear he would not tolerate the church being condemned without evidence. We came out smelling like a rose for once."

"So how does Dornan play into all this?"

"He's got a street rep of cleaning up other people's messes. That's how he's climbed so fast in the church. My buddy said the monsignor is known as the Enforcer. Uses unorthodox methods."

"What do you mean?" The more Riley heard, the more he wanted to dig deep on this guy.

"Back in San Fran, Dornan stopped two gangs from warring in his parish by riding with each one for a couple weeks. Word was, inside a month the gangs were more afraid of him than the cops."

Damn. "I'm sitting at St. Catherine's. He's supposed to have a press release for me."

"Don't pull them into anything, Walker. Dornan's a golden boy. They love him here. The city *and* WNUZ will come down on your ass if you mess with him."

Perfect. Riley hung up and turned off the engine. His instincts prodded him to find the truth, regardless of Dornan's reputation. If there was something to be learned about Sally's death, Riley would question anyone, even a priest, who had a piece of information that could make a difference.

Especially a priest with Dornan's reputation.

So why did Riley hesitate?

Because those same instincts had convinced him to interview a killer in Detroit.

Chapter 19

St. Catherine's Church mourns the loss of...

Margo started the first paragraph of the press release again. For the third time. Her gaze strayed to her stalled fingers, then to everything within the four walls of her office that had recently been painted Tucson Beige. A color she'd won the battle over after goin' head to head with Baylor and Icky, whose preferences both leaned to the bright side. She'd thought Icky was goin' to go over her head to Monsignor at one point, but he'd backed down.

The annoying priest could be reasonable on occasion.

Too bad he couldn't write a press release.

The smell of panic seeping out of her pores overpowered the fresh paint odor. She finally faced the clock on her laptop. It refused to help her out.

Two minutes past four.

If she could just get out of this office to walk and think for a bit she could come up with the right words. She missed the outdoors from when she used to help her Da on the crab boat he operated out of Portland, Maine.

Thinkin' had been easy back then. Too easy. She'd thought her way right out of a safe home and into the hands of a monster.

Focus on the task. Monsignor's mantra played through her mind any time she stepped backwards into that place in her head where the world twisted in a frenzy of pain and fear.

The therapist Monsignor had found for Margo had taught her how to deal with anxiety. External scars could be removed with plastic surgery, if she'd do it, but the internal ones were the truly disfigurin' kind.

Those clung more tenaciously than a leech to a healthy host.

Margo drew from what the therapist had taught her. She squeezed her fingers into tight fists then stretched them out like starfish, took a breath and focused on her task.

St. Catherine's Church mourns the loss of...

That's when she heard footsteps in the hallway, coming toward her office. She recognized everyone by the sound of the person's steps. Like Icky, whose snippy steps matched his attitude.

Icky's protégé Valdez shuffled quietly, reserved. She prided herself on not addin' "suspiciously" to the list this time. She wouldn't judge the young man unfairly.

Monsignor's bold stride could be heard the length of the hallway.

Deacon Grizzle lumbered along like the giant he was.

Baylor made no sound when he walked, which was why he usually caught her off guard.

But these new footsteps clipped across the hardwood hallway, each strike echoing with confidence...and determination.

She had a feelin' who she was about to meet. Time had run out. Apprehension clawed the inside of her chest. Couldn't he have given her a few more minutes?

The footsteps ended, followed by a brisk knuckle rap against her doorframe.

Margo snapped her outer personality into place and turned with the face of surprised innocence. "Yes?"

The visitor stepped inside her office, clearly used to lettin' himself into any situation. This guy stood just as tall and wide in the shoulders as Monsignor, and the two men's similarities didn't stop there. This man's eyes took in her, the office, the computer, everything with sharp precision, like that of an eagle on the hunt.

Eagles were also handsome. And dangerous predators.

"Is Monsignor Dornan here?"

"And who would be askin' for him?"

"I'm Riley Walker with WNUZ." His eyes were blue, but

not crystal clear like Monsignor's. The pair bearing down on her now had the deep-blue color of an ocean, the kind that hid as many secrets as the bottom of the sea.

Monsignor had warned her Walker was a barracuda.

Just as dangerous a predator as an eagle.

She had to tilt her head back, same as she did to address Monsignor when he stood over her. "Monsignor's not here at the moment. He's takin' confession."

"You're Irish." He smiled, eyes twinkling unlike any barracuda she'd ever seen, and flipped her initial impression on its keel. Then he offered his hand to shake.

As though she mattered.

"That I am." She *did* matter and deserved the respect he showed. Monsignor had told her that over and again. Unless you gave a person reason not to, they owed you respect.

But she had to admit feelin' a bit flattered for some reason.

Out of courtesy and professional habit, she stood and clasped his hand. He shook hers with strength yet gentleness. A flick of energy raced between her palm and his. She snatched her hand back the minute he released hers, then smiled to hide her reaction. That had been strange.

"I should have known anyone with eyes as green as yours came with a nice accent." He continued smiling, putting her at ease. A charmer, this one.

Who was here for a press release.

Shiftin' back to business, she pointed at a chair against the far wall. "You're welcome to have a seat over there and wait. Monsignor should be back soon." That would buy her some time and she wouldn't mind an attractive man decoratin' her office for a half hour.

"Are you Ms. Cortese?"

She shoved her hands in her pants pockets, foolishly bothered by the way he said her name. "That's right. You're here for the press release I'm workin' on. If you'll take a seat I'll finish it up for you and answer any questions you have."

"I appreciate your offer to help, but I don't think it's fair to ask the questions I have of a church secretary. The monsignor would probably agree with me." He whipped out a wider version of that smile.

A church secretary?

He hadn't been showing respect, but trying to lower her guard by actin' sincerely pleased to meet her.

She knew his kind. Riley Walker was a self-assured sexist dog who thought he could charm his way past any woman. There were two names outside the door on the wall. Hers and Monsignor's. Walker assumed the most menial of positions she could possess.

"I am the chief of staff at St. Catherine's," she said with a smile her father would have said indicated rough seas for Walker. Very rough.

Chapter 20

Damn. Major screw up.

Riley watched the ground he'd just gained with this woman – Chief of Staff Cortese – fall away faster than a mudslide in California.

He'd been making headway with her, anticipating how he might find out more through a secretary or receptionist – like in most companies – than he would from upper management.

Cortese had surprised him with a real smile a minute ago. The smile hadn't actually surprised him, but how that one simple expression had transformed her face. When she'd first turned those rich green eyes on him, Riley had been struck by the interesting composition of a wide mouth, narrow, almost-pointed nose, pale complexion and thick auburn hair springing in wiry curls to her shoulders. No makeup, fairly plain, but nice looking in a natural way.

Then she'd stretched those lips into a smile that ignited her eyes.

But the fire sparking there right now did not bode well for him. Arms crossed, soft brown eyebrows arched in challenge and those peach-colored lips tightened into battle-ready mode.

Riley lifted his hands in surrender. "My mistake." He wasn't above flirting with a pretty woman to smooth out a faux pas. "Sorry, I'm not familiar with the Catholic Church. When did they start letting attractive women run the place?" He winked.

"Let?" She glared at him like he'd killed her dog.

Hell. *Put the shovel down before this gets worse.* "Uh, we

were talking about the press release." What the devil had happened to the connection between his brain and his mouth? He'd just managed to demean the woman in less than five minutes. Twice.

"Sit." She pointed to a wooden armchair against the wall. "There. I'll have it in a minute."

Underneath that feminine exterior hid a general. One who had pulled inside the fortress and bolted the gate to any further conversation. His own dumbass fault.

Riley walked over to the chair and heard hers roll across the wood floor as she sat down at her computer. He ignored the chair she'd directed him to and remained standing where he could study the pictures pinned on a cork wallboard. Photos of children playing in the snow, a family in front of the church, a wedding party in simple attire...most had Cortese hugging a kid or hamming it up with another female.

She could be damned pretty when in full happy mode.

The sound of keys clicked rapidly behind him. He stepped over to an oak bookcase, the antique kind with glass doors covering each section. The model of a sailboat with graceful lines and a tall sail rising almost two feet high sat on an onyx base. The brass nameplate said "Emily's Dream."

He reached toward the glass door and heard, "Please don't touch that."

More typing.

Feeling like a scolded kid, Riley shoved his hands in his jacket pockets and turned around. "What do you know about Sally Stanton's murder?"

"Only what you and your associates report in the news. I'm almost finished with the press release. Give me a minute, and I'll have it for you."

Her jaw ground back and forth. A frown drew fine lines in her forehead. Was she stressed over writing the press release, or his presence?

A part of Riley wanted to leave her be, to type in peace, but the news dog in him could smell an opening to poke around. "I swung by Philomena House on the way here and asked a few questions."

She paused in typing, but didn't lift her head.

"Don't you think the circumstances of Sally's murder are a bit odd?" He didn't have anywhere to go with this, but that had never stopped him from scratching around until he found something of use.

"I'm afraid I'm unfamiliar with the investigation into her death." She pecked out a few more words on the keyboard.

"Probably wouldn't be so odd if not for Sally's death being the second Philomena House resident killed in the last two weeks."

Cortese placed her hands on the desktop and chewed on her upper lip as if she counted to ten before answering. "Yes, we've lost two parishioners in the last ten days." She lifted her head slowly. Eyes narrowed, hard as her battered wood desk. "This is a difficult time for everyone at St. Catherine's and Philomena House. I wish you'd respect our need to mourn in private."

He read the rest of her thoughts in the disgust lining her voice. She considered him one of the news vultures who ran down the families of victims to ask how they felt about losing a loved one who had been killed in a heinous way.

How would anyone feel who had lost someone that way? He shared her disgust and didn't care to be included in her loathing.

This wasn't the first time he'd faced that prejudiced attitude, but for some reason having her look at him that way stabbed him. "I didn't harangue your parishioners. I have sources in that area." Five punks not old enough to grow beards who'd better have answers the next time he saw them. "The other killing from Philomena was a gunshot to the head, too."

"So what?" Cortese countered, temper percolating. "The one two weeks ago was a drug-related death. Sally didn't do drugs."

People said too much when they got angry, stressed or both.

Why was she on edge? The monsignor Riley had met at the gun range wouldn't turn a press release over to a novice or leave her to face a reporter unless she had what it took. And he doubted they'd put a woman in the position of chief of staff who wasn't made of steel.

After what'd happened with the embezzlement and Philly's apologetic attitude since then, Riley would have expected a more confident air. Would she slip and give away something if he pushed a button or two on her?

Or did she even have buttons to push?

Riley offered a thoughtful look. "You sure that prior death was drug related?"

Her lips moved with silent words then she waved a hand, dismissing his question. "You'll have to be askin' the police about that. I wasn't there. We deal with the aftermath of these deaths." She bent her head and returned to typing.

That fit the confidence level tied to her position.

He'd let her stew a minute while she worked on the press release. People generally worried themselves more on their own once he planted an idea they hadn't considered.

She moved the mouse, clicked twice and the printer on the table behind her purred into action. When it finished printing, she reached over and snatched the paper off the tray then turned around and stood, shoving the document at him. "This should answer all your questions."

"So I contact you if I have more questions?"

"You shouldn't have *any*."

He reached for the paper and offered a slow grin. "Matter of fact, I do have a few more."

The disbelief that swiped across her face was priceless. A tiny slip in her facade. "About what?"

"St. Catherine's, this outreach center, Monsignor Dornan...?"

"You're just digging for no reason – "

"Everybody's got a story. Take you for example – "

"I don't have a story." She answered too quickly.

He dropped his voice. "When I hear that tone it just makes me want to dig deeper."

She clamped her lips shut and crossed her arms.

"Doesn't the fact that both victims were killed in one place then moved to another spot, that both were residents of Philomena House and both were killed by a .38 round to the head make you wonder if there's a connection at all?" Riley folded the paper without reading it, sure there would be little of value in the text. He could find two or three similar characteristics between murders in any low-income area so that didn't mean those two killings had any link, but he doubted Cortese would realize his ploy.

"You have our press release," she answered with rigid professionalism. "Discuss your theories with the police, if you actually do any research before reporting a story."

Scared animals attacked. Riley understood this, but his temper still flamed. "It's not always about a story. There's a kid at risk. Sally's little boy. The longer it takes to get him back, the less chance anybody has of finding him alive. Philly's police can only do so much with what they've got to handle."

Her stiff bottom lip softened, but she didn't give an inch.

"I'm going to push for answers with or without your and Monsignor's help. By not helping me, you ensure Sally's child stays in danger." He thought he'd pushed too far when she just stared in silence.

Her little finger trembled. "I gave the DA's office everything we had on Sally and Enrique. What do you want from us, Mr. Walker?"

Had that been a plea to back off or an honest offer? And what had she given the DA's office that Kirsten Massey hadn't shared? Riley had to give Cortese a reason to talk to him. "We can either work together or against each other. I believe there's a tie between the two killings and the common link is Philomena House." When she showed no sign of offering another shred of help, he used the only hammer he had in hand. "I'm running with this story soon unless you help me."

"Me?"

"You...or Monsignor. Somebody familiar with Philomena House or from St. Catherine's has got to answer questions."

She had a cocky little chin she shoved up at him, but she failed to hide the worry in her eyes that spurred his curiosity further. "*I'm* the media contact for St. Catherine's. We want Enrique found, too, *but* that doesn't mean I'm going to help you exploit his tragedy or use this situation as a means to attack St. Catherine's."

"Good enough. Looking forward to working with you." He said that to let her know he took her reply as agreeing to answer his questions. He wouldn't hammer on a church secretary who didn't get paid to deal with someone like him, but Cortese had made her position here very clear, *and* that she was the go-to person. That worked for *him*. She wouldn't be nearly as difficult an adversary as Monsignor.

"One warning, Mr. Walker – "

He sort of liked this tough side of her...

" – screw me over and hell's going to look like a good place to hide."

...or not.

Chapter 21

Riley found his way back outside since Cortese didn't offer to walk him to the door. She might not be as easy a nut to crack as he'd thought. But what had she given the DA that Kirsten hadn't shared? Now that his temper had cooled, he wanted another shot at Kirsten. She'd know if the police had anything on Enrique.

He just had to rile her enough to loosen her up, get her to say something. They mixed like a lightning strike and dry wood, so stirring her up shouldn't take much.

Getting her to meet him for dinner, now that would be the challenge. But then he hadn't been born of stubborn Irish blood for nothing.

When he reached the rear parking lot, he gave his truck a minute to warm up so the defroster could melt the ice on his windshield.

A flash of blurred silver sneaking slowly into the parking lot drew his attention. The car parked close to the building, forty feet away from his truck. He couldn't see through his iced up glass.

A cell phone beep alerted him to a text message. Lifting it into view, he read:

Philomena House 6 pm. *Baby G.*

The possibility of learning something on Enrique jacked his pulse.

Riley consulted the digital clock in his dash. He had eighty minutes, plenty of time, so he rolled his window down and tilted his head into the brutal air for a better look at the silver car.

Mercedes sports car, newer model...a striking woman with a scarf covering her head got out. She pulled on a black fur coat that might not be real fur, but based on the rest of the picture he'd bet someone in that household had dropped a nice chunk on it.

More telling than the scarf on her head were the darting glances as if checking her surroundings. She donned a pair of dark shades. Something about her tugged at a memory that wouldn't gel.

Interesting. Who was she? And who was she *hiding* from here?

Cortese indicated Monsignor was currently taking confession.

What had brought this socialite slumming? The need to confess a sin she couldn't tell her *own* priest?

One too embarrassing to admit?

Riley waited until she disappeared around the corner of the building before he revved the engine and turned his defroster on high. He drove down the row where she'd parked.

Her vanity tag read "KELSEY."

His cell phone rang again and he glanced at the ID to see if this meant Biddy had something new. The monitor ID displayed UNKNOWN. He answered, "Walker."

"You lost your job."

Riley's eyes bulged. His heart thumped fast. That voice. This time he was sure. The killer had called him back. *Think. Talk.* "No, just got suspended. What can I do for you?" He'd managed to keep his voice even and calm when he wanted to ask about Enrique in the worst way, but fear of making a misstep forced him to be cautious.

"We have a duty to the citizens of Philadelphia. To tell them the truth, let them know about the dangers of sin without repentance."

We? "I understand." Not even. With that opening, Riley had an idea he wanted to believe was a safe approach, but life had taught him there was no such thing. His skin felt clammy. *Don't screw this up.* He spoke carefully. "Sally must have been a sinner, but her little boy was innocent. You know where Enrique is?"

"Sally repented. Her soul is safe."

"But – " Riley swallowed and took a steady breath. Sweat beaded on his forehead. No risky statements, no gambling with this child, but he couldn't let this guy go and not find out what had happened to Enrique. "Is her little boy alive?"

"Of course he is. Children are held in God's hands."

Excitement rushed through Riley, rippling across his skin. "How about letting him go?"

"Not yet."

Riley closed his eyes. Not yet. What did this guy want with Enrique? *Don't make a misstep. Just keep everything nice and calm.* But his voice came out raw when he said, "Please, let the little boy go."

"We all must sacrifice in this war against Satan and his followers. For Enrique's sake, you must perform your duty and not fail me."

The bottom fell out of Riley's stomach. "What do you want? Just say it and I'll do it." Riley had answered in a level voice that hid the throbbing beat of his pulse. He'd do whatever this guy wanted even if it was to walk off a cliff.

"I'll be in touch." The line disconnected.

Chapter 22

Climbing the flat stone steps to St. Catherine's chapel was like navigating a tiered ice rink. Lucinda thankfully made it to the doors without breaking a bone, which would have created even more problems since she did not want to expose her identity.

She had no choice but to find someone who didn't know her, and it had to be now. All she needed was an objective sounding board to figure out which way to go next.

She needed to talk to someone she could trust who would understand her confusion. The church had battled troubles over abuse recently. Priests had spoken frankly with parishioners about the problem, sharing how they now knew where to look and what to look for to prevent the past's repeating itself.

By the time she left here she wanted to have a clear idea of her next step, no matter what the consequences were. Nothing mattered more than Kelsey's well being.

Still, she couldn't talk to her own priest about this. Stan had attended the same cathedral for the past ten years. The priest would never look at Stan – or her – the same way again if she spoke to him about her concerns.

A wave of nausea hit every time she considered what she'd have to say and the shame she faced, whether she was right *or* wrong. If she was right, she'd missed the signs before now and had allowed her daughter to be harmed. If she was wrong, she'd committed a betrayal by even thinking something so hideous about her husband.

Inside the front door of the chapel, Lucinda found a lean,

gray-haired man in coveralls standing on the top two steps of a ten-foot ladder. When the door closed with a soft nick, he paused from sanding the molding above an archway made up of curves and scrolls, and turned to her.

She waited for him to say something, but he must have had the same idea so she said, "I'm looking for the priest."

"Which one?"

She had no idea. "I, uh – "

He saved her by pointing at the door to the chapel. "Should find one in there." Then he returned to sanding.

Glad to not answer any more questions, she stepped inside the quiet chapel where her dark sunglasses blinded her. She removed them and pulled the cashmere scarf off her head. Her eyes adjusted. The chapel could hold about a hundred parishioners. Why had the parking lot been so empty?

Maybe because the majority of members in this parish had to work the kind of jobs that prevented them from going to confession during a workday.

These hallowed buildings always gave her a sense of awe, no matter the size or the condition. This one was on the road to recovery. Sleet heavy skies dulled the light seeping through the stained-glass windows.

Each side of the room had a confession booth built of dark-stained wood.

But the size and worn edges of this chapel gave it a lived-in feel that offered comfort. That and the loving polish someone had applied to the older wood so it shone. The touch of someone who cared.

Soft footsteps tapped down the center aisle toward Lucinda. She swiveled around.

A woman in black pants and a deep pink turtleneck pullover walked toward her. "Can I help you?"

"I called about confession." An hour ago, once she'd gotten Kelsey settled at home with Janeen.

"I'm Ms. Cortese." The late-twenties woman extended a pleasant hand with her welcoming smile. "I'm sorry, but I'm sure I mentioned confessions are only taken until 4:30 on Tuesday afternoons."

But it was only ten minutes past that. Lucinda couldn't go another week with this problem. "Yes, you did, but I have to see the priest, really, this is important."

A young man entered from the other end of the chapel and walked up onto the stage to the podium.

Ms. Cortese swung around, frowning at the young man. "What are you doing, Valdez?"

His head shot up from where he'd leaned down to look at something behind the podium. "Uh, trying to find the short in the audio system. Father Ickerson asked me to look into it."

"I see." Ms. Cortese took her time turning back around, as though she pondered his answer. When she faced Lucinda again, she started to speak but both doors to the confessional booth on Lucinda's left opened, snagging her attention.

One man stepped out sideways to allow clearance for his barrel gut, sort of a roughneck construction worker look. He mumbled something under his breath that might have been "thank you," but sounded like the same thanks a driver gave a cop for receiving a speeding ticket.

"Tell Lisa we're praying for her," Ms. Cortese told the heavy-set man as he lumbered past. The comment had sounded sincere, but had held another meaning that was hard to read.

The guy glared at Ms. Cortese and left without a word.

Lucinda didn't know what had just exchanged between those two, but she had her own problems. "I *must* speak to – " She shifted her attention from Ms. Cortese to the second man who had exited the booth. She'd plead her case directly to the priest.

He was tall, handsome, memorable.

Very memorable, now that she thought about it. Lucinda had met Monsignor Jack Dornan only a few weeks back at a fundraiser for a new art museum. Her stomach curdled at the possibility of being recognized. He'd been very nice when he spoke to her, Stan and even Kelsey, which meant he would very likely remember Lucinda. She could not talk to him either.

What the heck was Monsignor Dornan doing here? She thought he was at one of the other major churches in the area.

She'd picked this one as the least likely place someone would recognize her as Stan's wife.

The monsignor hadn't looked at her yet. The muscles in his face were tight with a stern frown, his eyes on the man whose confession he'd just taken. Some thought had trapped the monsignor in the moment.

But he was not as trapped as Lucinda felt. She still had a problem to solve and switched back to Ms. Cortese. Would it be insulting to ask for an after-hours confession *and* a different priest?

Ms. Cortese had been watching the priest with worried eyes, but now she blinked as if returning to the present, and swung her attention back to Lucinda. "I'm sorry, Miss...?"

Lucinda's heart thumped a loud warning that she might be making a bigger mistake by staying.

Heavy footsteps beat across the wood floors and echoed against the high ceilings as the monsignor walked up. "Hello."

Please, God, have mercy and get me out of this. Lucinda raised her eyes to the monsignor. "I...uh." She swallowed, buying time to come up with something.

Ms. Cortese spoke up. "She's here for confession, but I told her it's past the time."

Monsignor Dornan's face warmed with a smile, his gaze steady on Lucinda. "I can take one more."

Lucinda glanced at Cortese, whose eyebrows shot up in question. Ms. Cortese started to speak, but Monsignor Dornan quieted her with a look that passed between them.

Lucinda seemed to be the only one not in on these silent messages.

"I'll go over my last meeting with you after you've finished, Monsignor," Ms. Cortese said in an efficient, but brisk manner, then spun on her heel and walked back down the aisle to the altar and exited through a side door.

"Shall we?" Monsignor Dornan lifted a hand toward the confessional booth.

Like I have a choice at this point? Lucinda nodded and headed to the confessor's side of the confessional. Why was she worried? People remembered her husband, a high-profile television executive. Wives were invisible most of the time, at least she was. She wore conservative clothes and stayed out of the news, one of the few things that Stan had made very clear from the beginning of their relationship was not negotiable.

Lucinda had easily agreed since she had no interest in being in the media spotlight.

Once she settled on the bench and the door on the screen separating the two halves slid open, Lucinda took a breath and prayed he wouldn't tell her priest about this if he did recognize her.

He couldn't, right? Everything she said was in strictest confidence. That took some load off her chest.

"Bless me, Father, for I have sinned. It's been a week since my last confession. My husband and I argued today."

"And?"

"We don't normally argue, Father, but I got confused and I'm still kind of confused." She wished her mother was still alive, someone she could tell her blunt thoughts to who wouldn't condemn her for jumping to conclusions.

"Go on," he encouraged in a deep voice.

"Well, our daughter has been so quiet and depressed lately that I think I might have overreacted when she started crying and I blamed the problem on her father. I know that sounds wrong, and I've never blamed him for anything in the past. The last four months have been hard on all three of us. He's a very important man in a major company – high-profile company – so he's under a lot of pressure. I've tried to be there for him and for my daughter, too, but I think I might be hitting the wall on how much I can handle. I'm starting to wonder if I'm doing anything right these days." She stopped to catch her breath. Her heart had a stranglehold on her emotions, but she wasn't stopping now. Not with her family's future at stake.

The monsignor waited silently, which encouraged her to take another breath and tell him the rest of her thoughts. "I know it sounds like I'm weak, but I'm not. I had to raise my daughter alone after my first husband died. I can do it again, but I want this marriage to work."

"A solid marriage is built on communication and faith in God. Does your husband follow God's word?"

Thank goodness, an easy question. "Yes, he's a devout Catholic. Active in the church. He's never really raised his voice to me until today. He's been a good husband and father, even adopted my daughter so she's his child, too. She's so sweet and she *was* so happy, but now she's not, and I don't know what to do." Her voice broke on a sob she sucked down. He didn't need to listen to that.

"Why is your daughter unhappy?"

"I'm not sure, but..." Could she really bare her deepest thoughts? If she didn't, she couldn't handle another day of wondering what to do. "This is confidential, right? I mean you can't even tell another priest or anything, right?"

"Yes, that's correct."

Please tell me I'm doing the right thing. Kelsey is my world. She depends on me to keep her safe. Lucinda took a breath. This was a safe zone where she could say anything, no matter how bizarre.

"I'm worried that something has...has...happened to my daughter...physically." She choked on the last word. A bleak image rose in her mind. "I might be wrong, but she's been so withdrawn and she's so skittish around St...my husband." *I have to protect Stan, too, if he's innocent in all this.* "I don't mean to make it sound as though he did something, I mean, I know he loves both of us, but I...oh, dear God, I can't say it –" She cried into her hands, hard painful sobs that she couldn't stop. Just the possibility of what she suggested made her physically ill.

Silence answered her sobs until she finally regained control and sniffled. She coughed, pulled a tissue from the box next to her and dried her raw eyes. "I'm sorry, I just...I don't know. He's never done anything inappropriate before so I can't believe he would now, but my baby is so upset and won't talk to me or let me touch her. She used to spend hours with him on the computer and today she ran from him. I don't know what to do, but I won't let anyone harm my child."

There was a pause, a deep, silent pause, before he cleared

his throat and spoke.

"There is no question here." His voice picked up strength and power when he added, "A child must be protected...at all costs."

Chapter 23

Philomena House would never win an architectural award unless they gave one out for a brick box two stories high and twice as wide.

Riley took one last glance over his shoulder at his Tundra parked across the street on the curb. He hoped the truck still had those custom wheels when he came back out, given that the area was already shrouded in full dark.

His cell phone rang. Riley snatched it up, ready for some crap about Baby G running late. "Walker."

"Your ass is going to be parked in jail tonight if Massey pulls the warrant she's working on," Detective J. T. Turner growled.

Ah, hell, Riley didn't need J. T. pissed off along with Massey. "What the hell?"

"She thinks you're holding back information on that phone call. Said she pulled your records and the time stamps don't jive with what you told me. You doing that, Walker, holding back information? Because, if you are, I'll pick you up personally."

Riley opened his mouth, but had nothing to say. The break in time had been when he'd sat unable to breath or talk or think, but no one wanted to hear that.

No one would believe him anyhow.

"Goddammit, J. T. I told you and her both everything I knew at the time." Almost everything. Kirsten didn't know that the killer had his cell phone number. "But I left you a message to call because I have more."

"Like what?"

"The killer called back. He got my cell number, probably from the station. Not like that's hard to do in this business."

"Fuck. We need a tap on your line, but if the call was made from another Mickey Mouse payphone company it won't do much good."

"Why? Are they immune to a warrant?"

"No. The people who own those operations are impossible to find and even when you do they won't agree to a tap or doing anything to help. All they care about is collecting money. It's a nightmare to get anything out of them. Not like dealing with the big phone company. We're better off if it's a cell phone. We can track that as long as the phone's on."

"He didn't talk long, J. T., so I doubt you'd have gotten a location triangulated, but you set up a way to track the call and I'll do whatever I can to keep him talking. Can't promise how long I'll keep him on the phone. I won't push him."

"Why not?"

Riley wished just one person didn't think he was using this kid to get a story. "Because I'm worried about that child so I don't want to scare him off or cause him to do something...reckless."

J. T. didn't comment at first then said, "Good idea. What did he say?"

"That Enrique is still alive."

"Jesus."   The harsh sigh that followed was that of a detective who had been up too many hours with too few breaks. "What else?"

Riley related the whole phone conversation again then moved back to the issue of him going to jail. "I'll make you a deal. If you can keep Massey off me until later tonight I may have some information that will help you on the Stanton murder case and Enrique."

He hoped. Riley didn't have much at this point, but he had to stay free long enough to come up with something to trade with Massey.

She'd hang him on the time gap between receiving the call and reaching 9-1-1 if Riley couldn't convince her and J. T. the time difference had not been to get a jump on the case. He'd come up with a reason by tonight, something that wouldn't force him to admit he'd been close to losing consciousness during that phone call.

"Don't interfere with this case," J. T. warned. "Bad enough you're getting calls from the killer."

"You don't want what I've got then?" Riley had never known a detective to pass up a chance on any free information.

J. T.'s hiss of pent-up air filled the line, ragged and spent sounding. "Consider yourself forewarned that we'll be listening in on your calls so we'll know when to triangulate the killer's call. See what I can do with Massey. No promises. Meet me at Race Street Café at nine tonight." The detective didn't wait for an answer since it wasn't a question.

They both knew Riley would be there for any hope of sleeping in his own bed tonight, which wouldn't happen if he didn't come up with a lead of some sort.

Riley pulled on the warped entrance door to Philomena House. It groaned in protest and balked two-thirds of the way open. Once he passed through the gap, Riley yanked hard on the door to slam it shut behind him.

Smelled like dinner being cooked in a few apartments, a scent that reminded him of boiled cabbage and something with a pungent curry sauce. Stale odors lingered, a residue of bodies that had passed through the building and stayed long enough to leave a human imprint in the air – perspiration and desperation.

A last chance place.

Gray walls, but not recently painted. Shiny aluminum mailboxes covered the wall on his right, ten in all.

Had anyone picked up Sally's mail?

Only two boxes had names. No Stanton. Riley had a choice of taking the first floor hallway straight ahead or the stairs on his left to what was likely an identical layout above.

The front door to the building creaked open behind him.

Baby G squeezed through and left the door ajar. "You *do* have vehicle insurance, right?"

Riley pushed passed him to check his truck. Still there. He turned around in time to catch G's snicker. "Not funny."

"Depends on your point of view." Baby G wore a long-sleeved, robin's-egg blue pullover that hung loose over faded-red, baggy warm ups. Probably crossed town in that. Not the least affected by the temperatures outside.

"How you feeling?" Riley shouldn't be surprised to see Baby G without his sister. Street kids got patched up and moved on with little pampering.

Baby G lifted a fist with the thumb stuck up.

"What have you got for me?"

"A deal."

Riley crossed his arms. "Spit it out."

"Matching shirts for the team."

He'd lose less money in a mugging, but he didn't really mind buying shirts. Doing it this way would allow Romeo's team to feel as though they earned the booty, but only if Riley made Baby G work for it. "*Five* shirts for what? Police have probably been here, picked this place clean."

Baby G shook his head, slowly. "Eight shirts."

"You only have five players," Riley argued.

"All good teams have alternates. We've acquired three more players from extended family."

This whole basketball sponsorship was turning into a bottomless pit. Riley indicated the apartments with a head nod. "How good is this information?"

"Solid and the police *don't* have what I've got you."

Hot damn. "If that's so, you'll get your shirts."

"Follow me." Baby G headed down the hallway.

Kid noises scrambled with television racket behind the first door they passed. Baby G rapped his knuckles on the second one. When the door opened, a slender Haitian woman greeted him with a smile then pressed a wary gaze at Riley. Baby G said something, the dialect sounding like thick Haitian. He turned to Riley. "This is Titia, my brother-in-law's aunt's cousin. She didn't know Sally Stanton, but she knows the woman who was friends with Sally."

In a convoluted way, that made sense. "Okay."

The woman nodded at Baby G and stepped out in the hallway, closing the door behind her.

Riley and Baby G followed Titia to the first door they'd passed with the kid noises. She knocked. A pale dumpling-shaped woman with a head of frizzled black hair and swollen feet stuffed in pink house slippers came to the door. The apron over her flowery cotton dress had faded stains and bleach holes. A genuine cook.

Baby G's relative spoke to the plump woman who frowned as if working to follow what Titia said, then the talking ended and both women turned to look at Riley.

He didn't know what they wanted so he smiled.

"I'm Betty," the second woman said at last. "You know Sally?"

"No, ma'am." Riley chose his words carefully. "But I'm trying to find out who killed her and what happened to Enrique."

Betty studied him with faded brown eyes shaped by Hispanic genes and filled with a mother's concern. "Why?"

Riley shoved a "little help here?" look at Baby G, whose eyebrows lifted with the delight of a used car salesman seeing an easy mark.

This would probably cost him embroidered shirts. Riley rolled his eyes then gave Baby G a nod.

Baby G said something to Titia who spoke to Betty who rattled something unintelligible back, then the three of them talked at once.

Riley had seen discussions between two warring nations take less effort, but no one in Philomena House had a reason to trust him. Without Baby G's stamp of approval, Riley would be SOL. Shit out of luck.

Everyone stopped talking. Betty addressed Riley. "I tried to tell the police what Titia told me, but they just did a quick walk through Sally's apartment and left. They didn't think it mattered."

"What mattered?"

"Enrique's woobie blanket's gone." Betty lifted an index finger and waved like a first grade teacher. "I told the police I was sure Enrique didn't have his Diego blanket with him when I took Enrique and Sally to the hospital, but the police just wanted to get a photo of Enrique and look around the apartment."

That made sense. The police would have been searching

for pictures of a man or a phone number, some place to start. Riley didn't understand where Betty was going with all this, but patience played his role as investigator. "What's the deal about the blanket?"

"St. Catherine's staff gave it to him. Enrique called it 'his Diego.' Sally would wait up and wash it at night when the boy slept, washed it by hand so nothing happened to his blanket. She'd have it back on him before he got up." Betty's eyes watered up with the memory. "If Enrique hadn't been so upset and hurt bad last night he'd have pitched a fit when he realized he didn't have his Diego. He's a good little boy and loves that blanket so I figured he'd be crying for it by now."

Riley needed more than a child's attachment to a blanket. He frowned at G who lifted his heavy shoulders in a shrug. Baby G spoke to Titia in way that sounded like a question.

Titia fired off an answer that Riley didn't think Betty could even follow based on the way her lips parted in confusion. When Titia finished, Baby G turned to Riley. "Think I get the point now. Miss Betty has an extra key to Sally's apartment. She went upstairs to get the blanket this morning to take to the hospital and check on Enrique. When she couldn't find it, she called the hospital. They said Enrique left with his mama around eleven last night. Miss Betty found out about the killing this morning so when the police came by she tried to tell them the blanket was missing. They wrote it down, but didn't really listen when she described it, then they searched the apartment and left."

Riley could understand how they'd assume it wasn't a big deal and probably couldn't understand what any of this group was saying without Baby G.

To be honest, he wasn't seeing the significance of the missing blanket right now.

Baby G took a breath and continued. "Miss Betty was telling Titia the news this afternoon when Titia got in from work. That's when Titia told Betty about someone in Sally's apartment last night."

Now *that* could be important. "How would Titia know someone had been in there?"

"Sally's apartment is above hers. Titia heard footsteps and thought it was Sally at home, but now she thinks it was someone else."

"Why?"

Betty spoke up. "Because the news said Sally's body was found before 1:00 am this morning. Titia heard the footsteps when she went to the bathroom after 3:00 am. Sally couldn't have been in that apartment. Somebody stole that baby's blanket."

Riley's thoughts froze on the only person who had a reason to steal something personal of Enrique's, something special.

Just like in Detroit.

The Kindergarten Killer had taken favorite stuffed animals to bury with the children.

Chapter 24

Who should repent tonight? Choices, choices, choices.

All deserving. But he'd narrowed it down to two. Each required different...orchestration. Either way, he had the tools necessary.

His warm breath fogged the windshield. He rubbed his leather-gloved hands together, watching each scene in one of Philly's safe little suburbs play out happy as a Hallmark card picture. Shiny cars that benchmarked success arrived at tidy houses surrounded by perfect landscaping. Kids and dogs playing in the yards ran to meet the cars as they parked.

Sitting still this long wore on his nerves. If he could cull one more sheep out of Satan's herd early tonight, he'd have time to deal with another one before morning.

Getting away from St. Catherine's without drawing attention was getting harder, especially now with the flurry of activity created by the pope's visit, though that was a true blessing.

But to whip this parish into shape, he had to be more creative about his schedule, especially with Cortese.

Nothing eluded Margo Cortese, except having a life, but St. Catherine's benefited from that.

He could work around her, maybe come up with a way to get her out of the office more often. Just for a while, until he cleaned up around St. Catherine's. It all came down to time.

The clock's tiny arms fought him at every turn.

People demanded a few minutes here and there, chewing away his available hours like hungry termites. He'd never complained about hard work, never would. The rewards made it all worthwhile. This was another chance to prove his value to everyone. Especially Bishop Gautier who he owed for so much.

This parish *would* be ready for the pope's arrival.

But not if he didn't punish the sinners. The ones who confessed, rushed a few Hail Marys and went right back out to commit the same sins again and again.

That's why tonight had to be a special penance, something to make other sinners pay attention.

To fear the Lord is the beginning of freedom.

Riley Walker had been fearless in Detroit when he faced off with Satan's soldier and won. He should understand the price of fighting a war against sinners, that some sacrifices had to be made so that the world could learn the price of being unrepentant. But if Walker's inquisitive nature circled too close to St. Catherine's he could become a problem. One that could be managed, as long as Walker had motivation.

The weak in spirit always needed tangible motivation.

Walker would do as instructed for the sake of the child.

Every step in the plan had been worked through with precise detail, right down to choosing that specific newsman. Walker's news station had given out his cell number with little hesitation.

Another sign that everything I do is blessed. Because of his commitment, St. Catherine's would thrive and become a testament to other parishes around the country. He would not accept failure from anyone, especially himself.

Reputations weren't built on occasionally persevering.

Satan never dropped *his* guard or took a day off.

Besides, based on the confessions spun today at St. Catherine's, the children of this city needed someone to defend them against dangers that hid behind friendly faces...like parents.

Children deserved their own special heaven on Earth.

Adults had a duty to protect the innocent, but few would take on the tough jobs, not if it meant getting their hands dirty.

Or bloody.

A white sedan hummed as it passed his vehicle,

unobtrusively parked in a dark shadow. The sedan slowed three driveways up to turn in. The garage door opened. Lights flooded the driveway and across the car that slid into its warm nest.

And there was the dog, tail wagging, happy to see the dad.

Where was the happy homemaker standing at the door with a flour-dusted apron and a martini in hand for her husband?

Not a real homemaker, but the Feldman woman, a faithless wife who ogled the seventeen-year-old boy who did the yard work and shoveled snow while her husband worked hard all day. Worse than that, Feldman hit her kids when she couldn't handle her frustration.

Maybe that should be part of her penance, a sound beating.

As God said, spare the rod, spoil the...sinner.

Chapter 25

What would it take to back Massey off? Riley huddled his shoulders against the damp with the temperature diving ten degrees below freezing and the black night closing in around him. He walked stiffly toward the Race Street Café.

He had one idea, one chance at turning J. T. to his side. But that hope hung by a thread tied to a child's blanket.

Snow drifted lazily down to the sidewalk, adding to shoveled slush piles mixed with road grime from traffic along Race Street.

Christmas lights still twinkled on the second floor balcony of the stack of brick apartments on his right. A block away, the Race Street Café lived in the shadow of the Ben Franklin Bridge on the edge of the historic district some called Old City. Tourists visited the nearby U.S Mint and Betsy Ross House to find out what happened back when. But Philly's finest wound down with a Smithwick – pronounced schmiddick – beer to talk about what had occurred today and what they could do to prevent something worse from happening tomorrow. The café served all wallets, even the Philadelphia Flyers who frequented the place.

When Riley reached the dormer-style overhang above the entrance, he pushed the door open to a blast of warm air flavored by hops and spicy wings.

J. T. Turner sat at the bar, elbow propping the hand that held his head. He nodded at whatever the old guy in a police uniform next to him was saying, then his eyes drifted away, meeting Riley's gaze before giving a barely discernable nod.

Most of the tables still accommodated the café's heavy

dinner hour business. When three people at the end of the long bar closed their tab and walked out, Riley nabbed two of the three seats and waited as J. T. disengaged himself from the cop.

Riley ordered two drafts that arrived the same time J. T. sat down next to him.

J. T. lifted the beer, drank a long swallow then set the glass down and turned to Riley, who hadn't touched his. "Just got off the phone with Massey. Again. The only reason you aren't wearing cuffs is because I convinced her to wait until I had a chance to interrogate you. At least until tomorrow."

"Thanks."

"Wasn't easy after I told her about your latest phone call."

Maybe she'd back off if a lead came from the last call. "Any luck tracing it?"

"Another two bit payphone."

"Figures. What'd Massey say?"

"She wanted to put you and your phone somewhere you can be monitored. I told her the killer might be watching you. She finally gave in and said she doesn't want to hear anything else tonight unless we break the case. So you better have something worth me buying you a short reprieve."

One night. Not much, but a start. "Does she really think I didn't tell her everything I heard on that call?"

J. T. eyed him with the precision of an investigator who had seen and heard it all. "Don't know, but you're going to have to explain that time gap between getting the call from the killer and you calling 9-1-1. That doesn't match your statement. Minutes are a big deal in this type of case."

"I know that." Riley caught J. T.'s suspicion. The last person he wanted against him was J.T. Turner. And right now, J.T. was thinking he'd been played. "I gave you the time I got the call and told you I called as soon as I hung up. I didn't – "

"Cut the bullshit, Walker." J. T. leaned his head down and spoke low, just for Riley's ears. "I won't tolerate jeopardizing one of my cases just because you did that television special on the PD. Everyone on the force appreciates the funding for more equipment, but at the end of the day we're cops. So don't screw with me on this case. I don't give a fuck about WNUZ or your story."

Riley ground his molars so hard he could taste enamel. "I'm getting damned tired of being treated like the bad guy here. Not my fault Sally Stanton was killed or that her kid is missing, but I'm trying to help and all I'm getting is a hard time."

He took a breath, chugged a drink of beer and set the glass down hard. What the hell? Might as well stop dancing around the real issue. He knew what Massey had been digging at earlier today and what J. T. was thinking. "I am *not* going to ask this killer for an interview. I've got as much at stake as anyone else."

"Not as much as that little boy."

True.

J. T.'s jaw muscle twitched. "What the hell do you think you're doing to help this kid? Give me one reason to keep Massey off your ass."

Riley's grip on the mug tightened at the constant lack of faith in his intentions. He'd never live down Detroit. But he gave J. T. and the other cops more credit than everyone else. While newsies and City Hall postured, Philly PD faced these problems every waking minute. Riley looked at it from J. T.'s perspective.

Just a matter of point of view, as Baby G had said.

He stared past J. T.'s shoulder for a few seconds, at tables of diners in animated discussions. What would it be like to be normal again? To not spend every waking minute wondering what he could have done differently last year? He cut his eyes at the detective who nursed his beer, waiting.

Riley knew only one reason J. T. might give him a break and help with Massey. He'd have to explain the gap in time between the killer's call and dialing 9-1-1. He'd rather take a beating than expose his emotional state to anyone, but he'd put himself through far worse to help Enrique.

Swallowing a slug of beer first, Riley wiped his mouth and opened the wound. "When I took the call this morning, I had no idea who he was and still don't, but ten seconds into that call I *knew* he was a killer. Had to be. I – " He could do this. " – lost touch with reality for a bit. Didn't think it had been more than a minute, but must have been longer than I realized."

There were questions in J. T.'s eyes, but he was patient as an owl watching a mouse scurrying toward him.

"I froze." Riley continued staring at the dull bar surface. Perspiration beaded along his neck. "Couldn't believe another killer was calling me. Felt like a bad flashback." He lifted his gaze to J. T.'s face. "There's always a case...that wakes you up in the middle of the night, the one that haunts you. Never known a detective who didn't have one."

J. T. pulled back and propped an elbow on the bar to support his head, but still said nothing.

"Detroit's my nightmare. I'll never get that child back." Just saying that out loud hurt his soul. "Whether you or anyone else wants to believe this or not, I wasn't going after a story in Detroit. If you don't believe me, call the detective of record. I'd never do anything to interfere with finding a child and if you'll let me...I want to help you find Enrique."

Then Riley would go back to work, if he still had a job, and pick up where he left off, clocking a hundred hours a week to avoid sleeping. But he couldn't continue even that empty existence until this child was found.

Not after missing that sound in the background of the first phone call. And especially not after the killer had put the responsibility for Enrique's welfare in Riley's hands.

Seconds ticked so slowly while he waited, Riley could almost feel each movement on his watch.

"Okay, for now, but I'm not agreeing to anything." J. T. sounded ready to talk.

Riley could work with that. "I've got some ideas and some information from Sally's neighbors. I think the killer went to Philomena House last night."

J. T. sat up. "What were *you* doing there?"

"I was asked to meet a source there who found out about something your men missed." This was where J. T. had to make a decision to accuse Riley of interfering or accept that he might be a valuable resource.

Scratching his head, J. T. scowled. He tapped his fingers on the bar. "Okay, what?"

That sounded like an opening to collaborate.

Riley relaxed his grip on the mug and leaned in, keeping his voice down. He shared his conversation with Titia.

J. T.'s curse turned a couple of heads further down the bar. He shook his head. "What's that bastard going to do with the kid's blanket?"

"I don't know for sure, but the one in Detroit stole something important to every child he kidnapped...then he buried the keepsake with the child." Riley had spent some time on the Internet searching for any past cases that were similar, but had come up with zero. He did find a picture of the Diego blanket Miss Betty had described to him as Enrique's, printed with the words, "To the rescue, my friends!"

To the rescue, my friends.

"What else you got?" Turner stared at his beer, eyes glazed with frustration.

"I got a press release from St. Catherine's – "

"What the fuck were you bothering them for?"

Riley leaned back now, studying J. T. "I seem to be the only person not walking on eggshells around St. Catherine's. What's the problem with just asking questions?"

"You weren't here during the whole media storm they went through over a deacon embezzling money. By the time the bishop brought in an auditor and proved a deacon had been the only person who acted criminally, the media had turned that little church into a den of scam artists. Television and newspaper PR departments worked overtime to backpedal."

WNUZ would have been in the middle of that debacle if not for a board member telling them to stand down. "That's last year's news."

The detective shook his head in warning. "Pointing a negative spotlight at St. Catherine's – *without* good cause, which means *hard* evidence – is not going to help any of us."

"So you don't want to hear what I have?"

"I want to hear it, but I want you to understand how

sensitive the city is to picking on this church. Bishop Gautier didn't just clear the church's part in the embezzlement, he brought in Monsignor Dornan who has a spotless reputation. Dornan's known for cleaning up a mess. His presence alone is all the proof this city needed to believe in the church and start donating again."

"What're you saying? Dornan and that church are untouchable?" Riley didn't believe anyone was above questioning when a murder had happened and a child was missing.

"No one is above the law. No one." J. T. narrowed his eyes, not pleased with the insinuation that Dornan was above being poked at with questions.

But the monsignor was over St. Catherine's, which meant he was over Philomena House.

Riley lifted a hand in apology. "I wasn't insinuating that you'd let anyone slide who you suspected of a crime and I'm not insinuating anyone at the church is involved. What's the worst that will happen if they answer a few questions?"

That lowered J. T.'s ruffled feathers. "It's not that simple. If I show up at St. Catherine's asking about these murders, someone will talk and it'll hit the news no matter if you keep a lid on it. Dornan's got the ears and backing of powerful men in this city – Catholic and otherwise. After what happened last year everyone's over-sensitive about that group, but if Dornan thinks anyone is attacking something under his thumb he'll hand you more trouble than you can handle."

"I'm not attacking St. Catherine's." Yet. Riley shrugged, offering a relaxed attitude. "But they're attached to Philomena House where two people have been murdered in the last ten days."

"Tell me something I don't know."

"When I talked to their Chief of Staff Cortese today, she – " Riley noted J. T.'s slight eyebrow lift in surprise. " – couldn't get me out of there fast enough."

J. T. laughed sarcastically. "I should be surprised at that?"

"Point is that I've never had a church or anyone who needed donations not jump on the chance for free media exposure. I heard banging upstairs and there were construction trucks out back, so I asked about the construction going on. She said it was a new youth center then hustled me out the door. Why didn't she jump on that opening to ask me to do a special on the program?"

That sent J. T.'s stare into deep-thinking infinity. "Odd, but it doesn't mean anything."

"She pushed me out the door *after* I asked about the last killing at Philomena and suggested there might be a connection with the Stanton murder. I could tell by her face she didn't like that idea. Why not? Wouldn't they want to stop the killings if there's a connection?"

"That's a reach, Walker."

"Maybe, but both bodies were shot with a small caliber weapon and both bodies were moved after killing."

"Not that unusual."

"Both people had a child under the age of six."

"Still not that unusual."

But Riley could tell the seed was trying to take root in J. T.'s mind.

The detective held his thoughts closer than a gambler with a royal flush. "I'll put the Diego blanket description out with my men and talk to the profiler to see if this fits any profile, but the guy who killed Stanton could be Enrique's father."

"No. When I talked to Miss Betty, she told me Enrique was the product of a rape and the guy was caught a year after Sally gave birth." Riley seethed at what some animals would do to a woman, an innocent one who was mentally challenged to boot. "The bastard deserved more than prison time. They should've strung him up like a bull and neutered him without anesthesia."

J. T. flinched at the image then turned his mug around, hesitating about something. "You realize Enrique's probably dead by now, right?"

"No, I *don't* realize that." Riley refused to even consider the possibility even with all the statistics that backed it. "Not after talking to the killer today. He wants something from me and knows I want the kid back. Without Enrique, he has nothing to trade."

"Maybe, but he may just be leading you on until he runs out of options."

"We'll see, but I'm moving ahead based on Enrique being alive."

J. T. said nothing. He didn't have to when doubt oozed from his pores. "I'll see what I can find out about Sally's history." He pushed the mug away and waved off the bartender. "Now, tell me straight up you're not hiding anything about that phone call this morning if you want my help with Massey."

"I've given you everything I've got."

"Can't promise you Massey will let this go with that five minute gap of time. She may go for interfering with an investigation or she could decide to put you into protective custody and lock you up with your cell phone."

"Right now I only care if you believe me and if she pulls me off the street I think she'll be jeopardizing the best chance we've got at getting Enrique back."

J. T. stood up. "I'm buying what you've told me for now. You have my cell number. You need to call in anything, you call *me* first." His eyes turned into black stones. "Understand this, Walker. We have a common goal, but if you fuck me over, Detroit will look like a picnic."

Take a number.

Chapter 26

What was taking this sinner so long to wake up?

He hadn't hit him that hard.

A blustery north wind yanked at his robe, lifting the tail of the cloth to expose his thermal underwear. He sweated from exertion.

This body had been a chore to move. He'd loaded the unconscious man into a wheelbarrow, then rolled him to this perfect spot in the Laurel Hill Cemetery. He stepped back out of the beam from the flashlight he'd propped up on the overturned wheelbarrow so he could survey the image, assured the sinners would understand his message.

The motionless body rested with his back against a headstone that rose six feet in the air and read: "DEATH CANCELS EVERYTHING BUT TRUTH."

Fitting.

He patted the .38 in his right coat pocket. *Not yet.*

The man slumped forward, flannel-shirt-covered arms stretched out to each side with his forearms secured to wooden stakes in the ground.

"Wake up," he ordered. Nothing happened.

He shoved the flashlight into his left coat pocket, and pulled out a plastic bottle of water. He poured the icy liquid on the pig's face.

That resulted in a mouthful of gargled profanity that ended with, "What the fuck are you fucking doing?"

"Are you truly repentant?"

"Fuck you."

Guess that would be a "no."

The slob looked up, squinting. "What kind of fucking priest does this?"

"The same one who does this." He shoved a scrap of material in the guy's mouth, then stepped back and gripped the ax standing next to his leg. He lifted it high and swung down hard. The snap of the first wrist bone echoed a duet with a guttural scream muted by the rag.

This sinner would arrive in Purgatory without the offending appendages that had been intended for purposes other than hurting a vulnerable female.

Chapter 27

An irritating chime played once, twice.

Just ten more minutes. Riley finally figured out what the noise was. He came awake, cursed at the racket and snatched up the phone. Could be Jasper calling, even though his foster dad had gotten around the house fine last weekend when Riley visited.

Opening the phone on the way to his ear, Riley answered, "What?"

"You have another task."

He snapped wide-eyed alert. When did this killer sleep? Riley pushed up on his elbows, his gaze straying to the clock. Just after three in the morning.

"What do you need?" Riley reached over and clicked on the lamp next to his bed.

"Go to Laurel Hill Cemetery. Hunting Park Gate."

"Do you have Enrique?"

"I'll call back." He hung up.

Riley swatted the pillow aside and jumped up, ready to hurt somebody. But he needed this anonymous tipster, couldn't lose his temper now. Not with so much at stake. He wiped his eyes with one hand and scrolled through speed-dial numbers on his cell phone with the other then hit a key.

The second ring barely sounded when J. T.'s thick voice came on the line. "Better be worth waking me up."

"He called me again."

Didn't take a full heartbeat for J. T.'s voice to clear. "What'd he say?"

"Told me I had another task and to go to the Hunting Park

gate at Laurel Hill Cemetery. You got your call. I'll see you there." Riley closed the phone before J. T's string of foul curses burned his earlobe. He considered what they might find, but the caller hadn't said to look for a body. Riley still owed it to Biddy to help him keep his job, which meant bringing him along if there was a story to be had.

He keyed another call and headed to the bathroom.

"What the fuck you want?" Biddy growled into the phone after one ring.

"Want your job back by daylight?"

Breathing filled the pause. "I'm in."

Riley gave him the low down. "Meet me at the Hunting Park Gate of Laurel Hill Cemetery in fifteen minutes."

"You think I got fuckin' wings?"

"Okay, make it twenty."

In less than five minutes, Riley had splashed his face with water and dressed in jeans, boots and a sweatshirt. He snagged his leather flight jacket and keys on the way to the door.

Nothing stirred along 5th Street when he pulled out of the parking garage, heading to the Vine Expressway. WNUZ had rented him a condo in the Penn's Landing area where old mixed with new, modest apartments sprinkled among high-rise towers.

Home for only one more week unless he nailed this story.

If not for getting Biddy's job back and hanging close to help his foster dad, Riley couldn't care less about staying here or getting the story if he didn't find this kid.

He'd just have to make it all happen somehow, but right now he only wanted to know one thing.

Was Enrique really still alive?

Riley made the trip to the cemetery in fifteen minutes. When he turned on Hunting Park Drive both sides of the road were lined with six-foot high, wrought iron fence. Moonlight lit the piked tops of the support posts.

At the stone gate columns, he turned left. Two pikes were bent in as if pointing at the rows of limestone tombstones lined up inside.

Someone had snapped the flimsy padlock. Had a vehicle

nosed the gate open?

Riley left his truck running in park and stepped out. Headlights hit him from behind. He turned around to find a Land Cruiser, one of the original ones with rusted fenders and what was left of the finish that had been red twenty years ago.

Biddy must have wings after all. He parked off the side of the drive and got out carrying a duffle bag he dropped in Riley's truck bed.

A motor rumble and another set of headlights came toward Riley from inside the cemetery.

He stood very still and kicked himself for not putting his weapon within easy reach.

The Ford Explorer that parked in front of him dropped his pulse back to normal. J. T. Turner drove the pea-green hand-me-down from his lieutenant. Other detectives would get the truck next year, complete with the dented fender, cracked glass and six-digit mileage.

Seemed like the Philly P.D. guys who worked the front lines should get the new rigs then pass those down to the pencil pushers instead of the other way around, but what did Riley know?

J. T. climbed out and stepped into the glow of light, eyes swollen from too little sleep.

"He ain't happy," Biddy pointed out.

"No one's ever happy to see me."

"Just figuring that out?"

Had Biddy actually cut a joke?

"What are we out here for, Riley?" J. T. scanned around him, but everything was pitch black beyond the headlight beams.

"I was told to come here. You know what I know." Riley's phone rang. No one spoke while he answered. "Walker."

"Go to Millionaire's Row."

Could the killer see them right now? "Where's Enrique?"

"Can't miss him." The click sounded too final.

Riley's stomach did a twisted, double somersault when he closed the phone. "Said we'd find *him* on Millionaire's

Row."

No one uttered a sound. Riley knew the other two were thinking the same thing. Would they find Enrique?

A squad car pulled in behind Riley. Biddy climbed into the Tundra's passenger seat. Riley got behind the wheel and waited for J. T. to swing his vehicle around to lead the way, then let the squad car go next.

"So what's with this character who's calling?" Biddy asked. "What's he like? A wacko?"

"No. Calm and his voice sounds different each time as though he's trying to change the timbre and inflection. Can't tell what's natural or fake or even his age." Riley allowed a car length of space between him and the squad car creeping along ahead, running a handheld spotlight out his driver's window.

Riley didn't want to think about what they might find. His gaze roamed over the spooky landscape then he glanced at Biddy. "I get you in a jam by coming out in the middle of the night?"

Biddy shook his head and pushed a smirk back at him. "Nah. Wife's usually good about things like this. I don't give her enough credit sometimes. She's always taking my shit in stride." The smirk lifted into a sly grin. "I told her when you called we had a big news break and might get back to work today. She booted me right off the bed."

Riley smiled. Biddy's wife sounded like a nice girl, the kind all men planned to marry, but only the lucky ones landed.

A hundred yards inside the cemetery, J. T. made a quick left onto Millionaire's Row decked out with mausoleums constructed of stone. Some had stained glass windows glistening in the light of the full moon. Steel doors and sturdy wrought iron gates with heavy security locks protected the dead from marauders in the last home they'd have.

J. T. slowed at the top of the hill that boasted a view of the Schuylkill River some joked was almost worth dying for. Across the road from the mausoleums were humble family plots and headstones sans the spectacular overlook.

"It's like the city itself," Riley whispered, but didn't know why he spoke so softly. Wasn't like he'd wake the dead. "The rich get a room with a view. Everybody else is stuck with a view of their neighbor's tombstones."

Biddy sat up when Riley's headlights lampooned a tall headstone ten feet away. "There it is."

The two vehicles ahead of Riley had parked just past the body slumped over with his legs stretched out in front of the tall marker. Reminded Riley of a drunk passed out in an alley.

He was so damn glad to see an adult body and not a small child. That might seem unkind to think about someone who'd probably been murdered, but there it was.

He parked and jumped out. The bands of anxiety cinched around his chest finally stretched and let him draw a deep breath again.

When Riley and Biddy got within ten feet, J. T. stood up from where he'd crouched near the body. "Don't contaminate the scene."

The other officer was speaking in his radio, giving someone – more officers – directions to the location.

"We'll stay right here on the paved section." Riley leaned toward Biddy and whispered, "Any chance that was a camera in the bag you threw in my truck bed?"

"Good bet. I tossed an old BVP3 Betacam into the trunk. The picture won't be as high a resolution as the new ones, but that sucker is heavy and don't shake. Put a spotlight on anything and we'll get it."

"We better take whatever shots we want now before the rest of J. T.'s boys show up."

Biddy walked back to the Tundra.

When J. T. backed up from the body, Riley got a good look and cringed.

The guy's arms had been tied out to stakes on each side. He had bloody stumps where his hands should be. "He's not shot?"

"Yeah, he's got a bullet hole in his forehead." J. T. turned to Riley, a grim set to his mouth. He pointed to a spot of hard-packed gravel. "Take two steps to right *there*."

Riley very carefully moved closer, making a wide step to

hit the gravel mark.

"Put the light on this," J. T. told his officer.

The beam moved into place as J. T. used his latex-gloved fingertips to lift a foot-long triangle of fabric.

Riley swallowed. J. T. held the corner of a child's Diego blanket...covered in blood.

Chapter 28

Riley heard J. T.'s voice from a distance. He couldn't take his eyes off the scrap of material he knew had to be from Enrique's blanket.

He'd never been sick at a crime scene, but this one threatened to bring him to his knees.

"Walker!"

"What?" Riley shook off the wave of nausea.

"Do you know what Enrique's blanket looks like?"

Biddy came up and flipped on the camera, but Riley put his hand out to stop him. "Not yet."

When Biddy lowered the camera and pointed the lens at the pavement, Riley answered J. T. "I'm about ninety-nine percent sure that's the corner of a blanket identical to the one that belongs to Enrique. There's a cartoon character called Diego on the front with a couple of monkeys and a yellow Jeep-type truck in the jungle."

"We'll test the blood," J. T. said, his voice low and intense. "The chopped off hands were holding the blanket so the blood may not belong to Enrique."

"Yeah, that makes sense." Hope blasted through Riley at warp speed. He caught Biddy staring at him, waiting for a decision. His mind shifted into business mode for now. They didn't have a new lead to chase and they didn't have any reason to believe Enrique was dead or harmed. Not yet. And there was no reason not to report this cemetery death.

This footage should be enough to use as trade for getting their jobs back now and not harm anything on the Stanton case.

Riley called out, "J. T., you good with us filming the body, but nothing about the blanket or the kid? I'll label the killing however you say, and nothing identifiable, so it doesn't leak to next of kin before you reach them."

J. T. had returned to the scene. He stepped back to Riley, debate flickering in his gaze. But Riley had leveled with him last night and was giving him a chance to say no. "You got sixty seconds then you're going to have to back up to your truck. I'll have more officers here to secure the area and shove everyone behind the tape."

"Got it." Riley turned to Biddy who was already filming.

The vic was pushing close to forty, if not already there, thick neck like a man who earned his muscles with hard labor. Walmart clothes and a bad haircut. This was the only time that stiff would get to visit Millionaire's Row. The ground was black with blood, which explained the marble-white skin where the vic had bled out. His head was dipped forward...almost bowed.

Biddy paused from filming and cocked his chin toward the Hunting Park gate. "I hear sirens. Actually, I see blue lights. Anything else you want filmed up close before they run us out of here?"

"Get the tombstone. I'm thinking 'death cancels everything but truth' meant something to the killer."

He and Biddy were walking back to the Tundra when two more squad cars arrived. Riley would lay in some quick sound bites before waving the video under Lehman's nose. He had a right and obligation to report this killing.

Then everyone would be happy for once. Lehman would have the jump on the story, Biddy would be back at work and Riley...well, he wouldn't be content until he found Enrique – alive – but he'd be free to pursue leads, too.

Patrol cars rumbling into the park gave life to the chilled air. Officers strung up yellow tape from tombstone to tombstone, like a scene from the old movie, *Crypt*.

"Climb up in the truck bed." Biddy produced a mega-spotlight he handed to Riley then plugged the cord into an AC accessory port in the Tundra. When Biddy jumped up in the bed with him he lifted the camera to his shoulder. "They didn't say we couldn't film from here."

"Detective Turner?" one of J. T.'s men called out from the far side of the victim.

J. T. went over to see what they needed then yelled over his shoulder. "Riley, swing that light over here, would ya?" The detective motioned to his men to move aside.

Riley shined the light up the corridor the officers provided then looked at Biddy. "He wants our tips. He wants our light. He just doesn't want us here."

"You know what they say about wanting something." Biddy grinned, still filming. "He can shit in one hand and wait for the other one to fill up."

A dark sedan pulled in at the end of the current line of cars with another squad car close behind. Blue lights flashed on and off over the headstones and line of police cars.

When the lights on the sedan dimmed then disappeared, the driver's door opened. DA Investigator Massey emerged, dressed as though she was on her way in for a City Hall meeting.

"She ain't happy either," Biddy muttered, lowering his camera.

"Yeah, I'm two for two." Riley's chuckle died in his throat. J. T. wouldn't have had a chance to talk to her about not executing a warrant yet. This wasn't the place or time for the detective to put in a word for Riley.

Would she believe him if Riley told her he was just as surprised to be here as she was to see him here?

Chapter 29

"For the love of God, Walker, is that you?" Kirsten Massey's words pulsed out on angry white clouds in the chilled air.

Riley watched her silhouette split the patrol car headlights as she made a straight line to him, hips swaying with each sharp step, black hair flicking back and forth in angry sweeps. Direct contrast to her surroundings. She couldn't be more noticeable if she wore clothes outlined in neon lighting.

He checked J. T.'s men to see that they had extra spotlights in place now so he gave Biddy a nod then shifted the light to the side of Investigator Massey in a way that didn't blind her. Biddy panned his camera vertically from the ground up, which meant he was getting Massey from her short boots and black pants, beige sweater and a knee-length wool coat just as dark as the pants all the way up to her slinky black hair.

When she came fully into focus, Riley felt an unwanted stir at the sight of her that surprised him. Had to be the overwhelming sense of relief he was still experiencing over the possibility that Enrique might still be alive.

Or that he'd simply lost all sense of self-preservation.

This woman could do nothing but cause him more trouble than he was already in. Sure, he had all the freedom of speech rights he could ask for, but the killer had drawn Riley deep into this mess in a way that would be hard to explain soon if they didn't find the guy. In the meantime, he'd have to tap dance around Kirsten Massey.

She didn't hiss or show claws when crossed. No, she went

for the jugular vein when she rose to a battle. There was something about a woman with fire that spawned his interest. Go figure. Especially since this one would use that fire to incinerate him.

Just proved that the lower half of a man's body completely disconnected from the brain when introduced to a particular set of female pheromones.

She didn't change direction to see the corpse first, still pinning that formidable gaze on Riley. A crimson scarf wrapped her neck in a brutal slash of red.

His backup weapon had usually been charm and he needed it now in spades.

"How is it, Walker," she started before she even reached him. "That you manage to get here so quickly?"

Riley jumped down from the bed, diverting the light so that some still illuminated her face without broiling her skin. He shook his head, warding off the attack. "You wouldn't have known about this without my tip and we haven't gone near the body."

"J. T. told me you got the call again. Did you manage to get through to J. T. right away after the killer called or did your thumb slip and hit the 'end' button three times to buy you an extra ten minute head start?" She glared up at Biddy. "Cut that camera off right now unless you want to share a cell with Walker."

Her demand broke the fragile silence in the cemetery and shifted the macabre mood into business as usual.

"Turn it off, okay?" Riley asked Biddy before his cameraman gave her his 'freedom of speech' response.

"That's crap, but whatever." Biddy flipped a switch and the light on top of the camera died then he lowered the heavy piece to the truck bed.

Riley turned back to answer her, but she cut him off. "Do *not* waste my time with your well-constructed time line for calling Detective Turner." She shoved a hand on each hip. "Do you really think we're that stupid?"

"I don't think *you're* stupid," Riley answered in an innocent tone. "And I definitely don't think Detective Turner's stupid, so I'm not sure who you're alluding to with 'we.'" He figured he was hitting on all cylinders when she paused in silent thought.

Riley followed up with a smile.

Big mistake. That yanked the plug holding back her boiling temper.

"I'm so not in the mood for cute crap," she snapped. "I want answers, now. No bullshit or I'll add breaking and entering to your list of transgressions."

Riley lifted his shoulders. "I called J.T. the minute I got the killer's call. Gate was open when I got here. Hell, we followed Turner inside. I'm playing by the rules."

J. T. stalked up to them in time to catch the end of her spiel. He hiked an eyebrow full of doubt at Riley.

No help there.

Right now, Kirsten and J. T. were on the same team that Riley needed to divide for any hope of getting out of this.

As J. T. stepped into their circle of conversation and crossed his arms, listening, Riley asked Kirsten, "You don't want me to give Detective Turner my report first? I sort of thought *J. T.* did the initial investigation then sent his reports to you, but hey – " Riley lifted his hands away from his body in a what-the-hell motion. "If you want to take my statement first, that's fine."

J. T.'s dark eyebrows lowered and he opened his mouth to speak. If he appeased the investigator he'd ruin Riley's division tactic.

But Kirsten jumped in, unwittingly aiding him.

"Of course, not." The chagrined look she gave J. T. almost made Riley feel bad for putting her on the spot. Almost. "Give him your statement then *I* want to speak with you."

She was a spitfire with a straight-laced sense of duty. Didn't take much to get her ticked off, but she wouldn't dare cross the lines of protocol.

"In that case, I'll give my statement to Turner." Riley cast the detective a look of "do something" like take out a notepad, which Turner did.

"I'm going to take a look." Kirsten angled her head at the corpse. "Stay here, Walker. I'll be back as soon as Detective

Turner is through with you."

"Yes, ma'am."

Kirsten's lips tightened with irritation. She wheeled away and marched off.

Riley grinned at the rear shot. All passion and fury. Too bad she was with the DA's office.

J. T. shook his head and rolled his eyes as if Riley had made a big mistake.

"What?" Riley asked.

"She *hates* to be called ma'am."

"Really?" Riley chuckled. He'd tuck that away to use later. J. T. started writing as Riley rattled off his statement. Before finishing he had a question for J. T. "Any luck tracing that last call? He had to be on a cell phone watching us."

J. T. nodded. "That one *was* a cell phone."

"Really?" Hot damn.

"Don't get excited. They found it in a garbage can. The phone was a prepaid and the number fit a stolen phone report."

Shit.

When the detective walked away from him to where a cluster of officers now scurried around the site, Riley turned to Biddy. "Can you edit this tape?"

"Sure. Got it all set up in my basement."

"I'm stuck here until she's appeased or I'll end up in jail. J. T. told me last night she's got a warrant ready to process."

Biddy gave him an ah-shit sigh. "Told you she was a ball buster."

"First I'm going to convince her I'm worth more to this investigation free to move around than I am locked up then I'll see what I can get her to share." Be easier to open a clam with a toothpick, but he'd cracked hard nuts before. Riley checked his watch. "It's going on four-thirty. Why don't we meet at WNUZ at six so I can do the voice over and we'll offer Lehman a deal he can't refuse before we jump everyone on the morning news."

"No problem." Biddy loaded the equipment in the bag and carried it with the ease of toting a sack of feathers.

Riley waited in the designated spot.

And waited.

Massey ignored him for the next hour and then some, which started cutting him close on reaching the station in time with traffic piling up.

Two other news stations had already packed up and left. A flock of helicopters still filmed from overhead. Photographers traipsed all over the cemetery for shots, but nobody had the film Biddy had taken or the report Riley would voice over.

All he needed was five minutes to make Lehman capitulate. WNUZ's GM might be a bastard on his best day, but Lehman was serious about rebuilding that station. He wouldn't refuse a story that would help WNUZ's bottom line.

When Massey finally looked his way, Riley waved and tapped his watch.

She said something to J. T. who nodded then Miss Investigator Massey strode toward him. Light peeked over the horizon in waves of pink, orange and purple. When Massey finally reached him, Riley was prepared for anything she said except, "I'd like to see your cell phone."

Refusing her would put him on shaky footing immediately. "Sure." He fished the phone out of his pocket and handed it over.

"Thank you." Massey turned around.

"Whoa, wait a minute. I need that phone."

She looked over her shoulder. "Really?"

What the hell? But he wouldn't get anywhere by antagonizing her. "There's just an Unknown ID from the guy's call. How about taking a quick look and handing back my phone then if you're going to be tied up for a while we can meet over breakfast or lunch. My treat."

"I'll think about that." She took another step.

"What? Hey, we both have a job to do, but I've got less than thirty minutes to make it to the station."

Massey turned back around at that and walked straight to Riley.

"You were one of the first witnesses on this scene, and you know about the blanket, so you're not going anywhere until Detective Turner is ready to take you with him." She angled her head in a way that said she would not negotiate. "I'll allow you to remain uncuffed, but you are a person of interest in this case. Take one step away from where you stand and you'll land in lockup before you can say your name. As a minimum, I can put you in protective custody immediately. And this?" She held up his phone. "Is mine right now. You wanted to be in the middle of this investigation. Consider your wish granted."

Chapter 30

After an hour observing and talking to forensics while Detective Turner interacted with his men, Kirsten finally caught the detective's eye and waved him over from where the body was being removed from the headstone. Turner's teams still scoured the cemetery for evidence.

Was this killing tied to Philomena House, too? A serial killer picking on poor citizens?

Turner strode up to her, his boots crunching through frozen turf. When he got close, his gaze cut sideways then back to her. "What's Riley still doing here?"

"I told him not to leave. Not unless he wanted to wear handcuffs." The look that settled on Turner's face unhinged her confidence. A chill of warning traveled up her spine, that she wanted to attribute to the sub-forty-degree weather, but knew better. "I took his phone until I could confirm he'd called you immediately and isn't playing some game with this killer."

"What'd you find out?"

"I contacted his station on the way here. They hadn't received a call from anyone this morning for Riley, so *if* he heard from the killer it was most likely on this phone, which is suspect all in itself. There *is* an unknown caller right before he dialed you, but that would mean the killer has his cell phone number."

"Actually, he told me last night the killer had called him on his cell phone yesterday."

She'd been right to hold that lying media dog here. "Yesterday? And he didn't tell me? That just sealed his fate."

Turner held up his hand. "Wait a minute. He got the call *after* you told me not to contact you unless we had a break in the case. Technically, I didn't see that as a break so *I* didn't tell you. What's going on? You two have history?"

"Not even. I don't socialize with the media. They're all a bunch of cold-hearted vultures waiting on any bloody scrap for a story."

"I tend to agree with you in most cases, but I'm not sure it's fair to label Riley that way, any more than it would be fair to say everyone with a law degree is a blood sucker with no conscience." Turner's tired eyes creased with humor.

He had a point since she didn't lump herself in with attorneys who preyed on the naïve. Kirsten rubbed her eyes and raked a handful of hair back off her face and sighed. "Point taken, but the media can *not* be trusted. Especially not someone with his track record from Detroit."

"Yeah, well..." Turner shoved his fedora back and scratched his forehead. "I did some checking last night after I left Riley. Got ahold of the detective in Detroit that was on the Kindergarten Killer case. He said there's another side of the story that was never made public."

Kirsten raised an eyebrow in question. "Why not?"

"I consider this under the rules of confidentiality right now because this can't get out in public."

That he had to ask her to keep what he said in confidence stung her pride. She was the last person who would help the media. "I don't share anything that goes through the DA office or the police department with anyone."

"This isn't official business, but it was told to me in confidence. The detective in Detroit said they couldn't tell the public they were working with Riley to get a shot at tracking the Kindergarten Killer. Not even his station knew Riley had gone to the police with the idea of offering the killer an interview on the air."

"But the interview *was* Riley's idea, right?"

Turner nodded. "True. But, the detective said he warned Walker it was dangerous and Walker told him it was their job as adults to protect children. That it couldn't be any more dangerous for him than for the kids being grabbed by this nut case. Plus Riley put his job on the line and broke union rules when he went to do the interview because he wouldn't take a cameraman with him and wouldn't let the station know the location. That's why no one backed him from his station when everything went to sh...down the toilet. Not easy to watch someone commit suicide with a handgun in front of you either."

Discomfort dug into Kirsten's shoulder blades. She didn't want to feel bad about what happened to Riley in Detroit, but this put a new look on what she'd believed until now.

Turner added, "And one other thing – he ruined his media credibility by tricking the Kindergarten Killer. A lot of people wouldn't trust him again to be interviewed in secret. That's currency in his business."

"I have to admit I'm surprised."   Shocked would be a better word. Her father would fire someone over that. She mumbled her next thought out loud. "Why would he put his career and life on the line for the child of a stranger?"

The silence that followed her question all but slapped her in the face with Turner's unspoken reply. *Maybe for the same reason law enforcement puts their lives on the line for strangers every day.* "Never mind. I know the answer."

"What're you going to do about Riley?"

She'd made a grave tactical error. "I don't know. I may have turned our best hope of help on this case into an enemy."

"Talk to him. He's a reasonable person and I think he may have sources we can't get to."

She cut her eyes at Walker who leaned against his truck with arms crossed, jaw squared and eyes on the ground. "What about his phone?"

"Give it back to him. I think the killer was watching us this morning, because he called with final instructions right after we arrived. Probably best we leave Riley free to take calls. I believe he contacted me the minute he hung up from the killer's first call on this body."

"In that case, wish me luck."   She walked through the throng of officers who still searched the cemetery for evidence and dodged the ME waving the gurney over to load the body. As she got closer to Walker she noticed something she hadn't seen from a distance. He still leaned against his truck with his arms folded over his chest.

But he was fuming.

He hadn't stomped around angry or made sniping comments. Daylight had been a suggestion at that point. The sun blazed overhead now, melting pockets in the snow-covered ground, not warming Walker's disposition one bit.

His stare would back down an armed South American warlord and she had put the venom in that gaze.

But what was she supposed to think when she'd confirmed at four this morning that WNUZ had not received any call for Riley Walker since yesterday? In her mind, there was no way the killer's call had been forwarded from the station.

Thus, the killer had Walker's phone number. Those two were in communication. Looked guilty as hell.

Kirsten had come up with the logical conclusion that Riley had withheld information from the police, and her, yesterday. A valid reason to take possession of his cell phone this morning to determine if his story checked out.

She walked toward him, chin up, eyes steady, ignoring the chaos going on in her stomach. She *had* to make amends, because as much as she might not like the fact – they did need him on this investigation. For the love of St. Bridget, she hated kissing up to a man whose very profession put her teeth on edge.

At arm's length away, Kirsten stopped and held out her hand with the phone on her palm, positioned as a peace offering. She could be polite. "Here's your phone."

The newsman didn't move to take his phone, just continued to lean against the side of his truck and lifted that fuck-you stare to meet her gaze.

Crap. What happened to the flirt from earlier? "I've confirmed that you contacted Detective Turner immediately after receiving the anonymous call." She didn't try a smile since he clearly wasn't receptive to playing nice. When he still didn't speak or move, she accepted the obvious. She'd have to suck it up to take one for the team and apologize, but she wouldn't grovel to a newsman, not even for the team.

"Look, Mr. Walker, I apologize for jumping to the conclusion that you had delayed contacting the police. We're all under stress here and we all make mistakes." *Give me a break already.*

He stood away from the truck, arms still crossed.

She knew how a chipmunk felt sitting too far from protective cover when a hawk zeroed in on it for lunch. But her feet were staying planted.

"You're *sorry* about taking my phone?" His voice was so soft and dangerous the skin across her neck rippled. "You took my phone *after* Biddy left to edit the film then drive it to WNUZ to meet me so that he could sit down there for the past three hours and forty-two minutes pissed off since I didn't so much as call him as a courtesy to let him know I'd be a no-show. I could have called him on someone else's phone if you hadn't instructed every officer to refuse me that one request. But that's not even why a lame 'I'm sorry' doesn't cut it. The damn video was just a simple story." Riley's voice picked up volume.

She clenched her jaw to hold back her own frustration, sure that he wouldn't listen to anything right now. Riley was supposed to be on suspension. How was she to know he'd intended to report this story himself? She continued to hold the phone between them, determined to make him take it.

He unfolded his arms and put his hands on his hips, leaning his head forward until the veins in his neck popped out like thick steel cables under the skin. "I was *not* breaking a major story. I was *not* using this to advance my career. I was *not* jacking up the ratings for the station. But I could have negotiated getting us back on the payroll, which specifically – " Walker dropped his volume to a harsh whisper only Kirsten heard. " – would have given Biddy his job back *this week* since he's got a pregnant wife who can't be on her feet at all right now and doesn't need the stress of her husband being out of work. He needs this job for the insurance alone and you may have just cost him any chance of getting it back."

Mother of Mary... Not bad enough she'd destroyed the

best resource they might have, but costing the cameraman his job was unconscionable.

She'd never hurt anyone like that in her life.

Riley snatched up the phone and turned around, heading to his truck.

"I *said* I was sorry – " She bit off her words.

He slowed long enough to say over his shoulder, "Sorry? That's your best answer?"

The words she'd thrown at him yesterday in her office. Her sick stomach returned with force. "And I still need to talk to you – "

He never slowed his angry strides. When he reached the truck, he climbed in, cranked the engine and started weaving his way backwards through scattered police cars, officers and sightseers.

St. Bridget sucked big time if Kirsten could not find a way to mend this rift. She was a reasonable person, too.

She could admit she was wrong.

But she couldn't do it unless Walker would listen.

Chapter 31

Lucinda had never kept a secret from Stan, but she had to follow her instincts when it came to her child. She couldn't see Stan going along with what Monsignor Dornan had advised.

Not when it meant the chance of the public hearing about Kelsey being counseled for possible abuse.

So Lucinda had been on her own when she and Kelsey had talked to the doctor earlier.

She closed the door to Kelsey's bedroom and walked to the stairway leading to the foyer of her home, a place that should be a safe haven. Today's visit with the psychiatrist hadn't revealed anything specific since Kelsey shared very little with the doctor, but the visit had given Lucinda hope.

Dr. Adelaide Ziegler had a wonderfully calm approach with children and gave the impression she was prepared to spend whatever amount of time it took to convince Kelsey she could share her fears with Dr. Ziegler. She'd met Kelsey and Lucinda at their home instead of the office. Lucinda had Monsignor to thank for that courtesy since he'd made the call himself, and Dr. Ziegler to thank for coming at the only time Lucinda could assure that Stan had a full afternoon at the office. She couldn't risk Stan showing up unexpectedly.

Lucinda hadn't gone to Ziegler just because the doctor had been highly recommended by the Monsignor. She'd seen the television special on Ziegler that Stan's competition had shown over a week ago. What had impressed Lucinda about Ziegler was that she'd said not all withdrawn children were abused, but those who were lived in fear every day unless someone stepped forward. That had planted the seed of "what if" in her mind yesterday. The other saving grace that Monsignor shared, was that Ziegler would say nothing to anyone, like Stan, until Lucinda gave the okay. That had been her big fear until now.

She'd just reached the last step onto the marble foyer floor when the front door flew open, startling her almost as much as seeing her husband rush in. "Thought you had a lunch meeting, Stan?"

"I canceled it." Stan stopped halfway inside. He gave her an odd look. "What's wrong? I couldn't get you on the cell phone so I called here and Janeen said she wasn't watching Kelsey because you were at a doctor's appointment with her."

What's wrong? Lucinda had been asking herself, the priest, the doctor, God, everyone that same question. But she hadn't asked Stan, because she didn't know who to trust right now and that hurt almost as much as her fear over what Stan might have done.

Dr. Ziegler hadn't said anything definite, but she did say Kelsey was exhibiting the signs that someone might have touched her inappropriately.

Lucinda ignored the sick roll of her stomach and forced a casual tone, hoping not to raise his suspicions. The doctor had also said it was common for the abuse to be someone close to the child. "I wanted a medical opinion on Kelsey's behavioral issues."

That sounded like Kelsey was acting out, not in such deep depression and withdrawal that her own mother couldn't reach her.

"Did the doctor find anything wrong?" The way Stan said that sounded as if he thought she'd taken Kelsey to the medical group they saw as a family.

God forgive her, she wasn't correcting his misconception.

"Kelsey is physically healthy, as far as we know. I just wanted to be sure there wasn't something we were missing." If Lucinda told her husband Kelsey was seeing a psychiatrist, the renowned Dr. Ziegler, would Stan understand and be supportive?

Or would his first concern be that news of his daughter seeing a doctor as well known locally for treating child abuse as Dr. Phil was known nationally for relationship issues might create negative public perception for him?

Stan was in a business that exploited personal situations for the benefit of a news broadcast after all.

Until a couple of days ago, Lucinda would have known the right answer instantly. She'd have had no doubt that Stan would be more concerned about her and Kelsey than anything else.

But now she didn't know.

And at this minute, Kelsey was her priority.

Lucinda would worry about her marriage later. The possibility that she'd fallen in love with, and married, a man who could hurt her child nauseated her almost as much as it terrified her, but she would risk all to assure Kelsey's safety.

Even exposing Stan if she found him guilty. But she had to be sure first.

His shoulders dropped. "Okay, that's fine. I was worried. Did the doctor say anything about how she's...acting?"

Lucinda had never been adept at lying so she shook her head.

Stan raised his gaze to hers with the same love-filled look that had smitten her when he'd asked her to marry him. He started to speak, then stepped back and closed the door before turning back to her. "I felt so bad about losing my temper yesterday that I went to see our priest. I told you when we married I had grown up an only child and never spent much time around kids."

Her heart shook with tremors of guilt over the doubt firmly wedged into her every thought of Stan. He sounded so sincere. Was she overreacting to what she'd seen and heard up in Kelsey's room? Stan needed her as much as Kelsey did right now. *Please, God, help me find the answers. I don't want to destroy my marriage, but I have to protect my baby.*

Lucinda couldn't stand there with him sounding sincere and not offer him something. She still loved him and wanted to believe she was wrong to suspect him. "I understand the strain you're under and I'm trying to deal with Kelsey's problems so you aren't bothered."

Stan came over and pulled her into his arms.

She hated that she cringed inside, afraid to be touched by him until she knew the truth.

He kissed the top of her head. "I don't mind being bothered when it comes to Kelsey or you. She's important to me, too. Very important. I love her and it's my job to make sure she knows that. I feel like I've been neglecting both of you lately, but her in particular. That's got to be why she was so fussy around me the other day, but I'll fix it. I'm going to take her with me more often and spend some one-on-one time together. Maybe I'll plan a day just for the two of us."

Lucinda's mouth went dry.

Stan was not going to be alone with Kelsey ever again until Lucinda knew without a doubt that he had not molested her child.

Chapter 32

Turner scratched his ear and sat back in his creaky desk chair, considering the best way to broach a touchy subject with Investigator Massey, who had asked for a minute to reply to a text. The steady rumble of voices in the bullpen outside his office only quieted in the early morning hours when detectives were digging for information and thinking of possible leads.

"Sorry, Detective, but that was the DA." Kirsten shoved her cell phone into her simple black shoulder bag with no designer label swinging from a chain. She came from money, but a person would have to search for that information to know it.

"No problem, Ms. Massey."

"Could you do me a favor and call me Kirsten?"

He was genuinely surprised by the request, but nodded. "Sure thing, Kirsten. You're welcome to call me J. T."

She smiled as if she'd gained a small victory. "You were saying you had news."

"I got the results from the blood sample on the blanket piece we found at the cemetery and the blood doesn't belong to Enrique."

"That was quick."

"We got lucky, if you want to think of it that way, because Enrique had just been in the hospital and they drew blood. The rest of the evidence is going to take a while to get processed with the usual backlog."

"I'm working on getting funds to pay outside labs to process the evidence, but it's tough with the budget cuts."

"I understand." Turner wanted to lead her toward his goal for this discussion. "I think there's a chance Enrique may still be alive."

"I want that child to still be alive, too, but the odds are not in his favor."

"I know that. I have a profiler working on the evidence we have so far. She says it's erratic behavior for a serial killer and kidnapping a child doesn't fit any particular serial killer pattern either. That alone points to not relying on standard assumptions in a case like this. Walker said the guy told him the kid was still alive."

"Walker." She said the name with all the pleasure of discussing a poisonous snake.

"Does that mean your conversation didn't go well this morning?"

"He wasn't receptive."

"We need him."

"Why?"

"He's coming up with information we don't have. Walker found out the kid's blanket had been stolen from Sally's apartment after her body was found, which points to the possibility the killer knew Sally personally. Walker may be able to tap information we can't access or just don't have the warm bodies to run down."

"I hear you." She sat like a proper lady, but her fingers were never still, always moving as if she played an invisible piano. "I shouldn't have busted on him so hard this morning."

"Why did you?"

She shrugged. "I grew up around newsmen who sacrificed all for the almighty ratings points. I didn't expect to meet one with integrity."

"I've had my run-ins with the media, but Walker knows he's under a microscope. He's making every effort to work with us. If this cemetery killing is tied to Sally Stanton's by that caller and that scrap of blanket – if it is Enrique's, and I'm betting it is – then we have a serial killer. I've got men chasing down every possible connection between Stanton and Bruno Parrick. He's the vic from the cemetery."

"Did he know Sally or work around Philomena House?"

"Don't know. They were both killed by a .38 caliber. I'll have ballistics back later today. But if we're going to believe the same person is calling Walker, which I think is the case, and the killer told Walker that Enrique is still alive, we have to work on the premise the child's alive and these are related killings."

"Do we know if there are any other deaths tied to these two? Walker brought up the murdered vic from Philomena killed two weeks ago that was closed as drug related." Kirsten sat back, deflated. "This is not heading in a good direction. We can't drag anything connected to St. Catherine's into this mess without something concrete. Not after what they suffered over the last year."

"I understand, but we're going to have to dig deeper on this and Walker might be the answer."

"What do you mean?"

"We can tie his hands or let him run. He's already sniffing around St. Catherine's. WNUZ was the one station that did *not* hang the bishop out to dry last year so they aren't going to run anything sensational about the church. That's the best control over Walker right now. I won't let him interfere in my investigation, but I say we give him some room to move."

Understanding spread across Kirsten's face as she considered his suggestion. "You're right, but to do that I'll have to patch things up with him."

"I bet he'd let you if you gave him an opening."

"You'd lose money. I've called twice and gotten his voice mail. We know he's monitoring his cell phone so he's avoiding my calls."

"I've got something I don't think he has on this case that you can use to bargain with since we don't have the funds to process the evidence fast. But don't trade unless you can get us something that helps me solve this case."

She perked up. "Deal."

Chapter 33

All Riley's senses warned he was entering a hostile situation, but he had no choice if he wanted a chance to explain to Biddy. He stepped over the shattered beer bottle and newspaper on the sidewalk and pushed open a steel door similar to the kind found at the delivery entrance to a warehouse.

But the edges of this one had been chewed up with a crow bar at one time.

If parking his Tundra outside Philomena House had been a gamble, leaving his truck alone on Girard Avenue in this section of Ludlow constituted high stakes wagering.

Late 90s rock music pulsed in waves from speakers hidden in the textured black ceiling of Pete's Trapdoor Bar.

Riley hadn't seen a trapdoor outside or in here, but the minute his eyes adjusted to the low lighting he felt certain he'd found Pete. The mammoth bartender with skin like soot stood two inches under Riley's height, but outweighed him an easy seventy pounds in boulder-size muscle. He leaned on a varnished wood bar twenty feet long.

And gave Riley a dead stare that televised a mix of messages.

What are you doing here? Who are you looking for? I could kill you with the beer in my hand and not spill a drop.

At least, Riley considered that last one possible. Biddy picked this place and sent a text to be here by two o'clock, which passed ten minutes ago.

Of course, Biddy didn't say *he'd* be here at two.

Riley scanned the crowd that seemed busy paying

attention to their meals or in quiet discussions in small groups. Testosterone squeezed the air tight, as if this place stayed on alert for a threat.

Special Ops clubhouse.

Silent, Pete still eyed Riley as if sizing him up to determine how big a hole he'd need to dig to hide the body.

If Biddy didn't show soon, Riley had no doubt he'd be given one chance to walk out under his own power. Riley had been in, and started, his share of bar brawls in his early years, enough to know when retreat made more sense.

Biddy strolled into the room from the back, which probably housed the bathrooms. He slowed at the dartboard area to high-five a guy who could probably arm-wrestle a silverback ape and win. After a brief exchange of words, Biddy continued to the bar where he noticed Riley. He crooked his head at Riley and told Pete. "He's with me."

Pete nodded, which Riley took to be the equivalent of "Hey, nice to meet you."

"Let's go over there." Biddy angled his head at the corner.

Riley strode to the table. He'd seen plenty of joints like this, the floor stained with years of spilled ale, décor ala the local beer distributors and not enough lighting to order off the menu, because guess what? No menu. Just like the non-existent outdoor sign. The only identifying mark on the exterior of the building was a street number half-ass painted on the rusty corrugated metal siding as an afterthought.

Not even a local hang out. No one drank here without being screened.

Peanut shells crunched under Riley's boot when he stopped at an oil-colored wood table so abused it might have had a cinematic career at one time in western bar fight scenes. The chair he pulled out missed two rungs between the legs.

He sat down with his back to the wall where he could see the room and keep an eye on anyone encroaching on their conversation. A waste of time since practically all of the dozen men shooting darts or laughing over beers had taken note of Riley the minute he entered their space, then ignored him as soon as Biddy vouched for him.

Biddy took the chair on Riley's left, another gunslinger position where he could eye the room.

"Thanks for meeting me." Riley hadn't intentionally left Biddy hanging, but by the time he got his phone back the messages from Biddy had gone from trying to find him to one terse string of curses.

"Um-hm." Biddy folded his hands over his chest.

"Kirsten put me under arrest at the site this morning."

Biddy swung his gaze around, eyebrow cocked in question. "She arrest your phone, too?"

"Matter of fact, she did or I'd have caught you before you left your house for the station."

Pete plopped two draft beers on the table and walked off. No questions.

Biddy lifted his and killed a third of the brew on the first slug. "Okay."

Not sure what that noncommittal answer meant, Riley chugged a swallow of his dark draft and set the thick glass mug on the table. "Hear anything at the station?"

"Might say that. Fucking Lehman stormed the newsroom when he heard I was in. Face got all high-blood-pressure red. Thought he was going to flatline right there. Said the crew he sent out couldn't get close by the time they got there, but they saw you and your truck up at the front of the line."

Shit. Riley hadn't thought about Lehman's crew in the back row. "What'd you give him?"

"Not a fucking thing."

Riley considered that a minute while he drank a swallow of his beer that rolled cold and brisk down his throat. Biddy could have cut a deal with the film and let someone else voice over. "Why not?"

Biddy licked the foam off his upper lip and studied his mug with the interest of a glass collector contemplating an auction bid. "We only need one ratings point to make the three for your contract. Might have gotten that with this story, but if I'd handed him the film, Lehman would have used it and left you out in the cold." Biddy turned to Riley. "Would you have called another cameraman this morning if I couldn't have met you?"

"No."

Biddy sat on the film even though he could have gotten his job back.

Riley took a look around. He'd bet there wasn't a man in here that wouldn't follow Biddy out in the street to face an unknown threat. Biddy was the kind of man who lived by his word and expected Riley to live by his.

That had never been a problem for Riley. "Thanks."

Biddy nodded. "What's next?"

"We might pick up that last point for WNUZ with this killing if we can tie it to the Stanton one." Riley paused, calculating then seeing no way around his limited choices. "Except, I can't break the story on Stanton yet, not if we want to keep any kind of relationship with the police." And Riley wouldn't jeopardize Enrique's life. He'd err on the side of caution this time.

"Same people that arrested you this morning?"

"Not J. T. It was all Massey, posturing to make a point, and her little show backfired on her."

"How you figure that?"

"Now she knows we're on the right track and she wants to talk. I'll help J. T. and his men, but she's crazy if she thinks I'm sharing one iota with her. She can't take my phone, or she'll risk the killer will call and not talk to anyone else. Screw her. I need J. T. to know I'm being straight with him, and that's why I told him about Enrique's blanket." Riley flashed on that scrap of bloody material and kept telling himself Enrique might still be alive. Had to be alive.

"Any news on the blood samples?" Biddy asked.

"No. Doubt I'll get an answer from anyone but J. T., and he's up to his neck in bodies and a lost kid." Riley leaned forward to keep his voice low and still be heard. "Still interested in working on this?"

Biddy leaned forward, too, crossing his thick forearms on the table in front of him. "Whatcha got?"

"The monsignor at St. Catherine's is a crack shot with a .38 and he runs on ice water."

"Never heard of a priest who shoots, but doesn't take a

crack shot to kill at point blank range if you're thinking that way."

Riley scoffed. "Even I'm not going to point a finger at a priest, especially one who shoots at the police range, but this Monsignor Dornan is tough. He gets pushed he's going to push right back and probably harder. I asked about Sally's murder, if he could shed any light on it. He blew me off. Said to pick up a press release from his office, so I did and tried to get something out of his chief of staff, but she's evasive."

"She?" Biddy's eyebrows perked up.

"Yeah, quick, sharp, protective. Too groomed to be new, but she doesn't want me around. You'd think with them developing this outreach center they'd try to get some free publicity, but she couldn't hustle me out fast enough when I asked about another Philomena House resident murdered a week ago."

"Told you 'bout the media shittin' all over St. Catherine's. Might just be gun shy."

"Maybe, but I don't think so. I need information on any killings with a .38 shot to the head and the body moved. Want to focus on Philomena House and St. Catherine's parishioners. Narrow it down to a ten-mile radius. They released the name on the victim from the cemetery. Bruno Parrick. We need to find out if he's connected to Philomena House or St. Catherine's."

"If we drag St. Catherine's into this mess and find out they didn't need to be involved the WNUZ board will never put you back on as anchor. Might not get another anchor job. Anywhere."

Riley met Biddy's steely gaze straight on. "You don't want to do this, that's fine, I'll understand, but I don't care who goes down with a kid missing. And the only shot we have at getting our jobs back is breaking a major story. This case is all we've got."

No more questions, no extra clarification, Biddy just said, "Okay. Let you know when I have something."

There hadn't been a lot of times in Riley's life that he'd been given unconditional support, but he knew when he'd just received it. His cell phone chimed.

The caller ID was unknown. "Walker."

"Kirsten Massey here. Don't hang up."

He hadn't hung up on her today, but he *had* let her prior calls roll to voice mail. "What, *Investigator* Massey?"

Biddy eyed him with a this-should-be-interesting expression.

"I've got a deal for you." She let that hang between them without another word.

"Why should I care?"

"To help Enrique."

Damn, she played her top card, first hand out. "What's your deal?" Riley heard a tone beep on his phone that indicated a text message being delivered.

"You agree to meet so we can talk and I share information."

He ground his jaw, wanting to shut her out, but in the end he'd do a lot more than shove his temper and pride aside to help find Enrique and nail this murderer. "Okay, deal."

"The blood on the blanket is *not* Enrique's. It all belonged to the vic."

That earned her a few points. "What else?"

"The victim was killed at the location we found him. If you'll meet me, I've got something else to share about the bodies, but not over the phone."

She'd made Riley an offer he couldn't pass up. "When?"

"I can't get away until this evening."

"Meet me at the Alma de Cuba at seven."

"I'll be there."

Riley ended the call, not quite sure what had just transpired, but curiosity had sent him into worse situations than dinner with a woman. He told Biddy, "The blood on the blanket all belonged to the vic. Massey's willing to trade information tonight."

"Guess it was worth getting my ass crawled by Lehman this morning if it means Massey's gonna play ball."

Nodding, Riley lifted his phone again. "Had a text message from Lilly. I asked her to let me know if we got any movement in ratings." If anyone at WNUZ knew the pulse of the station, Lilly would. He normally talked to the receptionist everyday and brought her coffee that was drop-shipped in from Chicago because she liked it as much as he did.

"She'd know." Biddy nodded. "But I doubt WNUZ got a decent hike today since the crew was shut out of filming."

Riley read the text message. "Ah, shit! WNUZ dropped a point."

He'd felt pretty good about gaining one point in the next week, but *two*?

Not odds he'd put serious money on.

Chapter 34

"We need that done *now!* Why haven't you – "

Margo's head jerked up at the angry words that jumbled into a mottle of garbled sniping. That had sounded like Icky's snotty tone way down the hall. She quickly finished checking off electrical supplies being unloaded at the back door of St. Catherine's, calling goodbye to the delivery guy.

Once she shut the door and hung up the inventory clipboard, she took a fortifying breath to find out what Icky had started this time.

She hurried down the hallway past all the offices, making a mental note when she caught a glimpse of Monsignor in his office. When had he come in? Didn't matter. She had to see him, but not until she found out why Icky was on the rag again. She pulled up short at an eye-to-eye face-off, punctuated by Icky's low-eyebrow scowl and Baylor's defiant, jutted-out chin.

Baylor stood there holding two brand new five-gallon buckets of paint that had to be straining his arms. "Told you I called the company today. Can't do a thing about them not showing up to get the roll-off Dumpster. Don't know what's the big deal. Nobody's behind on the remodeling. *You* talk to them if you want to."

"*I* don't have time to deal with Dumpsters." Icky had probably perfected indignant by the age of five.

"My time's important, too," Baylor countered.

"What's wrong?" Margo asked calmly then prepared herself for the reply. Icky was as apt to snap at her as give a civil answer.

Grizzle walked out of the men's room. He was ghost-pale until he started coughing, then his face flushed more with each painful sounding draw of breath.

"What's *wrong*?" Icky asked, dragging out the last word. "What's right?"

Margo didn't know who to help first with Grizzle hacking so horribly he sounded as though he needed oxygen, but she couldn't stand by and let Icky berate Baylor, who sort of reminded her of her da some days. She offered, "*I'll* check on the Dumpster, but it's after four so I may not be gettin' them until the morning, Father Ickerson. Will that suit you?"

Icky turned his scowl on her.

"Probably be picked up by then."   Baylor turned dismissively and walked toward the stairs. "You want to do God's work? Come upstairs and get your hands dirty."

"Can I help you with those?" she asked, worried about Baylor carrying so much up the stairs at one time.

"No."   Baylor shook his head, waving off her question as insulting. "I got it."   He disappeared into the stairwell.

Icky was getting all worked up. "This building is not going to be ready on time."

Grizzle started to speak, but Margo held up her hand. "Save your throat. It sounds raw."   Then she turned to the walking hissy fit. "We'll be fine, Father Ickerson. We have a good two weeks until you-know-who visits."

"This place is nowhere. Near. Ready." Icky stomped back and forth, pacing the short width of the room. His face turned red as the top of a thermometer. "The police are crawling all over Philomena House as if they expect to find a killer visiting someone and that guy from the media has been there asking questions. Why isn't Monsignor dealing with that? I had Philomena House all cleaned up and now I have to send Valdez back over when we need him here." He stormed off.

Her anger flickered to life. Icky had no reason to take that tone or criticize Monsignor, who worked endless hours for this place. And Valdez might not be the best person to send to Philomena. The guy gave her the creeps some days and that was when she could find him.

Grizzle gave her a look of commiseration and strode down

the hall, hacking behind Icky. Poor guy sounded worse by the day.

Margo followed until she reached her office and stepped inside to find Monsignor's office door still open, but he was on a phone call.

She was not moving from her desk to do anything until she had a chance to speak with him. The stress of waiting to discuss her meeting with Riley Walker yesterday had ruined any chance of sleeping last night.

Monsignor had left St. Catherine's right after finishing his late confession yesterday. She'd been upstairs going over a question the construction crew had on the remodeling, then returned to her desk to find a note in Monsignor's script explaining that he had a dinner appointment.

The press release had been yesterday's crisis.

New day. New disaster. She went to her desk and scrolled through the online news stories once more. There was the headline again: Brutal Murder at Laurel Hill Cemetery.

She drummed her fingers. Riley Walker would be all over this the minute he figured out where Bruno and Lisa Parrick worshipped.

Margo had to tell Monsignor about Walker's insinuations yesterday. Insinuations...or threats?

A deep chuckle floated from Monsignor's office. He ended his phone conversation with, "I think we can work this out. See you tonight."

That was her opening. Margo grabbed the paper from her desk and scooted over to his office. "Could you spare a moment, Monsignor?"

He looked up, scratching his jaw. "Sure, if it's not a confession."

"Why?" She smiled at his teasing tone.

"Seems Father Ickerson *was* in the building yesterday after all when Bruno came in, but no one knew he'd returned. He takes confessions too personally, as if Bruno Parrick had snubbed him by speaking to me."

Icky had a temper tantrum over the smallest things.

Margo had no sympathy. Icky hadn't had to face Riley Walker yesterday, which reminded her...

"About that, first I want to give you the press release." She handed him the document.

"I don't have much time. I've got two appointments downtown and need to be gone in forty-five minutes to make the first one by five-thirty." Monsignor took the document and lowered his gaze to the page.

Margo should be used to so many meetings, but it seemed as though Monsignor had a lot of appointments lately, particularly in the evenings. Just like San Francisco. She'd arrived at the St. Peter Covenant House a week after he'd moved to the south side location. Inside a month, Monsignor had been booked with dinner appointments and late night meetings. He'd always been a night owl, which had been in his favor at that time, when he had to stay up all night for two weeks straight to deal with the pair of warring gangs.

When she'd expressed concern over his riding around with the gangs at night, he said he had no choice and in the end everyone would benefit. He'd said, "Blessed are those who hunger and thirst for righteousness, for they will be filled."

Margo stifled a shudder at that memory. Bloody memory.

Members from both gangs had died in shootings at night during the time Monsignor rode with them.

He could have died, too.

Settling deeper in his leather chair, Monsignor read the press release.

She'd sat in that chair once. The leather swallowed her, reminding her no one could fill his chair or his shoes. He was St. Catherine's best hope for rebuilding.

He lifted his gaze. "Okay, what else?"

"I think we may have a problem with the media." Margo tried for unconcerned and hit halfway between that and shaky.

Monsignor's forehead crinkled in confusion. "The press release is fine. Well done, in fact."

She'd like to enjoy the moment, to bathe in the pleasure of his comment, but couldn't preen with a possible disaster on the horizon. "Thank you, but after meeting him I don't think he's going to be satisfied with just a press release."

"He who?"

"Riley Walker."

"Was there a problem?"

"Walker's got it in his mind that Clayton Howell – you know the Philomena House resident who was killed two weeks ago? – that his death is somehow connected to Sally's."

"What is it with this guy?" Monsignor put the press release down slowly, perplexed at first, then the muscles in his face shifted. He showed irritation on occasion, such as yesterday with Bruno's lashing out at Valdez, but Margo rarely saw Monsignor's face turn to stone as it did now. "How does he think those deaths are connected?"

She ignored the frigid undercurrent since that hadn't been directed at her, but the newsman. "Both were killed with a small caliber weapon and both bodies had been moved to a second location after death." Margo rubbed the bridge of her nose with two fingers, buying a few seconds. "I told him to talk to the police, that we were more concerned with the families left behind. I got the impression he wants to do a story on St. Catherine's and you."

On her, too, but she was so insignificant that would never happen so why mention it, right?

Monsignor sat back, arms resting at each side and palms together in front of his chest, contemplative. "If we push Walker away, he'll work that much harder to get what he wants. He's no rookie. He knows how to turn anything into a story." Monsignor cocked his head to the side, eyes distant as he sifted through information mentally. "Walker's with WNUZ, the only station that didn't rip the bishop to pieces last year. Based on that alone, I'm surprised he's coming at us this way," Monsignor mused absently.

"I didn't realize one vulture missed the frenzy. Why did WNUZ hold back when the others attacked and, if that was the case, why would Walker come snooping around here now?"

"I recall the bishop telling me a board member at WNUZ had a personal interest in St. Catherine's – something about having come here as a child – so he called his news hounds off the hunt. But Riley Walker wasn't here when all that happened so he may not know the station's position on causing us undue problems." Monsignor raised his eyes to Margo, a gleam of confidence twinkling. "He needs to be informed. I'll contact Bishop Gautier as soon as I get a moment and find out who can enlighten Walker on showing the church respect."

Margo's chest relaxed like someone had opened a pressure valve. She smiled. "Great. But we have a new problem."

Monsignor sat forward, elbows on his desk, hands clasped, but the taut posture said *her* job was to solve problems. "What?"

"Bruno Parrick was found dead this morning. He was killed in Laurel Park Cemetery." She waited, but couldn't read what was going on behind Monsignor's closed mask.

"That's awful. What do they know about the murder?"

His undisturbed expression surprised her, but Monsignor had seen so much in over fifty years on earth than her mere twenty-nine, that she attributed his non-reaction to being better prepared at hearing of unexpected deaths.

She lifted her shoulders. "Nothing much other than his...hands had been cut off before he died." How gruesome. She didn't think Bruno was redeemable, but she'd never wish for anyone to suffer that way. "I'm worried about what Walker will make of this once he realizes Bruno and Lisa worshipped here."

If the police weren't holding the bodies for now there would be back-to-back funerals and that would draw every news station around like flies to syrup.

She wouldn't want that, but the dead deserved a funeral.

Monsignor stood calmly. "You're the computer whiz. Find whatever you can on Walker."

She wasn't exactly a whiz, but Monsignor spent as little time on the computer as possible, using it more as a word processor than a communications tool for other than email. "I thought you said you knew him."

"I know *of* him. Seems like there was something mentioned about his last job in Chicago or Detroit."

"How does gathering information on his background help us?"

"Because Walker's too sharp to be at WNUZ, the lowest ranked television station in Philly."

"So?"

Monsignor cut his eyes at her with a calculating gaze, the trademark of his success. "Information is power. If he's got any kind of negative media history, which I'll bet he does to be with WNUZ, Walker's name will be all over the Internet. Find out what you can and *you* field his questions when he contacts us. Don't let him around anyone else here. In fact, if you don't hear from him by tomorrow morning, *you* contact him."

Me? "Why?" She probably shouldn't have been quite so abrupt, but come on. What was he thinking?

"I want you to keep tabs on Walker, find out what he's up to and what angle he's playing for a story. *You* have to be proactive to keep a layer between St. Catherine's and Walker to prevent him from blowing this all out of proportion and pointing an accusing finger at us. If he does, by the time the media circus dies down we will have missed our small window of opportunity."

"The pope's visit."

Monsignor nodded. "If Walker gets away with tying these killings together and connecting them to St. Catherine's just to break a big story, the pope's security will deem this site a risk and advise against visiting."

The coincidence played on her conscience. "You don't think there's an actual connection between these deaths, do you?"

He stood up and lifted his watch into view, checked it then told Margo, "To have three parishioners killed so close together in time and circumstances might seem unusual in some areas, but if you'll recall we had two die violently in a similar socio-economic area of San Francisco within one week. This is more a matter of location than anything."

She nodded, trusting in Monsignor's evaluation.

He scratched his chin. "Talk to this reporter and make him see how unsupported claims will jeopardize St. Catherine's future. If that doesn't work, I'll talk to him, but that's exactly what he wants right now. If Walker wants a story, tell him to write one about how St. Catherine's influence is cleaning up this area."

She'd rather be snowed in with only Icky to talk to than have to dodge Walker's questions on another death related to St. Catherine's. She had to pinch back a sinful thought that involved physically harming Riley Walker.

The newsman would assume the three deaths had something to do with St. Catherine's.

And what if Walker *did* find a connection? Could there possibly be a killer targeting people in the parish?

Chapter 35

He paced his office, working on the plan for this evening. Mrs. Feldman still had to be dealt with before she put her hands on her teenage obsession, the young boy who shoveled her driveway. But that kid didn't live in her house. Wasn't in immediate danger.

Not like the two younger children who needed divine intervention now.

He only had time to save one tonight.

What was wrong with parents these days?

It was a mother's job, her most important duty, to shield her child from danger. That made a mother as much at fault as those who would hurt her little one.

Dark encroached outside with each minute he deliberated.

Make a plan and stick to it. But if he chose wrong tonight a child would suffer at the hands of a demon.

It was *his* duty to hand the children to God.

His duty to stop Satan's rule.

Blessed are those who hunger and thirst for righteousness, for they will be filled.

Chapter 36

Riley searched the six o'clock dinner crowd packed into the Race Street Café.

He spotted his target, who claimed to want media coverage even though he seriously doubted that excuse for the meeting. Wading through a mash of diners buzzing with conversation, he slowed his approach to Margo Cortese.

She sat alone, unfolding her napkin as though she didn't have a care in the world. Auburn hair with an electric-charge curl hung to her shoulders, a top layer of damp ringlets indicating she hadn't been here long enough for those to dry from the light drizzle outside. She wore a shamrock green sweater he bet would bring out the Irish in her eyes.

Riley sidled up silently to the table while she was distracted, placing her napkin in her lap. "I like green, reminds me of springtime."

Her head snapped up. "Oh, you're here." She smoothed the napkin again, then fiddled with her glass of water.

Was she on edge around all reporters or just him?

Or men in general? That didn't make sense, because she spent the day around primarily men.

Riley pointed at a chair. "May I?" When she nodded, he slipped into the one across from her, giving her plenty of space. "So you want some media coverage?"

"Yes, we'd appreciate any help you can give us on the youth program at the outreach center. That's what all the remodeling is about." Her demeanor segued easily into autopilot business mode. That gave him an insight into her comfort level, which meant her discomfort level would be personal. Interesting.

Especially since most people said too much when they were *not* comfortable.

"Be happy to come by and do a walk through to give me an idea of how to plan the video session." He used his most accommodating tone. Keeping things easy. Nothing confrontational at first, then he'd slide in a direct question when she wasn't expecting it.

"Wonderful. Anything you want to know about it right now?"

Her *wonderful* had been obligatory and her smile hid stress, covering what was really on her mind. He said, "Nothing that we can't discuss when I come back to St. Catherine's."

That stumped her. She'd clearly planned on his supplying questions on a mundane topic she could safely answer.

He smiled again. "But since you're here and we have a minute, I do have something I'd like to talk about."

Suspicion fanned across her face. "Don't you want to order?"

"I've got dinner plans. Can't stay." He caught relief in her half smile before she lifted her glass to take a drink so he added, "Not that I wouldn't enjoy a nice dinner with a pretty woman. Maybe we could do it another time."

She choked on her water, set the glass down and jerked her napkin up to wipe her mouth. "Sorry. That went down the wrong pipe. I, uh, keep a very busy schedule, but thanks for askin'." She moved her hands to each side of her plate, wrists against the edge of the table, then shoved her hands in her lap as though she had no idea what to do with them.

Riley suffered a moment of sympathy for her anxiety, but she'd instigated this meeting and he couldn't pass up an opportunity to catch her out of step. "Consider it an open invitation." When she didn't respond, he changed direction. "Let's talk about a missing child and who else at St. Catherine's can help with information."

Didn't take much to push her pissed-off button.

Her eyes narrowed to the point of slits. "What is it with you and St. Catherine's? Haven't we been under the microscope enough with the media? We're doin' all we can to help our parishioners with programs like Philomena House and the youth center, not to mention our other community programs. We worry about *all* the wee ones and will do anything to help the police. What else do you people want?"

You people? As if newsmen were all a bunch of vultures. Some might be, but he resented constantly being lumped into that group. His tone was no longer accommodating.

"*I* want to find someone who's willing to do whatever it takes to get a child back. You act like I'm accusing you of something. I'm not, but I am challenging you to share everything you and the rest of St. Catherine's staff can on Sally and Enrique Stanton."

Her lips closed tight. She shoved at a thick lock of curly hair that bounced right back into place alongside her smooth cheek when she let go. "We all want to get Enrique back, but I don't personally have anything to give the police."

"And the priests?"

"They've shared anything important already and you know they can't divulge what they hear in confession."

"I can appreciate the sanctity of confession, but a child's life is at risk. Doesn't that bother any of *you* people?" He dished that back with a heavy slap of sarcasm.

Restraint and fire clashed in her gaze. The blaze won. "You dare to question our priests who hold the trust of every member, no matter how important or insignificant those people and their problems may rank on your personal scale? And what about *your* interest in Enrique? You'd have me believin' you have a righteous reason for investigating these deaths?"

Deaths, as in plural? The first death two weeks ago wasn't tied to this killing, just something Riley had tossed at her to get a reaction. Did she know something she wasn't saying about that one or Bruno Parrick's body found in the cemetery today? All J. T.'s office had shared with the media about the body so far had been a name and that the man was survived by his widow. No children mentioned, which threw a new inconsistency into the mix of profiling.

But Margo's slip sent a quick surge of adrenaline through

Riley that he could be on the right trail. "You don't think finding a child is enough reason for someone to show an interest?"

She lifted her chin and met him eye-to-eye. "For someone other than a newsman."

"You always so distrustful of the media?"

"I never trust a man who flirts with me, because I don't know his motives. Just as I don't know your motive for hunting Enrique or knocking the scab off a wound St. Catherine's is just startin' to heal."

"What would prove to you I'm sincere about finding Enrique and not just searching for a story?"

"You'd have to convince me these people matter and I don't think you can do that. You expect everyone else to bare their souls and tell all but what about you?"

"What about me?" He didn't give a damn if he sounded hostile. He had an idea where she was heading with this.

"Bare *your* soul for once. Tell the truth about your darkest secrets. What was your motive for interviewin' a killer in Detroit? Would you have interviewed the Kindergarten Killer if you couldn't have told anyone you had an exclusive interview with a serial killer?"

Where others raised his fighting hackles when they took pot shots at him, this woman's direct questions sliced deep to the core.

He'd asked the man in his bathroom mirror harder questions than that since last year. Yes, he'd wanted to find that little boy, but any newsman would have been jacked up at the chance to get this guy on camera. The hole inside him opened and burned with pain, a black vortex that threatened to pull him in. That's why he couldn't go there, couldn't think about that day again. His heart pumped harder and harder. He swallowed down the anguish and forced the misery into a mental locker he slammed the door shut on.

He had to get through today and find Enrique, stay away from that bottomless hole he couldn't climb out of if he fell all the way in.

Riley forced his words from between tight jaw muscles. "What happened in Detroit is in the past. A child is missing here, today. What purpose would baring my soul serve?"

"I'd know if I could trust your motive for pushing this investigation, because I don't think you even know why you're doin' this."

She'd driven a spike deep into the core of the infection eating him inside out. He didn't want to think about the whys, just function, put one foot in front of the other with a purpose for each day. He resented the hell out of her disturbing the balance beam he teetered along between sanity and insanity. If he dipped too far one way, he'd fall back into the lost existence he'd lived in right after the Kindergarten Killer's suicide.

The waitress delivered a Shepherd's Pie and served it to Margo Cortese then left.

"I'd take care what you say about St. Catherine's," Cortese warned in a calmer voice as if she suggested using the correct fork. She'd regained her control, stabbing at the crust on her Shepherd's Pie. "Your television station was the only one wise enough not to attack us during the embezzlement debacle. Since you're suspended right now, I doubt your superiors would approve of your visit to St. Catherine's or even know about it. You might be wantin' to check with them before chasin' a wild-hair story involving St. C's that could have a negative connotation."

Riley had hit his limit of threats for the day. "I have no intention of putting St. Catherine's in a negative spotlight based on speculation."

She smiled, genuinely pleased and clearly relieved at his admission.

"But," he continued. "If solid evidence points to St. Catherine's or Philomena House being at the center of this, and it's clear that you and the monsignor's staff had prior knowledge I'll personally break that story wide open. And I don't care who on the board of WNUZ doesn't like it. I guarantee you I'll find a station to carry *that* story." Riley stood. "Thanks for the tip."

"What tip?" Worry wiggled in her voice.

He stepped aside and politely shoved his chair back under the table then leaned down and placed one hand on the surface for support so he could crowd her space. This was another wild shot, but he had her concerned about something. "When you referenced *deaths*, as in more than one. That tells me I should take a closer look at Bruno Parrick's murder."

Riley lifted up to his full height and peered down at her. "And since you're so keen on soul searching, ask yourself how much *you're* willing to risk to protect an organization when a child's life is at risk."

Chapter 37

The night belonged to the wicked and desperate.

He would take it back from the wicked, by using their desperation. Wind howled through the trees towering over each side of the dark path he followed, lit by his small LED flashlight. He'd grown up in dark places, lived in Montana where night fell like a widow's cloak over the entire house.

Used to scare him, late at night when the wolves howled and the coyotes yodeled to each other.

His father said facing your fears made a man tough.

Made a ten-year-old kid wet his pants when he'd gotten locked outside all night on the porch without even a flashlight.

He'd survived though and maybe if his dad saw him walking alone through these woods at night he'd finally say, "I'm proud of you."

Never would happen now with his dad long dead and buried.

It hurt to know he'd miss the chance to show his dad how tough he'd become, but he had a duty now, a way to prove himself to someone more important. When he got St. Catherine's straightened out, he'd be acknowledged for the results of his carefully executed plan. But success would slip from his grasp if Margo didn't keep Riley Walker reined in.

The newsman had been his best choice as a phone contact. Someone who understood the cost of failure. Walker's history would prevent him from becoming too ambitious. He was brilliant and recognized excellence. The time approached, and Walker was the perfect choice to show the world God's hand in action.

But if the newsman cost St. Catherine's a visit from the pope, Walker would pay the price.

Crack. Something else moved in the woods, hunting. He'd prefer the noise belonged to a deer instead of a dog.

A light glowed through the branches.

Just as he'd figured. The cabin was buried in a thick section of woods alongside the Evansburg State Park twenty miles northwest of Philly. The perfect place for someone to hide sinful actions.

But no one hid from God.

He hoisted the duffle bag with everything necessary for his task. He needed an armload of righteousness tonight. But he only had enough space for one small body to rest in peace, so he had two decisions to make. Which child stayed in God's care? And what to do with the other one?

He'd make it Riley Walker's problem. That should keep him away from St. Catherine's.

Chapter 38

Riley strolled into the Alma De Cuba a couple of minutes before seven, searching for a head of black satin hair. He nodded at the maître d' who knew his face, then tilted his head toward the bar, indicating his destination.

Cuban music throbbed at just the right level to allow conversation yet protect a private discussion. Located on Walnut Street, the restaurant served Rittenhouse Square residents. Alma de Cuba was relatively new to Philly, at least compared to restaurants established over past decades that had been built in neighborhoods of territorial ethnic divisions.

The mayor and DA preferred rubbing elbows late at night in those secluded neighborhood settings instead of the newer restaurants.

Another reason Riley had picked this place.

He wanted Massey out of her element and couldn't picture her frequenting a flashy nightspot that was so out of character with her power suits and inflexible attitude.

There she sat at the bar in a silky white blouse loose over a short black and green skirt. He didn't know why he noticed the polar difference between Kirsten Massey's designer look and Margo Cortese's not-quite-together appearance right then.

Maybe because both women made strong feminine statements in their own ways.

Either one would be an interesting – and challenging – dinner companion given better circumstances.

A female bartender in the restaurant's signature red blouse

and black pants paused in front of the DA investigator to ask, "Everything okay with your club soda?"

"Yes, thank you." Kirsten smiled politely and took a sip from a tall glass that appeared untouched.

Riley stopped behind her, ready to get this meeting over with when the delicate scent lifting off her skin stalled his thoughts. When was the last time he'd had dinner with a woman just to be with her? He couldn't remember.

But this was not a date.

He shouldn't start off by antagonizing her, but he still smarted from this morning. "You're early. That mean you're anxious to see me?"

She jerked in surprise then calmly swung around to face him. Her entire body shifted into immediate composure. "I'm always on time for a business meeting."

He glanced past her shoulder, nodded a silent message at the one bartender who winked a reply acknowledging she got his order before he settled on the barstool.

Massey might sound all hard edge and business, but she twirled the straw in her club soda, fidgeting.

He generally made it his priority to put a woman at ease in any social setting, but Massey had set the ground rules when she'd deemed this business. Plus, he'd been skewered by her prickly nature a couple of times and needed to capitalize on any advantage tonight.

She either didn't notice or chose to ignore his glare when she said, "Let's get one thing clear. Everything we discuss tonight is off the record."

Dalia, the bartender Riley had exchanged a silent message with, carried his drink to him on long legs that seemed to reach from the floor to her shoulders. Her flashy red shirt was slit from her cleavage practically to her crotch.

A fact that Kirsten Massey hadn't missed. She fiddled with her straw, not turning her head to outright look, but her eyes held a silent opinion.

"Here's your mojito, Riley." The mid-twenties bartender leaned forward a little extra when she served the drink. Sunny blonde hair flowed over Dalia's shoulder until the long strands almost, but not quite, covered the free show. As if that hadn't showcased all her attributes, she finished off the picture with ruby lips framing a bright smile.

"Thanks, Dalia. How's your mother? Get her out of the hospital yet?"

"Yesterday. Thanks for the number of that group who donates time to the elderly. I don't know how I'd be able to work and care for her without them."

"Glad it worked out."

Dalia served his mojito and glided away, giving everyone behind her a great retreating view in tight black pants.

Riley flipped his attention to Investigator Massey. "I give you my word."

Kirsten blinked away some private thought. "On what?"

"That everything we discuss tonight is off the record." He hid a smile over her momentary lapse. Dalia was as sweet as they came, but he had no interest past being casual friends with her. Kirsten Massey, on the other hand, didn't fit his picture of sweet, but something about this little hedgehog spurred his interest like no woman had in a long time.

"Good, now Mr. Walker – "

"*If* you agree to use first names," he added.

"What? No. We'll keep this on a professional level." She'd said that in her courtroom voice, the one that allowed no leeway.

One time when he'd been stuck at the courthouse with time to kill, he'd sat in on one of her cases and seen her in action. Impressive under cross-examination, she had an iron backbone and unwavering control. Sort of like a pro disarming a bomb as if there were days left on the timer instead of only seconds before the explosion.

A tough adversary.

Which meant he could push as hard as he wanted tonight and not worry about this one shriveling into tears. "You don't use first names at work with anyone?"

"That's different."

"Come on, Kirsten, lighten up if you want me to talk off the record. I'm not up for another power play."

She said nothing, but her eyes strayed away with guilt riding her gaze.

Riley pressed it to get the air cleared. "Or was there another reason for what happened in the cemetery?"

She blew out a breath of resignation that ruffled her hair. "You're right. I wanted you to know you couldn't play news games with an investigation"

"I didn't – "

She held up her hand. "I get it that you're sincere about helping. First names are fine, but for tonight only. I have a favor to ask, too."

"What?"

"I'd like to get a number for your cameraman and apologize to him for this morning. I wasn't doing that to punish you or him and I really hate that he got screwed...." Her voice trailed off.

"What? Didn't get the last of that."

"I really thought you had not been straight with us." She swallowed, her slender neck muscles moving with the effort. "Bottom line...I was wrong."

Da-yum. Choking down that apology had to hurt her throat. He'd faced unforgiving people for months on end and knew how hard it was to live with not being able to rectify a mistake. "I accept the apology and I'll give you Biddy's number before we leave."

Her eyes had strayed from his face again, but lifted in surprise. She'd expected to catch more grief.

He smiled to disarm her further. "What do *you* have to trade?"

Kirsten glanced at each side of where they sat. "Let's not talk here. I put my name in at the door, but they said the wait might be forty-five minutes."

As if on cue, Dalia walked up. "Your table's ready, Riley."

Kirsten's frown warned she didn't care to be one-upped. Too bad.

"Thanks." Riley finished his drink and sat the empty glass on the bar. "Shall we?"

Kirsten hooked the strap of her purse over her shoulder and reached for her wallet.

"I got this." He fished out his money clip and pinched a

chunk of cash, peeling off enough to cover the tab plus a healthy tip.

"Thank you, but anything else is Dutch." Kirsten issued that order and stepped away as the maître d' showed up.

Riley waved his hand. "After you."

Kirsten followed when the maître d' moved ahead, guiding them to the third floor seating Riley had called ahead to reserve.

Maybe he should have stayed on the main floor. Kirsten's hips swayed in rhythm to the erotic music in a way that reminded him of other things he was tired of doing alone besides eating.

Like Dalia, all the female staff here were hot as firecrackers, but Kirsten was in a different league. The kind of woman who wouldn't date someone outside the elite circle she traveled in.

Not a man with his past.

Regardless, he'd never be part of Kirsten's sanctimonious club that catered to the perfect male. Those who never broke a rule or made a mistake.

So why was he going off on that unproductive tangent?

Because he did enjoy a challenge and Kirsten wasn't trying to play him, to use him for her own purposes, the way his ex-wife had.

She paused ahead of him when she reached the second floor, head swiveling on that slender neck as she took in Latin décor like no other restaurant he'd visited since moving to Philly.

Alma de Cuba was built on three levels with black slats covering subdued ceiling lights. Photographic images of sugar cane and tobacco being harvested by Cubans were projected on the walls. Sweat dripped off the faces of working men and women in the pictures. Nut-brown, sunglistened muscles rippled on the arms of men swinging machetes that bit into stalks of sugar cane.

When they reached a table overlooking the lower floors, the maître d' pulled back a chair on one side. This was Riley's table, because he sometimes accessed this floor from the back stairs that lead straight up to the third level. From here, he could perch on the balcony like a voyeur watching the entire second floor below.

Their waiter appeared out of nowhere decked out in a white coat. After reciting several house mixtures with interesting names he asked for their drink orders.

Kirsten paused, her smooth forehead marred by frown lines of deep thought. Or confusion. She had that spent look he knew all too well after a long day when even a drink order was one more decision to make. A look that tugged on his instinctive urge to comfort a woman, even this one.

He offered, "I usually get an El Jefe. It's made with ten cane rum, sugar, lime juice and bitters, or for a little less bite you could try the Suave made with Bacardi Limon."

She smiled. Any other time he'd take that as a positive sign, but this was the smile he'd seen in the courtroom right before she torpedoed the defense attorney's entire case with one statement.

"I'll have Caiperinha – " She cut her confident gaze at Riley. "It's known as the little peasant girl." Then she ordered an appetizer, all in perfect Spanish, and said, "Gracias, Humberto."

Riley had to smile in admiration. She would be a worthy opponent tonight.

Chapter 39

That might take a notch off his cocky attitude.

Kirsten had no intention of letting Riley Walker toy with her tonight. He thought picking Alma de Cuba would put her in his territory?

"Impressive." Riley grinned, at least his mouth did. His blue-gray eyes smoked with some wicked thought.

That smile could be infectious if she weren't carrying plenty of built-in antibodies that repelled smooth talking newsies.

Humberto delivered their drinks.

Riley dialed up his grin. "That appetizer sounded pretty sexy to be food."

She would normally chuckle if someone other than Riley Walker had made that comment, but he was a rogue from top to bottom who would jump on the least bit of encouragement. "It's royal palm dates stuffed with almonds, wrapped in bacon, covered with a blue cheese fondue and served on a bed of red onions. Nothing sexy about that."

"Depends on how it's eaten, Kirsten."

Argh. She could nail him between the eyes in a courtroom, but he *was* in his element here and her powers waned when she was exhausted.

The minute the waiter withdrew to place their orders Kirsten slipped right back into attorney mode. She needed Riley to work with her and the police. "Back to why we're here. I'll admit that you've helped the investigation and you're important to the killer since you've been the only person he's contacted on these last two deaths."

"Last two? Like there were more? Am I hearing that the death two weeks back is tied to this...like I tried to tell you?"

"Yes, it could be, but don't try to convince me you knew for sure."

Riley lifted the glass to his lips, no doubt using the sip of his drink to weigh how much he should admit. "It was a hunch."

"And that's why we didn't jump on it."

"Not even to move a child's safety ahead of the mayor's business plans?"

"That's not fair. We're doing everything we can to find Enrique."

"As long as it doesn't put a dent in tourism or the city's image?"

"Look, I don't always agree with every decision that is made, but I understand what the mayor is trying to do." Was she really going to give credence to DA Van Gogh and the mayor's position when Kirsten had battled for every penny she pulled into law enforcement? She had to if she wanted to back Riley off City Hall. "Unemployment is at a record level, jobs are disappearing every day and tax money is drying up. He's doing what the people elected him to do – keep food on their tables. Putting criminals in jail is just one of the many balls he juggles."

"I realize the mayor has a lot more than crime to worry about, Kirsten, but we both know you have a killer on the loose. One who may kill again. That has to take precedence at some point. These murders are tied together somehow. The DA just doesn't want to admit it. If she did, she'd have let you interview Judge Berringer."

"What makes you think he wasn't interviewed?"

"Did *you*?"

She could lie and end this, but she'd never shied from the truth. "DA Van Gogh confirmed the judge has no past connection with Sally Stanton. We believe the location was a slap at law enforcement. And the DA doesn't want the media getting into the middle of the case, but I've explained your special situation to her." Kirsten couldn't believe she was arguing in Cecelia Van Gogh's defense. Especially after listening to Cecelia go off for a half hour about Riley's involvement.

"You know a good investigative newsman can ferret out a lot of things that may not show up in a police investigation, and before you give me a ration of grief to go with that insulted look, I'm not criticizing you or the police."

She noticed he hadn't mentioned the DA in his exclusion of criticism, grouping Kirsten on the side with the police. Riley Walker had just gained more ground in that one moment than all his flirting could get him.

But he used charm to get what he wanted with women, like downstairs with that sexy bartender, which only confirmed what Kirsten had always known about men like Riley.

They were smoother than fine whiskey and just as intoxicating if you had too much. When it came to his kind, a smart woman abstained.

"We didn't come to discuss politics, Kirsten."

She didn't hesitate to take the opening he gave her to move away from discussing the mayor and Van Gogh. "The vic this morning has been identified."

"I heard. Bruno Parrick. And no kid involved?"

"Right."

"What about the other killing two weeks ago. The other Philomena House resident?"

Kirsten nodded and shared information that any news group could get their hands on. "Clayton Howell. He lived with his girlfriend and her baby. She claimed a drug dealer was harassing Clayton to work for him. She said Clayton had been clean for six months, didn't do drugs and didn't mule them. She said the drug dealer had been pressuring Clayton to sell drugs at the factory where he worked."

"Was a child in danger?"

"Not really. Clayton's girlfriend got a threatening phone call one night that if Clayton didn't do his job the drug dealers were coming for her and the baby. Clayton was found a mile from Philomena House. A squad car passing through the neighborhood found the body so J. T. thinks the killer had to be watching, which would account for why he didn't call anyone then."

Riley scratched his jaw. "Doesn't sound like there is a direct connection, but I still think the kids are key. What if this killer thinks he's protecting the women and children?"

"By killing a man who was not a father and a mentally-challenged mother who had never intentionally hurt her child before?" Kirsten leaned back, crossed her arms and arched an eyebrow loaded with doubt. All negative body language she hoped he read to go with her disgust at even suggesting some bastard had noble intentions.

Riley calmly lowered his menu to the table. "I'm *not* defending this maniac. Just trying to figure out what drives him. He's still got Enrique so it might be centered around the kids." He continued calmly, his quiet tone making her feel rude instead of intimidating. "Come on, Kirsten, meet me half way on this. Think of it as brainstorming."

She hadn't heard her first name used this much since coming here and shouldn't notice the gentle way it rolled off Riley's lips.

Getting sidetracked on that avenue would lead her down a path she enjoyed even less than dealing with slick defense attorneys in court. "But I point out again that Bruno Parrick didn't have a child, so that blows a hole in your theory."

"That's why it's called a theory until it's proven." Riley waited as the white-jacketed waiter showed up to place more drinks on the table, take their order and leave. His gaze moved away from her, not focusing on any particular thing. "Anything   new   come   back   on   the   piece   of Enrique's...blanket?"

Kirsten heard suffering in his voice that had likely been there all along. *Have I been too bullheaded to hear it?* He'd asked about the bartender's mother and in spite of the woman downstairs oozing sexuality, Riley hadn't flirted with her. Just asked her like a friend.

Did he actually *have* any friends? His cameraman worked with him, but was Biddy a friend? Would anyone befriend a man with Riley's history?

The additional details J. T. had shared earlier today on what happened to Riley in Detroit had forced her to see him in a new light.

What had this man gone through the night he watched a kidnapper blow the top half of his head off only an arm's length from his face? How had he survived knowing the only person who could find that child had died in front of him? Riley Walker was no saint, but now she had to admit that he bled inside like most people would when a child was harmed.

He might still be hemorrhaging from Detroit.

Well, duh, he was human so of course he was. If she hadn't been laying the sins of her father at his feet she might have noticed sooner.

When the silence stretched too long she realized he was still waiting to hear what she knew about Enrique's blanket.

She shook her head. "Nothing new on his blanket and we sent a team to dust Sally's apartment, but that didn't produce anything either."

"Okay."   Riley   studied   his   glass,   finger   wiping condensation down the side.

"We matched the bullets in all three bodies. Definitely a .38."

"Not surprised by that."   He lifted his glass and took a drink.

Kirsten had one last bone to offer him, but it was her best negotiating piece so she had to make the most of it. "We do have one more piece of evidence that ties the killings together."

That pumped up his interest to high again. Riley put his fork down. "What?"

"This can't be leaked to anyone."

"I think I've proven I'm safe with evidence."

"I mean it, Riley. I *will* put people in jail for leaking anything to do with this case to the public, even if I have to dig up obscure laws to do it."

He didn't offer any more assurances, which she honestly didn't need from him, so what was she doing, other than covering her ass? She sat back in her chair. "We found a clear oil on all three victims."

Riley's forehead puckered. "What kind?"

"All we know right now is that it's a high grade olive oil."

"Where was it on the bodies?"

She was a DA investigator stepping over the line and had to figure how far she could go. But if she didn't give him an answer he'd go digging around to get it. She *could* give him a half answer that would protect pertinent information. "Inside the wrist."

And on the vic's forehead. Why she felt guilty about lying to Riley she had no idea, since he was media after all, but something had changed today. He'd given her a second chance when she hadn't been willing to give him a first one until now.

Riley frowned in concentration. "What could the oil mean?"

Kirsten had speculated and didn't like the direction she'd gone. She sure as the devil wasn't sharing her first thoughts, that priests would put oil on the head and wrist. Not with Riley, since he would see it as more reason to go after St. Catherine's. The bad thing was that she was starting to see it that way too. She needed to give Riley enough that he could help the investigation, without completely blowing the doors out of her sworn ethical standards.

She tapped the napkin in her lap then squeezed her fingers to stop the nervous habit. "Who knows? Maybe the wrist means something to the killer. That's why we need a lab to test the oil, but our labs are backed up for months. I've asked for special funding but it hasn't been approved yet, and even that will take six weeks at best. J. T. said you helped him with getting a DNA test run quickly on a case for another investigation recently."

He gave her a sharp look for that.

"J. T. trusts me with that information. The sooner we get the oil from these three vics tested, the sooner we find the origin and might have our first solid piece of evidence."

"I've got a lab that'll test it immediately."

A better answer than Kirsten had hoped for. "How much will it cost me?"

Riley sat still, contemplating so long that Kirsten started to withdraw her request.

"If I get the oil tested at no cost, I want a real dinner with no business talk after this is over as payment. I choose the place and pick up the tab."

Kirsten just stared at him, dumfounded. Like a date? No. She didn't date anyone here, didn't have plans to stay in Philadelphia past finding Elicia even if the city *was* growing on her.

The point was that she didn't want to date anyone, especially someone connected to the media.

Delaying her answer on Riley's offer turned the heavy silence into a living, breathing thing that could destroy what she'd worked to gain tonight.

But she couldn't just blurt out "no."

How could she reject his offer when the police so desperately needed this oil tested? What would J. T. say if he found out she'd refused to help with the case because she wasn't willing to go out to a social dinner with Riley?

And when had this pushy newsman become Riley?

She cleared her throat, acting as if that was the holdup to answering him. "I accept, but only after this case is closed." J. T. had to solve it first. "Thanks for getting the oil tested."

"Done. Now, what about looking into how St. Catherine's is tied to these killings?"

Kirsten shoved her plate away. "Unless you can prove someone directly connected to the church is either shielding evidence or involved in these killings, no one in the city or the police department is going to drag St. Catherine's or any other church into this when it's not warranted. Me included." She held up a hand to stall his protest. "But, I *will* do my part to put away any person we can prove is killing citizens and kidnapping innocent children. *Anyone.*"

Riley finished his meal. "Fair enough. I'm going to hold you to that when I hand you evidence."

If he found out where the oil had been on the bodies and the design created by the oil on the vics' foreheads, Riley Walker would have all he'd need to point a finger at a church, and St. Catherine's was first in the line of fire.

Which was why Kirsten and J. T. had to break this case before it exploded and left Philadelphia in a pile of ashes.

Chapter 40

Six in the morning and no call from the killer yet. Could that be good news or bad?

Riley poured coffee in the chipped mug with a faded fishing scene. One of the few things he moved everywhere he went that reminded him of his foster dad.

Jasper always had a simple way of dealing with problems. When Riley moved here three months ago, he saw Jasper first and told his foster dad how badly he'd messed up his life in one night. Jasper had listened then said, "Everything heals. Some cuts heal faster than others." Then he cooked up eggs and bacon just like he used to do after some scrape Riley'd gotten into as a teen.

Breakfast would be nice now.

Riley opened the door of his refrigerator and stared at the empty racks. Why would there be any food in here when he didn't like to cook? The financial package he'd been given by WNUZ was decent, but wouldn't cover a housekeeper, or cook, so food wasn't going to miraculously show up.

A phone rang. The landline in his condo, not his cell phone. Riley picked up the cordless receiver and closed the refrigerator, resigned to waiting for an early lunch since it was only mid morning. "Walker."

"Turner. Got your email with the address of the lab in Trenton and sent an officer with the oil samples." Someone in the background asked J. T. a question. He answered, then came back. "How soon you think they'll get the results back to me?"

Right after they call me with the results. "Might be

tonight, tomorrow worst case."

He wouldn't leak a thing to anyone, particularly the media, but Riley wanted to know what the oil on the bodies represented. Why had the oil been put on the wrists?

"Thanks for doing this."

"Glad to do it." Riley noticed J. T. didn't rib him about the dinner trade with Kirsten. So she hadn't told J. T. that she fell on the blade for the PD, huh?

Riley grinned, knowing she'd considered it a huge sacrifice, then he remembered something he had to tell J. T. about getting the samples tested. "Tell your officers delivering the oil samples to Jersey not to call Dink by his nickname if they happen to hear about it. He hates to be called Slim Dinkens."

"What's the deal? He some skinny little prick?"

Riley chuckled. "He's five-ten and weighs two-forty."

"I don't get the nickname Slim?"

"He used to weigh three hundred and sixty pounds."

J. T. snorted, then got right back to business. "No calls?"

"Can't believe you asked me that." Riley carried his mug to the living room where one wall of glass looked out toward the Delaware River. Some overpriced decorator his ex-wife would have loved had adorned the place in contemporary glass and stainless steel.

"Just surprised," Turner said. "I thought with the last two killings so close together we were seeing a pattern."

"You're sure this Bruno Parrick didn't have kids at all?"

"Married for five years. My detective who interviewed the wife said she had half-healed bruises. Massey said you think the kids are key to this. Think now it might be the women?"

"Not if he killed Sally."

"True."

"The killer said 'children are held in God's hands'. That still points at the church to me, but maybe he means figuratively and not literally." If Riley used cold logic he'd realize how ridiculous that sounded, but the killer hadn't given up a child's body yet so he had to believe Enrique might still be alive.

"You know how many killers have blamed God for

directing them?"

"I know. But Sally was a member of St. Catherine's and lived at Philomena. What about Bruno?"

"Stop beating that horse, Walker. Got another call. Let's touch base later." J. T. was gone in a flash.

Riley tried to convince himself J. T. really had another call, but his news sixth sense told him J. T. had just dodged a question. About Bruno Parrick and St. Catherine's.

Biddy might have information.

The chiming noise of his cell phone played once then repeated, growing louder from the bedroom. Hot damn, Biddy must be channeling him.

Riley hurried into the bedroom and dug the phone out of his coat jacket, but it stopped ringing by the time he flipped the device open.

He played the voicemail...one unplayed message. The recording started without any indication of the caller's ID, but there was no mistaking that scratchy male voice.

"Body's in the Dumpster behind the Philly police station. Kid's in a car in New Liberty at –" The connection died.

Riley played it again, but the message cut off in the same spot. No matter how hard he squeezed the damn phone it wasn't going to spill any more news.

Had he said kids as in "a kid is in the car" or as in "the kid's body was in a car?" Riley's pulse jackknifed through his body. And who had died?

Could the kid be Enrique Stanton?

Where was that car? Outside? The temperature had fallen to freezing overnight.

Riley hit the speed dial for J. T. When the detective answered, he told him, "Just heard from our caller again and the news is worse."

Chapter 41

Police buzzed around the back lot of the Philadelphia Police Station like a swarm of blue wasps.

Kirsten parked her city-issued Crown Victoria along 8th street. She kept scouring the area for Detective Turner as she climbed out and reached for her wool overcoat on the backseat.

The temperature was trying real hard to reach thirty with a bold sun doing its best to warm the brittle air, but wind sliced through her like a dagger of ice. She hustled the coat on and swapped her dress shoes for rubber-bottom snow boots then locked her car.

Parking this close to a police station should be safe, but what better place to pilfer through a vehicle than when all the cops were focused on a dead body in a Dumpster?

She picked her way across patches of dirty snow hiding slick panes of ice just waiting to twist an ankle or put someone's back out. The driveway to the back of the police roundhouse, or the cop shop as some called it, slanted downhill to the loading dock at the lower basement level.

Television vans with beanpole equipment sprouting out the top had parked as close as they could get.

She nodded at the officer manning the entrance who kept them at bay and scanned for Riley's silhouette, but he wasn't here. That shouldn't concern her, but it did.

Kirsten kept inching her way down, taking her eyes off where she stepped only long enough to keep from running into anyone.

One officer stood at the top of an A-frame ladder that had

been propped against the Dumpster. He was talking to the ME who stood several feet away, shaking his head. The ME pulled his ball cap off and used the same hand to scratch his head.

Who would have ever thought to look for a body in the police Dumpster? Why did the killer drop it there?

The aroma of coffee, in practically every hand circulating the area, was lost the closer she got to the Dumpster. A rancid smell snuck in on her next breath and threatened to ruin what had been a tasty breakfast an hour ago. The body wouldn't have decomposed enough to stink unless it had been there a long time. Not in this cold. She might toss her cookies later, but she damn sure wouldn't do it here in front of all these officers.

The next inhale undermined her conviction so she switched to breathing through her mouth.

Detective Turner met her halfway. From the strong whiff of his clothes she could guess where he'd been.

"We're securing the body and photographing before they pull it out for the ME." He sniffed at himself and moved downwind of her. "He saw rats running out of the bin and won't get inside."

"I don't blame him." She shivered against the visual *that* invoked, then glanced around. Still no Riley. "Same MO?"

"Best we can figure." Turner paused to yell at one of his men to keep the damn media from blocking the entrance. "The call Riley got this morning came from a phone booth. I sent a warrant over to get the location of the call, but getting an answer from one of the fly-by-night phone companies won't be easy or fast."

Kirsten felt for Turner. This had to be the most frustrating job on earth. "Hell of a place to dump a body. I suppose there'd be a certain irony to his choice of locations if not for the gravity of this situation."

Turner cut his head around, lips twitching. "Is that the same as saying this would be funny if finding dead people didn't suck so bad?"

"You could say that, yes." She licked her lips to keep from smiling over the macabre humor. Could they be getting a break? Had the killer made a mistake with this bold action of dropping the body here? "How long could the body have been here to smell that bad?"

"The body doesn't smell. Someone threw a dead possum in there right after it was last emptied. That's the odor."

Ah. "Anyone see a person or vehicle here last night?"

"Back here? Uh-uh." He was shaking his head. "No one's back here after 5:00 PM unless they're trying to sneak out early on a shift."

"Security cameras?"

"Here? Be serious."

Kirsten stared at his sarcastic laugh. "Are you saying *no one* saw this person drop a body at the back of a police station?"

Any soft line in Turner's face disappeared.

She held up a hand. "Hey, I didn't mean that to sound like criticism. I'm just surprised by a body dumped in the PD's backyard."

"Don't apologize." He crossed his arms and let a whistle of disgusted air slip past his lips. "I said almost the same thing but in a much more...colorful way when I found out. This is a brilliant place to dump a corpse. All they have to do is cruise along 8th Street then swing down to the Dumpster. No one would look twice at a vehicle coming back here, especially in the middle of the night. Hell, I wouldn't come back here after dark without my weapon drawn."

She stared at the scene of policemen scrambling across the lot looking for any piece of evidence and the tedious job of removing garbage from the receptacle before the body was lifted out. Hours and hours of work just sifting through trash when she knew they wouldn't find anything more than a body with no prints, no hair, no DNA. No calling card of the killer like a personal mark. Not if it was anything like Sally Stanton's body. Unbelievable.

She considered all the common denominators and one was missing from this picture. "Where's Riley?"

"Been here and gone. WNUZ got overhead shots, but nothing from Riley. He gave me a statement and left."

"Any idea who the vic is?" She'd walked out of a

meeting with the DA to find a blunt message to meet Turner about a body at the station. She could see how this was newsworthy due to the corpse being left at a police precinct, but not why she had to come immediately. Unless...they knew who it was.

"No ID yet. White male, mid thirties, dressed in discount store jeans, beer insignia T-shirt, stainless-steel biker emblem earring, calluses on his hands and work boots. I personally checked the body before anyone else got in there. Gunshot wound to the head."

Kirsten grimaced.

When Turner continued speaking his voice dropped down to a conspiratorial level. He glanced around then said, "There's a clear liquid on his head and wrist."

"So how *are* all these deaths related?" she asked in an equally low voice.

"Hard to say for sure. The profiler said so far the one constant is all the inconsistencies, but the kills are specific enough to not be random. I'll get a sample of this oil to Riley's lab."

He studied her for a moment, looked away as if considering something, then back at Kirsten. "Here's the thing. If you mention around City Hall that we got an outside lab to test the oil samples, they'll want me to move up testing on some other cases." He leveled her with a judgmental gaze, prepared to pass sentence on her response. Waiting to see if he'd offered a sliver of trust to the wrong person.

"You're absolutely right. I totally agree that we keep our source private."

The glimmer of admiration in his eyes counted as one of the best gifts she'd ever received, because it meant his trust came with it.

Turner yelled directions at two of his men then turned back to her. "If this oil comes back as all being from one source, we're going to have to at least consider Riley's point about looking at St. Catherine's."

"I agree. I've been thinking about oil being marked on the forehead in a cross design."

"Can't let Walker find out."

"No way." Kirsten shoved her hands in her coat pockets and worked her fingers to keep circulation moving. "That's all he'd need to add to his *theories*."

"Speaking of Riley's theories, that's the other thing I wanted to tell you," Turner added. "The caller said something about a child in a car."

"What child? Enrique? What car?"

"We don't know. The message on Riley's phone was cut off before the caller finished."

She saw kill-Riley-red. "If he's jerking us around to get to that child first – "

"Whoa." Turner chuckled softly, which surprised her. "I don't think he's yanking anyone's chain. I heard the message myself. Sounded legit, plus Riley's pretty stressed out over trying to find that kid. If it's not Enrique...." Turner shook his head in pity.

She hadn't even considered that possibility. Her heart had plummeted to her knees last night at how Riley had looked when she'd told him about the blanket. But that still didn't mean she could let anyone with something to prove screw around on this investigation. "Riley's suspended, so that means he's not reporting this at the station himself, right?"

"Uh, yeah." Turner scratched his chin and started looking around like he planned to exit this conversation the minute he saw a viable reason.

"So where is he?" She was beginning to feel like Turner and Riley's rapport was a little too solid, leaving her excluded. Silly, but that rubbed since she'd worked hard to build a professional bond with the police, and in particular Turner. She didn't like being odd man – woman – out.

"Said he was going to find out what he could about the call origination, hunt for the kid and let me know anything he discovered."

Great. Kirsten had just spent the morning going through the ringer about how much was leaking to the media and why they needed Riley Walker in the middle of this case. Couldn't Kirsten and the police handle an investigation without the help of a reporter whose track record was full of potholes?

Now Riley was off on his own hunt without clueing her in.

Kirsten had stood her ground, defending Turner and his team's methods and defending Riley, so she was in no mood for any shenanigans if he thought he could do what he wanted after last night.

Her cell phone played a jingle that indicated an unknown caller. "Massey."

"Kirsten, I figure J. T. has told you about a kid in a car by now," Riley said in a rush as though he didn't have time to chat.

"Yes. What else do you know that you haven't told me about? We had a deal that we'd share, which means you calling to inform me, too. I'd hate to lock you up and ruin your imposed vacation by spending it in a jail cell." Yes, that had come out of her bitchy side, but old habits died hard. Especially when Riley should have called her before this.

"You keep threatening me and I'm going to start thinking you want to put me in handcuffs...play cops and prisoners."

Leave it to Riley to flip that around on her.

She felt her face heat at the comment and hoped Turner thought the cold air was behind any blush in her cheeks. Thankfully, he hadn't heard Riley's comment.

"Excuse me." Turner cocked his head toward the Dumpster, indicating he had to get back to the scene.

She waved him off then lowered her voice to warn Riley. "You're not helping your *own* case right now."

"Lighten up, Kirsten. I've got an idea that might give us a chance to find this kid before he or she freezes to death. If the child is still alive."

That got her attention and forced her to overlook his use of her first name during office hours. "What is it?"

"Let me release the details about a missing kid in a car to the media so people will look for a child in an abandoned or parked vehicle."

She clenched the phone, cursing herself for believing his motives were honest. He wanted to break loose a story after all. "Why are you even asking? The media all of a sudden get a conscience, especially the one who stands to get the scoop of the day?"

The silence that answered her rolled on for a few seconds before Riley said, "When exactly did I become the bad guy? I thought we agreed that I was trying to help find this kid and help the police find a murderer. Just to be clear, I plan to contact *all* the television and radio stations at the same time so whoever gets the *scoop* can have it if they find this child. Give me a break, okay?"

Stop acting like an inconsiderate bitch. Riley is not your father or any of his team. His comment about being the "bad guy" hit too close to the truth. She'd ranked all media, especially the power players, as the evil ones who made life difficult for most law enforcement.

Like her dad and Landry, her father's right hand man, who would come down hard on one of the anchors at her father's television station for missing the exclusive on a story like this. But Landry had been there for her when her mother died, a decent guy in this business, too, even if he did harbor unrealistic expectations about her. *Not the time to dwell on that problem.*

Riley sounded sincere about putting this child's welfare first. And she was making his life miserable because hers was. What happened to being fair to everyone? Why didn't that reach to newsmen? Especially one who was doing everything he could to find a child.

That stirred something warm inside her chest for the renegade reporter. "Okay, fine. That's a good idea and we appreciate your help."

She'd ease up on him some, but he still needed to stop calling her Kirsten when she was on the clock.

"You're welcome. Got a list of pay phone locations in New Liberties owned by small companies – "

"How'd you find *that*?"

"I know someone in the business license department."

"They just handed over a list?"

"I was nice to the lady who helped me."

Only nice? More like charmed the woman into giving up everything, including her own phone number. A part of Kirsten wanted to applaud him for getting that much, but another part suffered a moment of an emotion that edged toward jealousy. Absurd. "When can you get this on the news?"

"Should be all over the place in the next half hour. Talk to you later...Kirsten."

She rolled her eyes. He knew how much that bothered her. But right now they had to find that child. How long had the child been in a car with the temperatures hovering in the low twenties? She doubted the killer left the car full of gas and running. A kid in a vehicle with no heat and vulnerable to someone who might steal the car.

Was the killer screwing with them, playing a tick-tock game? Giving Enrique back alive, but only if they found the child before he died of exposure?

Chapter 42

Riley made the corner from Lawrence Street to Vine in the Northern Liberties area, peeking into empty cars. Felt good to walk in the sun after the overcast skies first thing this morning. The sidewalk was filling up with office workers leaving early for lunch.

Using one earphone for his portable FM radio receiver left him with one ear open to hear a child's cry. Long shot to even think that would happen, but the impossible happened all the time in his business.

A patrol car cruised slowly down the same street toward him with two male officers, both scanning everywhere. But Riley had the better viewing point from the sidewalk. He recognized the officer in the passenger seat as Willie Malone about the time Malone's gaze snagged on Riley. The officer paused and nodded in acknowledgement as the cruiser kept moving.

At least some law enforcement believed he was helping them. What had happened to the alliance he'd formed with Kirsten last night? She acted like any ground gained had washed away at the strike of midnight and she'd returned to treating him as though he was a burr in her backside.

He intended to keep her a little out of step by cajoling rather than combating, but her assumption that he'd use a child in danger to pump a story for the station struck a nerve he hadn't realized he'd left exposed.

What would it take to shake up her rigid, biased opinion of him?

He reached the end of the street and crossed with the light

to walk down the other side.

What made this murderer tick? If Turner released information on a serial killer, copycats would pop up, and the flood of calls from every person who thought they knew who the killer was would bog down the investigation.

But if this child wasn't found alive or another became connected to the case, the police might have no choice but to expose the threat to protect innocent kids.

The DJ chattered away in Riley's ear on the talk radio show that hyped the missing child again. Hopefully all the stations were putting out the word every ten minutes like this station.

Riley's phone rang. Unknown caller. He answered it quickly. "Where's the kid?"

"In an '88 Chevy parked in a shutdown garage on Lawrence Street. Auto repair with a checkered flag sign."

"Who is – " the call ended. Riley swung around and took off at a run. He'd just passed that closed down garage about ten minutes ago. The police cruiser was nowhere in sight. Shoving the radio and earphone into his pocket, he hit the stored number for J. T. on his cell phone.

The minute Riley heard the click and J. T. start to answer he cut him off. "The kid's at an abandoned auto repair..." He took a breath that froze his lungs. "Over on Lawrence Street, west of Vine. Concrete block building...got a checkered flag on the sign."

"Where are you? Why can't you breathe?"

"I'm a street over and running that way."

"Don't have a heart attack. I'll have a squad car there by the time you get there, maybe *before* you get there, for once." J. T. hung up.

Riley would have laughed if the stitch in his side didn't hurt like a mother. In less than a minute, he scrambled around the turn onto Lawrence. In the distance, he saw the checkered emblem on a plastic sign that had one corner shot out.

Adrenaline kicked in and gifted him with a second burst of energy.

When he reached the building, Riley raced around toward

the back, looking for a window not boarded up. He found a broken window on the side and climbed through.

Approaching sirens whined. J. T.'s men were on the way, but Riley couldn't wait for them to arrive. Not if the child – Enrique – was alive. He could be suffering from hypothermia.

Every second counted. He couldn't think about the possibilities or it would paralyze him.

Riley stepped carefully through the building, the air rank with mildew, grease and oil. This guy calling in dead bodies and missing kids was a nut case. There could be a booby trap, so Riley hesitated to call out and unintentionally put the child in danger if he moved toward Riley.

When he reached the garage part of the building, there was an overhead door on his right and a dishwater-gray Chevrolet that had to be late 80's on his left. In two strides, he was looking into the back seat where a lump the size of a child was wrapped in layers of blankets. Not moving.

Too late? *God, no.*

Chapter 43

Riley tried the door handle first. Locked. He rapped his knuckles on the window.

Sirens screamed then shut off. Car tires crunched gravel outside. Doors slammed.

Nothing stirred under the pile of gray and brown blankets in the back seat.

He needed something he could use to break the window. Riley looked around and found a two-foot-long piece of angle iron, checked once more to make sure the child – or whatever was under that blanket – was protected from falling glass, then bashed the corner of the front driver's-side window.

Men shouted outside the garage door for him to open it.

Riley couldn't stop to do that. He didn't know the condition of the child. Wouldn't waste another second that might make a difference.

He reached in and opened the door then hooked his arm around to open the back door.

Voices filtered in from the direction of where Riley had climbed through the window.

Not wanting to get shot, he yelled, "I'm in the back. Got the kid."

The voices silenced and when Riley leaned inside the back seat he heard, "Step away from the car with your hands up."

"Then shoot me, Malone."

"What the hell?" Malone lowered his weapon. How'd you get here before we did?" The two other officers with him holstered their weapons as well.

"Got a tip on the location right after you saw me. There's something wrapped up here in the back, but it hasn't moved." Riley glanced at the officers as they surrounded the front of the car.

Every face in the room looked as gut shot as Riley was going to feel if they found Enrique Stanton's lifeless body in that small bundle of blankets.

"Let me help." Malone stepped up as Riley leaned in. Riley lifted the bundle into his arms, then backed out and held the padded weight as Malone unwrapped the layers and layers of blankets.

The prettiest little girl with black hair and smooth pink skin lay in the nest of blankets. Sleeping. Not dead.

Thank...God. Riley had never been a religious man, but even he had to admit this kid had an angel watching over her. The crazy caller had put her in a relatively safe place and protected her from the weather by insulating her in the blankets, the car and the garage.

"Any idea who she is?" Riley asked, as the other officers gathered around for a view of what was, for once, good news. He tried not to be disappointed this hadn't been Enrique.

"I don't know," Malone shook his head. "We got a list of missing kids. Be nice to tell the parents the kid's alive for once." He spoke into the radio mic at his shoulder, reporting the discovery and that the child was alive.

Riley tried to wake the little girl by talking softly to her, but she didn't stir. "I think she's drugged or she would have heard me smash the window."

"We'll take her to St. Joseph's first to get medical attention. You got wheels?"

"My car's about two miles away. I'll get it later. Let's get her to the hospital."

"Let's go."

Once Riley was settled in the back seat of the car with the little girl, Malone hit the lights and siren. The run to St. Joseph's wouldn't take long. Malone was talking into his radio, rattling off instructions to send out the crime unit. He'd left the other patrolmen to secure the building.

Riley's cell phone rang. No caller ID. "Walker."

"You get the little girl?"

Riley didn't know what to think about a killer who kidnapped a child then worried about the kid's welfare. "Yes. Your first message cut off before – "

"Then answer your phone next time."

"Is she drugged?"

"Cough medicine to keep her calm. Take care of Pia." The line went dead.

What the hell was going on with this guy? Riley gave Malone the information he'd just received and Malone radioed ahead to the emergency room. Then Riley keyed J. T.'s number. When the detective answered, Riley shared the name Pia.

"I'll send someone to get her fingerprints and run those, along with the vic from the Dumpster and see what we got," J. T. said, thinking out loud.

"When you see Kirsten, tell her – "

J. T. cut in. "She's right here. You tell her."

"What, Walker?" Kirsten sounded tired, but sharp as usual.

"My theory is back on the front burner. Maybe someone at St. Catherine's knows this kid. Her name's Pia."

"We can't go blowing in there asking questions without probable cause."

"What? You afraid to find out there *is* a connection?"

"Tell you what I'll do, Walker. If I find out her parents live within a five-mile radius of St. Catherine's, worshipped there or lived in Philomena House, I'll share that information with you and question everyone around St. Catherine's myself."

Finally. He didn't know what had gotten through to her but was glad something had. Maybe finding this little girl. "Glad to hear that."

Kirsten added, "But if there is no direct connection to St. Catherine's you have to let this go and let J. T.'s people investigate the best way they see fit."

Shit. He didn't like that idea one bit, but the killer had been consistent so far. This little girl had to be tied to St. Catherine's somehow. The sooner Riley could prove that, the quicker they could figure out who had Enrique.

Riley had lost his desire to take a gamble in this business that night in Detroit, but backing away from Kirsten's deal could mean getting his hands tied, and that could mean the difference in finding Enrique or not.

And Riley held proof in his arms that Enrique could still be alive. "Agreed."

Chapter 44

Why had the killer given this child back?

Riley had worn that question out the entire time he'd paced the halls of St. Joseph's hospital, waiting to find out the identity of little Pia. He was in the ER treatment area now, just outside Pia's curtained-off area. The staff bustled from one end to the other of the emergency center with cases far more dire than the child's, but Pia was being seen.

J. T. had told Officer Malone to stick around and talk to the little girl when she regained consciousness. At half past one, Malone heard it might be another hour before he could see her. The officer had left to grab a bite in the cafeteria, telling Riley he'd be back in twenty, which meant any minute now.

Once Malone returned, there would be no reason for Riley to hang around since he'd be barred from hearing anything the child said.

Riley could sit in the waiting room where the air didn't reek of blood and alcohol, but there were still several newsies perched there, ready to leap on him for a story. He found a certain irony in hiding out on this side of the door.

A sixty-ish woman in a simple paisley cotton dress, plastic boots and a black overcoat entered through a staff-only door on the right side of the triage area. She limped to the nurse's station, guided by the lady Riley had seen at the emergency check-in desk earlier.

"Where's my granddaughter?" The elderly woman wheezed out her question in a teary voice. She leaned on a metal cane and didn't reach Riley's shoulder. She was solidly built, reminding him of German bone structure.

The check-in clerk spoke to the nurse, and then said something too soft for Riley to hear and pointed down the hallway to where he stood.

The grandmother nodded and limped toward him, then paused outside examination room four, where little Pia was being checked over.

When she knocked on the door a nurse in scrubs stepped out to talk to her. "Can I help you?"

"I think you have my granddaughter," the woman said.

"The doctor is examining her. If you'll have a seat over here – " The nurse pointed to a line of three chairs. "I'll come for you as soon as he's finished. Pia is still groggy."

When the grandmother was settled and alone, Riley moved over to sit next to her. He eyed the door Malone would enter through. If Malone caught him talking to a potential witness, Massey wouldn't have to execute a warrant for his arrest. J. T. would order his officer to cuff Riley and bring him in.

But J. T. and Kirsten had jobs to do, neither of which included sharing vital details on the investigation with an out-of-work reporter. "My name's Riley Walker. I found your granddaughter."

The grandmother's blue eyes watered. "Bless you."

"Do you know who might have taken her? Or would her parents know?"

"That worthless mother of hers probably left this baby sitting out on a corner somewhere." Grandma gripped her cane with bony fingers. Her voice shook. "My son's been raising Pia. He's a good boy who loves that baby, but he doesn't think straight when it comes to her mama. Girl's a drug addict, probably holed up somewhere with a needle in her arm."

Riley hadn't expected the child's mother to be so bad. He'd started thinking the body in the Dumpster was possibly the little girl's father, but that would pop a hole in his theory about the killer protecting children. "Does your son live close by, maybe in the Northern Liberties area?"

"Oh, no. He's a country boy. Got a cabin about twenty

miles out of town near Evansburg State Park. I left two messages. He'll be here soon as he finds out about Pia. Next time he won't let that little whore convince him to leave Pia with her again."

Pia's father being a good man and living twenty miles out in the country put another nail in Riley's theory. One of them had to be the link to St. Catherine's. "Do you or Pia's mother live in this area or worship at St. Catherine's Catholic Church?"

The grandmother gave him a strange look then shook her head. "I live further out than my boy, Vance, and that slut lives in New Jersey. We're Baptists."

Chapter 45

Bodies were piling up and every decent lead came with a lit stick of dynamite.

Kirsten strode into her outer office, the space used by her assistant. Taylor Funk could usually be found at her desk, positioned just right of the door to Kirsten's office. Taylor was rarely MIA, especially at three in the afternoon, which meant the young woman had probably made a run to the ladies room.

Stifling a yawn, Kirsten kept walking. She didn't mind losing sleep if it was productive, but these multiple killings took a left turn every time they got a solid lead to work with.

"News flash. DA Van Gogh's gunnin' for you," Taylor called, walking into Kirsten's office.

"And here I thought you had *real* news." Kirsten turned to face her. "Give me about five minutes then you can unleash her on me."

Taylor got points for wearing a mauve pant suit that flattered her plump body instead of the too-snug and too-revealing clothes she'd first worn to work, but that hair color had changed twice in four weeks. Today the short locks spiraled out in wiry black curls with red streaks.

"You got it, boss." Taylor's phone rang in the next room. She stopped chewing her gum and dashed back to answer the phone in a voice so smooth she should be doing voice-overs for radio or television. She ran her fingers over the springy hair clipped back at each side, exposing a row of pierced earrings lining the outer edge of her right ear.

Kirsten dropped the file in her hand on one of two boring-brown side chairs that faced her desk. She punched the voice mail retrieval button on her desk phone then shifted her attention to scan notes on her desk.

After the beep, a cultured male voice said, *"I tried your cell phone several times, but you haven't deemed my calls worth returning."*

Her father? Kirsten stepped over to close her door.

He would never admit to anyone in his circle that his only child would not give him her cell phone number, which meant he'd spent money to get it. *"I have the time for the memorial ceremony,"* he continued on the recorder. *"If you'd answer my calls once in awhile."* His smooth corporate tone disintegrated into irritation on that last part.

Kirsten moved a finger to end the message.

" – you think I had something to do with your friend leaving, but I didn't and don't know where she is."

Her hand stalled.

She'd assumed he'd hired a private investigator to get her phone number. But maybe that had been a byproduct of his hunt for Elicia?

Or this could all be wild conjecture on her part.

Get it together Kirsten. He was not going to make her doubt herself.

But had he figured out why she'd *really* come to Philly in the first place?

A short knock on the door was the only warning she had before Cecelia barged in.

Kirsten put the receiver down.

"What's going on?" Cecelia had a habit of expecting everyone to know what she was thinking. She could be asking that about the jackhammer outside vibrating the windows or she could be asking about a budget overrun for their department.

But Kirsten was getting better at reading her mind. Cecelia wanted to know whether or not Kirsten had closed the Stanton case yet.

"We can't dismiss the Stanton killing as domestic violence any more than we can dismiss the murder this morning." Kirsten prepared herself for the battle ahead.

"We're running out of time to get this shut down."

Since when did murder cases get solved on a schedule? Kirsten let Cecelia ramble. The DA really didn't care for anyone's opinion but her own anyhow.

"The media is beating down the doors to find out about the body in the Dumpster. On city property, no less. Right under the noses of the police. This is getting out of hand." Cecelia stuck her arms out and shook her head as she walked to the window, acting as if Kirsten had control over an unknown murderer. The DA had poured her gym-toned body into a cerulean blue dress that hit about an inch above the knees and at the last hint of a modest neckline. The shoes matched so exactly that Kirsten wondered if the dressmaker whipped out the pair from scrap material.

Kirsten could not allow Cecelia to screw up this investigation. "The police are doing everything they can, but we can't release any details about these murders to the press that would allude to a serial killer. We don't know what we're dealing with yet."

In another of her dramatic motions, Cecelia dropped her arms by her side and turned around. She pursed her lips much like an annoyed guppy. "That's why we *have* to call a press conference and give the media something that will keep them happy."

Kirsten crossed her arms. "We have to be careful about any news the killer hears. He's a strange bird. Even though we have matching bullets and oil on all four heads so far – "

"Four?"

"The body this morning appears to be consistent with the other three. Why not just release the standard statements about being unable to share more at this time, etcetera?"

"Let me walk you through this," Cecelia said in a voice that insinuated Kirsten had gotten her law degree from a school for mentally challenged attorneys. "There's no guarantee this killer will continue to use the same MO based on the inconsistencies so far. This department's best move would be to say the crimes may be connected, but we're leaning toward domestic violence being at the center of the killings rather than suspecting a classic serial killer."

"But that's not true."

"It is true until it's proven otherwise, Massey."

"Talking to the media could create problems with this case." Kirsten had to get Cecelia to see reason.

"If we avoid the media the leaks will get us. It always happens. Best to create suspicion that someone is doing this to cover up a domestic homicide. Otherwise, the minute the media releases secret information on the case copycat murders will pop up with just enough similarity to convolute the investigation and stretch police resources beyond where they are now."

Much as Kirsten hated to admit it, Cecelia had a point. She just did not trust the DA's motives.

"Plus," Cecelia went on with her oration, using her hands as a symphony conductor. "If it leaks about the oil on the head being drawn in a sign of the cross similar to last rites, it's going to sound like a religious nut out killing people, which throws speculation on the church. Again. None of us want another fiasco like that last one with St. Catherine's."

"I'm taking precautions against that."

Cecelia continued as if Kirsten didn't exist. "If we have fallout against the church again the national media will pick up on what's going on in Philly and turn this into an anti-Catholic city. With the business symposium around the corner everything the mayor has worked for will disintegrate."

Now there was the Cecelia that Kirsten knew who was more concerned about the mayor's ability to generate positive PR for the city.

"Plus," Cecelia went on. "We just got word the pope will be visiting. Bishop Gautier pulled a coup in getting the pope to visit St. Catherine's."

"St. Catherine's? Not the Cathedral Basilica?"

"He's going there, too. But having the pope visit an inner city program will be a huge boost to the mayor's plans. When the pope visits Philadelphia the rest of the country will sit up and take notice. They'll realize this is truly the city of brotherly love for all." Cecelia stared above Kirsten's head. Her voice took on a lofty air.

Patriotic music should be playing in the background.

In the abstract, Kirsten could clearly see the DA's point in not wanting to turn these killings into a national news story, but Kirsten didn't work in the abstract. She dealt with real people who had suffered from real crimes.

Cecelia had given her another way to attack this. "Well, that's a surprise and I'm thrilled to hear the pope is coming, which means we also have to assure everywhere he visits is safe. I don't want to point a finger at any church either, but we have evidence to vet. I'm thinking we need to ask for oil samples from churches in the areas of the killings as a start on figuring out where the oil on the victims originated."

Cecelia gave her the I-am-your-superior eye and stuck a matching hand on her hip. "And what if that gets out? People will be afraid to attend church if they think a serial killer may be watching for his next vic during Mass. Nothing stays private once you have cops sniffing around a place, not even a church. Anybody can get olive oil, for Christ's sake."

Kirsten quelled the first comments racing to her tongue. Pointing out that the DA's office had a few leaks of its own would only give Cecelia a reason to continue this going-nowhere conversation when Kirsten had work to do on the case.

But Cecelia wasn't finished quite yet.

"Bishop Gautier made a brilliant move by bringing in Monsignor Dornan. Everyone has calmed down about St. Catherine's. Dornan earned his take-no-prisoner reputation by turning around every disaster the Catholic Church has handed him. Philly is crazy about this guy and the city will go wild once there's a formal announcement about the pope's visit. This is everything the mayor could hope for."

Kirsten tried to feel a sense of celebration, but couldn't see the fireworks for the additional burden this would put on Philly's PD.

Undaunted by Kirsten's lack of enthusiasm, Cecelia continued. "You and Detective Turner need to find this murdering SOB before he causes any more problems."

Any more problems? As if they'd been discussing a prankster spraying graffiti on buildings? Kirsten made a show of lifting her watch into view and stepping behind her desk as if to check on an important appointment. She hoped Cecelia took the hint and left. Nope.

"You've got two days, Massey."

"To do what?" Kirsten crossed her arms, annoyed at the underlying threat in Cecelia's tone.

"Or you're off this olive oil killer case. It's not technically yours until Turner has something for us to prosecute. We have other cases that need your attention."

"What happened to 'make this your priority'? Now you expect me to just drop it in two days if we haven't found the murderer?"

"Yes, I do. If this ends badly, I don't want someone from my office in the middle of the news frenzy. Especially someone seen spending too much time with Riley Walker."

First she throws me into the melee and now she condemns me for being there. The bitch. Kirsten was not getting bumped off this case so Cecelia could shove it into filing cabinet obscurity. "Every case I have is up to date. Nothing has been ignored and any time I've spent with Riley Walker has been in the interest of solving this case. I have no intention of backing off now."

"Two. Days. Need I remind you that the mayor has to make budget cuts? Having a DA investigator is a luxury, not a requirement for this office." Cecelia left on that not-so-subtle threat.

Chapter 46

Lehman's text message to Riley had been blunt: Come to my office at 4:00 to discuss your job.

Not a big surprise since Lehman's message had come on the heels of Lilly telling Riley WNUZ's rating was taking a nosedive. Seemed every station but WNUZ had a video of Riley carrying Pia into the emergency entrance of St. Joseph's.

Why hadn't Lehman just couriered his termination papers?

But then Lehman wouldn't get to gloat in person.

But Riley hadn't received his walking papers yet so he couldn't be sure that was the reason behind the message. And Biddy's future was tied to his so he couldn't blow off Lehman.

Not after talking to Biddy on the way here and finding out the cameraman was headed with his wife to the hospital again. High-risk pregnancies came with all sorts of problems. The doctors hadn't given good odds on her carrying this baby to full term, and warned her that getting pregnant again after this would put her own life at risk.

This might be their only child.

She had seven weeks to go and medical bills filling up the nursery. Biddy needed his job and the insurance.

If Riley had known all this back when he came to WNUZ he'd have refused to work with Biddy just to keep him safe from any fallout Riley had to endure.

Once again, history couldn't be rewritten.

He walked into the Liberty Building's granite and glass

foyer. He flashed his WNUZ ID badge for security who checked the list then allowed him to take the elevator to Lehman's ivory tower.

If WNUZ cut him loose right now his credibility would plummet faster than the stock market in the Great Depression. And Lehman would put the screws to him with the other stations. He'd leak rumors that would prevent Riley from selling any story, because a station was only as good as the reputation of the people on their news desks.

His cell phone chimed as the doors opened for the elevator. Riley backed away to take the call rather than lose it in the car. "Walker."

"Is Pia okay?"

The killer? "Seems to be. Still groggy. What about Enrique? Is he okay?" Riley forced himself to maintain a slow conversation in an even tone in spite of the adrenaline that jacked through him every time this guy called. The key was to not lose this connection. One set of J. T.'s technicians would be listening in and another group would be racing to triangulate the call.

"Enrique is in good hands."

Riley hated the cryptic way this guy talked. "What do you want now?"

"The news stations are making the sinners out to be victims. They slander me for helping a child. Their vile reports mock repentance and death."

Guess throwing one body in a Dumpster or staking another one to a cemetery headstone didn't count as mocking the dead. Riley stepped further away from the elevators when one car belched out a wad of people.

The security guard cast a suspicious look in Riley's direction.

Riley kept his voice low. "I have no control over what any of the news stations report."

"I will not tolerate you sharing what I tell you with any of them or the police."

Unless you want a body picked up.

The caller continued. "We have a duty, you and I. I'll let you know when it's time to inform the people."

"Got it." Riley would say anything to keep this guy calm and on the line. He searched for a way to keep an open dialogue. "So you've been calling me because I'm a reporter?"

"Not just any reporter, but the one who faced Satan and won. You taught Detroit to be vigilant and protect their children."

Riley nearly sank to his knees. His mouth turned raw as an open wound. This bastard had chosen him *because* of Detroit?

The killer's voice picked up volume and strength like a Sunday morning television evangelist. "*You* forced Satan from Detroit. Together, we can do this in Philly, too, but only if you do not fail me."

Riley blinked away the haze of shock and disbelief and found his voice before this guy thought he wasn't listening. "If you want to protect the innocent, why give me Pia and not Enrique?"

"Pia needed asthma medicine."

So this guy knew specific details about the children he nabbed. "But what about Enrique? Is he still...alive?"

"Of course, he's alive."

Hearing that gave Riley a surge of faith he'd find this child.

"He has to be alive. We all must sacrifice in the war against evil. I have plans for him tomorrow."

"What plans? What's tomorrow?" Riley yelled. "He's a kid, don't hurt him – "

The call ended.

He couldn't speak until he caught his breath and his heart stopped beating like a war drum. Riley punched J. T.'s number and started in on him as soon as the detective answered. "You get that bastard on this call?"

"Hold on." J. T. barked out orders at someone for a report. A muffled exchange followed then J. T. cursed as he came back on the line. "Got an area, but not a specific location. I'm betting even if we do nail down a location that we'll just find another prepaid cell phone wiped clean of prints and tossed away."

Fuck. "What part of town was it in?"

"Close to City Hall. Sounds like he's pissed off at the news stations. Doesn't like being criticized for brutal killings and abducting a little girl then leaving her in a car."

"I caught that." Riley watched for an elevator, saw one empty and jumped on, closing the doors before anyone joined him.

"Enrique might or might not be alive – "

"He *is* alive." Riley didn't want to hear statistics on how children missing for more than twenty-fours hours were rarely found alive.

"Okay, fine, but this guy is getting agitated. Sounds like he plans to use Enrique to make a statement."

All Riley could picture was the corner of that Diego blanket covered in blood. Would this maniac spill a child's blood to fulfill some duty he imagined had been decreed by God?

Based on the gruesome killings so far – yes.

"I'm telling you J. T., too many things point back to that church."

"I'm not disagreeing. My men are running down every possible lead, including a background check on the vic from this morning. In the meantime, I don't have to worry about you leaking anything now, do I?"

"You never did. Think I'd risk a killer snapping and using that kid to prove his point?" Riley didn't give J. T. a chance to answer that question as he exited the elevator on Lehman's floor. He tried for a quick shot at information. "So you got a full ID on Pia, huh?"

"Little bit. Not much. Talk to you later."

Riley figured that question would get J. T. off the phone.

Didn't matter. He'd found out Pia's father's name and Biddy would check on it...once he got his wife back home. Or maybe Baby G or Romeo would come through.

Lehman's receptionist said Lehman was expecting Riley, and to go on in. He stepped into the office that spread across three hundred square feet, with a sofa and two comfy chairs in a more personal sitting area where coffee was usually served.

Lehman turned around from hanging up his phone and pointed at one of the two office chairs facing his desk.

Guess that meant no coffee. Riley sat down and propped his elbows on the chair arms, lacing his fingers at his chest.

"Our ratings are sinking faster than a lead weight," Lehman started. "The other stations have scooped us on every one of these killings. The board is livid after watching every station in the city – but us – covering you with that kid at the hospital. It's clear you have an inside track on these killings."

Riley didn't agree or disagree. He still couldn't see where Lehman was headed, but so far the GM had laid out plenty of reason to cut him loose. Or to bring him back. Riley thought about Biddy with his wife in the hospital and mentally crossed his fingers, but kept his body and face calm and unmoved.

"I don't know what game you're playing, Walker, but if you're trying to make the board come to you with a deal, it's working. They've authorized me to offer you a permanent contract. Two-year deal."

Now this was an interesting turn of events. Riley had wondered if his absence from the anchor chair and the subsequent crash in ratings might make the board think twice, but honestly, that had been a result of the other stations getting scoops that Riley had but couldn't use. His presence on camera—or the lack thereof—likely hadn't made a dime's worth of difference.

Who would have thought the crash in ratings would work in his favor? Riley could see the possibility of negotiating a sweet deal for him and Biddy both.

But Lehman hadn't delivered the punch line yet.

"I'm listening." Riley kept a blank face.

"If you can wrap up an exclusive on these killings, something no other station has, we'll work out the rest of the details."

Riley couldn't believe how calm Lehman was being about having to tuck his tail to make this offer. This might work once the case was solved, but if Riley delivered what the board wanted now he'd go back on his word to J. T.,

Biddy and Kirsten. Worse, if he stepped behind a camera at the anchor desk he'd jeopardize Enrique for sure after that conversation with the killer.

"I'll think about it." Riley pushed himself up.

Lehman's eyes gave him away before the smile. "You've got until tomorrow at noon to make up your mind. Their offer is contingent on you coming in then and delivering an exclusive story that will rock every station in town. If you can do it, the board will give you two years to rebuild ratings. If not, WNUZ's crash will be laid at your feet alone. If that happens the only anchor position you'll find will be in a town with one stop light."

Give the board of directors what they wanted to get his and Biddy's job back so Biddy's wife and baby had a fighting chance, or walk away and keep Enrique safe?

Either way, it came down to a child for a child.

Chapter 47

"Janeen?" Lucinda walked in with the mail and dropped it on the counter in the kitchen. She couldn't shake the bad feeling she'd had all day, not since this morning when Stan said he was planning a surprise.

She didn't need a surprise. She needed her life to stabilize, to be able to believe in her husband again. But nothing would get better until she knew what was going on with Kelsey.

That's why she'd spent the day at the library digging into books Dr. Ziegler had recommended on child abuse. She'd left angry and depressed, now more convinced than ever that someone had...*touched* her child. Most likely a male, based on what Dr. Ziegler had told her. But one thing the doctor had said kept playing over and over in Lucinda's mind.

Child abuse perpetrators are too often someone the child trusts, a family member...their own parent.

Lucinda grabbed her chest, sure that her heart was ripping in half. The only male who spent time alone with Kelsey was Stan.

Why now? The question had been running through her brain until she'd read that not every pedophile fit a specific pattern. She took a couple of deep breaths to stave off the anxiety attack waiting to strike. She finally dropped her hand and pulled herself together, determined to stay calm when her head was a chaotic minefield. Every thought about Stan and Kelsey threatened to destroy her sanity. But she had no proof and would not condemn any man without it. Still, until she knew for sure one way or another, he was not going to be alone with Kelsey no matter what Lucinda had to do to prevent it.

She walked into the kitchen and tossed her keys on the built-in desk in an alcove they used as a small office center for the house. Her keys landed on a note. Janeen's little boy had broken a tooth on the playground, but Janeen would be back in time to meet Kelsey's bus.

Lucinda checked the time. The bus wouldn't arrive for another ten minutes. She laughed at herself. Maybe her motherly premonition had been for Janeen's little boy.

Of all the people Lucinda had tried out as a housekeeper, Janeen had proven to be the most competent and responsible. She'd been a Godsend in part because Kelsey loved her.

Lucinda hoped Kelsey would open up to Dr. Ziegler soon so the doctor could start piecing together what had happened. *Find out who hurt my child.* She clutched her stomach at the wave of nausea that rushed up her throat over Dr. Ziegler's initial reaction. Ziegler believed Kelsey had experienced inappropriate contact and felt so strongly about it that she'd gained permission from Lucinda to contact Kelsey's school to inquire about any reported problems or charges of misconduct.

The head of Kelsey's exclusive private school had told Ziegler they reviewed the background of every teacher. All were above reproach and there had been no cases of inappropriate behavior reported or any hint of misconduct that would lead them to suspect a teacher.

That pointed back to one place. Home.

Lucinda sat down at the built-in desk off of the kitchen and dragged a hand through her hair. She loved Stan, but she was too strong a woman to give blind faith where Kelsey was concerned. She hit the button for the house phone voicemail and frowned when the ID came up for Kelsey's school. They had Lucinda's cell phone for any emergency.

"This is Miss Johnson. Mr. Myers forgot to take Kelsey's homework when he picked her up this morning. Kelsey was a little upset so I didn't think to check before she left. I realize she's only missing a day, but I don't want Kelsey to fall behind."

Lucinda's ears buzzed. She grabbed the edge of the desk

to keep from losing her balance. *Dear God.*
    Stan had taken Kelsey.

Chapter 48

Where were they?

Riley tapped the Tundra's steering wheel, scanning the urban terrain for any sign of the marauding blackmailers. School had let out a couple of hours ago. Romeo and his bunch were usually here by five in the afternoon, regardless of temperatures dropping with the sun. They knew Riley's truck and couldn't miss it sitting next to the curb a stone's throw from the pitted parking lot edged in weeds and fast food debris they called a basketball court.

If Riley didn't figure out how to give WNUZ a story by noon tomorrow without putting Enrique at risk, hanging around long enough to sponsor this team would be a false promise. The least of his worries with Jasper's eyesight failing. Riley couldn't keep tabs on Jasper if he had to leave Philadelphia for a job in another state.

If anyone would hire him after tomorrow.

Jasper's disability payments didn't cover squat. Riley had no other expertise to fall back on if he had to find a new way to make money to pay his and Jasper's bills.

How could he possibly walk into WNUZ to report details he'd assured J. T. and Kirsten he wouldn't share? Details that could push a maniac to hurt a child? On the other hand, how could he let down Biddy, who would end up out in the cold with a pregnant wife?

Shit, he didn't have answers, but he couldn't walk away from this as long as there was a chance of getting Enrique back alive.

A hand slapped the window next to him.

Riley jumped at the noise then scowled at Romeo's grinning face on the other side of the glass. Another trait of street kids was invisibility.

He opened the door and stepped out to find all five draped along his truck bed, each wearing similar versions of ragged sweatpants and hooded jersey pullovers.

"Looking for a game?" Tusk, the tallest at just over six feet, had the basketball Riley had given them tucked under his arm. His name came from the acronym Tall Ugly Skinny Kid. Only the height and bony frame fit. Tusk's pale skin, straight brown hair and attractive hazel-green eyes rivaled Romeo's much darker hip attraction.

"No time for a game today," Riley answered

Baby G had his arms hooked over the top of the tailgate. "That must mean you're here for another *business* transaction."

Arnie's laugh came out something like a snort a donkey would make. Short, wiry body with squinty eyes behind a pair of black-rimmed glasses and wavy brown hair. He slapped the side of the truck, hooting at Baby G who frowned when Arnie snorted again.

Boris studied the others with hazel eyes that spoke for him since he rarely used his voice. A few inches shorter than Tusk, but built a lot heavier, Boris played hard, took his licks quietly and acted disinterested even though he didn't hesitate to back up the team if the others were threatened. With that body, he could probably bench press small cars.

Riley nodded at Baby G. "I'm here to deal."

"Step into my office," Romeo cut in then swaggered around the front of the truck, headed to where crates, cement blocks and a discarded car seat from an Impala served as their meeting space. The group followed with Riley bringing up the rear.

Once everyone had knocked off the ice and residual snow, Romeo got down to business. "Whadda you want?"

Nothing in trade first? Riley didn't question his luck. Maybe Romeo had decided they'd hosed Riley enough for now. "Looking for anything on Bruno Parrick."

"The one got capped in the cemetery yesterday?" Romeo

asked.

Riley gave him a short nod. "That's the one. I found out he worked construction and went by his job site. They wouldn't tell me anything, but when I asked about his wife one guy said she just got out of the hospital."

Baby G sat on the Impala seat, a finger laid alongside his cheek. He looked over at Tusk who dribbled the basketball around his legs. "Your aunt should know something."

"Maybe." Tusk never lost his concentration. "Got a phone?"

Riley didn't want to hand his over with the killer calling at any time. "Who's his aunt?"

"Does hair over on the west side. Big salon. They got television going all the time. All those women talk."

Romeo produced a banged up phone and tossed it to Tusk, who stopped dribbling and punched keys. Riley didn't want to know if the phone was hot or not. While Tusk talked in a hushed voice to someone, Baby G shifted his almond shaped eyes at Riley. "What else?"

"Any of you see the news on that little girl we found this morning? Pia?"

They all nodded or murmured an affirmative answer.

"Any of you know her or her family?"

They all shook their heads.

"What do you know about any of the other staff at St. Catherine's besides Monsignor?"

"You mean like Icky?" Romeo said.

Arnie snorted another laugh. Baby G chortled and even Boris chuckled.

This bunch had clearly been busy scavenging information to trade once Riley pointed them in the right direction. He smiled along with them. "Who's Icky?"

"Shoes." Baby G said that and they all clammed up, even Tusk who closed the phone and flipped it back to Romeo.

Riley squatted down to be eye level with the two negotiators, Baby G and Romeo. He should have known better than to think he'd get anything for free with this bunch. "What about shoes?"

"Team needs socks and shoes. Five pairs of Nikes and

three pairs of Adidas. Two pairs of socks each."

Riley saw his next paycheck disappearing faster than sand through an hourglass. "For all that, I want *good* intel on Icky, Bruno and Pia."

Romeo exchanged a loaded glance with everyone before he told Riley, "Hundred cash in advance for two out of three right now."

Riley would pay more than that, which was why he had to let the offer sit for a minute to cure properly. Otherwise next time he'd be paying double. He blew out a breath, making it sound like they had him by the short hairs. "Okay, what have you got?"

Baby G cleared his throat. "Father Ickerson is the other priest at St. Catherine's. Remember Titia?"

Riley lifted his chin in a "yes."

"Titia said Father Ickerson is in charge of Philomena house, his personal project. He has an ex-con, Valdez something, doing electrical work and odd jobs around St. Catherine's and at Philomena House. Deacon Grizzle works primarily with Father Ickerson, but he's also the replacement deacon for the crook who got them in so much trouble. Titia said Grizzle comes to Philomena House sometimes, too, but that new lady assistant hasn't been there."

"Margo Cortese?"

"That sounds right."

"What about Monsignor? Does he have any contact with Philomena House?" Riley had learned years ago the tiny pieces of an investigation were what made the big ones fall into place.

"Titia hasn't met him. Don't know if anyone else at Philomena has."

Riley pondered that a minute. "Who's the other one you've got something on?"

Tusk spoke up. "My aunt said one of the customers in her salon yesterday told everyone in the shop about the guy the police found in the cemetery. She said the customer's a nurse who works at St. Jo's and the police had to come there to tell Parrick's wife he'd been killed. The Parrick woman was in being patched up for a broken arm and black eye. Had a run in with a door knob."

Not a surprised expression among the team at Tusk's joking reference to the fact Bruno had probably put his wife in the hospital with his fists.

And not one of them smiled at the joke, not even Arnie.

"Okay, that's two of the three." Riley stood up. "Let me know if you get anything on Pia or Enrique."

Romeo had his hands hooked behind his head. "Why you still lookin' for him? Kid goes missing this long don't show up talking again."

"Let's just say I have confirmation he's still alive – "

Eyebrows shot up all around at that.

Riley continued, "So anything you find on him or Sally is still important. Like why her body was dropped on a judge's lawn?" He searched their faces. "Anybody know of someone with a beef against the judge?"

"Ah, shit, everybody pissed at a judge." Romeo shook his head. "That ain't nothing. But nobody talkin' trash about the judge. What about Mrs. Judge?"

"Yeah," Tusk broke in. "My aunt says someone in her salon is always yammering about a rich-ass bitch who pissed them off. Maybe the judge's wife got gambling debts – "

" – or she ran over somebody's dog with her car," Arnie added.

Then Baby G suggested, " – or she's sleeping with somebody's...wife." He grinned.

Boris rolled his eyes and said nothing.

Riley held up his hand before they had Berringer's wife killing Sally. But they'd given him a reason to take a closer look at the entire Berringer household.

He fished out his money clip and handed Romeo two fifties. Before heading to his truck, Riley told the group to text him with anything if they couldn't reach him to talk. Riley's cell phone rang as he climbed in. He cranked the engine and answered to find Kirsten calling.

"Where've you been, Kirsten?" He smiled at her sigh and knew it was because he'd used her first name. "I called you half an hour ago."

"I've been busy. We've confirmed the identity of the body

this morning and that the deceased *is* little Pia's father, but he isn't married to her mother. Philly PD is releasing his name to the press."

Ah, hell. The grandmother had bragged about Pia's dad being a model father. But was that a mother's opinion or the truth?

"What's his name?" Riley had found out the vic's first name was Vance and that he was an electrician, but Officer Malone had returned before Riley got Pia's grandmother to share her son's last name.

"Vance Montoya."

"Did you find out if he's connected to St. Catherine's in any way?"

"That's why I'm calling. I'm sure you recall the woman you spoke to in the hospital," Kirsten added with a tinge of annoyance. "Pia's grandmother is Vance's mother. She said her son had been trying to work things out with Pia's mother who is a drug addict living in New Jersey. The grandmother had tried to talk her son out of letting Pia stay with the child's mother in Ludlow, because the grandmother didn't believe Pia's mother was ever going to stop doing drugs, but she says her son loved the woman."

"Guess what they say about love being blind is true," Riley quipped.

Kirsten ignored him. "The grandmother said Vance told her yesterday he found Pia's mother overdosed so he called for an ambulance, but he couldn't find Pia. He rounded up people to help him search for his little girl, which has been collaborated."`

"Are you sure his girlfriend died of an overdose?"

"Yes. And Vance was a good father, based on what his mother said. The last she heard from Vance was when he went home to an old house he has in the woods near Evansburg State Park." Kirsten paused. "That's twenty miles away from St. Catherine's and the grandmother said they were Baptists and she'd never heard of St. Catherine's. That absolves St. Catherine's of being linked to all these murders so I don't want to hear anything else about them."

"Then don't ask me questions."

"We had a deal, Walker."

"I don't see how that clears anyone from suspicion." Riley had thought they were on the same side...until now.

"Pia's mother never lived in Philadelphia. No one in that group had any connection to St. Catherine's or Philomena House." Kirsten all but shouted that.

Riley slapped the console cover. "We're running out of time to find Enrique so while you and the rest of City Hall sits on your collective hands I'll be asking the questions you're all afraid to ask."

"In case you haven't heard, the pope is coming to Philadelphia. This city will go crazy if we put pressure on a church that was verbally trashed last year on assumptions."

Screw all of them. He'd find Enrique even if it cost the pope's visit. Seemed like the pope would put a child's life first. Right? "I heard the pope was coming, but losing that visit wouldn't keep me up at night."

"Don't make me do something I don't want to do, Riley."

He heard regret and worry behind that threat and caught that she'd used his first name, but it didn't change anything. "Lock me up if you can live with the consequences. But make sure you show up with enough to put me away for a long time, because I'm not stopping until this is over. And it's not over until the killer is caught and we find Enrique."

Chapter 49

Lucinda forced a smile through clenched teeth and hoped she possessed a smidgen of natural acting ability. She had to present a composed image to get past security at Stan's building where he managed a television station from his office as senior vice president.

The security staff knew Lucinda. Treated her as the wife of a very important executive in the company. She had a photo security badge that cleared her to come and go any time.

When she stepped up to the security desk, the officer on duty smiled, gave an obligatory look at her badge and wished her a nice day, clearing her so she could continue to the elevators.

They wouldn't be smiling for long.

Stan could not hide from her, not even here.

Nothing could stop her from getting her baby back.

She'd called Ziegler, but the doctor had been at the hospital with a critical case. That had left Lucinda no choice but to call Stan or the police.

A bell dinged, announcing the elevator stopping at the lobby floor. Lucinda waited for the car to clear then stepped in, thankful to be alone on the ride to the tenth floor where no one was expecting her. Definitely not Stan.

She'd considered calling him for all of a nanosecond. He hadn't called her before taking Kelsey out of school. Lucinda could think of nothing but getting to her child first and talking to Stan later. She'd had another reason for not calling. If Kelsey wasn't in this building, where she'd better be,

Lucinda didn't want to give Stan a chance to leave before Lucinda got here.

Please, God, keep my baby safe, Lucinda prayed for the millionth time.

If Stan had a reasonable explanation for taking Kelsey out of school – Lucinda hadn't come up with one possibility on her frantic drive here – she'd listen and come clean about taking Kelsey to the specialist so he'd understand why his taking Kelsey on his own had terrorized her.

Then she'd take Kelsey home and...do what?

Continue to live with a man when she still had no conclusive proof for or against his being a child molester?

She clamped her hands on her head to stop the mental noise before she lost her mind over all this.

The one thing that stuck in her thoughts from everything she'd read on child abuse were stories of the mothers who couldn't forgive themselves for not acting fast enough. Too afraid of accusing a family member of harming the child, when a family member had the best opportunities.

Women who had given the benefit of doubt to the wrong person out of love and commitment.

She was no freaking trophy bride who lived in fear of her husband or any other man who would touch her child. Tears stung the corners of her eyes. She hated feeling vulnerable, but more than that was feeling helpless to protect her child. Fear flipped to anger in the next breath when the elevator doors opened to the land of power players with corner offices and personal assistants.

Powerful people didn't scare her. A predator did.

Lucinda nodded at people who spoke, but couldn't trust her voice. Not with hard tremors shaking her body. She'd called and asked Stan's assistant to clear her through security so Lucinda could surprise her husband.

Literally.

Tears threatened with every step she took, her heels sinking into the thick Persian carpet. She angled down a walkway lined with precious metal awards covering the walls.

Stan's just-out-of-college assistant lifted a perky smile to

Lucinda. The nice young lady tried to greet her, then panicked and jumped up when Lucinda didn't pause. "Hello, Mrs. Myers."

"Where's my husband?"

"Your husband's in a meeting with the CEO and… Mrs. Myers, please wait!"

Lucinda didn't say a word or slow down. She wanted one thing and nobody was stopping her.

A glass wall separated Stan's office from the sprawling reception area. The door and a bushy plant blocked her view of whoever sat facing Stan's desk, but her husband was in view behind his desk, intently listening to someone.

Until her movement must have drawn his attention.

Stan glanced around and did a double take when his gaze snagged on her. He stared as though trying to assess why she was heading toward him like a runaway train. Two men in suits sat in cushy chairs facing her miserable dog of a husband who had taken her daughter without telling her.

Stan stood. His face creased with confusion. He spoke to the two men and walked out to where Lucinda stood with her hands curled into fists at her side. He hurried up to her. "Honey, what's wrong?"

"Where's Kesley?"

"Come over to the conference room so we can – "

"Where. Is. She?"

"Lucinda?" Stan looked around at the people who were pausing to watch. He took Lucinda's arm and started toward another glassed-in room with a large table and twelve chairs.

She yanked her arm back and pleaded, "Tell me what you've done with her!"

"She's fine, Lucinda," Stan said, his voice getting harsher. "I'm trying to tell you where she is, but this is not the place to talk about it."

Lucinda couldn't take this any more. She reached up and grabbed his shirt, not caring that she sounded like a lunatic. "I'm calling the police if you don't tell me *right now* where she is."

"What?" He looked down at her hands then at her face. "What's wrong with you?"

"Nothing is wrong with me. It's Kelsey, dammit. I took her to Dr. Ziegler. I know Kelsey's been abused."

Emotions raced across Stan's face from shock to disbelief to hurt and finally settling on anger. "How *dare* you accuse me of something like that?" he whispered in a chilling voice.

"I dare anything when it comes to my baby. I want her back. *Now!*" She was close to hysteria. Her entire body shook.

He grabbed her hands and shoved them off his chest, furious. When he spoke, he squeezed the words out between clenched teeth. "You're not seeing Kelsey until you calm down."

That did it. Rage blinded her to all else but finding her child. In a crazed moment fueled with adrenaline, she started beating on his chest. "I. Want. My. Daughter."

Someone yelled, "*Call Security!*"

Chapter 50

J. T. Turner studied the wall of leads, photos, brainstorming and evidence notes, and tried to connect dots on the killer who had little Enrique.

A .38 caliber bullet in the same spot on each forehead.

Oil wiped on the forehead in a cross mark and on the inside of each wrist.

Three had children.

Two were Philomena residents and one had worshipped at St. Catherine's.

"Let's work through this again," he told the two detectives he'd pulled off other cases to work on this one. "Start with enemies of each vic beginning with Clayton Howell."

Anthony Greco was a chain chewer, his jaw always grinding on a stick of gum now that he was no longer a chain smoker. He leaned a hip on the table shoved against one wall and covered in files. "Howell was catching heat from his old business associate from his muling days, but that one had a solid alibi. Howell had been quiet since moving into Philomena. Neighbors say he wouldn't even talk to Ickerson's new assistant Valdez once Howell heard Valdez had done time."

"What about Stanton?"

"Stanton did not have enemies anyone knew of. Neighbors say she got upset about losing her job at the grocery store, but she didn't kick a fuss until she got home and that was more about being upset than angry. Neighbors believe she fell on the little boy by accident."

"I spoke to Bruno Parrick's wife," Miron Zwolinski said,

picking up the next vic in line. "Figured since he put her in the hospital she might have told a brother or boyfriend on the side, but her family's in Canada and she said they didn't have friends come over. She said she didn't discuss family business with anyone outside of her priest."

That threw another red flag at the church. Turner wouldn't ignore the possibility of someone from the church being involved. But he would be damned sure before moving in the wrong direction.

"What about Montoya?"

Zwolinski used his toe to wheel the desk chair he sat in back and forth several inches. His face was a narrow oval that fit his tall, thin, stretched-looking body. "Everyone who worked with Montoya considered him a likeable guy. No real temper. In fact, a couple of them called him a pussy for letting his crack-head girlfriend yank him around. He's the one who found her comatose in a flop house, no clue her kid had been missing. Mom was declared DOA at the hospital."

"Our best connection is the oil on their heads and wrists," Greco said. "Don't mean it's got a thing to do with a church since anyone can get oil, but we can't rule out the proximity to St. Catherine's."

"Montoya has never been to the church," Turner said in a non-defensive voice. He wanted his men looking at everything behind closed doors, no matter who that was. "Looks like someone from the Northern Liberties area except for the Montoya guy."

Turner scratched the beginning of a beard from lack of shaving this morning. "We're missing something. This guy calling Walker has been involved in all these killings in some way and with the missing kids. Have to assume he's the trigger man, but even if he isn't he's still the nucleus for the deaths."

"The kids tie Montoya to the others," Greco pondered aloud.

Zwolinski stopped rolling his chair. "Except for Bruno. I asked if they'd ever considered adopting and his wife broke down in tears, saying they wanted children. Don't know if wanting them constitutes a tie in. But the killer did give the little girl back because she needed asthma medicine so he could still have Enrique alive."

Turner moved across the room, rubbing eyes that felt like he'd rinsed them with sandy water. "Okay, let's go for the kid connection. If that's the case, someone could have killed Howell because of the drug dealer threatening Howell's girlfriend and her child, but that would have meant his girlfriend told someone about the threat and she said she only told Howell."

"Stanton was in the emergency room with Enrique right before she was killed." Greco chewed, chewed, chewed then said, "Someone could have thought she wasn't a decent mother because she was mentally challenged and seeing Enrique hurt would have snapped the guy. That would point at someone in Philomena, which might be the case with Howell's killer."

Zwolinski shook his head. "But how does that link to Montoya who lives out in the country and had never been to St. Catherine's or Bruno who had no kids to hurt?"

Something on the hospital clicked in J. T.'s mind. "Enrique went to St. Joseph's Hospital that night. Bruno's wife was treated there and Montoya's little girl had been there, because they had her on file. What about Howell's girlfriend? Her kid ever at that hospital?"

"Sort of." Zwolinski frowned deep lines into his face. "His girlfriend had her baby there, but hasn't been back since."

Turner heaved a sigh. "Okay, that leaves us with the oil. We need samples from local churches, including St. Catherine's."

"Who's going to pull that one?" Greco asked.

"I'll get that sample." *That's why they pay me the big bucks.* Turner would laugh if that wasn't so depressing. He headed for his office to make a call to Kirsten Massey. When shit started rolling down hill it would stink up the DA's office, too.

Chapter 51

"What can I do for you, Monsignor?" Kirsten settled into the chair across from where Monsignor Dornan sat back in his leather one. She kept her smile in place. Fighting rush hour gridlock to reach his office had been a bitch, but she wouldn't have passed up this opportunity for anything.

He'd surprised the socks off her when he'd asked her to meet him at St. Catherine's.

Once she finished this visit she intended to find Riley and let him know she'd been here.

That should shut him up. *Yeah, right.*

"I've heard a rumor there is speculation regarding a possible link between the bodies that have been found this past week and St. Catherine's." The Monsignor reclined his leather chair slightly. Behind him, beyond a paned window, clouds gathered into one giant blanket of stormy weather above the tree line.

"What speculation?" Kirsten knew exactly whom Monsignor referenced and wanted to choke Riley for stirring up trouble. "I don't believe anyone in Philly PD or the DA's office has come around asking you questions or made accusations, have they?"

"No, you've all kept your distance, which the bishop and I appreciate, but I've come to the conclusion the best thing for everyone involved would be to establish that we have no possible association with these deaths beyond aiding those in mourning."

She had to admire his deal-with-the-problem-straight-on approach. "If that's the case, answering some questions would provide me with the ability to alleviate your concerns." When he agreed, she asked what he knew about each of the victims, jotting notes as he spoke, then pointed out that Clayton Howell, the first of the documented murders, and Sally Stanton had an association with St. Catherine's through Philomena House.

"Those two deaths could also be associated with the welfare system, but I doubt that implicates them any more than it should us." His elbows were propped on his chair arms, palms together, fingers laced. Absolute power radiated behind that unflinching gaze.

She could see how he came by a reputation for being so persuasive and imposing. No wonder the DA held this man in such high esteem. She had past experience with Monsignor Dornan. Before returning to Philly to accept the DA position, Cecelia Van Gogh had been in San Francisco during the time the Monsignor had been there.

Was that where he'd gotten the nickname Enforcer?

"I certainly agree with that line of reasoning," Kirsten admitted. "But we have to keep an open mind – "

"I suggest you look at those who prey on the less fortunate and sooner would be better than later. We both understand the significance of the pope's visit to this city."

Had she detected just a hint of threat in that? "The police are following every lead they find and doing their best."

"But no one can keep this from the media for long. They must be given more than that press conference today. Give them something else to focus on, or some prejudiced newsmen will share their misdirected opinions on these killings the minute they get back on the air. I doubt the mayor and governor will be happy if the city's image is destroyed on the brink of a papal visit or if you allow St. Catherine's to be victimized by the press...again."

Kirsten didn't need a crystal ball to know who was stirring up Dornan. Prejudiced newsmen like Riley.

She hadn't been involved in the first attack on St. Catherine's and resented the insinuation of guilt by association. "My job is to help convict criminals, not worry about public image for *anyone*. Just to let you know, we *are* getting closer to finding this killer." She wished that were true, but now was the time to put up a strong front. "We will catch him. St. Catherine's will be blemished *only* if someone from here is involved."

"You have *no* evidence connecting these crimes to us," Monsignor continued in a voice hardening more with each word.

"I can't comment on all the evidence collected so far – "

"The fourth death, the Howell man, had no ties to St. Catherine's, wasn't even Catholic." He steepled his hands beneath his chin, speaking as though he was educating her. "There must be other common threads between the four victims – like all lower socio-economic situations, drugs involved with two of the victims' families, at least two had recently been to the local hospital, three from New Liberties which meant they shopped at the same grocery stores, frequented the same pubs. Surely, you and Philly PD have come up with a better connection than St. Catherine's."

She had the oil on the wrists, but that still meant nothing if the oil didn't match the sacrament oils from a specific church. "We aren't jumping to conclusions, but we are open to all possibilities."

"I haven't asked for help with this...yet."

He was insinuating his powerful contacts in the city. Was he threatening her?

Kirsten sat forward, her fingers gripping her knees. "I have a great respect for God and the church, Monsignor, but you should know one thing about me. I come from a family of men who are pros at intimidating. Far more powerful than you. I am in awe of God. Not you. But if you're really serious about smothering any speculation that these deaths could in any way be linked to St. Catherine's I can offer you a simple test."

His eyes narrowed so imperceptibly she wouldn't have noticed if not for learning as a child how to watch for that in her father's gaze. She'd intrigued Monsignor Dornan.

"What?" he asked with an air of indifference she didn't believe.

"Give me a drop of your sacrament oil."

Right after she'd gotten the Monsignor's phone call asking her for a meeting, J. T. Turner had caught her on her way out the door. She'd told him where she was headed and that with any luck she'd leave St. Catherine's with a sample of oil.

If the Monsignor didn't throw her out of his office.

And call the mayor.

Chapter 52

Margo washed her ceramic soup bowl in the parish kitchen. Eating here by herself didn't feel so alone as when she ate at home in the little rental house a half-mile away. The kitchen still smelled of butternut squash soup she'd heated from a can and Baylor's stinky sardines.

Yuk. How could he eat those things?

Television chatter played in the background behind her. Baylor sat with his attention glued to the television in the middle of their white pinewood table. He liked to watch the six o'clock news while he ate, but left the racket box on every time as he finished his meal...like he was doing now.

He carried his plate and utensils to the sink where he washed everything and set the pieces in the drain rack. "Won't be in 'til seven in the morning. Picking up supplies on the way."

Took her a minute to realize he was talking to her and not just mumbling. "That's fine Mr. Baylor."

"Don't want Ickerson jacked up when I'm not here."

Neither did she. "I'll make sure he knows. Father Ickerson is – " *Anal, cranky, annoying...* " – particular about things, but I'm sure he appreciates the fine job you're doing. We all do. Monsignor comments all the time on your work." Sometimes more than she wanted to hear, but telling Jack Dornan so would make her sound guilty of some sin. She had enough faults without coveting the Monsignor's attention to an old man.

Baylor shrugged off the compliment and left. The television blared on, but Monsignor expected her to stay in the know so she tuned into the chatter. She dried her hands on a dishtowel and swung around to give the news her obligatory few minutes of attention.

A squawking commercial ended then the polished talking head flashed on the screen for a few seconds. The next image was of police dragging a woman dressed in a corporate-looking skirt suit out of a high-rise building downtown.

Margo lifted the remote control from the counter and stepped closer, because the woman being arrested seemed vaguely familiar.

"Where was Deacon Grizzle this afternoon?" Monsignor came sliding into the kitchen with an empty mug he placed in the sink.

"He sounded so awful at three I suggested he leave and get some rest before his cough turned into pneumonia." Margo returned to the news report and raised the volume.

A disembodied reporting voice said, "Police say Lucinda Myers has been arrested for threatening to kill her husband."

Monsignor's sharp intake of breath snatched Margo's attention. Her gaze bounced between the television and Monsignor. "What?"

But he didn't answer, his eyes locked on the disturbing images. When Margo turned back to the monitor the camera had zoomed in tight on Lucinda Myers's tear-streaked face.

Margo's mouth fell open.

Wasn't that the woman Monsignor had taken confession for after hours on Tuesday?

Lucinda struggled against the police, crying her heart out and begging anyone who would listen to save her baby. The reporter followed up with a last bit about how Lucinda had admitted taking their daughter Kelsey to a well-known child therapist, Dr. Adelaide Ziegler, without the adoptive father's knowledge. Then they showed a canned shot of Dr. Ziegler's photo from her new weekly talk show with the voiceover touting a high-profile child abuse court case involving a celebrity earlier this year, then segued to her celebrity status in her own right with her own weekly television show.

Margo backtracked mentally to connect events. Ziegler was the doctor Monsignor had asked Margo to locate contact information on *after* hearing Lucinda Myers's confession.

But Margo hadn't known who Lucinda was that day. Based on the timing and this news report, Monsignor's request for the doctor's information now made sense. Did that mean if Kelsey's father didn't know about the doctor visit, and Lucinda was threatening his life, that Lucinda thought her husband had physically abused her daughter?

A logical conclusion based on the facts presented, but Margo had learned a long time ago not to assume anything.

Especially when someone was tried and convicted by the press.

When the news changed to a car crash, she lowered the volume and flipped around to find Monsignor's face ashen.

"You obviously recognized her," Monsignor said, indicating the television with a dip of his head. "I have to go see Lucinda. She'll be in jail for at least several hours, if not overnight depending on whether she can be bonded out. The media is going to be a problem once I walk into the jail, but that woman needs someone to help her."

"But you're the PD's chaplain," Margo argued in what she thought was a reasonable counterpoint.

"That won't matter once the news vultures find out I'm there on the heels of these killings." Monsignor stared off, thinking. He muttered, "Who would have thought..." He shook his head, returning his gaze to Margo. "While I'm gone, find Riley Walker and figure out a way to stop him from creating a sordid special on St. Catherine's. If he discovers Lucinda came here and went to Ziegler on my recommendation, I don't want him using her pain to smear St. Catherine's."

"I put in two calls to him, but he hasn't called back so maybe he's not interested in us anymore."

"He's still interested, but he's lying low until he finds something juicy to use. He'll get wind of my connection to Lucinda the minute I enter that jail."

"Maybe someone else should go to see her." Margo regretted the words as the last one slipped from her lips. The censure in Monsignor's eyes told her she'd just disappointed him.

"The only other person who could do this is Father Ickerson and he left a little while ago to drop his car to get tires put on for tomorrow. The weather is supposed to be sleeting and he's running on bald tires. Besides, I wouldn't ask him anyhow as I'm the one she trusts. Priests can't sift through problems that land in their laps, choosing which ones to handle and which to avoid. I have a duty to help Lucinda and her family. She needs to know her child is safe. First I'm going to find out how much trouble Lucinda is in and reassure her she has someone to turn to then I'm going to..."

"What?" Margo had twisted the dishtowel in her hand to a spastic looking rope.

"I'm not sure, but Kelsey is at the center of this and her needs come first." Monsignor gripped his forehead with his hand. "And to think I came here to rebuild the members' faith in St. Catherine's."

He dropped his hand. "I'll see what I can do about Lucinda, but I need you to deal with Riley. Find him and stop him from making this any worse, which he will once he connects me to Lucinda."

Margo didn't envy Monsignor's wading through the media chaos to see the Myers woman, but she would've taken that over facing Riley Walker.

Stopping Riley from reporting *any* story would be about as likely as preventing Monsignor from walking into that jail tonight.

Chapter 53

Pete's Trapdoor didn't seem to have a rush of business whether it was mid-afternoon like yesterday or now at almost seven at night.

Everyone tipping glasses of beer and mowing through platters of food had problems, but at this moment Riley doubted any would trade places with him. He needed Biddy's expertise now more than ever.

The same reason the cameraman who had stood by Riley should walk away.

Biddy chomped down on a hand-pressed hamburger loaded with all the trimmings. Pete didn't skimp on food for warriors. Juice ran down the side of Biddy's chin. He swiped the liquid with a paper napkin and slugged back a swig of his draft beer before he leaned back and pinned Riley with a squint. "What's so important that you had to buy me dinner?"

Riley looked away and chuckled. He hadn't offered to buy squat, but could still manage a couple of brews and burgers. Maybe eating something would back off the headache chewing its way through his skull.

"Lehman called me in today." Riley gave up on finishing his own gut grenade and put his hamburger down to give Biddy the short version. When he finished sharing the conversation in Lehman's office, Riley said, "You should cut your losses and walk away from this. I can't tell you I'll have Enrique back by noon tomorrow. Give Lehman that video. It's still the best tape of the week and the stations are hungry for anything new. Use it to negotiate your job. If you don't, Lehman will bury you right behind me."

Biddy listened, not rushing to voice his opinion. He lounged in the chair, fingers tapping on the wooden arms.

Someone had changed the overhead music to an acid rock tune. Riley wished for the days when beer and music would solve most problems.

"What are you going to do?" Biddy finally asked.

Riley wished he knew. He only knew what he couldn't do. "I'm going to do whatever I can to find Enrique and I'll do nothing that will jeopardize his safety. But that doesn't mean you should get screwed over in the process. You've got a child to worry about, too. You're one of the best cameramen I've ever worked with. If Lehman doesn't take you back, I still have some friends at stations in other cities who'll give you a job."

"Can't move from Philly now that we're here."

"Why?" Riley hadn't expected that since Biddy's wife wasn't tied to a job at the moment.

"This is home. I grew up here and so did the wife. We want to raise our kid here."

Just the fact that Biddy hadn't said kids, as in plural, told Riley the cameraman believed he and his wife might be blessed with only one child. If that.

"What is it about Philly? The history?" Riley had rolled from place to place without looking back. He'd lived here as a teen, but couldn't understand what appeal any one town had over another.

"Philly's always been a blue collar town, rough around some edges, but it's a city with heart. People care what happens here. I want my kid to grow up somewhere that feels like they got roots." Biddy scratched his nose and exhaled a long, slow breath. He stared at Riley the whole time. "Besides, I can't move Sissy for a while once the baby's born."

Riley hadn't considered that. He liked knowing the name of Biddy's wife. Didn't know why, but he liked it.

"The only mistake you're making right now – " Biddy paused. " – is not trusting your instincts."

Riley raised his hand to stop that direction of conversation. He'd trusted his instincts once.

during the same time in St. Louis."

Riley rubbed his head. The hamburger had taken the edge off his headache, but he hadn't slept more than two hours a night in the past three days. "They ever catch the guy?"

"This is where it gets interesting. Guy who kidnapped her had a criminal record and history of gambling debts to mob-operated games. Two days before Margo was released from the hospital, Boston PD found the rapist's body in Back Bay floating along the St. Charles River. Police figured his past caught up with him."

"How'd he die?"

"Gunshot to the head. .38 slug."

Damn. Riley sorted through all the implications, mentally comparing that with the current killings. He thought out loud. "Any oil on the body would have been washed off...*if* the police had even known to look for it."

Biddy tapped his thumbs on the chair arms. "That's right. You thinking what I'm thinking?"

"Yep. We need to get a spent round out of Monsignor's .38."

"You got a home address on him?"

"I asked about St. Catherine's construction work when I was at Philomena House. The top floor of the three-story building next to the church is going to be the vicar's residence so Monsignor's probably got an apartment somewhere nearby, but I don't have an address yet."

Lines of concentration formed above the bridge of Biddy's nose. "I hear the Monsignor spends more time at St. Catherine's than at home. He might keep his piece in his office. How tight's the security there?"

"Nothing that would stop you, but Cortese left me a voicemail to call her and said she'd be at the office late tonight."

"Give me thirty minutes in that place and I'll either find the weapon and come back with a spent round or determine the weapon is not there."

"How you going to shoot it without someone hearing the shot?"

Biddy just lifted an eyebrow.

"Right. Stupid question." Riley tossed plenty of cash on the table. "I've got another idea, but it might involve bail money before the night's over."

Chapter 54

Lucinda shivered and swallowed another sob. How could she have screwed up so badly?

Stupid. Stupid. Stupid.

Kelsey was at the mercy of a predator.

My fault. Lucinda shouldered all the blame, from marrying Stan to confronting him this afternoon. Rage and terror had stripped her sanity, leaving her lost to any thought except getting her child back. She still should have calmed down and thought it through, considered the ramifications of attacking him and threatening to kill him. What had she been thinking?

That Stan would just hand over Kelsey?

No, she'd lost all ability to think past getting to her daughter. Seeing that she was safe.

Stan claimed Kelsey *was* safe. He said he'd brought in a highly touted female tutor who specialized in dealing with troubled and withdrawn children. The tutor was working with Kelsey in a private space just one floor below his office.

By that point, Stan had been shouting everything he said and Lucinda had been screaming that she wanted her child.

Did she believe Stan? She didn't know. He could have just been covering his backside with so many people listening. On the other hand, she still couldn't reconcile the man she'd married with the man who would harm Kelsey, but too many women had fallen into that trap and failed to put their child's safety ahead of love for a spouse.

What made her any different than those women?

Nothing. She was just a woman who had fallen in love

with the *perfect* man, and then trusted the person she loved.

Love. Lucinda didn't know what that meant anymore.

Cursing erupted ten feet away and behind her. She shuddered and kept her back turned to her cellmates.

Another whiff of urine and body odor struck her so hard she almost threw up on the concrete floor. She curled into herself on the metal bench, fear tearing her apart.

Fear for Kelsey. And there was no one to call since the only friends she had now were those she'd met through Stan.

Fear for herself locked in this jail cell with two women who smelled of cigarettes, cheap perfume and hard nights on the streets. One of them made Elvira look like a poster child for Mother of the Year.

She was alone in this battle.

Heavy footsteps pounded down the hallway and echoed against the concrete walls in sync with the beat of her thumping heart.

What time was it? Seven, eight o'clock? No windows to see if it was dark yet. They'd taken her watch along with her clothes and given her an orange jumpsuit.

Like a criminal. That happened when you threatened to kill your husband in public, and acted like you might do it right then.

Footsteps kept heading her way. She knew it was unrealistic to think someone might be coming to help her, but Lucinda sat up quickly, anxious to see who approached.

One of the women laughed. "You think somebody gonna throw you a scrap, dog?"

Another one said, "Shut up bitch. She was tryin' to help her little girl."

Lucinda didn't care what anyone thought or how she looked. She just wanted to know if anyone had believed her and gone to take Kelsey from Stan.

A police officer stopped in front of her cell then an angel of mercy appeared at his side. She recognized her angel by the black pants and matching shirt with a white clerical collar.

Monsignor Dornan thanked the officer then stepped closer to the bars once the policeman faded from sight. "How are you, Lucinda?"

She burst into tears that came from so deep inside she couldn't stop the geyser to answer him. She sobbed into her hands, her heart breaking into pieces that would never go back together the same way again.

"Here, take this." His gentle words drew her head up.

Lucinda could barely make out his face through her watery gaze. She took the handkerchief he offered and wiped her eyes. He waited silently while she pulled herself together.

"Thank you for coming." Her voice sounded tiny and desperate to her own ears. She'd always been strong. What had happened to her? She'd gotten complacent, comfortable with depending on someone else. She'd trusted too deeply.

"I spoke with the officers about your charges," Monsignor told her. He hooked a hand over one of the bars. "I've left a message for an attorney I know. What else can I do to help you?"

His kindness almost undid her again. After the humiliation of being handcuffed and booked into jail where everyone treated her as though she'd lost her mind or was on drugs, she bled adoration for this man who'd come to help her.

He could have sent the attorney and kept himself from being associated with this sordid mess. With her.

"You don't know how much seeing you here means to me. I took your words to heart when you said we have to fight the good fight of the faith. I tried, but I failed." She squeezed her eyes to stop the weeping. She wouldn't waste the time he was giving her. "Please find Kelsey and get her away from Stan."

Monsignor glanced back at where an officer stood not far away. "Keep your voice down, Lucinda. You're not helping yourself."

"I don't care what they do to me if Kelsey is safe." She reached for his hand, gripping the long fingers between her palms. His hand felt warm and strong, capable of anything. "Please promise me you'll save my baby and keep her out of Stan's hands. I can't make it through tonight knowing she's out there alone and vulnerable. Talk to Janeen. She'll help you."

Monsignor Dornan put a fist against his head, took a deep breath then lowered his hand and met her gaze. "I'll see what I can do."

Chapter 55

How could the police lock up a mother for protecting her child?

He didn't know who deserved his anger the most – the mother, the police or Stan Myers. What had Lucinda Myers been thinking to go after her husband that way?

She should have been more vigilant in watching her little girl to begin with.

Now he'd have to add saving Lucinda's daughter to his plan, but he could be flexible and add one more item to his list. In fact, Kelsey would prove valuable in helping his cause.

But he'd have to watch for the perfect opportunity.

A stream of headlights flowed into the neighborhood across the street from where he'd parked in a subdivision with houses still under construction. He'd waited until dark to find the Myers house in Germantown, a northwest section of Philadelphia.

Stan Myers could thank the media for showing everyone where he lived. Reporters interviewed neighbors as if people who waved at Stan and Lucinda in passing knew what really went on in the Myers house.

Stan Myers would probably have a realtor searching for a gated property by tomorrow.

But for now, the degenerate had to deal with a load of media camped outside his house. What did they expect? That Stan would run wild through the front yard, admitting he was a pedophile?

After that scene Lucinda made in Stan's office, the media

might have good cause for any expectation. Both parents had failed Kelsey. Her mother would be in jail for a day, maybe two, depending on whether her husband pressed charges or not.

Then who would stand guard over her child?

Neither Lucinda nor Stan was a worthy parent, but Kelsey had a savior.

He was the only one willing to battle sin while others stood by as Satan built a path of corrupted souls.

Satan was attacking St. Catherine's through law enforcement. The DA's office pumped garbage into the media then sent a disciple under the guise of trying to clear St. Catherine's name.

Investigator Kirsten Massey was crazy to think she could have a drop of sacred oil. God did not have to prove himself to anyone, particularly the DA's office.

We must fight the good fight of the faith.

Massey pretended to care while persecuting those who served God. She'd sealed her fate when she'd threatened St. Catherine's.

Chapter 56

Tires groaned against the pavement and horns squawked along Race Street with traffic churning in as much turmoil as Margo's conscience. She stomped her frozen feet up and down the sidewalk in front of the Race Street Café, preferring the miserable cold to being seen inside with Riley Walker.

Couldn't he have picked an earlier hour than ten at night? She had to get up for work even if he didn't have a job. If he didn't show up soon, she'd have to reconsider or freeze to death.

Wind pulled at the hood of her old parka, a battleship gray jacket with wool lining that blended in with the shadows where she huddled close to the brick building.

"What are you doing out here?" Walker stepped into her field of view.

So much for being incognito.

Jeans and the bomber jacket, five o'clock shadow darkening his cheeks and a razor sharp slant to his eyes. Everything, right down to the way he stood, vibrated danger toward anyone who got in his way.

She crossed her arms, ready to give Walker the brunt of her discontent. "I'm not hungry."

"Tell the truth. You didn't want to be seen inside with me."

She ignored his astute observation and looked around, checking the area. A middle-aged couple huddled close together as they headed toward the restaurant. "Let's go somewhere we can talk."

"My truck?"

"No." She was never getting into a vehicle again with any man who was not her family or Monsignor. "Follow me to where I'm parked." Margo walked off, not doubting for a minute that Walker would stay close behind.

At the door to her minivan, she swung around to face him. "You said you would trade information. That you had a way to shift attention away from St. Catherine's with these killings."

"If you brought something to trade with."

"I did, but I'm not handing over anything until you convince me you won't drag St. Catherine's into some sensationalized story about these deaths."

He crossed his arms and stepped close.

It took all her power not to take a step back, but he'd know she was terrified of him, of his size, if she did. She fingered the blunt knife in her pocket. Pepper spray could only be used once or twice. She never wanted to be defenseless again.

"I'm not sensationalizing anything, Cortese. I report the truth. I have not said one word about St. Catherine's – "

"You threatened to."

"No, I warned you I would not shy away from reporting the truth, but this isn't about a story. I'll share some things with you that only three people besides me know. So if this information comes out I'll know you leaked it. If that happens, all bets are off."

"I'm the last person who's going to share a word with anyone, particularly the media." She realized that statement conflicted with her standing here talking to Walker. "With the exception of right now."

"Enrique is still alive."

She sucked in a breath at that news. "He is?"

"Yes, so far. But the killer has alluded to using him for something tomorrow so we have to find this guy fast. I have a question for you. Do priests ever put a drop of oil on the arms or hands of a confessor?"

She considered his question carefully and couldn't see any reason not to answer. "Sometimes in absolution we put the sign of the cross on the forehead and another mark in oil on the wrist. Now I get a question. Why have you been targeting St. Catherine's?"

"Because Sally Stanton and Clayton Howell lived at Philomena and were members of St. Catherine's, both killed by a bullet from the same weapon, both marked in the same way."

She put the next piece together. "Oil was found on the bodies."

"Right. Two more victims killed in the same manner are being researched that I'm betting have a tie to St. Catherine's. Did you know Bruno Parrick?"

Monsignor was right. Riley Walker was only going to dig deeper. If he caught her in a lie, she'd lose what little negotiating room she had. "Yes, Bruno worshipped at St. Catherine's, but that doesn't mean anything. All these people live in the same proximity. Northern Liberties is not the safest area either."

"The victim found this morning didn't live in this area." Riley's eyes left her face and moved to take in their surroundings before coming back to her. "That's why I said if you believe everyone at St. Catherine's is innocent of any involvement to bring me a couple of drops of the oil used for dabbing on someone who's dying. Did you bring the death oil?"

She corrected him. "Sacrament oil. Like I had a choice with you breathing down our necks?" Or with Monsignor on the other side telling her to shut down Walker? What if Riley was on to something and the killer was using holy oil? Didn't matter. Monsignor was the only person with a key to the stock of oil at St. Catherine's, which she'd borrowed from where he kept it tucked away in his desk. She was the only other person with a key to his desk so there was no way the oil on those bodies had come from her church, right? Therefore, Riley was testing her to see if he could catch her trying to hide something.

Margo withdrew an empty aspirin tube the size of her little finger from her coat pocket. She'd scalded the tube in hot water and dried it before placing two drops inside.

He stretched out his hand.

She started to place the tube in his palm then pulled it back, terrified at what she was doing. Her heart climbed her throat with needle sharp fingers.

Monsignor expected her to handle this problem and she believed this would be an easy way to get rid of Walker.

He'd challenged her to prove no one at St. Catherine's had been at the crime scenes and she'd pretended to fall right into his trap by asking how.

Walker kept his hand extended. "I give you my word that I won't say a thing about getting this oil *unless* it can be proven that it matches what is found on the bodies." He must have thought her hesitation came from worry over what he'd report. "If it doesn't match, you'll have blown a huge hole in my theory about the connection to your church."

All well and good, but the damage would still have been done. She understood Monsignor's point of not being able to choose which problems she could deal with. She'd been given this one and made the best choice she could.

Like Monsignor, she was willing to accept the consequences.

Margo laid the tube of oil in his open palm.

"I have to say I admire your belief in your faith and the people you work with," Walker told her. His voice had been tender, almost apologetic. "More than that, I admire your guts in showing up here with this sample."

Margo didn't want his praise any more than she wanted to feel warmed by the respect she heard in his voice.

Tomorrow she'd have to confess to Monsignor that she'd taken oil from the chest and given it to an adversary of the church, one who was not of their faith even.

She'd just risked far more than any future with the church. Margo prayed Monsignor wouldn't discharge her from being his assistant. This was the only life she knew.

The only life she wanted.

The only place she felt safe.

Chapter 57

A walk in the night air should clear Kirsten's head, not drum up visions of what kind of animals stalked the city after hours. She carried her briefcase in one hand and jangled her keys in the other hand.

Downtown Philly smelled tired, the pavement holding fuel and tire odors to tangle with succulent wisps of Philly beefsteak still being cooked somewhere. Her stomach growled. She didn't like to eat after ten at night so she'd missed her window of time a half hour ago.

Keeping to the right of oncoming foot traffic, she passed beneath the protective catwalks covering the sidewalk along University Avenue. Two more hours at her desk should catch her up enough for tonight so she could thumb her nose at Cecelia Van Gogh's back tomorrow. The bitch had dumped two cases back on Kirsten's desk that had been ready to go when Kirsten delivered them last week. Cecelia's note indicated she wanted additional research.

No, Van Gogh wanted to load Kirsten to the point she couldn't expend any extra time on the serial killings until Philly PD made an arrest.

The strange feeling of being watched interrupted Kirsten's mental crabbing. She slowed as she exited the covered walkway and peered into the areas illuminated by streetlights. Buildings soared above her, the tops vanishing into a black void of night. Some people strolled and others fast-walked, none of them paying her any attention.

Then she saw him.

Riley stood away from the building where he'd been

leaning. He moved with an easy stride, meeting her halfway to the corner then falling into step beside her. "Got a minute?"

"Depends on what you want to talk about." Did she believe someone with a church was involved in these killings? Sadly, yes, she couldn't deny the evidence, but neither could she continue to collaborate with Riley. Not and do justice to her position with the DA's office.

"I just want to know where you're going to be at eight in the morning."

She stopped and cut a suspicious gaze at him. "Why?"

"Because I may have the hard evidence you're looking for."

Kirsten sighed. "Still determined to prove St. Catherine's is harboring a murderer?"

"I'm only here to give you a heads up. Just tell me where you're going to be."

"In my office."   In spite of all that was going on and having her butt chewed over associating with Riley, Kirsten was glad to see him. And had been thinking about their deal for dinner. Not a date in the serious sense of the word, but she'd thought on that potential dinner more than once. Paying up might be interesting.

Riley leaned close and whispered for her ears only. "What if I can deliver a sample of oil and a bullet that matches the ones found on the murder victims?"

His warm breath rushed against her skin, soft and inviting.

A professional wouldn't notice things like that, but a female couldn't ignore the way her skin tensed, wishing for more than his breath along her neck.

"Kirsten?"

That had come out sounding like a caress.

Her mind finally caught up to what he was asking.

She hadn't gotten a sample from the Monsignor so she doubted Riley could have finagled one. Doubted, but couldn't dismiss the possibility. "What are you telling me?"

"Nothing yet."   When he lifted his head away, he staked her with an uncompromising stare. "If I deliver you a match on those two will you follow through on your end?"

"The chain of possession won't hold up in court," she countered, not willing to give him any answer until she knew everything.

"I'll tell you exactly where I got both so you can search for your own evidence."

"You realize if I stick my neck out on this we'll both lose our heads if it goes bad."

He studied her, his gaze probing for something. She fought the urge to fidget under that assessment.

"We're going to lose Enrique tomorrow, Kirsten, if we don't do something. I won't call you with anything less than what I'm willing to stake his life on."

She believed him. Riley might have his faults, but she knew enough about him by now to believe the depth of his commitment. He'd cut his arm off before he'd endanger that child. "You have Dink and J. T. call me with the lab and ballistics results. If you get a match on both, I'll pull a warrant. But if not, all bets are off."

"Agreed. Thank you."

"Don't thank me, Riley, because I can only do so much," she said, exhausted and worried about him. "Please don't break any laws. I don't want to face you in court." She expected him to come back at her with a joke or sly comment, not for him to nod silently. His eyes drooped at the corners from lack of sleep and strain. He couldn't keep running on fumes for much longer. "Go home and get some sleep."

He just smiled and touched his fingers under her chin, holding her entire body hostage with that tiny connection. Her heart thudded a fast beat. If he kissed her right now, what would she do?

The kiss was only a touch to her forehead, but even that took her breath.

Why did this man, of all the ones she'd met, stir feelings she worked so hard to suppress? Why did she want to see him smile, to be genuinely happy? Why was she thinking about how much that dinner date was starting to matter to her?

"Go to your office while I can see you...Kirsten." He

smiled when he said her name.

"I work late a lot and I don't need you to watch."

He moved his hand to stroke her hair. "But I need to know you're safe inside before I leave."

Warmth fingered through her at having someone concerned over her safety. She'd dated men who respected her independence almost too much at times, never thinking twice about her walking home alone. In fairness, that's the message she gave off. *I don't need anyone.* And she didn't.

But she'd be lying if she said Riley's concern didn't feel nice. "I'll go. You call me if anything changes."

He nodded and stood where he was as she strode to the glass doors of her office building and stepped inside the warm reception area. When she glanced outside, he was melting into the dark.

He should have questioned her easy agreement to pull a warrant if he really had gotten a sample of oil and it matched the oil found on the victims.

If Riley knew what she'd found out an hour ago on Vance Montoya, the vic dug out of the police Dumpster this morning, he'd be tearing the doors down on a little church in Northern Liberties. But if Riley's evidence corroborated her findings, Kirsten would be the one tearing down St. Catherine's doors with a warrant.

And if she made a wrong decision, Van Gogh and the mayor would expect her resignation by dark.

When she reached her office, the message light was blinking. She unloaded her arms while the messages played. All were calls to do with work until the last one.

"Kirsten, I hope you enjoy the surprise I've planned for you."

What did her father have up his sleeve now?

Chapter 58

First he had to convince J. T. to get someone to test the bullet tonight, which would piss off J. T., then Riley had to drive like a madman to New Jersey where he'd piss off Dink.

Can't please all the people all the time, right?

The only thing that mattered was that a new day would start in one hour and sometime during that day – or night – the person who had mutilated and killed human beings had "plans" for Enrique.

Riley made the three-block hike through downtown to the parking garage where he'd left his truck to go find Kirsten. She smelled so nice tonight he'd wanted to pull her into his arms and just hold her. Not entirely true. He'd wanted to kiss her and the only thing that stopped him was the possibility of destroying the tiny bridge he could feel building between them.

When this was all done, he'd take her out for a dinner she'd never forget and do his best to make her want to do it again.

He jumped in his Tundra and let the motor run a moment to warm it up while he rubbed his hands together.

His cell phone rang. Unidentified caller. He didn't need a number to know who was calling. "Want something?"

"What were you telling Investigator Massey?"

The killer had seen him talking to Kirsten? "Are you following me?" Or her? This bastard better not touch her.

"The DA lied to the people today. How can I make sinners repent when the citizens are fed garbage through the media?"

"That was not my doing," Riley argued.

"The Lord does not abide those who scoff at justice. Punishing evil is not something to be taken lightly."

Chill bumps raced up Riley's arms at the warning in those words. "So you're only punishing the evil adults, right? Not children."

"I deliver the children to a safe haven."

"What kind of safe haven? Where is Enrique?"

"Somewhere nothing can get to him."

Riley had asked the Detroit killer the same question and heard, "Somewhere no one can find him."

Frustration had become Riley's constant companion, and it took everything he had to remain calm. "You gave me Pia, why not give me Enrique?"

"Enrique is part of God's plan to save more children." The killer's steady tone and emotionless delivery could raise chill bumps on a death row inmate. "He'll be with me tomorrow when I show the sinners the consequences of their choice. Then I won't need him any longer."

Riley hated this bastard with all of his being. Hearing this killer talk about Enrique and sinners as though they were pawns to be captured in some twisted game then waved under the nose of the loser threatened to make him lose his cool and do something stupid. What little was left of his soul leaked out with every reminder of Detroit and everything about this killer took him back to that awful night.

Biddy was right.

Riley had lost faith in his instincts after Detroit. He'd been playing it safe with this killer, afraid to make a wrong move when there was no guaranteed right move. He should be using his investigative skills to garner information J. T. could use.

Before his time ran out, Riley asked, "Why are you doing this?"

"To make the sinners repent and change their ways. It's my duty to confront those without conscience, to show them actions have consequences. Everyone is depending on me to clean up the garbage."

"What's your measuring stick? How can you be so sure someone is definitely guilty of a sin?"

"Because they know they're guilty when they confess their sins. I will give you all you need to know tomorrow. You tell Investigator Massey and the DA to prepare more graves if they don't tell the people the truth then. If a child is sacrificed because you don't follow instructions the blood will be on your hands."

The call ended before anyone could have triangulated.

Riley called Kirsten and warned her to be careful, that the killer had been watching them.

Kirsten argued, "He'll probably leave now that you know he was out here."

"Maybe. Just take a cab home, okay?"

"I will. Thanks for calling."

His next call was to J. T. who cursed him like a redheaded stepchild before agreeing to run ballistics overnight on the spent .38 bullet that Biddy had managed to find in Monsignor's office while Riley had drawn Margo away to meet with him. The cursing stopped abruptly when Riley explained that a match would mean Riley could tell J. T. the identity of the killer.

Chapter 59

He'd followed Kirsten Massey on foot through the dark streets to where she'd stopped to linger with Riley outside her office building on University Avenue. That had been an hour ago. Philadelphia howled softly with a harsh wind running most late night pedestrians off the streets. But he'd worn plenty of layers, prepared for the weather, so he found a place to curl up in a corner and wait.

When Massey came down from her lofty office, she took a cab. He hailed one right behind her and pretended not to know the address he was looking for, but gave directions the cabbie didn't realize were based on the taxi they followed.

She got out of the cab on 18th Street in Rittenhouse Square.

Nice area...for those who could afford one of these places. White lights twinkled from trees in the park that centered the square. A heavy guy who didn't look too happy walked his terrier that darted everywhere looking for the perfect spot to hike his leg.

As his taxi rolled past slowly, Massey paid her cabbie and hurried into a highrise that topped out over twenty stories. She smiled at the doorman who whipped open the glass door of the luxury apartment building.

So that's where she lived. How'd she pay for that on a government salary? Did Walker know about this place? Had he been to her apartment?

Walker had been a perfect choice, because he seemed to have no attachments to anyone. Until now. The woman had to be why Walker was getting testy and questioning so much when they talked. So the newsman had an interest in the DA investigator?

That could present a problem tomorrow if Riley balked at reporting the story of his career.

The last story of his career.

But on second thought, Walker's interest in Investigator Massey could turn out to be a benefit after all if he hesitated to perform on command.

Once the true story was reported, the city would see what a dedicated servant had done. They'd praise how he made the sinners realize what they faced if they did not repent and the pope...that visit would be the pinnacle of all he dreamed about.

Everyone needed incentive.

In the end, Riley would take responsibility for Enrique.

Chapter 60

Riley carried two cups of gas station coffee into the Certified Labs of Trenton in New Jersey and wasn't leaving until he got what he needed. J. T. had made him wait for the ballistics technician rather than just drop off the bullet, which meant Riley didn't reach Dink's lab until just after one in the morning.

Yanking Dink out of bed at that hour would cost him more than money. "You finished testing the other oil samples?" Riley asked.

"All top shelf olive oil with identical trace elements of herbs." Dink ran his fingers through his bedhead hair and flipped on lights. "You owe me forever for this one."

Riley smiled at the guy he'd met while covering a report on problems with a sewage treatment facility in Atlanta. "Got a possible supplier?"

Dink sat down on his rolling stool. "Maybe for the original base material, but the herbs and stuff? Not a standard mix of any retail operation I've found. Appears to be hand mixed, a custom or homemade concoction."

"That's not much help." Riley frowned at the limitless possibilities a hand-mixed potion created, but he couldn't have a better chemist running slides. CLT of New Jersey had lured Dink away from Atlanta and now he specialized in water treatment testing for city and state. Dink was one goofy looking, bohemian type with flame-red hair that would rival Carrot Top and a pair of Harry Potter glasses, all camouflage for the kind of brainpower they could use at NASA.

Riley drummed his fingers on the blue-gray Corian

surface of Dink's work center. "I have a hunch this oil comes from a church."

"Could be." Dink swung around on the stool. "Made a few calls to some buddies in the business. One of them said the components of the oil sounded like the kind used in his church for sacraments."

Riley stopped tapping his fingers. "Like a Catholic church, right?"

"Sure, but it could be Episcopalian or some other one. I don't go to church so I don't know who uses oil during the service."

"Can you reach your buddy now and ask him a church question for me?"

"Sure, if he's online." Dink pushed his bulk over to a keyboard. "Lives in San Diego." He typed with quick keystrokes, never backing up to fix a typo.

While they waited on a reply, Riley asked, "So you can tell if two oils are from the same batch, so to speak?"

"Sure." Dink was as good as the confidence in his voice. He could probably tell if two gnats had been hatched from the same gnat egg.

Riley pulled out the aspirin container and passed it to him.

Dink held up the small tube and gave Riley a tired look. "You're a pain in my neck, but I'm more of a Jack Daniels kind of guy, not the aspririn kind."

"That's got a couple of drops of oil. I need to find out if it matches the other samples...tonight."

Dink's eyes squinted then widened behind the glasses. "Dude, I thought you wanted something quick and *easy*. You think because *you* don't have a life I should give up my nights, too?"

"If you want four tickets to the Eagles playoff game."

"You're getting closer to my happy spot."

Riley released a tired rush of breath. "Plus this killer has a five-year-old little boy he's threatening to use to make some statement tomorrow...today. We have to catch him before he hurts that child."

"Ah, well, that's a righteous reason. Give me the sample and I'll do my Superman routine." Dink's computer dinged with an incoming message. "My boy's online. What do you want to know?"

"Ask him if a Catholic Church might use one exclusive type of oil?"

Dink zipped that question out and had another ding almost as quickly. "Not really. Olive oil is fairly universal."

"Ask him if all churches put sacrament oil on the arm of a terminally ill person, like on the wrist?"

After another series of lightning keystrokes, Dink hit the send and watched the monitor expectantly. "He says only in the Catholic Church. The priest makes the mark of a cross on their forehead and sometimes touches the oil to the inside of the dying person's wrist."

On the forehead, too. Had Kirsten held out on him? If so, Riley couldn't do anything about that now. "That helps, but it's going to mean more if there's a match with these oils."

"I'll know in four hours or less." Dink got busy.

Riley had settled back to wait when a text came through on his cell phone from Baby G...news on Lisa Parrick. Bruno's widow.

Chapter 61

Not his normal night of exterminating Satan's disciples from the world, but one that had been productive. He'd even managed to sleep for four sound hours. He needed to be rested.

Today would be monumental to St. C's future.

He opened the driver's door slowly, but no one would hear a thing in the back parking lot of St. Catherine's at four in the morning. He'd disconnected the interior light a long time ago to provide complete darkness when he needed to arrive and slip inside St. Catherine's undetected. He had work to catch up on, then he'd go shower. The porch light above the rear steps to the administrative offices was out.

That suited him since the whole point was to enter without notice.

His wool cap and thick gloves insulated him from the teeth-chattering frigid air, but the brittle cold cut through the thin material of his pants and tore at his exposed face with icy fingers when he stepped carefully toward the building.

Had to be careful not to fall. A broken arm or leg would ruin what would be one of the greatest days of his life.

No one would interfere with his plans.

Boom!

He swung around and waited for another gunshot. His heart pounded from shock that turned into laughter when he realized the source.

Not a gunshot. A backfire up on the Vine Expressway interchange.

Didn't wake anyone living around here, a pretty area at

one time before crackheads set up housekeeping in the old neighborhoods.

He zipped his jacket up closer to his neck and stuffed his hands in his coat pockets. Wind whistled through the naked trees surrounding the parking lot, branches iced just enough to tinkle when they touched.

When he got closer his feet slowed, senses alert. Fingering the .38 in his pocket, he considered the possibility of being mugged, then chuckled at the absurdity.

No one would harm him, not a servant of God.

A tiny light glowed from next to the roll-off Dumpster then a shadowed figure moved with the light between him and the rear door of the building. "I thought you were up to something."

The one person he hadn't wanted to face.

Chapter 62

"I've got a match on one of two things." Riley held his cell phone in one hand and a steaming cup of coffee in the other. He sat back on the sofa in his apartment, gazing at the lights of Philly that ended along the Charles River.

"You told me you had *two* pieces of evidence." Kirsten didn't harp at him, just grumbled in a voice thick with exhaustion. "You woke me up at four-thirty in the morning to tell me what?"

"That you better be ready with that warrant."

"I'm in no mood to guess at what you're talking about."

"The oil sample I took to Dink tonight matched the ones off the victims. If I tell you where I got it, will you not go off-the-charts crazy?"

"I do not act crazy. I've figured out you got the oil from St. Catherine's supply, but I don't know *how* you got it."

"It was actually a legitimate get."

"So does that mean the bullet was obtained through less-than-legal means?"

"Let's not get off on that just yet until we find out if ballistics has a match or not." He rubbed his neck and blinked to stay awake. "This oil *is* a match, which means someone has been using the oils from St. Catherine's."

"Not necessarily. It depends on where the oil came from originally. Could have been part of a larger batch that went to more than one church."

"That's true but what is the possibility of matching a church that has three victims connected to it and all with children?"

"Bruno and Lisa Parrick didn't have kids," she corrected.

"I found out that Lisa is two months pregnant."

"Really?" Kirsten whispered in surprise.

"She was in the hospital when she heard about Bruno and broke down in hysterics, telling one of the nurses she hadn't even told Bruno yet. She said the priest had urged her to tell her husband, but she was afraid he wouldn't be happy so she kept procrastinating." Riley had gotten that on a text from Baby G while he was at Dink's lab. No telling if Baby G had been up that late last night or had gotten up early this morning.

"That makes four," she said with glum resignation.

He sat up so fast he almost spilled his coffee. "What'd you say?"

"Four victims connected to St. Catherine's. I'll tell you about the fourth one only if you keep the hell away from that church while I work through due process."

If the gravity of what they discussed wasn't so serious he'd kid her about cursing. Miss Manners not on her game early in the morning? "You act like I'd go busting in there demanding the killer turn himself in."

She didn't respond.

"Come on, Kirsten, give me a little credit at this point." But Riley made no promises about what he'd do if Enrique got hurt while waiting on due process. "What have you got?"

"Turner's detectives had a breakthrough. Vance Montoya was one of the electricians who wired the Philomena House. His mother remembered that he'd mentioned once that he'd talked to someone from St. Catherine's about the problems with his drug-addict girlfriend when he wired the housing units, but didn't say who."

Riley wanted to rail at her for keeping this from him yesterday, but she didn't have to give it to him now. That she did made up for some of the things she'd done to cause him grief.

Speaking of access to information, Monsignor was privy to everything on St. Catherine's and Philomena House. Very few other people on his staff would know what, and who, he knew.

Kirsten added, "Every resident of Philomena House was handpicked and screened by the same person who took confessions for Sally, Bruno and Clayton's wife."

Still within Dornan's access and the Monsignor took confessions. In fact, he'd been in confession the first time Riley stopped by St. Catherine's offices.

Riley's only regret in all this was the fallout Margo would face once Dornan was arrested. The Monsignor had been some form of anchor for her after Margo's brutal attack.

But she was the kind of woman who had a steel core and would survive.

The kind of woman who would not want to back a killer.

He eased back on the sofa, ready to hear Kirsten finally admit the name of the person he'd suspected for three days.

"Has to be Father Ickerson."

Chapter 63

He froze when the small beam of light moved from the shadows between St. Catherine's and the construction Dumpster. A familiar figure holding the flashlight emerged from the dark. Of all the people he'd been concerned might trip him up he hadn't expected Ickerson to be the one to catch on.

The tiny light jostled with each step Ickerson took. "Answer me."

"About what?"

Ickerson stopped two steps away. "You know what I'm talking about. You come and go all hours of the day and night. Now the police and media are snooping around, asking questions at Philomena."

"You're the one at fault for the problems there, not me."

He had no patience for this man's insolence.

"I'm disgusted. You're quite an actor."

So the priest was smarter than he appeared.

He now had two choices. Keep bluffing and hope this did not create a complication or deal with the problem straight on.

Since his calling didn't allow him to sift through problems to choose which ones he took and which ones he passed on, he accepted the only option. Deal with this problem now.

"Snooping around was a mistake on your part, Father Ickerson." He pulled the .38 out of his pocket and fired as the priest dove at him.

Chapter 64

"I understand how the weather has caused a delay in your schedule, but we really need the electrical wiring completed as soon as possible." *Yesterday, to be specific.* Margo rubbed her gritty eyes and stretched the phone cord to reach her coffee mug on the file cabinet.

She hadn't slept so badly since leavin' Boston eight years ago. That's the only reason she was in the office at daylight.

"Sorry, Ms. Cortese," Gonzalez said, just as he'd said the day before and the day before that. "We do the best we can. I call you tomorrow. Maybe come then."

"Thank you, Mr. Gonzalez." Margo hung up and finished gathering the trash in her office. She went down the hall to Deacon Grizzle's office since he was still out. Nothing had been cleaned in here. Why couldn't Valdez help with this? She couldn't decide if Valdez was really tryin' to do a good job or just puttin' on a good show for the monsignor. He came and went like the wind, answering only to Icky and preferrin' to tinker with the audio system as if this were Carnegie Hall. If Icky expected Valdez to be an assistant of some sort he should tell the kid about how collecting garbage in the offices would be a good way to jump right in.

She paused in mid-step. *Admit the truth.* Her foul mood had nothing to do with Valdez's lack of help with the garbage. Worry over facin' Monsignor had kept her up all night and worn her nerves down to the point everything bothered her.

She'd do whatever was asked of her if he did not make her leave, but she had to tell him what she'd done. Had to unburden her soul.

With one large black plastic bag in hand, Margo headed to the rear of the building where she'd stack the bags for Valdez when he showed up. She'd ask Valdez, nicely, to toss this and the other bags into the back of Baylor's truck so he could haul them to the dump. The roll-off Dumpster was for construction debris only.

What was the chance that company had picked up the Dumpster yet? Not one worth a decent wager if she were one to gamble. Just as she reached their small kitchen, the back door flew open ten feet in front of her.

Baylor rushed in with Valdez right behind him. "It's Ickerson. Looks bad."

"I think he's dead!" Valdez shouted.

Margo dropped the bag. "What happened? Where is he?"

Baylor waved a hand toward the door. "Out there. Been shot. I'm calling 9-1-1." The old guy took off at a run.

Margo ran past Valdez and out the back door with the young boy on her heels. Icky lay on his back. Blood trickled down the side of his head. She looked closer. Not trickling. Already congealed.

She checked for a pulse, but couldn't find one. It might just be low.

"Me and Baylor almost fell over him," Valdez said, his words falling out in a ramble.

"Help me get him inside so we can warm him up," she told Valdez who didn't look convinced she could revive Icky. Where was Grizzle when she needed someone with muscle?

She hooked her arms under Icky's upper body and grunted when she lifted. His shoulders were like ice sculptures. She didn't care for the short-tempered guy, but she didn't want him to die. They walked his limp body to the kitchen and lowered him to the floor. Margo sent Valdez to get blankets from the storage room. She pressed two fingers against the bone-white skin on Icky's neck. His skin was so cold it hurt to touch him.

Still no pulse.

Valdez rushed back in, panting, and his face almost as void of color as Icky's. He threw blankets on the floor and started covering the priest.

"Can you find me a small mirror?" she asked.

The kid gave her a thousand-yard stare for a moment then nodded and ran out of the room as if a mirror could bring someone back from death.

Where was that ambulance? Margo rubbed her palms together quickly then placed them against Icky's cold face, tryin' to bring blood back into his skin. How long had he been outside like that? What had he been doin' outside so early?

Valdez's footsteps pounded toward the kitchen. He hooked the side of the door with his hand and swung into the room on a slide and handed a chunk of glass the size of a business card to Margo. "We broke an old mirror upstairs when we were taking it off the wall this week."

Margo took the mirror. Was the old wives tale true? Could this be the beginning of seven years of bad luck?

Baylor rushed in. "I called. Everybody's on the way." The old guy was shaken, face so flushed Margo worried about his risk of heart attack.

Monsignor would be here by eight, but she'd call him as soon as she knew Icky's condition. Nodding at both of the men, Margo carefully moved the piece of mirror under the frozen priest's nose to see if he was breathing.

Chapter 65

Lucinda drew a shaky breath and folded her hands on top of the metal table between her and the attorney Monsignor had found for her. Her handcuffs clanked when her wrists touched the metal. They sat in a small meeting room the jail allowed for client-attorney conferences.

From what she could tell, the only requirements needed were a locked door, dull-white walls, a metal table and chairs in a space that smelled depressing.

She couldn't stop her knee from bouncing. "I'm sorry to ask you to wait, Mr. Urlich, but I'd really like the monsignor to be here when we talk."

"That's fine. I'll step outside and give him a call." Mr. Urlich had a doughy mid-fifties body, but he dressed up well in a tailored suit and silk shirt. She'd shopped with Stan enough to recognize distinctive men's clothing.

"Thank you." She needed to hear how Kelsey was doing more than how the attorney thought to get Lucinda out of jail. And she needed the Monsignor's input to keep from making another bad decision.

A few minutes after Urlich stepped out of the room, an officer stuck his head in. "Your husband wants to see you, Mrs. Myers."

She opened her mouth to refuse Stan when the officer added, "Said he has something to tell you about your daughter."

"Let him in." She prepared herself for this to be some excuse to get past her attorney.

The door opened and Stan burst in with an officer who

stopped her husband from going further than a step inside the door.

"What'd you do, Lucinda?" Stan's normally soft-gray eyes teemed with dark anger...and disappointment.

"I'm allowed to have an attorney." She lifted her chin to let him know she wouldn't be cowed.

His eyebrows dropped over eyes that thinned to slits and his lips parted as if he didn't comprehend what she said. "I don't care how many attorneys you get. What'd you tell Janeen to do with Kelsey?"

Lucinda rose to her feet. "I don't know what you're talking about. What have *you* done with Kelsey? Don't come in here trying to make me look guilty of something."

"You've done a better job than I ever could have."

"Where is she?" Lucinda yelled at him.

Stan's hands curled into fists. "I was willing to give you the benefit of the doubt. I figured you must have snapped from all the stress you've been under, but I would never have thought you could be like this. Stupid me, I still love you."

How could four words rip her heart even more?

"I'm getting you out of here – "

Thank God.

" – as soon as they have a bed at the hospital, but you're staying away from Kelsey until you get your head straightened out."

"You're trying to have me committed?"

He actually looked pained and hurt. What an actor. "I'm trying to figure out how to help you and take care of Kelsey. So tell me what Janeen did with her."

"You leave my baby alone!" she screamed. "Don't you go near her!" She pounded her cuffed hands against the table.

Her attorney rushed in. "What happened?"

The officer explained that Stan had come to see Lucinda.

The attorney snapped, "No one is to see her from here on unless I'm present."

When the officer made Stan leave the room, Lucinda sat down hard on the metal chair, dropped her elbows on the table and covered her face with her hands. What was Stan talking about? Where was Kelsey?

Wait a minute.

She'd begged the monsignor to help her. Told him Janeen would know what to do. Relief fingered through her, massaging the pain in Lucinda's heart and soothing her worries.

That's why Monsignor was late. He had Kelsey tucked away somewhere safe.

She lifted her face to Urlich who did a double take and frowned, asking, "Are you alright, Lucinda?"

"I'm going to be fine." She smiled and wiped her eyes. Monsignor chose this attorney and trusted him. Now that Kelsey was safe, she wouldn't continue to delay the meeting. "Let's get started."

Chapter 66

What had happened to the ballistics report?

Riley woke with a start on his sofa. He scrubbed a hand over his face, surprised to see daylight.

No phone call? He'd left his cell phone on loud in case he fell asleep. But had the battery worn down without him realizing it?

No, the monitor showed the time in bold – 9:37 AM – and that the phone had plenty of battery left.

He flipped it open, dialed J. T. and got a voice mail, dammit. But J. T. had said he'd call.

Riley ran through the shower and felt a little more human. The two hours of hard sleep would hold him for the rest of today. He'd just poured a cup of coffee when his cell phone chimed.

"Walker, this is Turner. Got a match on that ballistics report."

Riley had expected this, but still couldn't believe he'd really been right. Not exactly, since Kirsten was convinced Father Ickerson was their man.

"Walker, you hear me?"

"I heard you. Now you want to know where the bullet came from, right?"

"No, I'm thinking about making a charm bracelet with these things, asshole. What do you think?"

Riley lifted the phone away to spare his eardrums. Not the day to screw with J. T. He pulled the phone back. "I have to call Kirsten first. I made a deal with her."

He had to pull the phone away again. J. T.'s curses

bruised the airwaves. When Riley could get a word in, he said, "I'm calling her now. She'll call you next." He hung up before the conversation turned any more vile.

Kirsten answered on the second ring.

"J. T. got a match on the bullet I dropped off." Riley just realized he hadn't told Kirsten something. "The gun belongs to Monsignor. He's a crack shot. Ask anyone at the PD shooting range."

"Monsignor Dornan?"

"The same. I know how you feel about shaking up the church, but you've got all the evidence you need to act."

"I'm still going with Ickerson as my suspect, but I'm not picking up anyone yet until I walk the mayor and the DA through all of this."

"Dammit, Kirsten – "

"Listen to me, Riley. We don't know that he'll give us Enrique back for sure. I need to make this iron clad so no one will overrule me if I bust a priest. The last thing we want is the suspect to walk because we have nothing to hold over him."

He didn't want to admit she was right, but that didn't change the fact that she was. "Call me when you know what you're doing, okay?"

"I will if I can. I've already shared more on this case with you than I should have, but I did so with Enrique's best interest in mind and to find justice for the victims."

"I understand. You know where to reach me." He hung up and called Biddy who had taken his wife home from the hospital last night. All was okay with her and the baby for now. Riley caught Biddy up on everything. Biddy had located much of the same information on his list of suspects.

"Hot damn, that nails him," Biddy said, indicating Monsignor.

"Not yet. Kirsten is convinced it's the other priest, Ickerson."

"Ah, man. She's going to let the big fish slip through her fingers. What if the killer makes his move while she's processing paperwork?" Biddy scowled and muttered something under his breath about red tape.

"I've thought about that. I'll just deal with whatever he throws at me. Do me a favor – " Riley took a breath. He'd spent part of last night doing more than shagging evidence. "If anything happens to me, there's a file in my nightstand for my foster dad. Has his address in it. Would you get those papers to him?"

"Sure." Biddy was silent a minute then said, "Only if you meet me at Pete's."

He hung up before Riley could tell him he didn't have time to eat or drink.

In fact, he didn't think Pete even opened until eleven so what was Biddy up to?

Chapter 67

He ended the call to Stan Myers's television station and dialed the cell number the executive's nice assistant had shared.

His plan had gone into motion sooner than expected at six this morning when Stan's housekeeper had arrived at the Myers's home. She'd stayed fifteen minutes then driven away alone.

Following the housekeeper had been a brilliant move and proved to be a stroke of luck. He'd originally thought the only benefit would be pulling information out of the woman that would help him find Kelsey.

God smiled on those who did his work.

Stan Myers must have thought he was slick hiding Kelsey in the backseat of the housekeeper's car and sending her to the woman's home. No doubt thinking to keep his daughter away from the prying media who might ask the little girl questions Myers wouldn't want answered.

 Not a problem now. He placed the call to Stan and took a moment to enjoy the peaceful rural setting while he waited on the cell tower connection. This area on the north side of Philly would be perfect. A short drive for a distraught father even if the weather threatened to interfere. Ripe clouds ganged up, building into a confrontation that promised to turn into one devil of a sleet storm.

Mattered not. He was prepared for inclement weather.

The phone connection clicked. "Stan Myers speaking."

"I hope you don't mind, Mr. Myers, but I got your cell phone number from your assistant. I told her I had important information about your daughter."

"Who is this?"

"I'm Father Ickerson." He smiled. Ickerson should enjoy having a notorious reputation for a while. "Your wife came to see me, because she didn't want to talk about...some things with the priest from your church. I believe I can help you understand what is going on with Lucinda."

Myers muttered something acidic in a dark voice. "I can't believe she talked to all these people behind my back." He paused a moment. "What did she tell you about...us?"

"I can't share what was said in confession, even with you, but I do feel that I can shed some light on your situation."

"I'll deal with Lucinda later. All I want to do right now is to find Kelsey. Do you know where she is?"

"Yes, I believe I can help you locate your daughter."

"So tell me."

"What I have to share has to be said in person. It's not something I feel I can discuss over the phone."

"That's ridiculous. I have to find my daughter! Just tell me what you know so I can tell the police." Stan Myers might be accustomed to expecting people to jump when he shouted at work, but he couldn't call these shots.

"I'm sorry, Mr. Myers. Calling you was a mistake. If you don't want to meet I understand and I'll just – "

"Wait! Look, I don't mean to be rude to a priest, but I've got to find my daughter. I've been driving around for hours trying to figure out where Kelsey might be." Stan grumbled something about bullshit. "If you don't tell me what you know, I'm calling the police so they can talk to you."

"That would put me in the awkward position of having to tell them what your wife shared outside of confession about you and...Kelsey."

Stan made a noise that sounded like a pressure cooker getting ready to blow. "Okay, I'll meet you. Where?"

"I'm not far from downtown and hope you'll understand that I don't want to meet somewhere I'll be caught by the media."

"I don't want that either. I'll come to you. Just give me an address and tell me what you look like."

He gave Stan directions to a funeral home in Roxborough, northwest of Philly. "I'll be wearing my cassock."

Chapter 68

That hadn't been pretty.

A better description would be disastrous.

Kirsten hiked through Three Penn Square to where she'd parked her BMW coupe in a prepaid lot. She hadn't expected a short meeting, but neither had she figured it would run an hour past the ten o'clock time frame she'd promised to call J. T.

Ticking off the detective had become way less important since Van Gogh dropped a bomb on Kirsten's future.

Once Kirsten had the mayor and Cecelia in the same room, she announced her intentions of gaining a warrant to search St. Catherine's offices and church. Kirsten finished by explaining how the evidence gave probable cause to bring Father Ickerson in for questioning.

The silence immediately following her thorough presentation sucked the air out of the room.

Took about half a second for Van Gogh to blow her top, but that was mild compared to the mayor whose face turned beet red from his chin to his gray hairline.

The man should drop fifty pounds or go on blood pressure medicine. At close to sixty years old, he was a heart attack on legs.

Kirsten went over and over her methodical process in reaching this decision. Most damning had been the bullet and oil match. Everything settled down and seemed like it was going to work out until the mayor had to step away to take a call.

That's when Van Gogh got in Kirsten's face and said, "I

understand Riley Walker has been to St. Catherine's offices asking questions and harassing the Monsignor at the shooting range."

Kirsten hadn't heard that, but arguing with Van Gogh at that moment would have only wasted precious time.

Van Gogh wasn't through with her yet. "You're going to get your warrant, but you better be damned sure about what you do with it and that Walker is not using you. His ass is on the line with WNUZ. I found out he's got until noon today to file a major story to get his job back. They're offering him a cherry deal for this story in fact." She'd stabbed her sharp fingernail at the file in Kirsten's hands. "I heard about you and Walker having dinner the other night."

That was the minute Kirsten knew she had both feet in hot water.

The DA had shaken her head in a piteous way. "You have a lot of potential, Massey. But I think you've let Walker influence your decision-making. Be forewarned, if anything goes wrong in this case, it's not just your job, because with your connections I doubt that's a big deal."

Van Gogh had no idea how wrong she was, but Kirsten kept her mouth shut rather than give the DA any more ammunition.

"Screw this up and I'll put you in jail, because I'm betting you've broken more than a rule or two."

Kirsten hadn't managed a deep breath since leaving that meeting. No sane person connected to law enforcement wanted to end up locked inside a prison with hardened criminals who wanted revenge. Could she go on a leap of faith and trust Riley?

She did believe Enrique's life was in danger, *if* the child was still alive.

Ice drops tapped the sidewalk and pinged her skin. She gazed up at the low-hanging clouds darkening the sky. Would sleet change the killer's plans? She had no idea, but it was time to get off the fence and take a side.

Kirsten pulled out her cell phone and called J. T. to give him time to round up his troops while she hand delivered the warrant for Judge Berringer to sign. She didn't expect any trouble once she informed the judge of his wife's connection to Sally Stanton – a connection that Kirsten hadn't shared with Van Gogh or the mayor once things had gotten heated.

"Turner here. Been waiting to hear from you, Massey."

"I know and I'm sorry, but I had to run the gauntlet to assure City Hall stood behind us today." She passed the last building before the parking lot and turned right to weave though cars packed tight. She'd parked in the very back of the self-pay lot, the only spot she'd found open this morning. "The spent bullet your ballistics people matched last night came from a weapon that belongs to Monsignor Dornan."

"No way."

"Way. But the rest of the evidence all points to Father Ickerson so I think he's our man and I – "

"Can't be Ickerson."

"Why not?" She stopped in between two rows of vehicles.

"We dispatched men and an emergency vehicle to St. Catherine's this morning. Someone shot Ickerson in the head, but the bullet skimmed the skull. He's in a coma from loss of blood and hypothermia. We found the bullet. It's a .38."

"Was Dornan at the church?"

"He showed up while they were stabilizing Ickerson and rode to the hospital with him."

"Get a security team to the hospital. Find out where Dornan is right now then let me know and I'll meet you at the church with the warrant first then we'll have to bring in Monsignor Dornan."

She hung up and walked as fast as she safely could in short boots, glad she'd worn a pant suit today. Some truck covered in snow grime had backed in next to her car.

She slid carefully between the vehicles to keep from getting her navy pants and jacket filthy. When she put her hand on her door handle something hard that felt like what she'd imagine was a gun barrel stuck her in her back.

"Get into the truck quietly and move across to the passenger seat."

Chapter 69

Seeing the rear exit to Pete's Trapdoor Bar in overcast light of late morning gave Riley a better appreciation for the anonymous front entrance. While Biddy wired, grunted and cursed beneath the Tundra, Riley took in the clutter of mismatched lumber, rusted auto parts, bald tires and a couple of banged up trash cans.

Anyone who had not seen the inside of the Trapdoor – who was not aware of the backgrounds of the members of this clubhouse – would dismiss the ice glazed debris as junk and lazy housekeeping. The casual observer might miss the security camera concealed in the dangling light fixture with a broken spotlight, or two dime-size holes at knee level facing each other where someone trying to enter the bar uninvited would trip a laser beam.

"That's got it." Biddy slid out from under the truck bed. He looked more natural in camo fatigues with a navy blue T-shirt spotted with grime than he did in jeans and a clean white T-shirt with a camera hoisted on his shoulder.

"I don't get the point in all this tracking equipment on the Tundra." Riley shook his head. "I doubt the killer is going to let me just drive to some location when he knows I'm in contact with the police." Today was testing the limits of his patience.

Biddy had insisted on installing a tracking device under the Tundra in a way only a pro could detect the equipment if someone looked beneath the truck.

"So, now you're questioning *my* instincts?"

"Hell, no, but this seems like overkill." Either that or

Biddy wanted a way to find Riley's body to hand Lehman as a peace offering if they didn't get a story out of this.

With an hour to go until noon, it didn't look promising.

Wiping his hands on a red shop rag, Biddy faced Riley. "Sounds like this guy has an end game plan for today. Might call you in closer. Might not, but we don't send a man out in the field, particularly into a covert situation, without some way to extract him if everything goes to shit. I want to have a way to find you even if you can't tell me where you are."

Riley looked at the truck then at Biddy. "You can do that?"

"Yep. So why do you think it's taking so long to hear back from Massey?"

"Who knows? Probably wading through red tape."

"Bet I know why. Remember me telling you I had a lead on something to do with the pope's visit?" When Riley nodded, Biddy said, "Got a text while I was under the truck. Pope's not just coming to Philly. He's visiting St. Catherine's."

"Where'd you get that?"

Biddy just rolled his eyes in a "be serious" way as if Riley should have known better than to ask for his source.

Riley put it together. "So that's why Kirsten and the DA's office has been dancing even harder around investigating anyone at the church." Kirsten hadn't shared that either.

"Most likely."

"Shit. Kirsten said she had to clear the warrant with the mayor and Van Gogh." Riley clamped a hand on his forehead and tried to rub away the pain in his temples. "If she backs off, this killer will get away." Or...Riley didn't want to consider that the killer might take his own life and leave Enrique missing.

Biddy lifted a handheld GPS unit into view and punched buttons. When he seemed satisfied with whatever he read, Biddy put the electronic unit down on the open tailgate. "Here's how we're going to play this. The killer wants you to do something today. I'll be your last line of defense, but if he's good he may not give you time to reach me. That happens, you need plan B to alert me and I just gave you that."

Laid out in those terms, Riley couldn't argue the point. "Got it."

"What time you have?" Biddy lifted his watch into view, fingers on the stem to adjust.

"Eleven-fourteen." Riley couldn't believe J. T. and Kirsten hadn't called by now. Were they really going to lock him out of what was going on now? After what he'd done last night?

Or had Kirsten been shut down by the mayor and Van Gogh?

"We're synced." Biddy packed a handful of tools and wires into a scarred canvas satchel. "I'm not sold on this Ickerson guy being our man. I'll have something on him in a couple hours. Going to dig deeper on Dornan and Cortese, too, plus run the others through the intel gamut."

"Kirsten should have gotten to J. T. by now, but I haven't heard from him." The mood J. T. had been in this morning, Riley didn't expect to hear from him soon, though. "Of course, I haven't heard from the killer either."

"He'll call. This guy needs the recognition or he wouldn't have picked a reporter." Biddy's half smile lacked humor.

Riley would pull every marker he could find when this was done to see if anyone had a contact in Philly that would help Biddy. Getting the cameraman a job came before solving any of Riley's problems. But he had to come up with a plan for Jasper, too. He backed the Tundra out the narrow passage, thinking how this one-way drive had not happened by accident.

With the sun unable to pierce a thick canopy of bloated clouds, late morning felt more like twilight.

J. T. would call back once Kirsten told him who owned the .38, but Riley might find out sooner if he was sitting in J. T.'s office. When he reached the interstate, he headed to the police station. Worst case, one of the other detectives could tell him something.

The traffic had just lightened up when a cell phone started ringing inside the truck cab. His phone was in the console cup holder. Silent. Sounded as though the ringing was coming from the back seat of his dual cab.

He whipped to the shoulder of the road just before an exit and jumped out to search behind his seat. Over-the-road transport trucks blasted wind as they passed him and cars whizzed by, rubber whining over asphalt.

In the pocket on the back of his driver's seat he found a phone he'd never seen before. No reason to have a phone stashed there in his truck unless...the killer wanted a secure line.

But the caller ID indicated Kirsten's phone.

Riley's throat closed.

Chapter 70

"It's time." The voice coming through the cell phone in Riley's hand was familiar, but male. The killer had Kirsten's phone.

Riley's skin chilled and not from the sleet pelting his body. "Where's Kirsten?"

"Keeping me company."

"If you hurt her – " Riley lifted his fist to slam against the truck, but forced himself to stay under control. Kirsten's life depended on it.

"You'll do what, Walker? I'll be monitoring your location."

The need to reach through the phone and squeeze the breath from this guy shook Riley to his core, but he kept his voice level. "What do you want me to do?"

"Get back in your truck so we can talk." Riley did as told while the killer continued, "Massey is currently breathing and untouched. Stay on the line and do as you're told to assure she remains safe. If you drop this call, you have exactly fifteen seconds to get back to me. Pray the cellular service is your friend today, because if you don't reach me in under fifteen seconds there will be no reason for me to answer. You now have two reasons to follow my instructions to the letter."

In other words, Kirsten and Enrique were both at risk.

"I get it. You don't want me contacting anyone else. I'm not going to do anything to risk her life." Riley tried to sort through the changing nuances in this guy's voice, but nothing gave him a clear identity. Was he Monsignor? He'd know soon enough.

The killer began giving instructions. "I know the route you'll be on and how long to drive each section as I narrate directions. Drive north on Interstate 76."

Riley bit down to imprison words that wouldn't help. Brutal determination flushed away thoughts of anything except getting his hands on this man and making him pay for all the deaths, but most of all for what he was doing to Kirsten and Enrique.

Riley considered all the possible delays he might hit. "Weather's turning bad, so figure that in, too."

"I don't see that being a problem for a motivated driver."

Pulling to the bottom of the exit ramp, Riley turned under the overpass but did not whip back on the interstate. Instead, he drove past the northbound ramp, but he had less than a minute to make a maneuver that *might* alert Biddy. If Riley couldn't find a place to execute two back-to-back U turns – a pre-agreed upon signal to Biddy – he'd have to return to the interstate immediately or risk agitating this killer if he ran late.

In the meantime, Riley and Biddy had devised a way to send J. T. a message if Riley needed the police to triangulate his position. But that plan required calling J. T. and leaving Riley's call engaged, which would bleed the battery down. His phone had half a charge left. He'd intended to plug it in the minute he got rolling.

"You're not talking, Walker."

"Trying to maneuver around traffic to make a U turn and get back on the interstate quick. Give me a minute, okay?"

"You've got thirty seconds to start talking."

Riley lifted a knee to steady the steering wheel and shot his hand to the console, moving quietly to open the cover so he could pull out the DC power plug.

But there was no plug in the console. That bastard had taken the cord *and* the extra ammo Riley kept in there.

Riley couldn't use the cell phone idea yet, not until he knew what he was walking into. What if he drove to a location where neither Kirsten nor Enrique was being kept? He might still need the cell phone at that point.

No, Riley would have to depend on Biddy for now and save the phone battery until he had a better plan and more information.

"Thirty seconds are up, Walker."

Riley still hadn't found a place to do a double U-turn yet either. "Is Enrique with Kirsten?"

"The sooner you arrive, the sooner you'll know."

Chapter 71

Suburbia gave way to the countryside northwest of Philly. Ice formed on branches dripping with sleet along the Ridge Pike Highway. Riley watched for the next turn, noting a sign that indicated he was in the area of Evansburg State Park. He'd turned off the main road before reaching the park and now kept track of his trip odometer, as instructed.

He had two minutes to make the noon deadline Lehman had set. Wasn't going to happen. He'd let Biddy down big time.

"Can't hear you, Walker." The killer wanted a steady stream of conversation in between giving Riley directions.

"I'm on North Grange Road – " Riley switched the killer's cell phone back to his left hand again. " – looking for the gravel road on my left. I see it. I'm turning left...now."

"Almost here. The road will curve in a half mile. Take a right on the first dirt road."

Sleet chattered against the roof of his truck.

Riley drove around wallowed out holes in the rutted path and dodged low hanging branches in an ice forest. The road appeared used on a regular basis though. He slowed for a deer that bounded across an opening in front of him.

Now was the time to give a call to J. T. so his team would at least get to this location. Riley would let the connection run for two minutes, unless his phone got taken away.

He divided his attention between driving with his knees and juggling two phones to key in J. T.'s speed dial number and hit send. "Talk to me, Riley so I know we're still on the line."

"I'm on the dirt road. How far does this go?" Riley checked his personal phone. The signal was good. The call connected, timer started, fifteen seconds...then nothing. Damn. Had J. T. even realized it was him? He shoved the phone in his coat pocket.

"I see your truck coming through the woods."

Riley looked around until he spied the roof of a cabin on his right through the sparse woods. The road curled back toward the old dwelling and ended in what could loosely be described as a yard. Weathered boards sealed to remain natural looking held together the small structure that had a porch running the width. The compact size probably meant a one-room design.

"I can see everything you're doing," the killer warned.

Riley cut off the engine and climbed out still holding the phone to his ear. "Now what?"

"Drop the tailgate of your truck. Empty all your pockets on the tailgate and take off your jacket. Then take off your boots and socks. Then you can put it all back on once I see you don't have a weapon."

Riley did as told, first putting the cell phone on the tailgate. He removed his wallet and loose change from his pants pocket then reached into his jacket pockets. Clutching his cell phone in his hand, he grabbed a wad of the liner in each pocket and pulled them inside out to show he had nothing. He shoved the liners back in place, hiding his phone again and lifting the killer's cell phone.

"Okay. Now your shoes and socks, Walker."

Again, Riley carefully removed his shoes and socks to stand barefoot on the frozen ground, gritting his teeth when he stepped on a patch of ice.

The front door opened and a man in a black robe over long pants stepped out on the porch. Seeing someone who looked like a priest at this point didn't surprise Riley, but it wasn't who he'd been expecting. This guy was older than Monsignor.

"Put your shoes and socks back on."

Riley pulled socks over wet feet then shoved them back into the boots and palmed his wallet. "Who are you?"

"Don't play games. You know me. I have something to show you before we leave." The priest backed into the cabin.

The priest did look familiar. Had Riley seen him at the church or in Race Street Café?

A million new questions hit him in the face, but he moved forward, too anxious to find Kirsten and Enrique to question what he'd missed in his theory about the monsignor. When he stepped inside the warm cabin – a one-room building just as it appeared from the outside – he smelled the propane gas heater and something recently cooked that could have been soup.

His senses picked up a stronger sensation that caused the hairs on his arm to stir and lift.

An intense wave of...fear.

"Stop there," the priest – if he really was one – ordered.

Riley kept his attention on the .38 the priest held on him. From his peripheral gaze he could see a small kitchen ahead in the left corner and a rumpled bed in the far corner.

A whimper reached Riley. He swung his head to the right.

"*Kirsten!*" Riley started toward her.

"Move and you'll kill her," the priest warned.

Riley's next breath froze with all the muscles in his body.

Kirsten's frantic gaze clouded with fear, desperation and...hope. She kneeled in a corner, gagged and tied up with duct tape wound around and around over her clothes, pinning her arms to each side of her body and handcuffing her feet.

Twine had been secured around her neck then run in a taut line up to a small wooden table and continued across the surface to where it was tied to a thin wire protruding from a contraption with wires and...dynamite? A bomb?

That would be Riley's best guess, especially based on the situation.

Could be bullshit, but he wasn't a demolitions expert and Kirsten's life depended on him not making wild guesses.

Riley's entire body clenched at the sight of her terrified and in danger. Every nerve demanded he lunge at this maniac and stop him from whatever insane plan he had. But doing so would likely end in Riley's death.

That would leave Kirsten defenseless and Enrique,

wherever he was, with no hope.

"You've seen her." The killer wore a black down jacket over his black robe, similar to the one Riley had seen Monsignor Dornan wearing at the police range when they'd first met. The priest/killer reached over to a hook on the wall next to a dormant fireplace and snagged a set of keys. "We have to go."

Did Biddy's tracking device work this far away? Could Biddy find this place? If so, he'd be here soon. *If* he'd figured out that Riley needed help.

"Turn slowly toward the door," the killer instructed Riley. "And don't encourage her to do anything. If she so much as wiggles she'll blow up. Massey is insurance for you to do your duty."

"I'll do whatever, just don't hurt her." Riley cut his gaze sideways. When Kirsten's wild eyes met his, he winked, hoping she understood he wasn't abandoning her.

Dammit, Biddy, where are you?

Riley walked out to the porch then down the steps to the yard.

"Stop there."

When Riley spun around, he watched as the killer carefully hooked the end of a string into place then gently closed the door the last inch. The killer smiled at Riley. "If someone walks inside who doesn't know about that — kaboom."

Booby trap? Riley hoped if Biddy did make it here that SEALs were as indestructible as advertised. He couldn't consider the alternative of losing *both* Biddy and Kirsten.

"Go over there." The killer waved his weapon to the far side of the cabin. "Just so you understand the importance of being on time, there's a digital timer on the bomb. If I'm not back in ninety minutes, she's history."

That got Riley moving. He consulted his watch while he walked. Twelve-fifteen. At the end of the building, he found an old green step-side Chevy pickup truck. Hadn't this same truck been at the back of St. Catherine's Outreach Center the other day with a guy in coveralls unloading materials from the bed of it?

Riley stopped.

A gun barrel hit him in the back. "Keep moving. Go around the other side. You're driving."

The minute the truck bed was between Riley and the killer, Riley slipped his fingers into his jacket pocket. Working by Braille, he hit a preset number for J. T. and the send button on his cell phone. He hoped like hell the phone battery charge would last long enough for whatever was coming.

Riley climbed inside the musty cab at the same time as his unholy passenger. He sat still, waiting to be told exactly what was expected of him. "Who are you?" Riley asked again.

"Cut it out, Walker. You know I'm Monsignor Dornan."

This priest was *not* Monsignor Dornan. So he was delusional *and* a psychopath?

Why was he emulating the monsignor? Did he think killing sinners made someone a priest with a higher calling or was he trying to please the monsignor, and God?

The killer put the keys on the dash. "Crank the engine."

Reaching slowly, Riley took the keys and started the engine. He had to be careful how he handled this guy. Challenging this pseudo-priest could be dangerous since the guy clearly believed he was Monsignor Dornan.

At this point, the killer could pretend he was the pope and do anything he wanted with Riley as long as Kirsten and Enrique lived. And Biddy.

Riley hadn't seen any other building or a place that might be hiding Enrique on this property so he hoped the child would be wherever they were headed.

But what did this delusional priest want then? And *if* Riley returned to this cabin in time, would Kirsten still be there?

Would the cabin still be there? He gripped the steering wheel with sweaty palms.

Chapter 72

"I'm tracking Riley's truck and it's gone off the reservation," Biddy told J. T. "Have you heard from him?"

"Yeah, but the asshole wasn't on the line."

"Ah, hell. That's a bad sign. Riley planned to call you as soon as he left me to let you know the backup plan if he got in trouble. We decided if he got somewhere he couldn't talk he'd call you and let the connection run so you could triangulate his position."

"Fuck! I hung up on the damn call and I can't find Massey either. Dammitall to hell."

Biddy beat the steering wheel of his Land Cruiser. "I'm headed to wherever his truck is just in case Riley's there. Why don't you – "

"Hold on. Got a call coming through." J. T. came right back. "It's Riley."

Chapter 73

Riley forced every move he made with the steering wheel to be slow and easy. Sleet had changed to rain that beat across the old truck to the point he could hardly hear the directions his passenger issued at times. Riley took care to use his turn signals and stay under the speed limit. Drawing the attention of a cop right now would be dangerous for everyone involved. He drove a route through an even more rural area, headed east-northeast.

"What's this all about?" Riley asked, trying again to engage this priest-wannabe in conversation. Doubted he was a real priest. Probably someone who *wanted* to be in the clergy, but didn't make it.

"You'll see when we arrive."

Asking the killer to repeat his directions once before had annoyed him so Riley dropped the question. He hoped the cell phone connection was still engaged, but doubted anyone on J. T.'s phone could hear the conversation over the loud rumble of the diesel engine. *If* the line was even connected to J. T.'s phone. He couldn't exactly pull the phone out of his pocket to check it.

Riley had tried to ask about Kirsten and the bomb earlier, thinking to feed information to J.T., but the killer shut down any conversation about her or anything else for that matter.

"What am I looking for next?" Riley asked.

"A four-way stop, then about a mile after that there'll be a gate on your left. We'll go in there."

A few minutes later, Riley spoke loud enough he hoped someone on the phone would hear. "Is it that rotten gate on the left?" Stupid question with no other gate within view, which drew a frown from the killer, but he nodded.

After opening the gate, Riley climbed back in soaked to the bone. His teeth chattered from the cold inching into his bones. With the storm getting worse, his flipped on the headlights to counter the loss of light deep in the woods. The truck bounced and jostled, scraping between leafless branches that had encroached into the trail over time. This dirt road was in far worse condition than the one leading to the cabin where he'd left Kirsten.

Was she still alive? What about Biddy?

Worry about one person at a time. He had to focus on getting Enrique right now.

"Just tell me one thing." Riley used his most humble tone in addressing the killer.

"What's that?"

"Will you release Enrique after this?"

"Depends."

"On what?"

"If you report this story exactly the way I tell you."

Déjà vu hit Riley square in his chest. His heart took off at a loping pace. "Is Enrique really safe right now?" The vision of Kirsten tied to a bomb trigger rose to the forefront of his mind, suggesting Enrique might be in a similar situation.

The killer ignored him, pointing to the left. "Turn here."

Riley spun the steering wheel exactly as instructed and the wheels bounced over muddy ruts and downed branches. There was a path, but not much of one.

"Is he safe?" Riley pressed carefully for more information, even though nothing about this scene offered hope of him or the child escaping alive.

"Enrique? Snug as a bug."

"Where is he?" Riley hoped like hell the child was not exposed to the elements.

"Safest place he can be. Underground."

Chapter 74

The child was underground.

Tight-knuckle grip on the steering wheel, Riley looked straight ahead, trying to breathe. If he turned his head and saw that murdering bastard smiling, Riley would kill him with his bare hands.

The only thing saving this killer right now was the possibility of still finding Enrique. If that went away, if Riley had any reason to believe that child was no longer alive, the beast of pain he'd kept chained inside since Detroit would unleash with a fury that would shred anything in its path.

"Stop here."

Riley parked in the middle of the woods, black shadow from the storm closing in. His muscles vibrated with tension. Breathing came in short chops.

"Get out." The killer waited, not opening his door.

Riley climbed out into ankle-deep mud. He slammed the door and heard the passenger door slam before he trudged around to where the killer waited in a drenched robe. When the guy waved his weapon toward a break in the trees, Riley marched forward.

After something like fifty paces through a tangle of weeds, the killer ordered him to stop and don't move.

Riley had gone past cold to numb. He could hardly see where he was in the downpour until a powerful spotlight beamed on to expose the concrete foundation of a house. No framed structure, just the base of a foundation constructed of concrete blocks with five steps leading from the ground to what had been the main floor.

"Go up the steps," the killer directed.

As soon as Riley's foot hit the first step, he was able to see ragged boards two feet high and charred black at one corner. A fire had gutted the house many years ago.

When he reached the surface of the foundation, Riley took in everything with a quick visual sweep. Bloodstains spread over one area of the concrete, as if something had been dragged. The only other thing on the slab besides a couple of trees that had fallen across one end of the foundation was a hump in the middle of the space with a black tarp covering the mound.

Too big to be Enrique. He had to keep telling himself that.

Forcing himself to play this game, Riley asked, "Where are we?"

"This place? Used to be a halfway house until some heathen burned it to the ground. But he paid for taking our home." The killer jabbed his gun in Riley's back again. "Go pull the tarp off."

Riley moved forward, repeating to himself that the shape couldn't be Enrique. He ignored the obvious possibilities, that the shape might include more than one body, and reached down to grasp the tarp when the hump shook all of a sudden.

He snatched his hand back.

"Do it!"

Riley forced his hand out, grasping the cold plastic slick from rain and ripped it away, letting go. The wind caught the covering and blew it off the foundation. He stared at the figure huddled in a knot with his arms bound with rope against his body, the business suit he wore saturated with water. His ankles had been tied securely then tethered with a length of rope to his neck. No way to move without choking himself.

The figure lifted his head. "Help me!" he croaked.

Took Riley a minute to realize he stared at Stan Myers, vice president of one of the top networks in Philadelphia. Riley knew that because he'd seen Myers on television this morning. Something to do with Stan's wife getting arrested and threatening him about their daughter.

Stan's body shook hard, trembling from cold, fear or both. His face contorted with anguish. "Please, help me. He's going to kill my little girl."

Another child.

Riley turned to find the killer had shed his jacket and wore only the black cassock, but he'd produced a long white silk scarf from somewhere that now hung around his neck and down each side of his chest, very formal looking. A sharp gust flapped the tasseled ends.

"Catch." The killer kept his weapon pointed at Riley when he tossed a cell phone in a clear plastic bag. Riley caught the phone then the killer indicated a direction with his head, and said, "Move over there, about fifteen feet back to the spot marked on the cement."

Wiping water from his eyes, Riley looked around until he found an X the size of his two feet in black on the concrete. He moved to the spot. "What do you want me to do?"

"Open the phone to the camera. Use that to film and do the commentary. You show the world that I – " The killer lifted his chin, proud and defiant. " – am stopping the sinners who prey on children. They can depend upon the monsignor."

Riley couldn't believe he was going through this again. He couldn't let this happen. Not again. He pulled the phone out of the bag he discarded, then lowered it to his side where he could hide the way he carefully moved his thumb around pushing buttons. He couldn't key the wrong number. He wouldn't get a second chance.

"What'd you do with Kelsey?" Stan pleaded with the killer in the voice of a parent living a nightmare.

"She's safe from you *and* your wife." The maniac held his head high as if he'd performed the holiest of duties by taking Stan's child. "You'll no longer abuse her innocence."

"No! I didn't touch Kelsey. My wife is crazy." Stan looked at the killer then Riley. "I swear it on my daughter's life. I wouldn't hurt that child. I don't know what got into Lucinda."

The killer faced Stan and raised his weapon.

"Wait." Riley fumbled with the phone. "I've got the

video cued up, but you have to prove to the viewers you're really doing all this to protect children."

The killer lowered his weapon and stared at Riley as if *he* was the crazy one. "I don't have to prove anything."

"It's good PR, Monsignor." Riley couldn't believe he was having this conversation with a killer, but the guy was delusional and wanted to be treated as if he was the monsignor. "Tell the viewers where Kelsey is. You can always edit out anything you don't like later."

Squinting against the rain, the killer thought for a moment then nodded. "Okay. Start filming."

Riley made a show of hitting a button on the cell phone, but not the one to start videotaping with the phone. He'd just hit the send button for the number he'd keyed in he hoped like hell was J. T.'s. Then he turned the camera eye of the cell phone toward the killer. "You're rolling."

Straightening his shoulders as if he were addressing a congregation and not standing in a downpour with a weapon in his hand, the Killer smiled. "I'm Monsignor Dornan of St. Catherine's Parish. Today I'll show you what it takes to stop those in Philadelphia from continuing to sin without remorse. Here – " He pointed the .38 at Stan. " – is a man whose child has endured a terror no child should."

Stan mumbled in a barely audible broken voice. "I didn't do it, didn't do it..." He dropped his head, moaning then shook his head and raised grief-stricken eyes. "You kidnapped my child!"

Undaunted, the killer continued. "No, I saved that child and left her in the care of Janeen in a safe basement. Once I've redeemed the parents, I will bring Kelsey into the fold of the church where she'll be cared for."

Riley played the role of interviewer. "You sure the basement is secure?"

"Of course it is. Janeen lives in a nice neighborhood."

Riley hoped someone caught that and could locate the little girl and Janeen.

The killer stopped and looked expectantly at Riley.

What'd he want? A thumbs up?

"Sounded great." Riley shoved dripping wet hair off his

face with his free hand. "Now, about Enrique – "

"Not yet!"

Dammit. What was it going to take to get this bastard to tell him where Enrique was hidden?

Stan lifted his head and looked to Riley. "Please save Kelsey. You can't believe anything on the news. Kelsey knows I never touched her any way but as a father. *She knows*. Please save her."

Riley had nothing to base it on, but his gut told him Stan Myers was telling the truth and about to die at the hands of a lunatic for a sin he hadn't committed.

"Don't do this," Riley told the killer. If J. T. wasn't here yet that meant he and his men were having a tough time finding this location fifteen miles outside of Philly or that J. T. had to work through jurisdictional issues...or the call from the phone in Riley's pocket never connected.

"*We* have to do this, Walker," the killer ordered.

With nothing to go on but instinct at this point, Riley lowered the phone. He wanted to save Enrique more than he wanted to continue breathing, but he had to stop this guy from killing Stan. If Riley didn't play cameraman and anchor for this nutcase then the killer couldn't act. "I thought you said you were here to save children. Men of God are supposed to help people, not kill them."

"Turn on that video and start filming *now!*" the killer screeched, water spitting from his lips. Veins stood out on his forehead. His eyes blazed with insanity. "Sinners will repent or face the Enforcer." He took a step and swung his .38 at Stan's forehead.

"No, don't!" Stan jerked his body, trying to get away. The ropes cut his neck.

"Ready?" The killer struck a pose, head high, eyes challenging Riley.

Riley didn't lift the phone. "No! I'm *not* filming this or telling your story." He didn't know what else to threaten. The only possible thing nearby to use for a weapon were the two monstrous trees that had fallen crisscross over the last twenty feet of the foundation. Nothing useable there.

The killer snorted at Riley, the sound degrading. "I

thought you cared about Enrique. He's not far away, you know. You can have him once this is done."

Was Enrique really still alive? Was this all one big scam? "How do I know you aren't lying?"

"You have to have faith. Now, start filming." The killer turned back to Stan and lifted the weapon again. "I'll hear your confession now, sinner." When Stan just dropped his head, crying, the killer screamed, "Then prepare to meet the devil because the gates of heaven are closed to you."

Riley had never prayed in his life, but he prayed now. *Please, God, don't let this be a mistake.*

"The video isn't working," Riley shouted. If J. T. hadn't gotten his last cell phone call by now, Riley had run out of options.

The killer turned, confusion locked on his face. "What?"

Riley dropped the phone to the concrete and slammed his boot heel down on it then rushed the killer. Wind galed across the foundation and icy rain slammed Riley in the face.

The killer screamed, jerked his weapon around and fired at Riley.

Pain burned through Riley's side when he took two steps.

Another shot blasted and another.

Riley kept moving forward, adrenaline and fury driving him. He rammed the killer's chest, rocketing both of their bodies into the air. They went down together. Riley rolled on his side that hurt like a mother. He shoved up to his knees then to his feet.

Men shouted beyond the tree line. Police?

The killer was down on his back, jerking spasmodically and holding his throat.

Blood gushed through his fingers.

The priest had been shot.

"No!" Riley dove down on top of him. "Tell me where Enrique is. *Tell me*! Don't you die!"

The killer's free hand grabbed Riley's arm. He coughed and choked, blood drizzled out the corner of his mouth. His eyes bulged but then his lips moved, trying to say his last words.

Riley lowered his ear. "What? Say it. Where is Enrique?"

Gurgling noises pulsed from between the killer's chattering teeth. His body clenched once and shuddered.

Then nothing.

The hand clutching Riley's arm let go and slipped away.

Riley jerked his head up and stared down at the blank eyes of death.

Enrique was underground. Somewhere.

Riley shook the killer's dead body and screamed. *"Noooo..."*

Chapter 75

Police swarmed all over the foundation and through the encroaching woods.

Someone was talking to Riley.

He could hear his name, but couldn't comprehend the words. Didn't want to. Then a hand clamped down on his shoulder and Biddy squatted into view.

Riley stared at Biddy, who waited patiently. When Riley found his voice the words came out thick and rusty. "Thought you might have gotten blown up."

Biddy's answer was a wry smile that didn't match his sad eyes.

Riley would never question Biddy's abilities again. "You get Kirsten?"

"Yep. She's here. Wants to talk to you, but J. T.'s keeping everyone back."

Riley nodded.

Biddy asked quietly, "Who was the crazy priest?"

"J. T. ran the license. His name's Oscar Baylor. Worked at St. Catherine's." Riley stared at the house foundation. He'd ended up on the ground with his back against a tree, but couldn't recall exactly how that had happened. He swallowed. His words came out wounded, scraped along his raw throat. "He wouldn't tell me where Enrique was."

"I know, buddy." Biddy's voice was rough as Riley's. "Fuckin' bastard, but we're not giving up. We'll keep looking."

Riley had searched for the child in Detroit for another six weeks until he finally accepted that the first two bodies had only been found after the Kindergarten Killer had sent a tip...two weeks after the children had died.

The third child – body – had never been found.

Was Enrique still alive, scared, running out of air in some hole? Riley cupped his eyes, but horror coated the inside of his eyelids. He dropped his hand and took a trembling breath.

Biddy stood and gave Riley a hand up to his feet.

Headlights blazed through the forest from all the squad cars. Blue lights spooked through the dark afternoon.

Stan Myers stood shivering with a blanket around his shoulders. Medics and a dozen squad cars had shown up minutes after J. T. and his men arrived on scene in time to see the killer fire at Riley. Shooting the killer at that point was SOP for any law enforcement.

When Riley's gaze clashed with Stan's, the executive walked toward him. Agony wrinkled Stan's forehead.

Biddy started to intervene, but Riley put his hand out to let Biddy know it was okay. He understood the helplessness and terror Stan had suffered.

Stan seemed unsure what to do or say then his face crumpled and he hugged Riley, sobbing. "Thank you, oh, God, thank you."

Riley patted his back, unable to offer a word of comfort. They stood like that, lost in the moment. Riley had stopped caring about time when he watched Enrique's lifeline die.

Stan released Riley and stepped back. "The police found Kelsey and Janeen alive. My baby is alive because of you. Thank you."

All Riley could do was nod then Stan walked away.

The medics made a second attempt to approach Riley. Biddy took one look at where Riley held his side and waited. Riley shook his head. He wasn't hurt that bad. The bullet ripped a cut across his side, but nothing that would kill him.

If he did die from the wound, so what?

Biddy waved off the medics. Kirsten appeared out of nowhere. She rushed up to Riley and folded into the arm he hugged around her. His heart took a crazy leap. He wished he could hug Enrique, too. "How could I fail another child?"

She pulled back and looked up into his face. "You didn't.

This isn't your fault."

"Yes it is. If I hadn't come to Philly the killer would have – "

"Picked another news reporter who might not have saved Stan and Kelsey," Kirsten finished.

Riley's gaze strayed to the ME standing over the killer's body. "He put Kelsey in a basement. Why couldn't he have done that with Enrique?"

"I don't know." She lifted a hand to his cheek. Tears shimmered in her eyes. "He gave back two children, but he was crazy. We'll pull together search parties for Enrique."

"But where..." Something the killer had said clicked in Riley's mind. He stared hard at the foundation, wondering, then slipped out of Kirsten's arms.

"What is it, Riley?"

He started walking to the steps, holding his side that burned with each breath. He might be injured worse than he'd thought. Climbing the steps took some grit.

J. T. stood over the dead priest, holding a small vial of what appeared to be oil in his gloved hand.

Riley didn't slow down, just kept striding to where the trees had fallen – one a giant evergreen, the other a naked oak.

"What're you doing, Walker?" J. T. asked in a guarded tone someone used with a person about to leap off a bridge.

Riley grabbed a branch on the evergreen and yanked. Biddy appeared beside him, not saying a word as he added his strength and snapped branches thick as three fingers. Riley plowed into the dense mangle of limbs, pushing his way through and under.

Biddy stayed right beside him, muscling more wood out of the way.

Down on his hands and knees, Riley's fingers bumped something an inch thick and flat. A sheet of wood. He pushed to his knees. Branches held his back down as he tried to lift the edge of the plywood and pull, but it was stuck.

"I got it," Biddy said. "On three. One, two, three."

They yanked together and the sheet of wood slid free.

Riley went back down on his stomach and rolled under

branches, gritting his teeth against the pain. He felt his fingers slip over the lip of a concrete edging then squirmed until he was lying along a square opening. On the next move, he pushed sideways to lower his feet into a void and wormed his body under a gauntlet of branches.

Then his feet bumped a support.

Steps. He climbed down slowly until his shoe soles touched a solid bottom, soft and shifting like dirt. Musty smelling.

"Here ya go." Biddy lowered a small flashlight already turned on into view and let go.

Riley caught the light and started fanning it around the underground space. The beam shook in his hand. When his eyes adjusted, he saw something that jacked his heart with hope and scared the hell out of him at the same time.

He took four long steps across the earthen floor to where a glow leaked around the edges of a makeshift wooden door. The covering had been secured with a wooden bar.

Riley stuck the flashlight in his back pocket and grabbed the round pole that was thick like a shovel handle. Not a good visual. He jerked the bar up and flung it to the ground.

In too much of a hurry to consider what he might have to face inside, he jerked the covering away.

A Diego blanket covered a small mound.

His heart threatened to explode. A battery-operated lamp lit the cramped eight-foot- square area. He rushed over and reached for the blanket, lifting slowly to uncover a child lying on a small mattress.

Riley swallowed and scooped the dark haired little boy into his arms. He laid an ear against the tiny chest.

Where a heart beat.

Thank God.

Riley hugged the child. Miracles did happen.

Enrique was drugged, but alive.

Chapter 76

Margo stood at Monsignor's doorway, working up the courage to have this final talk. The monsignor sat hunched over a file at his desk, so intent he hadn't noticed her approach on silent feet. That or he was so exhausted from the last two days he was oblivious to any commotion around him.

He'd been absent from St. Catherine's all hours of the day and night, meeting with the mayor, the DA's office and law enforcement about everything from Icky's shooting to those poor people Baylor had killed. She hadn't found the chance to tell Monsignor about handin' over the oil, but he had to know by now.

He'd arrived early at St. Catherine's administrative offices this mornin', even ahead of Margo who thought she'd be first when she walked in a few minutes ago at seven. She couldn't stand waitin' another second to hear his ruling on her conduct.

"Monsignor, I'm needin' to speak with you. Please."

He lifted his head and showed her a face she couldn't read. His disappointment would cripple her more than anything else, even leavin' the church.

"Have a seat." He laid his pen down and sat back, elbows on the arms of his chair and hands clasped in front of his chest.

"I wanted to tell you this two days back, but Father Ickerson was injured, then everything...happened." She twisted the material on her corduroy pants, finding it hard to breath. Her eyes searched out everything on his desk, looking anywhere but Monsignor's eyes.

"Tell me."

Margo stopped fidgeting. "I gave the reporter a drop of sacrament oil the night before Ickerson was hurt." Her insides ached, just thinking about her betrayal, but she still believed in her reason for doing it. She licked her lips and continued in a coarse whisper. "When Walker asked for the drop of oil, I believed it would prove St. Catherine's was not involved

and – " Her voice fell off. Anything more would be whining.

"You believed in me," he finished.

She lifted her damp gaze to meet his quiet one. "Of course, I believed in you. How could I ever think you'd be capable of somethin' like...*that*?"

"Many others stood ready to accuse me the morning Baylor set out to kill Stan Myers."

"Because I made a terrible mistake." She turned her head then realized she was actin' as a coward and faced her mentor.

"Mistakes were made everywhere. I came here to rebuild the faith of this community and help Bishop Gautier overcome the damage done by a thief. I allowed a murderer to walk among us. No, it was worse, from what I now understand." Monsignor shook his head and the grim line of his mouth flattened more.

"None of us suspected Baylor."

Disappointment lining Monsignor's face said he wouldn't let himself off that easily. "The police profiler believes Baylor was like a mortar round, filled with potential to kill but not dangerous until activated. My presence was the catalyst. I'll spare you the classic symptoms of psychotic background, but he had a delusion that fixated on someone...who – " Monsignor paused, searching for a word.

" – was powerful and respected," Margo filled in. "A leader everyone looked up to." A man she revered more than any other person on this earth.

A sigh laden with lament escaped Monsignor's lips. "Yes, I suppose that sums it up. Baylor had once worked at the cemetery where one body was found and he knew all the victims well, having worked here and at Philomena House. Once the police knew it was Baylor and dug into his past, they found out he spoke easily with strangers, spinning all sorts of tales about his background."

"He was well liked at Philomena."   She might be committin' the sin of procrastinating but this would be her only chance for answers. "How did he come by the cassock and oil?"

"The tattered cassock he was wearing that night was not mine. Must have been stolen at another time. As for the oil, he probably took the key from your desk and opened mine and found where I hid the key to the chest."

Here was her opening to admit what she'd done but Monsignor continued, allowin' her a few more minutes of reprieve.

"I can tell myself that my .38 would have been just as accessible if I'd locked it up, but I was negligent in simply sticking the weapon on a high shelf in my closet."

She offered him what solace she could. "Children are never down here unsupervised, and we've never been robbed even when we operated in dangerous areas."

He waved that off with his hand. "Still my responsibility."

"I shudder to think how long he might have continued foolin' everyone," she murmured.

"Unfortunately, the authorities suspect this isn't the first time Baylor has adopted an identity. They believe he's killed before. He was living in the halfway house that had stood on the slab where he'd hidden Enrique. A pyromaniac resident suspected of burning the building was found dead soon after the incident and they think Baylor may have killed him. He'd been beaten as a child by his father. The profiler said he had likely never measured up to his father's expectations."

Margo wanted to feel sorry for Baylor, but that would take more prayin' than she could handle right now with her world collapsing. "Baylor knew about Stan and Lucinda Myers. Lucinda spoke only to you in confession. How'd he find out so much on the victims?"

"That's the worst part, but at least everything Baylor heard died with him." Monsignor rubbed his hands over his face and stood up, then walked to the window to look out. "When the police went through his office in the basement – "

"Yesterday?"

"Yes." Monsignor shifted around and leaned against the window frame, arms crossed. "The police found a camouflaged door to a room where he'd hidden notes and details on all the victims and their families. Baylor also used that area to listen to conversations held everywhere in this building. He was in the perfect position as handyman. He'd wired an audio transmitting system throughout the offices and the church. He could even tap into the system at different locations as well. Baylor was very bright and deeply disturbed."

Margo's eyes strayed up to a vent cover on the wall above Monsignor's head. "Could someone be hearin' us now?"

"Yes, if Baylor's office was open, but I'm leaving it locked until the police finish processing evidence, then we'll obviously have everything removed."

"We" had once included her, but she'd destroyed his faith in her. And she'd put off the moment long enough. Monsignor had always been there for her so Margo had to make this easy for him. "About what I did. I've proven I'm unworthy of your trust, so I'll accept my penance and leave."

"Is that what you think your penance will be? To be relieved of duty?"

Margo flashed a look at Monsignor before she could mask the hurt. What could possibly be worse? "I assumed as a minimum I'd be sent away."

"Then you'll leave me in dire straits."

"Wh-what do you mean?" Could he be sayin'...

"Father Ickerson will return, but not for another few weeks. He'll be here for the pope's visit, but he still needs to heal. Valdez thinks you raised Ickerson from the dead so he's now willing to be your new intern until Ickerson is back." Monsignor cocked his head to the side in that thoughtful look he struck when he wanted to impart some advice. "You committed no error in judgment. Your goal was honorable and your motivation pure. Sometimes we must risk much to do the right thing. I don't believe you betrayed me, but *supported* me. I've made mistakes reaching this point in my life, but my father used to say you can't make an omelet without breaking eggs. If you're looking for forgiveness, you'll have to discuss that with God, because I won't fault you for your faith in me."

"Thank you." *And thank God.* She wiped the tear that escaped down her cheek. "I promise to be the best chief of staff ever and won't let you regret keepin' me." Thanks be to Mary, she was stayin' and being given a second chance.

Chapter 77

His cell phone chimed, but Riley took his time reaching into his pocket for the electronic device that had turned his world inside out for over a week. "Walker here."

"Want to grab a beer and burger?" J. T. had been in touch over the last two days since finding Enrique and finishing up the investigation on Baylor, but not for anything social.

"Can't tonight. I'm on my way to the mayor's reception for the business symposium." Riley walked past a gilded ten-foot-tall mirror in the lobby of one of Philly's more spectacular downtown hotels and paused long enough to decide he looked pretty damned good decked out in a suit and tie.

"Ah, hell, that's right. I forgot we sent extra men over on security for that. Never figured you for hanging around City Hall cronies."

"I don't plan to stay long." Riley eyed the subtle wall clock that showed quarter after seven and smiled. "Someone owes me a dinner." Kirsten had agreed to a bona fide, no business meal if Riley got Dink to turn the lab work quickly and for free. He'd done both. She was supposed to arrive at this shindig by seven-thirty and he didn't want to miss her.

"That dinner's not with a certain DA investigator, is it?"

"If I told you, I might incriminate myself. Throw on a monkey suit and come on down if you want to scope out the ladies in the room. I'll get you in." At the elevator to the ballroom level, Riley stepped in along with another couple.

J. T. laughed. "Nah, I don't think so. I got a date with a few stiffs. Morgue must be running a special. Just got four bodies in over the last three hours from different areas."

"Oh?" The elevator rose carefully, so as not to disturb an eyelash on the elegant pair sharing Riley's ride. "I can always use a good story."

"Don't get excited. Sounds like someone jacked up some of the homeless. If there's a story, you're the only one interested. Catch you later."

Would there ever be an end to the killing? Riley could see how this great city came by its infamous nickname "Killadelphia," but that didn't reflect the heart and soul of Philly that Biddy had talked about. Biddy was right, too.

This was a city a person could grow to love.

Riley hung up and exited the elevator on a floor thick with money and prestige. He wove through clutches of Philadelphia's elite dressed to the nines, mingling with glasses of champagne and mixed drinks. Inside the ballroom, tables decked out in black and white bore elegant centerpieces of candles and flowers. Philly's notable citizens clustered near the cash bars that bookended linen-covered tables of food thirty feet long. More of the city's glittery socialites meandered along an endless selection of hors d'oeuvres, fruit, exotic cheeses and a carved ice sculpture of City Hall with champagne pouring through a chute from the front entrance.

He angled toward the bar boasting the fewest number of hovering patrons, a spot that also offered a decent vantage point for the whole room. He'd ordered a scotch on the rocks and turned around to find Stan Myers in a small group fifteen feet away.

Stan noticed Riley at the same time and offered a polite smile to his associates then disengaged himself before walking over to extend his hand to Riley.

When they shook, Riley asked, "How you doing?"

Stan nodded the equivalent of a "not bad, not great" answer. His eyes were still haunted, but from what Riley had learned the man had good reason. His wife had mistakenly thought Stan had abused Kelsey, her daughter that he'd adopted when they married. When it all came out, Kelsey had been touched inappropriately by a man, but a temporary IT person at her school had done the damage. Stan and his wife were both in counseling along with the little girl, who was now at a new school, some top dollar place Stan had found for her.

Stan cleared his throat and lowered his business mask into place. "Wish you'd reconsider my offer."

"I appreciate it, but I'm happy where I'm at." Riley couldn't believe he'd said those words, but he and Biddy were back on at WNUZ. He wanted to show WNUZ how to build a successful station based on solid reporting. The board had met his and Biddy's contract requirements, plus a bonus Riley negotiated so that Biddy and his wife could breathe easier.

To tell the honest truth, now that Riley had been at both the top and the bottom of this business he wanted to take on an underdog to rebuild. WNUZ's board wanted to see what he could do.

"Just remember to call me if you ever change your mind." Stan shook his hand again.

"You may not still feel that way when we trounce you in the ratings next year."

Stan smiled. "Bring it on." But he'd said that in the spirit of a fair challenge and walked away.

Riley's cell phone buzzed. He lifted it to find he had a text message and keyed the button. The brief message was from Baby G: Be here at 2 pm tomorrow. First game next week. A picture of the team in matching shirts and shorts and bright new mismatched shoes accompanied the message.

Riley grinned, keyed a brief reply that he'd be there and stuck the phone back in his pocket.

Several couples filled in the small gap of space between him and the food so Riley shifted over several feet until his gaze hit on DA Van Gogh. She wore a black cocktail dress like a second skin and obviously had to spend every day in the gym to maintain that zero-fat looking body.

Van Gogh gave him one look, wrinkled her nose then turned to the mayor and two of his friends, and rewarded the trio with a brilliant smile.

Geesh. Women.

Riley listened to the crowd with half an ear. He'd spoken with Kirsten earlier to let her know the bullet from the body found in Boston when the monsignor and Cortese were there had not matched the ballistics on these killings. That cleared the powerful priest of any suspicions. Kirsten had thanked him in a breathless rush, saying she was on her way home to get dressed.

A strip of neon red slashing diagonally through a midnight black dress stalled Riley's gaze. There was Kirsten and, man, did she look like a million dollars he wanted to unwrap one dollar at a time. She smiled and the room faded away.

He could stand for hours watching her walk toward him.

When she reached him, he just drank in the vision of her wearing a dress that dared him to flirt with her. She smiled, probably because he was grinning like an idiot.

"Hi, I – " Her eyes slipped off him and to the right of his shoulder. Surprise flashed, darkening the green in her eyes. "What are you – "

Riley swung around to see who had caught her attention.

A man who looked as though he'd stepped out of a fashion magazine photo shoot swept up to Kirsten. "Hi, babe."

Kirsten clearly knew this guy but her face was a picture of confusion.

What the hell? Riley took in the guy who stood eye-level with him and wore a dark Italian suit. Custom job.

The guy wrapped Kirsten in his arms. "Man, I've missed you."

Kirsten pulled back sounding breathless. "Landry."

Riley watched as though he'd stepped out of his body and observed from above. She was involved with this Landry guy?

Riley couldn't make sense of it, but his eyes didn't lie.

Landry beamed like the happiest guy on earth. He turned to Riley and stuck out his hand. "Sorry, but I haven't seen my fiancé in too long." He turned back to Kirsten who stared at Riley. Landry said, "Your dad called you, right? Told you he had a surprise."

Kirsten sputtered, "Yes, but – "

"Probably claimed credit, the old rascal." Landry hugged Kirsten tight to him, lifting her up to her toes.

Riley had envisioned doing that with her himself the whole time he'd dressed for this stupid party.

When one of the food staff walked by with an empty tray, he deposited his glass on it.

Landry finally put Kirsten back on her feet and grinned at Riley. "Didn't mean to interrupt, but I've missed my girl."

Kirsten shook her head. "I need to talk to you, Riley."

"No apology needed, Landry." Riley shoved a we're-done-here look at Kirsten. "Have a nice time tonight, Investigator, and consider the lab invoice settled."

He left before his brain had to process any more unwanted images. Why hadn't she told him she was engaged when he made the deal about dinner for the lab work?

Riley paid the valet, climbed in his truck and yanked the tie off then sped over to the morgue.

Might as well work on tomorrow's story. No one reported homeless deaths.

J. T.'s Explorer waited outside the morgue close to where Riley parked. He doubted staring at corpses would help him forget the look of Landry holding Kirsten, but maybe the beers he'd share with J. T. at the Race Street Café later would dull the memory. Maybe he'd even swing by Jasper's place and take his dad a six-pack of beer and a pizza later. Now that Riley still had a job, he had a few things in mind that would make Jasper's life a little easier.

When Riley reached the morgue, he found J. T. frowning over a body covered from the waist down with a white sheet and stretched out on a rolling table. Four more bodies were laid out on double-stacked carts and another one alone on a table in the corner.

"Thought you had hot plans," J. T. said, looking up.

"Nope. My date had a prior commitment."

J. T. studied him a minute then let it go, but muttered, "Kirsten's not going to be too happy tomorrow."

"Why not?" *And why the hell should I care?* Riley needed to do a head adjustment about Kirsten real quick.

"She's been looking for a woman named Lucy for a while,

some hooker a friend of hers is searching for." J. T. nodded over his shoulder. "Found her."

Riley walked over to a gurney where two attendants were transferring an over-made-up woman who needed the cosmetics to a stainless steel table. She'd been a rough late twenties, maybe mid-thirtyish when she died. Short brown hair with black stripes and earrings all up one ear. The other ear looked like a dog had chewed it off.

That probably hadn't hurt as bad as getting her throat slit. "Damn."

J. T. moved around and stood next to Riley. "I've got bigger problems than a dead hooker."

Riley canted his head at J. T. "Thought this was a slow news night."

"Starting to wonder." J. T. moved around as he spoke, studying each body. "My officers swept the area where all four of these bodies were found. The local homeless in each case said the victims were new to their area, just showed up a week ago. People living on the street are territorial so they know who's from here and who's not. And this last one? He doesn't fit."

Riley pulled his gaze from the hooker and moved around to see what J. T. was talking about. "What doesn't fit?"

"This guy's got expensive dental work."

When Riley leaned past J. T. to take a look, he did a double take. His stomach lurched. "That's not a homeless man."

"How do you know?"

"Because he's won eighteen Emmys for award-winning reporting. Name's Victor Sunderson. He goes undercover for months to get a story. Or he did." Riley faced J. T. "But the kicker is that he doesn't report here. He's from Chicago. And he had enemies."

The End

ABOUT THE AUTHORS

Thank you for reading book one in our new Riley Walker series. We hope you enjoyed it and, if so, will post a review. Please visit our websites for information on book two. Wes and Dianna

As a former Emmy award-winning journalist and NYT best seller, Wes Sarginson had a broadcasting career that spanned forty-six years. He anchored and reported first in Montgomery, Al, then Pittsburgh and Philadelphia, Pa.; Cleveland; Detroit; then in Washington D.C. two different times. He worked in Tampa, Fl. for ten years, then to Atlanta where he retired. Sarginson started "Wes Side Story", a successful daily feature, in Tampa and took it on to Atlanta where it continued to deliver a loyal audience. In addition to publishing a New York Times best selling nonfiction book on a famous bank robber, Sarginson has covered presidential campaigns; international events; and wrote and produced many documentaries. With his vast experience in covering a wide variety of news stories, most of which he has documented in over 40 journals, his stories and imagination are boundless. NYT best selling author, Dianna Love was one of his Wes Side Stories and that led to their collaboration in the Riley Walker series.

http://www.WesSarginson.com

New York Times bestseller Dianna Love once dangled over a hundred feet in the air to create unusual marketing projects for Fortune 500 companies. The first book she wrote won a RITA® Award and sold out in six weeks. She writes high-octane romantic thrillers, releasing three novels in the Slye Temp series during 2013. Dianna also co-authors an edgy thriller series on Riley Walker with NYT bestseller Wes Sarginson. When not in her writing cave spinning tales, Dianna tours the country on her BMW motorcycle, visiting readers and finding new story settings. She lives in the Atlanta, GA area with her husband, who is a long-distance motorcycle rider and safety instructor, and their tank full of unruly saltwater critters.

http://www.AuthorDiannaLove.com

~ Next is a sneak peek at one of Dianna's romantic thrillers ~

LAST CHANCE TO RUN

Chapter 1

Lightning crackled nearby. Close, but not close enough.

Escape tonight or ... there was no second option.

"Come on, God, *please*." Angel whispered the desperate prayer for the hundredth time since midnight. But lights still burned through Mason Lorde's opulent compound where she'd been imprisoned for the last ten days.

She had to get over this compulsion about being honest. The last time she'd done the right thing, she'd landed in a real prison with a warden and crazy female inmates threatening her life. That had been thanks to her father.

One more thing she had to get over. Trusting any man.

Wind howled across the beveled panes, rattling the French doors and sounding cold when August weather was anything but.

"I should have asked for a hurricane instead of a thunderstorm," she muttered under her breath. But hurricanes weren't as prevalent along the North Carolina coast as lightning storms. All she needed was a brief power outage. Not that she had any reason to believe in divine intervention at this point in her life.

A short life if she didn't get out of this place now.

She rolled a golf-ball-shaped compass in her hand, a dangerous stress reliever. She'd stolen it from his office, and to hell with any guilt she felt.

It would get her fingers snapped like twigs if Mason caught her with his solid gold desk toy.

No chance he'd let her off easy.

She'd learned that the hard way. Just like everything else in her life.

Mason Lorde, her dream employer. The bastard had turned into her worst nightmare. But with a conviction in her past, who could blame her for jumping at a chance for a job with a highly reputed firm? Assisting the manager in one of the warehouses for Lorde's revered import enterprise beat cleaning toilets or scavenging aluminum cans any day.

She'd thought.

Brilliant light flashed across the heavens, illuminating the edges of the brass bed at her shoulder. She glanced at the burgundy silk duvet covering the lump she'd built with pillows. Would that gain her an extra minute?

Maybe. She hated maybe. Reminded her how often her worthless court-appointed attorney had spouted that word.

Maybe you'll receive leniency for a first offense.

Maybe you'll get out early on good behavior.

Neither happened.

Maybe men would stop screwing her over at some point, but she wasn't counting on that, either.

Angel consulted her black plastic sports watch.

In sixteen minutes Kenner would begin his two a.m. round.

On the dot.

Unlike the rest of the security, the knuckle-dragging commander now in charge of Mason's thirty-room mansion lacked any tolerance. Kenner had been brought in from another of Mason's locations to replace Jeff, who'd overseen the property for the past ten years, according to his last screaming words.

He'd pleaded for his life.

Then Mason had ... nausea rolled through her stomach.

Another glance at her timepiece. Fifteen minutes, forty-eight seconds left.

She reached for the doorknob, desperate to flee, but paused short of touching it. She had no allies beyond patience. It wasn't as if Kenner would repeat Jeff's mistake. Poor Jeff, too slow on the uptake to be hanging with a bunch of killers. He'd smoked one too many cigarettes a week ago while she'd scurried down the Italian marble hallways in a fevered attempt to escape.

One of the other guards had caught her.

Mason didn't tolerate mistakes. He'd ordered everyone to witness Jeff's punishment. Angel, in particular. She still had bruises from where she'd been dragged outside and shoved up front for the show being performed for her benefit.

The citizens of nearby Raleigh would never believe what went on inside this private compound belonging to one of their most prominent city businessmen.

Just over six feet tall, with thick golden hair and a champion's physique, Mason, the Nordic antichrist, had calmly raised his .357 magnum revolver to Jeff's head and squeezed the trigger.

A deafening explosion. Then blood. *So much blood.*

She clenched her fists. The horror lived on, burned on the insides of her eyelids.

And the smell. Who could forget the god-awful coppery stench of fresh blood? Her stomach roiled again.

Hard to believe a week had passed. Seemed like just minutes ago. She squeezed her eyes shut and saw it all again. The hole in Jeff's forehead. His eyes locked open in horror. The back of his head ... she swallowed and took a breath. She'd carry that brutal image for as long as she lived.

Along with the responsibility for his death.

And all because of a job she'd thought was a godsend. What had she done so wrong in her life to have ended up involved with a criminal *again*?

The first time, she'd been eighteen. And naïve to the point of being clueless about drugs. *That* had cost her.

She'd had no reason to think her own father would take advantage of her job as a city courier and use her to mule drugs without her knowledge.

Then throw her under the judge's gavel to save his own hide.

This time, she was not going down without a fight.

If she got out of here tonight, she had the hammer that would bring down Mason. And prove her own innocence. She patted the heavy band wrapped around her waist like a money belt. The strip of plastic held a fortune in gold coins that would bring her salvation.

Or the end of her life.

Twelve minutes, forty-two seconds until room check.

Jagged sparks flashed across the eerie sky, nearer, but still too far away. Her heart pounded against her breastbone.

Come on, God. Don't I deserve one break?

Thunder rumbled through the black heavens, longer than it had during the two power outages earlier in the week. They were common occurrences at the estate, cured each time temporarily by generators. She'd timed the last two blackouts. Should the Almighty-in-charge-of-weather deign to knock out the main electrical feed once more, she'd have nine minutes until three thousand volts surged through the chain link fence again.

Three thousand volts or face Mason when he returned tomorrow morning – not much of a choice.

The goal was simple. Escape or die trying.

She still nursed wounds from her penance for that first attempt. Her hand unconsciously went to her sore ribs and she licked her cut lip. The guards hadn't harmed her beyond bruising, but Mason enjoyed doling out his personal brand of punishment.

The psycho had actually gotten aroused as he'd beaten her.

In the dignified tone of a pompous professor, Mason had explained his actions. "Consider this step one in teaching you compliance and submission, Angelina."

He'd wasted his time.

There would be no step two.

Thunder barreled across the sky, directly overhead this time, rattling the delicate glass panels between her and the storm.

Ten minutes, eighteen seconds left.

Her restless fingers worried the cold silver band Mason had locked on her wrist. He'd smiled when he assured her the tracking device was for her own protection. That had been right before he promised to return by the time she'd healed.

Cracked bones and bruises weren't major concerns, but

living to see her twenty-sixth birthday had become questionable.

The guards had breathed a collective sigh of relief after her beating, sure that she would stay put.

Only a crazy person would try to escape again.

"We'll see who's crazy," she whispered. "You son-of-a –"

Lightning exploded in a clap of thunder, so close her arm hairs stood on end.

The entire compound fell dark.

Angel hit the self-timer on her watch and dropped the compass down the front of her Lycra running top beneath a butter-yellow T-shirt. Mason's choice of color. Not hers. Combined with matching shorts, she'd stand out like a beacon when the first lights popped back on.

She pushed the French doors open and rushed into a cool rain that battered the second floor private balcony. She nudged the doors shut behind her. A worn navy blue ball cap shielded her eyes from the downpour and hid shoulder-length auburn hair she'd fastened into a ponytail.

No going back now. Guards would enter the empty bedroom by the time lights flicked on.

Feeling blindly in the dark for the rail that enclosed the balcony, she gripped the ledge, climbed over then locked her legs around the ten-inch thick center column. Her arms strained to hold her body's dead weight. Tremors shook her at the fear of falling twenty feet. Wet polished marble offered no traction to slow her descent.

She slid down the soaked surface. Friction burned both her hands and exposed legs in seconds. Tears, mixed with rain, poured down her face from the searing pain.

She lost her grip ... and clenched her muscles, waiting for the impact. She plummeted through a black vortex. Sharp points stabbed into her shoulders and hips when she landed, but no excruciating pain from a broken bone.

She'd been spared by a boxwood hedge.

Like a turtle on its back in a bed of nails, she lay still, panting hard against the pain in her ribs. The insides of her legs throbbed and wet bullets of rain pelted her face.

Drawing a deep breath, she kicked both feet and rolled to her side, dropping into a crouch to listen.

No thud of heavy footsteps – yet.

Time to get moving. Through the darkness, she counted memorized steps across the lawn. Lightning crackled and fingered through the dark sky. When grass changed to concrete, she sidestepped around the Olympic-size pool. Raindrops slapped the chlorinated water.

Her feet met grass again exactly on count. She picked up the pace. Her shoulder bumped against a stone arbor strangled by jasmine vines. She tripped on a thick stem and went down hard, scraping her palms.

She gulped a deep breath. Listened for shouts, boots splashing across wet ground, any sound of being hunted.

Still clear.

Jumping up, she lunged into the blackness, running hard, fighting the panic exploding in her chest.

Heel to toe, heel to toe. Don't smack the ground.

Finally, the big elm came into view during a quick flash of lightning. She stepped around the tree, sucking in short gasps of air. Running a marathon was easier than racing a hundred feet through the dark, expecting to get shot. Her heart hammered with terrified beats. She had to calm down and stick to her plan. Her hand shook violently as she made two stabs to press the button that illuminated her watch face.

Four minutes and twelve seconds.

Plenty of time if everything stayed status quo.

For the past ten days she'd pretended to be afraid of her shadow. Maybe the ruse had paid off. As long as no one rushed to be Mr. Efficient and cranked the generators ahead of schedule.

She sprinted eight big steps forward and stopped. Drenched to the bone, trembling from fear, she reached out in the darkness to grasp the ten-foot-tall security fence. Survival instincts stayed her hand at the last second, but there was only one way to know if the electricity was activated.

She stuck a finger on it.

No tingle.

She glanced up at the angry heavens. *Thank you.*

LAST CHANCE TO RUN

The current normally surging through the steel mesh could toss a grown man like a discarded rag doll. She grabbed a handhold on the fence.

Kenner's roar of anger from the balcony reached her.

He'd found her empty bed.

Clenching one handhold then another as fast as she could, she struggled up the fence.

Freedom was only a foot away. She hauled herself over the top. Her hand slipped. Soft flesh tore on the twisted ends of the chain link. She bit down hard to swallow a cry of pain. No sense giving Kenner a tip on which direction she'd run. He'd find out soon enough anyway. She slipped, kicking frantically for any foothold. Falling from this height could mean a snapped ankle, and speed was her best weapon right now. She caught a toehold, scrambled down the other side, and leaped away from the fence.

Lights blazed on across the compound. Two minutes early.

She froze. Wet chain link sizzled with renewed power.

Every survival instinct she had screamed at her to tear through the woods like a madwoman. But hitting a tree might knock her out or daze her. Instant capture. Instead, she backed away from the fence, her feet on autopilot when she turned and plowed forward. Every time lightning streaked across the sky and lit up the woods, she raced ahead, dodging trees. Thick underbrush clawed at her arms. Pain from the cuts burning her skin demanded attention.

She pushed harder.

Sheets of rain blasted through breaks in the trees. Thunder boomed overhead.

How far could Mason's men track her?

Would the storm interfere with the bracelet's signal? She hoped for that miracle since God had been accommodating so far.

A jagged branch snagged the edge of her thin shorts and ripped a searing gash across her thigh. An adrenaline spike masked the pain, but her lungs begged for oxygen.

She was an endurance runner, not a sprinter.

At an unexpected opening in the brush, she stumbled to a

stop, sucking air. Snatching the gold paperweight from between her breasts, she flipped it to the compass embedded in the top. She got her bearings during the next brilliant lightning display.

The small airfield she'd seen on a map in Mason's office should be dead ahead.

Tucking away the compass, she started to move then jerked around at a noise.

Distant barking and howls broke through the deluge. Mason's dogs trained by expert trackers. Between the animals and the stupid bracelet, they were on her trail. She pushed on with one thought – surely someone at the airfield would help her.

What if they knew Mason? *What if someone at the airport worked for Mason?* At the very least, he flew in there and might be a client who paid for hangar space.

"What ifs" would get her killed if she slowed down.

She ran her fingers compulsively over the band of coins strapped around her waist. Those eight rare coins were as important as her next breath.

She'd sworn once that she would *never* go to jail again. Her one and only conviction had not been her fault. The police hadn't believed her story then.

They'd laugh in her face this time – right before they handcuffed her.

Taking Mason's *Saint-Gauden's Double Eagle* coins had stamped her death warrant. But they didn't belong to Mason either. He'd stolen the rare pieces from a museum to trade for what he called a once-in-a-lifetime find. Some panel made out of amber from back in the fifteenth century.

She smiled in spite of her pain.

Mason would be empty handed when it came time to deliver the coins on Sunday.

One more way to pay that bastard back. If she didn't get caught by Mason or the FBI first.

The FBI should be thrilled to have the stolen coins returned, and her testimony on Mason's international crime ring. But no one would listen to her until she could prove she had no part in the original theft.

LAST CHANCE TO RUN

Mason claimed he had evidence that would implicate *her* in the theft. And who would the authorities believe? A local dignitary or a nobody ex-con?

As if someone had thrown a switch, the downpour fizzled into a steady shower. She burst through a break in the trees and slowed while her eyes adjusted, but moved forward steadily.

The ground fell away. She stumbled down a short drop into a ditch, landing on her knees. No pain because adrenaline still rushed through her, but she'd have bruises on bruises after this. She climbed up and touched pavement.

The runway.

The good news? No fence around this airport. She scrambled to stand and drew a quaking breath. Freedom got closer by the minute.

The bays of pursuit dogs pierced the night. They were closing in.

A fence at this point might've had merits.

Searching past the runway, she spotted the bright glow of an open hangar a quarter of a mile away. With no time to waste, she sprinted toward the illuminated area.

Running felt good in spite of how her thigh throbbed. Blood trickled from the deep gash. Forcing her heart to pump harder only made her bleed more, but she'd survived worse.

She softened her steps as she neared the hangar then crept to the edge of the building. A tall, lanky man in mechanic's coveralls loaded boxes into a sleek twin-prop cargo plane.

When the worker finished, he walked across the spotless floor toward a brightly lit office.

She could just make out two men on the other side of a glass door. The mechanic pushed the door open and announced the airplane was ready to go.

Angel hesitated. She'd always obeyed the law before. Now, the "slightly illegal things" she never would have done in the past just kept stacking up. Clenching her jaw against the unavoidable twinge of guilt, she made her decision.

That was the old Angel.

The new one wanted to survive and accepted that she'd never outrun those dogs on the ground.

DIANNA LOVE

One way or another, she was leaving on that plane.

Chapter 2

Zane peered through the dull glass office door into the pristine hangar where Hack's man loaded the last box into Zane's Cessna 404 Titan. He moved over to the pot of strong coffee always ready for pilots and filled his thermos.

"You ain't listenin', son."

"I have to make this run," Zane answered Hack absently, then shifted around to face the terminal manager.

"You cain't be serious 'bout flyin' in this mess." Hack laid a dog-eared queen of spades down, completing another game of solitaire.

Oh, yeah, dead serious. He had five days left to prove he deserved the charter contract High Vision Enterprises had up for grabs. The other two charter groups had enough equipment and personnel to cover deliveries *anywhere* in the continental US. Zane was already at a disadvantage in that he only wanted the southeastern region, but he'd impressed High Vision last week by delivering a shipment the other two carriers had turned down. This was another opportunity Zane wouldn't pass up.

Couldn't pass up.

Zane's skills as a pilot had given him a reputation across the business for doing what couldn't be done. His roster of clients had grown steadily since he'd opened for his first cargo flight. But he had other reasons for going after High Vision's business. He had a deal on the side nobody knew about. That deal hinged on getting contracts with companies like High Vision – companies of interest to the DEA.

The money he made on the side as an undercover

informant would save his baby sister's life. He'd almost lost her to her demons once.

He'd unintentionally abandoned her when he went into the military. Not again.

"I'll be fine," Zane said. Genetically engineered white mice, packed in the six cases being loaded on his plane, had to arrive alive and on time. He didn't give a rat's ass about the mice. No pun intended. But he also didn't plan to blow the best chance he had at cinching the deal with High Vision.

"H-o-o-wee!" Hack raised one gray eyebrow at the weather radar on the huge, outdated CRT computer monitor to his left. The dial-up connection was deadly slow, and the animated radar loop crept across the screen. "Nobody oughta fly in a front like this. Don't be fooled none by that little break out there. It's a comin' in hard."

Zane grunted just to give the old guy a response.

Hack shifted his bulk to lean forward, and the vinyl office chair squeaked in protest. "You hear 'bout that fella down in Montgomery? Told his wife he *had* ta fly in that bad squall come off the Gulf. Said he'd lose his contract with Shoreline Delivery if he didn't. They used a bag to pick up parts of that man. He was scattered plumb across Alabama."

Zane shrugged. Life was a gamble.

Odds were no worse now than when he'd put everything on the line for his brothers in arms, which he'd do again in a minute.

It would take more than lousy weather to make him pass up a chance to get one step closer to security for him and his sister.

Everyone vied for High Vision's business. If he didn't meet the delivery deadline, somebody else would the next time.

"Don't you git it?" Hack continued. "That pilot didn't keep the contract noways. He shoulda just stayed home. If he had, he'd be alive an' flyin' today."

Sure, bad weather upped the potential for a problem, but compared to Zane's combat flight experience, making Jacksonville tonight would warrant only a little more attention than usual. Of course, his military record, training, and background appeared nowhere on the credentials for Black Jack Charters.

And neither did his real last name, Jackson.

As Zane Black, he kept his personal life separate from work, and from the sometimes-rough characters he encountered. People who wanted him to fly cargo that was illegal at best, a danger to American citizens at worst. His alter-identity had been part of the deal he'd cut with the DEA when they'd become his partner in the charter business.

They bought the plane and set him up. He busted ass to get contracts of his own – and contracts that interested them.

Damned lucrative work that was filling up a bank account for his sister's business scary fast.

Beyond that, doing this for his country was work he believed in. Something that made hauling around smelly vermin a little easier.

He'd flown more than his share of dangerous missions in his career as a pilot. On the last one, he'd barely walked away. In the Air Force, he'd been a respected fighter pilot instead of humping commercial cargo for a living.

But that was three years ago and this was today.

Hack's police scanner crackled with a short conversation in law enforcement code.

"Slow night for the boys in blue," Hack declared.

"What happened now?" Zane asked with feigned confusion over the cryptic announcements. He'd spoken 10-codes like a native language in his former life. Police agency codes were different than military, but since he'd been doing the side work for his friends in the DEA, he'd learned the police agency usage. He knew exactly what the codes squawking on that radio meant, and what had transpired.

"Got a couple hotheads havin' at it in a beer joint parkin' lot down the road."

Hack's man loading the Titan shoved the office door open and announced, "All fueled and loaded. Ready to go. You got to feed those critters if you're late?"

Zane lifted a shoulder. "Beats me. Vision doesn't make allowances for late. Thanks, Tyler. I'll close it up." He preferred to shut the cargo hatch himself and know for sure everything was buttoned up tight.

With a nod, Tyler pulled the door closed, strolled across the hangar, and disappeared into the maintenance shop.

Rain drummed against the metal roof.

"H-o-o-wee. Listen to it come down out there. You hang around and we'll have us a couple hands o' poker."

Zane ignored Hack. A blur of yellow in the hangar caught his attention.

He couldn't believe his eyes.

Had a woman just slipped into his airplane?

Was she nuts?

And where in the hell had she come from?

Zane snatched up the thermos. "Thanks for the coffee." He left before Hack could offer one more warning about aeronautic suicide. The last thing he needed tonight was trouble, even if it came in a long-legged package.

When he stepped outside, an odd sound carried on the swirling wind. Misting rain drifted through the haze of light beyond the hangar.

He stopped to listen.

Dogs bayed in the distance. Bobbing lights flashed near the woods at the far side of the runway. It didn't take a detective to figure out they were hunting something – or someone.

His stowaway was sadly mistaken if she thought he'd help a fugitive.

Zane paused.

A fugitive on the run from the law would be all over Hack's police scanner, but the only alert sent out in the last thirty minutes had been the parking lot bar brawl.

Concern tapped along his spine.

He stuck his head inside the cargo door of the Titan and scanned the secured load. The tie-down straps were cinched tight, as they should be. Hundreds of tiny toenails scratched frantically against the aerated crates. A faint putrid smell accompanied the chattering racket.

In the shadows at the rear, he spotted a bruised leg. Blood trickled from deep scratches. His vision adjusted. Two enormous, terrified, whiskey-dark eyes came into focus between a break in the crates.

Who was she and why were they after her?

And if the police weren't the ones chasing her, who had turned dogs loose to track her?

Amplified barks and howls echoed louder across the airfield. The bleeding leg disappeared and the two eyes ducked away. A memory crashed into him of his younger sister, battered and bleeding, in the wrong place at the wrong time.

No one had lifted a finger to help her.

Three years of buried guilt roared to the surface. He'd cursed the spineless men who'd turned deaf ears to his sister's screams.

He'd cursed himself worse for not being there to save her.

Zane climbed inside, slammed the cargo door behind him, then tossed the thermos into a bag on the floor. He moved forward into the left seat, cranked the engines, and jerked on his headset.

As he pulled out to taxi, he passed two black Land Rovers screaming into the airport, sliding to a stop on the taxiway to his left. Out jumped five men in dark suits with bodies the size of refrigerators.

Static crackled in his ear. He keyed the radio to activate the automatic runway lights then spoke into his headset microphone. "November Zero Niner Niner Five Papa preparing for takeoff."

Two trackers with dogs appeared in his headlights, further down the runway. The ensemble raced toward him. Both men struggled to keep up with hounds charging against their leashes, amped up on the scent of the hunt.

Zane gunned the engine, taxied straight ahead.

Hack's excited voice burst inside his headset. "Zane, come on back. Got some men here want to see you."

What if the brutes were with law enforcement? He'd have to hand her over. No woman was worth getting arrested and having people digging around into his background.

A hundred yards ahead, men dove away from the churning props, dragging the bloodhounds with them.

He clicked on his mike. "Are they Feds?"

"No. Private security, but they really want to talk. Says there's big money in it for you."

Big money had a suspicious ring to it. Zane continued to flip levers. "What type of security?"

He swung around the far end of the taxiway, barely slowing. A squeak sounded in the rear, but he couldn't decide if it had four legs or two.

Two sets of high beams shot around the opposite end of the runway thirty-five hundred feet away to face him. What was the chance those headlights belonged to the two sport utilities full of muscle? Pretty fucking good.

He eased the throttles forward.

What kind of trouble was this woman in?

To keep an eye on his cargo, he'd installed a rear view mirror. He shot a quick look at the cargo hold. A pair of wide eyes stared back, more panicked than before.

He understood that look.

She was running for her life.

After a long silence, Hack finally answered his question. "Private security, uh, like ... Big Joe Levetti."

Hair stood up across Zane's neck.

Hack had always joked that Big Joe had D-E-A-T-H tattooed across his knuckles. No way would Zane turn that haunted, frightened woman over to a bunch of hired guns.

He barked one last message into the radio. "You're breaking up. I've got IFR clearance from center. I'm gone." As the aircraft picked up speed, the four headlights racing toward him grew larger. Zane gripped the controls tighter. His pilot's manual didn't cover playing chicken in a loaded Titan on a rainy night. But his military experience made this an easy call.

Besides, he'd never been one to play by the rules.

Buffeted by the wind, the plane rocked and careened closer to the Land Rovers, the distance between them shortening with every second. He mentally calculated the added weight of the stowaway in the back.

He'd never get this aircraft up before reaching the vehicles if they held their ground.

He'd never be able to stop in time either.

LAST CHANCE TO RUN

Last Chance To Run – December 2012
www.AuthorDiannaLove.com

www.ingramcontent.com/pod-product-compliance
Lightning Source LLC
Chambersburg PA
CBHW071159250626
47159CB00001B/133